Praise for Radclyffe's Fiction

"…well-plotted…lovely romance…I couldn't turn the pages fast enough!" – Ann Bannon, author of *The Beebo Brinker Chronicles*.

"…well-honed storytelling skills…solid prose and sure-handedness of the narrative…" – Elizabeth Flynn, *Lambda Book Report*

"…a thoughtful and thought-provoking tale…deftly handled in nuanced and textured prose that is both intelligent and deeply personal. The sex is exciting, the story is daring, the characters are well-developed and interesting – in short, Radclyffe has once again pulled together all the ingredients of a genuine page-turner…" – Cameron Abbott, author of *To the Edge* and *An Inexpressible State of Grace*

"With ample angst, realistic and exciting medical emergencies, winsome secondary characters, and a sprinkling of humor…a terrific romance…one of the best I have read in the last three years. Highly recommended." – Author Lori L. Lake, Book Reviewer for the *Independent Gay Writer*

"Radclyffe employs…a lean, trim, and tight writing style…rich with meticulously developed characterizations and realistic dialogue…" – Arlene Germain, *Lambda Book Report*

"…one writer who creates believably great characters that are just as strong as mainstream publishing's Kay Scarpetta or Kinsey Milhone…If you're looking for a great romance, read anything by Radclyffe." – Sherry Stinson, editor, *Outlook Press*

DISTANT SHORES, *SILENT THUNDER*

2005

DISTANT SHORES, SILENT THUNDER

ISBN 1-933110-08-2
This Trade Paperback Original Is Published By
Bold Strokes Books, Inc.,
Philadelphia, Pa, USA

First Edition: March, 2005 Bold Strokes Books, Inc.
Second Printing: May 2005 Bold Strokes Books, Inc.

Credits
Executive Editor: Stacia Seaman
Editor: Ruth Sternglantz
Production Design: J. Barre Greystone
Cover Photos: Lee Ligon
Cover Design By Sheri (GRAPHICARTIST2020@HOTMAIL.COM)

By the Author

Romances

Safe Harbor
Beyond the Breakwater
Innocent Hearts
Love's Melody Lost
Love's Tender Warriors
Tomorrow's Promise
Passion's Bright Fury
Love's Masquerade
shadowland
Fated Love

Honor Series

Above All, Honor
Honor Bound
Love & Honor
Honor Guards

Justice Series

A Matter of Trust (prequel)
Shield of Justice
In Pursuit of Justice
Justice in the Shadows

Change Of Pace: *Erotic Interludes*
(A Short Story Collection)

Acknowledgments

In many ways, this book, the third in what has evolved into the Provincetown Tales, represents a milestone in my writing career. *Safe Harbor*, the first book in the series, was also the first book I published. *Distant Shores, Silent Thunder* is the twentieth. In the interim I have moved through several phases of publishing, finally forming Bold Strokes Books, Inc. in 2004.

Writing is a singular pleasure made sweeter by sharing it with others. Publishing is a demanding, exhilarating, and humbling experience. Being entrusted to assist others in the achievement of their creative dreams is awe-inspiring and a reward unto itself. I am fortunate to have a fabulous team of talented, dedicated professionals who make not only my writing better but Bold Strokes' publications exceptional.

Thanks go to Stacia Seaman, executive editor, and Ruth Sternglantz for their outstanding editorial input; to first readers Athos, Diane, Denise, Eva, Jane, JB, Paula, Robyn, and Tomboy; and to the diligent proofreaders, Eva, Denise, Diane, Robyn, and Shelley, for assistance with this book.

Even before the presses roll, the work of "getting out the word" is crucial. Many individuals have supported me over the years by bringing my work to the attention of readers and booksellers, and I will never be able to thank everyone. Every member of the Radlist has been an emissary at one time, and I am in your collective debt forever. As I embark on this new stage of creating the fiction I love so much, I especially want to thank Linda Hill and Bella Distribution for broadening the horizons and extending the reach of Bold Strokes Books.

Now, with so many books and so little time—when every moment is spoken for—Lee continues to be my champion. *Amo te*

Radclyffe, 2005

Dedication

For Lee,
For Whom No Horizon is Too Far

Prologue

Early August, 2002, Boston, Massachusetts

Trauma alert STAT...trauma admitting. Trauma alert STAT...trauma admitting. Trauma alert STAT...

Dr. KT O'Bannon sprinted down the crowded hall toward the trauma bay at Boston Hospital, dodging stretchers, visitors, and hospital personnel with the agility that had made her an All-American hurdler in college, one hand pressing the stethoscope draped around her neck against her chest to prevent it from flying off. The emergency call being broadcast through the overhead speakers was the sixth trauma alert of the day. That often happened on weekends in the summer, especially when the weather was as hot as it was this particular Saturday evening. Drivers were short-tempered and drove too quickly on roads that were too congested for even the normal speed limit. People partied too hard and too often in backyards and bars, becoming victims of accidents and assaults. And of course, there were always those individuals who chose to settle their disputes with knives and guns rather than fists. Regardless of the mechanism of injury—vehicular, blunt, or penetrating—KT handled them all. And she loved it. Loved the excitement of never knowing what challenge the next crisis might present, the rush of being on the firing line—of being the one making the life-and-death calls—and the incredible high of beating the odds one more time and snatching another life from the jaws of death.

Security STAT...trauma admitting. Security STAT...trauma admitting. Security STAT...trauma admitting.

KT hesitated for only a second, wondering at the unusual request, before she shouldered through the double doors of the trauma admitting area. Unlike the emergency room proper, which was partitioned into multiple curtained cubicles for the treatment of patients with minor injuries or medical problems of all types, the trauma area was designed as a fully functioning operating room. As such, it consisted of a single forty-by-forty-foot room with several adjustable padded operating tables aligned in the middle of the space beneath huge circular overhead halogen lights. Every available inch along the walls was occupied by bins of supplies, including full surgical packs containing all the instruments required to perform any type of invasive surgery. There was even a power drill to perform a craniotomy—the removal of a section of the skull in the event that it was necessary to relieve acute pressure on the brain.

Even though KT did not know what life-threatening problem awaited her, the basic routine, repeated thousands of times over the past fifteen years, was so familiar that the natural surge of anxiety evoked by the disembodied voice over the hospital intercom system was softened to a distant thunder in the background of her consciousness. She *did* know with absolute certainty that the nurses, residents, EMTs, and trauma techs would already have the resuscitation well underway, functioning efficiently without her direction. Establishing the ABCs of resuscitation—airway, breathing, and circulation—was second nature to even rank beginners after a few days in the trauma unit. In all likelihood, an endotracheal tube would already have been placed into the trachea to deliver oxygen, IVs started to augment blood volume and support circulation, and drainage tubes inserted into the bladder and stomach to monitor output and control secretions. *Her* greatest contribution was going to be organizing and prioritizing treatment, including managing the often complicated drug therapy, and performing whatever urgent surgical intervention might be needed to control hemorrhage or maintain an airway.

Mentally gearing herself for battle, KT swept the room with a confident gaze and a split second later realized that something was terribly wrong. A patient *did* lie on the table in the center of the room—a middle-aged Asian male whose short-sleeved, checked shirt was soaked with blood—but the usual milling mass of individuals who made up the trauma team and who *should* have been surrounding him was absent. Instead, three women and two men huddled in a semicircle on the far side of the room facing the door that KT had just barreled through, and they all appeared to be staring at another man, who jittered from foot to foot at the base of the patient's bed, his back to KT.

"What's going on?" KT said abruptly as she started forward. She didn't even have time to flinch away when the man pivoted sharply and slashed her right cheek with a long, thin-bladed knife. Shocked more by the absurdity of the act than the pain, KT jerked to a halt. "What—"

Out of the corner of her eye she saw the knife arcing back—a glinting slice of deadly silver, and this time it was headed for her throat. She did the only thing she could. She blocked the weapon with her open hand. The blade, honed to a razor's edge, sliced with terrible efficiency across her palm. Someone screamed in the distance.

KT's vision wavered as blood splattered her face and chest. Her legs were suddenly so weak that she dropped to her knees. The sudden change in position probably saved her life, because the next thrust of the knife passed high over her left shoulder without touching her. Then as she hunched forward, cradling her injured hand against her chest in an attempt to stop the bleeding, the room exploded into pandemonium. Three security guards burst through the doors amidst chaotic shouts and the clatter of instrument trays being knocked to the floor. Kneeling in the center of the room, surrounded by the glittering stainless steel instruments and swatches of blood, KT was unaware of her assailant being subdued and dragged away, oblivious to the blood streaming steadily down her face, soaking into her scrub shirt, and pooling on the floor between her legs, unconscious of the frantic voices calling her name. Her attention was riveted to her hand. Her befuddled mind couldn't make sense of what she saw in the depths of the wound, but in the core of her being, she knew.

"Oh God," she whispered. "Oh God, oh God...I can't move my fingers."

Chapter One

Four Weeks Later, Provincetown, Massachusetts

Love? Come here and look at this," Reese Conlon said with a note of wonder. "She's following my finger."

Tory King placed a hand on her lover's back and looked over Reese's shoulder at the baby cradled in her arms. Reese, seated in a rocking chair in front of the double glass doors that led out to the deck overlooking Provincetown Harbor, was feeding their infant daughter from a plastic bottle filled with the breast milk that Tory had pumped that morning. Regina's deep blue eyes were open, and occasionally she blinked as she sucked on the soft plastic nipple in her mouth. Intermittently, Reese held her index finger in the air a few inches above the baby's face and waved it. "See that? Just then."

The excitement in Reese's voice was so endearing that Tory had to catch her bottom lip between her teeth to stifle a laugh. "It's still a little soon for her to be focusing, honey. It'll probably be another month or so."

"Well, she does *everything* early." Reese's tone was only slightly aggrieved. "She showed up almost two months early, then she was ready to come home from the hospital three weeks sooner than the pediatricians predicted, and she already sleeps through the night. Well, *most* nights. At the rate she's going, she'll probably be walking by the time she's six months old." Reese turned her head and glanced up at Tory, her generous mouth quirked into a grin that deepened the dimple low on her right cheek. "You have to admit she's amazing."

It was hard for Tory to decide which of the two was the more beautiful: Reese with her coal black hair, deep blue eyes, and heart-stoppingly handsome features, or the baby whose eyes were as blue as Reese's, but whose dark brown hair held hints of red and gold like her own. Together, they stilled the breath in her chest. Afraid that Reese would see the tears that quickly rose to tremble dangerously on her lashes, Tory pressed her cheek to the top of Reese's head and wrapped both arms around her shoulders from behind. "I love you."

Reese tilted her head back again and kissed the side of Tory's neck. "You just love me because *I* got up at four o'clock the last two nights."

"Mmm, there is that, I suppose." Tory's tone was teasing, but she felt a twinge of guilt knowing that she'd been only dimly aware of the baby fussing and of Reese getting up to see to her. It was hard to admit that she was just recently beginning to regain her strength after the tumultuous emergency Cesarean section that had been necessary when she'd gone into labor prematurely. Precipitous labor and emergency surgery took a toll on anyone, but she was nearing forty, and her recovery had been slower than she would have liked. Although Reese would never complain, Tory knew that her lover had been shouldering more than her share of the household chores as well as the child care while still fulfilling her obligations as Provincetown's deputy sheriff. "Things should get easier next week when the tourist season is over and the activity quiets down in town. Then you won't be working quite so hard."

"I'm fine," Reese said quickly. And she was. She'd never been happier in her life. She had never expected to fall in love or to have a family. Not because she didn't believe in those things, but because all she had ever envisioned for herself was a career in the Marine Corps. She'd been raised in a military family, had trained from the time she was a teenager to follow in her father's footsteps, and had become an exemplary career Marine officer. It wasn't until four years earlier that she had grown restless, plagued by the persistent sensation that something in her life was missing—something that she could not name because she had never thought to seek it. It had taken leaving active duty and traveling across the country to a small fishing village on the very tip of Cape Cod for her to discover that what she longed for was a love of her own. She had that now, with Dr. Victoria King, Provincetown's resident physician, and their newborn daughter, Regina. "Everything is perfect."

The words made Tory tremble because she believed them while still fearing, in the deepest recesses of her heart, that happiness might be a transient accident destined to disappear. There was a reason for that fear, but it lay in her past, and she would not allow the past to follow her here. Banishing old disappointments, she tightened her hold on her lover and kissed her neck. "Do you mind watching her while I run over to the clinic?"

"Uh-uh." Reese turned in the chair and checked the wall clock that hung in the alcove between the large open living room and the adjoining kitchen-dining area. "I have to be at the *dojo* in two hours. Think you'll be back by then?"

"Absolutely. I'm sure Dan is swamped. I'll probably be lucky to catch him free for a few minutes between patients."

Reese rose, shifting the baby into the crook of her arm, and crossed to the kitchen where she deposited the empty baby bottle on the counter. "Is he definitely leaving next week?"

"I think so." Tory tried hard to keep the worry from her voice. Dan Riley was a general practitioner from Pennsylvania who had worked for the last few months in the East End Health Clinic, Tory's medical facility. Tory hadn't anticipated that Dan would need to shoulder the entire weight of her practice, but Regina's early arrival had altered those plans. Since the baby's birth in July, Dan had been doing the work of two doctors. During the summer, when Provincetown's population swelled to thirty thousand or more, the clinic staff was constantly busy caring for tourists with minor injuries and medical problems in addition to providing routine healthcare to the three thousand year-round residents. Now, an emergency had arisen with Dan's wife's family, and *he* needed to return to Pittsburgh as soon as possible rather than in December, when he had expected to leave. "I managed to get an ad in the Boston papers yesterday, and I've got every contact I can think of putting out the word that I'm looking for someone to fill his spot right away."

"You'll find someone."

"Of course." Tory tried to sound optimistic, but they both knew that Provincetown in the off-season was not the kind of place that people flocked to. The winters were long and cold, and the village was very quiet with almost nothing to offer in the way of entertainment from November to May. Even the cinema and many of the restaurants closed during the off-season. She would be very lucky to find someone to take Dan's place at this time of year. "I thought I'd talk to Kate later and see if she'd be available to watch Reggie a few more hours every day."

"I'm sure my mother would be delighted to watch Reggie all day, every day," Reese said quietly, leaning back against the waist-high breakfast counter and regarding Tory solemnly. "But you're not thinking about trying to handle the clinic yourself, are you?"

"I know it's soon, but babies younger than Reggie go to day care without any problems—"

"Tor. I'm not talking about Reggie. I'm talking about you." Reese crossed the room and lifted her free hand to Tory's cheek, trailing her fingers into the thick hair at the back of Tory's neck. "You've lost weight, you still tire easily, and—"

Tory turned her head and pressed her lips to Reese's palm, then wrapped her arm around Reese's waist. "I know. But I'm feeling much better every day."

Reese kissed Tory softly. "Let's wait and see what happens with the ads."

"All right," Tory relented, not wanting to worry Reese any further. She returned the kiss swiftly and forced a smile. "I'm sure something will work out."

"Me, too."

"I'll see you soon."

"Be careful," Reese called as Tory gathered her things and started out the door. She tried hard to keep the frustration from her voice, because she knew how seriously Tory took her responsibilities to the community. Still, the only thing that mattered to Reese was that Tory, and now Reggie, were safe and healthy. *Provincetown will just have to get along without a full-time doctor if Tory can't find a replacement.*

❖

Tory walked into the busy waiting room at her clinic and felt instantly at home. Two months away, and despite the daily joy of her new daughter, she was starting to seriously miss her medical practice. Randy Schuyler—svelte, blond, and almost too pretty to be a man—looked up from behind the reception counter, a single frown line marring his otherwise flawless forehead. Beautiful long lashes that made many a woman weep lowered over his liquid brown eyes as he fixed her with a steely stare. "Go away. You're on maternity leave, and Dan is far too busy to talk to you."

"Hi, sweetie," Tory said brightly in passing. She edged around the counter, sidling between the chairs crowded into every inch of floor space. *I'm going to need to put on an addition at this rate.*

"Tory," Randy said, a pleading note in his voice now. "Look at the waiting room."

She didn't need to. Her practiced eye had already taken in the more than half dozen adults and children waiting to be seen. She stopped and picked up the top chart in the pile by Randy's left hand.

"Martha?" Tory called.

"Hello, Dr. King," an elderly woman responded from a seat in the corner. "How are you, dear?"

"I'm wonderful. Come on back, and let's see how your blood pressure is doing."

An hour and fifteen minutes later, she'd seen six patients and was sitting behind her desk charting when Dan Riley walked in. Tory smiled. "Hi. Let me just finish this note, and I'll get out of your way."

Dan, a solidly built forty-year-old with curly hair just beginning to gray, rimless glasses, and an angelic face, shook his head and flopped into one of the two chairs. "No problem. It's your desk, after all."

"How's it going?" She hadn't seen him for several days, and he looked thinner than she recalled. Certainly the circles under his eyes were darker. "How's your wife's dad?"

"He's holding his own, but I think it's going to be a long haul."

"Listen, Dan, I know it's hard for both you and your wife with you not being there. As soon as—"

"Ruth understands," Dan said swiftly. "She knows I can't just leave without someone to cover for me. I've talked to all my father-in-law's doctors about his treatment, *and* I check in a couple times a day to make sure his condition hasn't changed."

"It's still not the same as being there." Tory made a decision, the one she should've made eight days earlier when Dan's father-in-law suffered an intracranial hemorrhage from a ruptured aneurysm. "If I don't have someone to replace you in a day or two, I'll take over myself so that you can join her. I'm sure the entire family will feel better if you're there in person to handle things."

"I thought your obstetrician said you couldn't go back to work for a full three months after your delivery."

"It's been two—and I'm doing fine." In truth, it would be difficult, because she still couldn't make it through the entire day without a nap in the afternoon. Nevertheless, she could split up the patients between morning and evening hours if she needed to take a break in the middle of the day. At least her leg had improved to the point where she no longer used her cane and only occasionally fell back on the lightweight ankle cast for support. The muscles in her damaged calf would never regenerate, but with steady, persistent training she'd regained enough strength in the surrounding musculature to support her damaged ankle without the heavy, hinged metal brace. Standing all day wouldn't be as difficult as it had been in the years just after her accident. "I can handle it, especially now that the season is almost over."

Dan looked skeptical. "Most of the patients I'm seeing every day are regulars. This isn't a very big town, but you're the main primary care doctor. The patient load's not going to get that much lighter, even without the tourists."

"I'll manage," Tory said firmly. She glanced at her watch. "I need to get home so Reese can get to class. Tell your wife that Saturday morning, you'll be on your way to Pittsburgh."

"It's Labor Day weekend! I can't leave you then."

Tory simply shook her head. "I mean it, Dan. It's time for you to go home." *And for me to come back to work.*

❖

Reese tied the belt of her *hakama* over her *gi*, bowed to the *kamiza*—the ceremonial altar which consisted of a simple shelf of hand-carved wood on which stood a small vase of dried wildflowers—and stepped barefoot onto the tatami mats that covered three quarters of the main floor in the Provincetown Martial Arts Center, the *dojo* that she ran out of a converted garage on the far east end of Bradford Street. Her senior student was already present, sitting on the far end of the mat in *seiza*—knees bent, weight back on her heels, hands resting palms down on her thighs. Bri Parker's eyes were closed as she readied herself for training. Reese crossed quickly to the center of the room and assumed the same position, facing Bri and the other students who were beginning to line up silently side by side. Reese also closed her eyes, cleared her mind, and slowed her breathing until she was in a state of relaxed readiness. Her mind and body were united, and from that place of harmony, she was prepared to do battle.

Expelling her breath slowly, Reese opened her eyes, bent her forehead to the mat between her steepled hands, and greeted her class in Japanese. The ten students returned her bow and her greeting, and for the next hour, the men and women trained in the art of jujitsu. Reese moved silently between the partners, observing and occasionally stepping in to demonstrate a technique before moving off again. Her classes were traditional in the sense that the students learned by performing and by watching Reese and Bri. Before Tory's pregnancy had become too advanced, *she'd* been one of the senior students, although her formal training had been in hapkido, a Korean style similar to the Japanese martial art of aikido. All three styles, however, bore similarities in their use of joint locks, shoulder throws, and defensive blocks and kicks.

After Reese dismissed the class, Bri approached and waited a few feet away. Other than the fact that Reese was an inch taller and thirty pounds of muscle heavier, they were so close in appearance, with the same thick black hair and cobalt blue eyes, that strangers often mistook Bri for Reese's younger sister. Reese removed her *hakama* and held it out to Bri. "Thank you."

"It is an honor, *sensei*," Bri replied as she always did, for it was customary for the senior student to fold the *sensei*'s ceremonial outer garment.

Reese nodded in acknowledgment and glanced toward the door, where a petite brunette with whiskey-colored eyes waited, her gaze focused intently on Bri. Allie Tremont was Reese's newest student as well as the newest member of the sheriff's department, having just transferred from nearby Wellfleet. The look of unguarded appreciation on Allie's face took Reese by surprise. Surely Allie knew that Bri was involved. Reese turned at the sound of Bri's voice.

"Here you are, *sensei*."

Reese took the folded garment, and the two women walked together to the end of the mat, bowed, and then stepped off.

"The second Sunday in October," Reese said. "I've asked a test board to convene for your black belt test."

"I...oh wow...I..." Bri's voice caught and she swallowed. "Yes, *sensei*. Thank you."

For the first time, Reese smiled. "No need for thanks."

"Oh, man. Wait until I tell Carre." Then, remembering that *telling* her lover about one of the biggest events in her life was the only way that she would be able to share it with her, a cloud passed across Bri's face and the light in her eyes dimmed.

"I'm sure she's going to think it's great," Reese said as she clapped Bri on the shoulder.

"Yeah. She will." Subdued, Bri looked over to where Allie still waited and forced a smile. "Hey," she said as she started toward the brunette, "guess what?"

Reese waited for them to change and followed them to the door. As she locked up, she watched Allie climb onto the back of Bri's motorcycle and wrap her arms around the rangy youth's midsection. A few seconds later, Bri gunned the motorcycle down the driveway and onto the road with Allie pressed tightly to her back.

"Perfect," Reese muttered to herself as she walked toward her Blazer.

Chapter Two

Bri and Allie left class together today," Reese announced as she stripped down in the bedroom in preparation for a shower.

"Hmm?" Tory, who'd just fed the baby and put her down for a nap, sat on the side of the bed buttoning an oversized man's shirt—the only thing she happened to be wearing. Finished, she looked up in time to see Reese, who hadn't bothered to pull on underwear after changing out of her *gi* at the *dojo*, kick out of her jeans. Tory caught her breath, ambushed by the unexpected sight. Whereas her own body, even at the peak of conditioning, rarely looked more than sleekly toned, Reese's was a study in richly sculpted muscle. *How many times have I seen her this way? A thousand? How many times have I touched her? Too many to count. And still she makes my heart stop.*

"Your shift starts at four?" Tory's question was casual but her voice was husky and low. The stirring in her belly was welcome after the long abstinence. They had been carefully intimate a few times since Reggie was born, at least to the extent that Tory was able to caress Reese to a gentle climax or hold her while she brought herself to orgasm. But Tory had been so exhausted from the difficult labor and subsequent surgery and then the demands of a hungry newborn that her own sexual satisfaction hadn't been high on her list of needs. Suddenly, it was. Out of nowhere, desire flared, hungry and hot—not the slow ignition of simmering coals that she might have expected after such a long period of quiescence, but a full-force blast of heat that left her instantly wet and craving Reese's touch. "You've got a while yet before you have to leave for the station, right?"

"Uh-huh." Reese glanced over and stopped in midmotion.

A faint flush rose on her chest when she registered the look on her lover's face. "Tory, come on." Her voice held a hint of both warning and plea.

"I've missed you touching me."

"I've missed you, too—like crazy." Reese's eyes darkened with the need she had no desire or ability to hide. She crossed the room quickly, knelt in front of Tory, and rested both hands on Tory's thighs. The tail of the loose cotton shirt brushed the backs of her hands, gentle as a kiss. "But Wendy said—"

"Wendy *said*," Tory repeated firmly as she cupped Reese's breasts and leaned to kiss her, "that I couldn't have vaginal intercourse for eight weeks. She *didn't* say I couldn't come." She found Reese's mouth just as she closed her fingers around the small, erect nipples. As she slid the tip of her tongue teasingly over Reese's lips, she tugged her nipples to the same tantalizing rhythm.

Groaning, Reese surged against Tory's body, pressing her breasts hard into Tory's palms. She smoothed her hands under the shirt, her thumbs stroking the insides of Tory's thighs.

Tory lifted her mouth away, murmuring throatily, "Oh yes. I'm not the only one who misses it, am I, baby?"

"You know how much it excites me when you touch me." Reese's blue eyes had gone nearly black, her breathing reduced to short, swift gasps. Having the baby in their life was a miracle, but it was Tory she lived for. Tory who defined her existence, Tory who gave purpose to her days. "I'm most alive when you have your hands on me. I love it when you make me come."

"I haven't been doing enough of *that* lately, that's for sure." Tory stretched out on the bed, grasped Reese's hand, and drew her down, too. Then she turned on her side and edged a knee between Reese's thighs. "Going from every other day to once every couple of weeks is a big change."

Reese laughed softly, insinuating her fingers beneath Tory's shirt again to stroke her back. "We've both been pretty busy with Reggie, and you *are* recovering from surgery. I haven't felt neglected in that regard."

"Neither have I, really," Tory murmured, trailing her fingers along Reese's thigh. "Until today."

"Mmm. I'm not complaining." Reese caught Tory's lower lip in her teeth, bit gently. "These are extraordinary circumstances." She touched her tongue to the spot that she had just nipped. "But I miss touching you. I miss hearing you, feeling you come."

Moaning softly, Tory smoothed her hand down Reese's flank and over her hips. "I'm so ready to come for you now."

Whatever protest Reese might have made was lost on a moan as Tory slid a hand between her legs and squeezed gently. Tory whispered, "Let me come for you, baby." She squeezed again. "Let me come *with* you. You want to, don't you?"

"Oh yes. Yes." Reese's vision was hazy, her stomach in knots. Tory. Touching her, loving her. Tory. Needing her, wanting her. "Oh, Tory."

"It's okay, baby," Tory soothed, pressing her fingers into the waiting wetness.

"Don't touch me yet," Reese warned breathlessly. "You know I'm no good at holding back. Let me make *you* feel good for a while first."

"Good?" Tory's laugh was shaky. "It can't get any better. God, I'm so ready now I could burst."

"Just wait." Ignoring the steady surge of blood pulsing through her depths and the almost painful need to push into Tory's palm, to rub against the fingers that she knew could have her rocketing to orgasm in a matter of seconds, Reese rested her forehead against Tory's and anchored herself in her lover's eyes. Watching Tory's eyes grow cloudy with pleasure, she caressed her breasts, swollen and heavy, and squeezed the dark, full nipples. She thrilled to Tory's soft cry as she smoothed her fingers down the center of her abdomen, still gently rounded with the memory of pregnancy. Tory's fingers twitched against her clitoris, and she struggled not to come. "Careful," she whispered urgently.

"Oh God," Tory sighed, "I love to feel you like this, so hard, so ready for me." The feel of Reese's pleasure, hot and wet against her fingertips, made her body soar. "It's been so long. I need you now, baby. Please don't make me wait." Her hips bucked as Reese fondled her. "Oh, I want to come."

Reese brought her mouth to Tory's and kissed her deeply, stroking tongue to tongue as her fingers swept up and down the length of Tory's clitoris, circling harder with each long caress. Tory, caught by surprise by the swift rise of her orgasm, closed her fingers convulsively around Reese, jerking her clitoris spasmodically as her own climax peaked. With a cry, Reese flooded Tory's hand with her passion.

"Oh my God," Reese murmured, staring at the ceiling as she waited for her limbs to make their way back to her body. Tory curled against her side, her head on Reese's shoulder, making small, contented sounds of happiness. Reese threaded shaking fingers through Tory's hair and caressed the back of her neck. "How is it... that I never remember just how wonderful it is making love with you?"

"It's some kind of protective biologic mechanism," Tory advised sleepily. "Like labor. If women had clear memories of giving birth, they'd only do it once." She rubbed her hand over Reese's stomach, then indolently rested her fingers between Reese's legs—not to arouse, merely to possess. "And if we really thought about how great making love was, we'd probably never get out of bed. We'd lose our jobs, end up on the streets, and our children would starve."

"If you don't move your hand," Reese growled halfheartedly, "*my* job is going to be in jeopardy. I've got twenty-five minutes before my shift starts, and I still have to shower."

Tory merely burrowed closer and flung her leg over Reese's thighs. "Tell me after all those years in the Marines that you can't be ready in five minutes."

Reese caught Tory's hand before she really did forget what she needed to do. "Rolling out of the rack is a little bit different than this."

"Mmm, I should hope so." Lazily, Tory nuzzled Reese's shoulder and bit down on the firm muscle, eliciting a groan that was more pleasure than pain. Then, relenting, she rolled away. "All right. Go now. I won't be responsible for my actions otherwise."

With a sigh, Reese swung her legs over the side of the bed, stood, and headed for the bathroom. As she reached in to turn on the shower, she heard Tory behind her in the doorway. She looked over her shoulder at her naked lover. Tory's face was soft with the aftermath of their lovemaking, her body lush with motherhood.

Reese's stomach clenched and another flood of wanting coursed through her. "Tor. For God's sake. Give me a break here."

The corner of Tory's mouth lifted with satisfaction. "I was just going to talk to you while you got ready. I won't touch."

"Promise?"

"Can I wash your back?"

"*No.*"

"You're no fun at all." Tory pulled a robe off the back of the door and shrugged it on. "Safe enough now?"

"Just stay out there," Reese said threateningly as she stepped under the spray.

Tory plunked herself down on the closed toilet lid as the bathroom filled with warm steam. "What were you saying earlier about Bri?"

Reese stuck her head out of the water. "Huh?"

"Bri. You said something about Bri and Allie before."

"Oh yeah," Reese shouted above the sound of drumming water. "They left together after class today—on Bri's bike."

Tory waited until Reese finished her shower and stepped out to reply. "What about it?"

"Allie was plastered to her."

"At the *dojo*?"

"No," Reese said testily as she toweled her hair. "On the bike. You know, arms around her waist, pressed up against her back."

"I think that's kind of required on a motorcycle."

Reese tossed the towel into the hamper. "Bri should know better."

Tory's expression grew serious. "Honey, it makes sense for them to be friends. They're the same age, they're both police officers, they're both lesbians. It's probably completely innocent."

"And what if it isn't?"

"Bri is pretty young still, and so is Caroline, for that matter. Caroline being in Paris for most of this school year is going to test their relationship, perhaps even more than it can withstand." Tory rose, reached for another towel, and stepped around to dry Reese's back. Then, appreciating her lover's worry by the stiff set of her back, she threaded both arms around her waist and rested her cheek between Reese's shoulder blades. She could hear Reese's heartbeat, steady and strong and sure. That sound and everything it represented was what she counted on; that was what she had built her hopes and dreams and future upon—the solid surety of Reese's love. She turned her face and kissed Reese's back. "Remember that Bri worships you. No matter what happens, she's going to need you on her side."

"I know." Reese covered Tory's hands with her own and sighed. "I just don't want her to do anything stupid."

"Try to trust her...and be there for her if she stumbles." With another kiss between Reese's shoulder blades, Tory stepped away. "You should get dressed. I can't seem to keep my hands off you this afternoon, and I know you need to go."

"I didn't ask you about how things went at the clinic this morning," Reese added as she combed her hair.

Tory hesitated, then kissed the tip of Reese's chin. "Go to work. I'll tell you when you get home."

❖

When Reese reached the station, Bri's motorcycle was parked in the small side lot. The sheriff's department on Shank Painter Road was a single-story box of a building with the crowded office space taking up the front half and the rear housing several holding cells that were rarely used. Reese stepped inside and scanned the room. Gladys Martin, the day dispatcher, was just gathering her things in preparation for leaving. An efficient, even-tempered middle-aged woman, she looked up at the sound of the door opening and sketched Reese a wave. Bri, in a crisply pressed uniform, sat behind one desk, and a middle-aged man with thick dark hair, winter gray eyes, and wide, strong features occupied another. The broad planes of his face had been tempered in the more refined lines of his daughter's, but the resemblance was clear. Nelson Parker was the sheriff, Bri's father, and Reese's immediate superior.

"'Lo, Gladys. Anything happening?" Reese asked as she pushed through the creaky gate in the waist-high dividing partition that separated the tiny waiting area from the space beyond that held the officers' desks, file cabinets, and an industrial-sized coffeepot.

"The biggest excitement we had all day was when a couple

of tourists sank one of Flyers' rental boats out in the middle of the harbor."

"Huh. That must have taken work. Everybody okay?"

"The tide was out," she said derisively. "They could practically walk back to shore."

"Someone take the report?"

"Ted Lewis."

"Good enough." She settled behind a desk piled high with papers. A small, silver-framed photo of Tory and Regina sat next to a pencil holder with the emblem of the United States Marine Corps embossed on its side. "Hey, Bri. Afternoon, Chief."

"Hi, Reese," Bri replied.

"Conlon," Nelson grunted as he set aside the report he'd been reviewing. "When you have time, let's talk about the duty assignments for the weekend."

Reese held up a sheet of paper that had been divided into neat columns and rows, the grid meticulously filled in with times and names. "Got it right here."

"Should have known," Parker muttered to himself. His second in command was the best officer he had ever worked with, and he'd slowly turned over the day-to-day running of the department to her. The other officers respected her, she worked tirelessly, and she was professionally above reproach. "It's the last big push of the summer. The town will be jumping."

"I doubled the swing and night shifts. That means overtime."

The big man grimaced as he took the schedule from Reese. "Fine." He fumbled on his desk for his Tums and chewed one absently. "Who did you assign as Tremont's training officer?"

Bri's head came up as she regarded Reese and her father intently.

"Lyons. They'll work the swing Friday and Saturday."

"What about me?" Bri asked quietly.

"You'll ride with me," Reese replied.

"Yes, ma'am," Bri said with a smile and went back to her review of the updated firearms manual. She wouldn't have minded riding with Allie, but she knew Reese would never put two rookies together. Even though technically *she* wasn't a rookie. She had a solid three months under her belt *and* she'd taken fire. Still, if anybody was going to partner with Reese, she wanted it to be her. She pointedly ignored the faint twinge of jealousy she'd felt when she'd thought Reese might take over Allie's training herself—mostly because she didn't know which one of them she'd been jealous over.

Chapter Three

"Wanna drive?" Reese asked as she and Bri walked to the patrol car after finishing an early dinner of fish and chips at one of the takeout stands on MacMillan Wharf.

"Yes, ma'am!" Grinning, Bri caught the keys one-handed and jumped behind the wheel. "Where to?"

"Let's take another slow run through town." Reese fastened her seat belt and angled her back against the door so that she could look out the windshield as well as see Bri. "So, did you get a chance to tell Caroline about your test?"

The corner of Bri's mouth dipped but she kept her voice light. "Not yet. I called, but the time difference is a killer. Half the time I can't catch her in or I wake her up." She sighed. "Plus, even with cheap rates, long distance gets really expensive, and now that I have to pay for the apartment all by myself, we're trying to be careful. I sent her an e-mail, though."

Reese nodded sympathetically, eyeing the cluster of scantily clad men clogging Commercial Street in front of the Boatslip. The afternoon tea dance had just let out, and the night's revelry was about to begin in earnest. Despite the fact that Provincetown in the summer was filled to overflowing with vacationers and day-trippers, there was very little public drunkenness or disorderly conduct. The town didn't need a very big jail, because crimes requiring detention occurred very rarely. However, crowd control, the increase in drug use among both the town's youth and tourists, and vehicular accidents kept Reese and the other members of the department busy. As Bri carefully maneuvered through the oblivious throngs, Reese asked, "Is she settling in okay?"

Bri kept her eyes fixed straight ahead, her hands clenched on the wheel. "Yes, as near as I can tell. It hasn't even been a month yet." *But it feels like forever.*

"It's tough," Reese remarked, "that she's so far away. It probably wasn't as bad earlier this year when she was in Manhattan and you were here."

"I always knew I could see her if I wanted to. All I needed to do was get on the bike and go. Now..." Bri blew out a breath and consciously forced herself to relax. *It's just that we've never been apart, not really, since we were fifteen. Those four months in the spring when I was being a jerk and Carre wasn't talking to me don't count. That was just plain hell. This is different; this is something we both agreed would be good for Carre's art career. So I just have to suck it up.* "It's okay. I knew it would be hard at first. I'll get used to it."

"Well, you know...you're welcome at the house anytime."

"You must be pretty busy, with Reggie and all."

"She's settling in. And you're like family, too, Bri."

Bri flushed. "Thanks. I...uh...appreciate it."

Reese wanted to ask her about Allie but didn't quite see how she could. She didn't *know* that anything was going on between them, and if she were in Bri's shoes, she wouldn't want anyone making assumptions *or* prying into her private business. On the other hand, she didn't want to wait until there actually was a problem to do something about it. *As if you could. As if it's even any of your business.* A muscle in Reese's jaw jumped. If Bri had been a recruit, it wouldn't have been an issue. She could've demanded to know what was going on and would have been well within her rights. A lot of things were easier in the Corps.

Knowing Bri was unhappy and feeling helpless to help her made Reese think of her infant daughter. She decided on the spot that she was completely incapable of being a parent. All she wanted to do was keep Reggie in the house, safe and secure, for the next twenty years or so. She certainly didn't want to think about her getting involved with anyone, male *or* female, where there was the slightest possibility that she could get her heart broken. However, Reese was certain—as well as eternally grateful—that Tory would know exactly what to do about any problems that Regina might face.

The radio crackled, flooding Reese with a sense of welcome

relief. She wouldn't have to pursue the conversation with Bri any further—at least, not until she had something concrete to discuss. She grabbed the microphone and clicked receive. "Conlon."

"Passerby reported an abandoned vehicle, late-model Aerostar or similar, dark blue or black, on 6 just west of the turnoff to Race Point," Paul Smith, the officer assigned as dispatcher, reported.

"We'll check it out," Reese advised. "ETA two minutes." She swiveled to face front, her expression intent. "Go east on Bradford and cut over to 6 at the end of town. Come up on the vehicle slow and park twenty feet behind it so I can check the plates. Keep the engine running."

"Yes, ma'am." Bri's expression and tone were calm and controlled, but her heart was racing. Vehicle stops and domestic disputes were the most dangerous situations a law enforcement officer could face, because the call could be something as routine as a flat tire or as potentially lethal as a psycho with a gun. Bri put the worries from her mind and focused on following orders. After all, she was trained for this. And she was with Reese.

In just over a minute, she pulled up behind a dark green van with tinted windows parked on the sandy shoulder of the double-lane highway. "Tires are okay. The hood's closed. Doesn't look like a breakdown."

"I see that." Reese strained to see through the dark glass into the interior as she keyed in the license plate number on the remote computer terminal. She waited. There didn't appear to be any motion inside the vehicle. The relay to the station house was slow, but eventually Smith's disembodied voice returned.

"Vehicle registered to Thomas Bridger of Chelmsford, Mass. No wants or warrants. The vehicle, however, was reported stolen sometime last night. You need backup?"

"Have Lyons and Tremont swing by," Reese replied curtly. "Code two."

"Roger that."

Reese flicked on the loudspeaker. "Anyone in the vehicle, step out with your hands in the air."

Five seconds. Ten. Reese repeated the message. When there was no movement in or around the van, she unsnapped her holster, drew her weapon, and opened the patrol car door. "I'm going to have a look inside. Back me up from here—stay *behind* the cruiser door."

"Yes, ma'am." Bri eased out, rested her forearms on the top of the open door, and trained her weapon on the rear of the vehicle. The metal door in front of her wasn't bulletproof, but it afforded her some protection. Reese, on the other hand, was out in the open and vulnerable.

With her weapon at her side, Reese put her back to the driver's side of the vehicle and inched forward, hesitating for a second to peer through the rear window. She reached out and tried the rear door. Locked. With continued caution, she moved forward and attempted to open the driver's door. As it swung open, she crouched instinctively and trained her weapon on the interior. A millisecond later, she hastily holstered her weapon and leaned inside.

A boy—he didn't look older than fifteen—lay slumped on his side, his legs under the steering wheel, his head leaning toward the passenger seat. His eyes were closed, his face gray and sweat coated, and his limbs loose and lifeless. He didn't appear to be breathing. She would have thought him dead except when she touched his neck, his skin was warm. As she pressed two fingers to his carotid artery, she scanned the rest of the van. Empty. A faint, weak pulse trilled beneath her fingers.

She backed out and straightened, then turned to Bri and waved her forward. "Got a casualty here. Unconscious male." As Bri rushed to join her, Reese continued, "We need to get him to the clinic."

"Should I call for the paramedics?"

Reese shook her head. "It'll be faster if we take him ourselves."

"Is it okay to move him?"

"It doesn't appear that the vehicle has been involved in an accident, and *he* doesn't show any evidence of trauma. I doubt his neck is at risk." As she spoke, Reese levered the front seat back carefully and bent over the victim once again. "Just to be sure, I'll support his head and shoulders and you get his feet."

"Here come Allie and Jeff," Bri announced as the second patrol car pulled in front of the van, sandwiching it between the two cruisers.

The four officers easily lifted the boy out and carried him to Reese's patrol car. Once they had him secured in the backseat, Bri climbed in with him and Reese got behind the wheel. She looked up at Jeff Lyons through the open window. "We can't be certain he was alone. Check the vehicle for any evidence of illegal substances, and then search the scrub in the immediate area to make sure there isn't someone else out there in need of help."

"You got it, boss."

Reese sped with lights and siren clearing the way toward the East End Health Clinic, hoping that after 8 p.m. on a weeknight, the clinic wouldn't be too busy. The parking lot was nearly empty when she pulled the cruiser up to the front door and bounded out.

"We need a stretcher out here," Reese called in Randy's direction as she stuck her head in the door. Then she hurried back to help Bri lift the youth out. By the time they maneuvered his inert body from the vehicle, Dan and Randy had the collapsible stretcher open and waiting for them. Within a matter of minutes, they were back inside the clinic and heading down the hallway toward the treatment rooms.

At the commotion in the hall, Tory stepped out of her office wearing her white clinic coat and stared at the group. "What's going on?"

Reese's face never changed expression, despite her surprise. "Found unresponsive in a car out on 6. He's barely breathing."

"Bring him in here," she directed briskly, leading the way to a treatment room. "Accident?"

"No sign of one," Reese replied.

Dan steered the stretcher to the side of the examination table and, while Reese and Bri stood out of the way, he and Tory moved the youth and began resuscitation. They worked together efficiently, with very little conversation.

Reese had seen Tory in action many times, but her lover's focus, skill, and confidence never failed to impress her. Even now, although she was baffled and uncharacteristically angry, Reese was spellbound.

Tory placed her stethoscope against the boy's chest, frowning as she listened. "Respirations shallow—four times a minute." She reached up and thumbed his right eyelid open. "Pinpoint pupils."

"Pulse and pressure low," Dan said tersely.

"Overdose." Tory turned to an open tackle box that stood on a stainless steel tray next to the examination table. She pulled out a tiny glass ampule, snapped off the top, and filled a syringe with the clear liquid. As she worked, Dan started an intravenous line in the boy's forearm. Tory passed him the medication. "Amp of Narcan. I'll push the D50."

Dan injected the drug intravenously while Tory prepared a bolus of glucose, just in case the problem was a diabetic complication and not a drug overdose. If it was insulin shock, the concentrated sugar solution would bring him around. Within seconds of the injection of antinarcotic, however, the boy's eyes flew open, and he began to thrash and cough.

Bri stared, then asked in a low, urgent voice, "What's going on?"

"They just gave him an antidote to a narcotic overdose. It works almost immediately, especially if the narcotic is the only drug he's taken."

The boy stared wildly about before lunging upright on the table. Before Dan could restrain him, the patient grabbed Tory's arm and pulled her off balance, nearly causing her to fall. Reese was at her lover's side in an instant, grasping the youth's shoulders and pushing him back down on the table.

"Easy, buddy." Both her voice and her grip were kind, but her eyes were sharp and hard. "We're just trying to help you out here."

"It's all right," Tory said quietly. "He'll settle down in a second."

"I'll just stay here until he does."

Tory recognized the intractability in her lover's tone and made no reply. Glancing across the boy's supine figure to her associate, she said, "We should probably put him on a Narcan drip so he doesn't go out again. I'll draw blood for a tox screen first if you want to set up the infusion."

"Sure."

While Dan was busy mixing the intravenous drip, Reese motioned Bri closer with a tilt of her chin. "Check his pockets for ID. We need to notify family."

Bri patted him down and pulled a wallet from the voluminous side pocket of his tan canvas cargo shorts. She flipped it open and sorted through the cards inside. "Robert Allen Bridger. Fifteen years old. Same address as the registration."

"Robert," Tory said sharply, attempting to get the confused boy's attention. "Robert, can you hear me? I'm Dr. King. Robert? You're going to be all right."

The young patient turned unfocused eyes in her direction and mumbled incoherently.

"He's going to need to be transported to Hyannis for admission," Tory informed Reese. "Until we get the labs back, we can't be certain exactly what he's taken or what other problems might develop." She smiled faintly at Reese. "You can let go of him now that Dan has the drip going."

Reese stepped back, keeping one eye on the restless youth while she spoke to Bri. "Check with Lyons and Tremont to see if they found anything else with the vehicle. Particularly any sign of what he might have ingested. I'll give his parents a call. Looks like he stole the family car and set off to have a little fun." She shook her head. "Some fun."

"I'm on it," Bri replied and headed for the door.

Tory rested her hand lightly on Reese's forearm. "Why don't you use my office to make your calls."

"Where's the baby?" Reese asked quietly.

"With her grandmothers." Tory brushed her fingers over the top of Reese's hand, noting that her lover made no response. Gently, she repeated, "Go ahead, darling. I'll be there in a minute."

Silently, Reese turned and walked away.

❖

Twenty minutes later, Tory slipped into her office just as Reese, who sat with a hip on the corner of the large walnut desk, hung up the phone. "Did you reach his parents?"

"Yes. They're on their way to the hospital in Hyannis. It will take them a couple of hours to get there."

Tory nodded. "The EMTs are just leaving. By the time his parents arrive, he'll probably be settled in."

"How's he doing?"

"He's stable. He'll bear watching for a day or two, depending on what kinds of drugs he's been doing. Relapses are not uncommon with some of the popular cocktails nowadays." Tory crossed the room and stopped a few inches from Reese. "He's very lucky that you came by when you did. Another ten or fifteen minutes and he would've been in full arrest."

"One of the townspeople noticed that the car had been there all afternoon and called it in." Reese shrugged. "I didn't have much to do with it."

Tory lifted a hand and brushed the dark hair from Reese's forehead. "You recognized the problem and acted quickly, Sheriff. You saved his life."

Reese caught Tory's hand and held it, rubbing her thumb slowly across the top. "What are you doing here?"

"When I stopped by this morning, Dan was really swamped." Tory sighed. "I kept thinking about it, so I came in to help him out. Kate and Jean said they didn't mind watching Regina."

"It seemed pretty quiet when we arrived a while ago." Reese traced her fingers along Tory's jaw. "And *you* look beat. Are you leaving now?"

"In just a little while." At the look of confusion on Reese's face, Tory continued quickly, "I need to go over some of the inventory and look at the patient schedules for the next week or so." She laced her fingers through Reese's. "I told Dan to go home, Reese. His family needs him, and he needs to be there."

"Permanently?"

"Most likely, yes."

"And you're planning on coming back to work?"

Tory nodded.

"And you decided this already?" Reese spoke quietly, her face composed. "Without talking to me about it?"

"It just came up today, when I was here. I'm sorry. It just seemed like the right thing to do."

Reese stood, nodded once, and settled her brimmed hat low over her brows. "I have to get back to work. If you need me to pick Reggie up later, I can do that."

"I won't be here that long. I'll get her." Tory placed her palm against Reese's chest. "Reese—"

The radio clipped to Reese's shoulder crackled.

"Sheriff?"

"Go ahead, Lyons," Reese replied sharply.

"We've got a problem out here."

Reese's jaw set. "I'll be right there." She brushed her lips over Tory's forehead. "I'll see you later."

Tory watched her lover walk away, wishing she could call her back, wishing she could erase the disappointment she had seen in Reese's eyes. But Reese had a job to do, as did she. Forcing back the sadness and the small sliver of self-recrimination, she sat down behind her desk and reached for the first chart on the ten-inch-high stack that awaited her.

Chapter Four

After thirty minutes of fruitless effort, Tory realized that she wasn't going to be able to concentrate enough to efficiently finish her chart work.

"I'll just have to come in tomorrow morning and do it," she muttered as she tossed her pen aside and rose from behind her desk. Ten seconds later, the cell phone on her belt vibrated. Hoping it was Reese, she snapped it open. "This is Dr. King."

"It's Reese. I need you to come out to the scene on 6."

Tory tensed. "Another victim?"

There was a beat of silence, then Reese's voice, flat and low. "No. A DB."

In addition to her clinical practice, Tory also acted as the county coroner in those rare instances when it was necessary. It wasn't unusual in small communities where suspicious or unanticipated deaths were rare for a local physician to perform the basic duties of confirming death, noting the time and circumstances, and signing the death certificate. Thankfully, it wasn't a responsibility she needed to fulfill often.

"I'll be right there."

Reese gave her the directions and signed off. On the short drive to the other end of town, Tory tried not to think about what might be waiting for her. No death was ever easy or routine, but at least there was some small comfort in knowing it was part of the natural cycle of life. But violent and senseless death, so often a result of man's careless or brutal action, was unforgivably tragic. She saw the line of emergency flares isolating the vehicle from the road and slowed to a halt on the shoulder. In the eerie red-orange glow of the magnesium torches, she could make out the silhouettes of figures moving around the vehicle, stringing crime scene tape.

One of those shadowy forms, she knew, was her lover. Uncertain of her footing in the semidarkness on the soft, shifting sand, Tory moved forward slowly. When she'd almost reached the rear of the vehicle, Reese materialized from the darkness and extended a hand.

"She's back here in the brush. Here—hold on to me. The slope here is tricky."

There had been a time when Tory would never have accepted assistance, even from someone who loved her. The accident that had occurred in the midst of the Olympic rowing heats over a decade before had nearly cost her her leg, but she'd lost more than her ability to compete. For a very long time, she'd lost her independence as well as her health. Her recovery, both physical and emotional, had been slow and hard-won. Only in the last few years had she regained enough confidence to allow help and enough strength in her damaged leg not to need it under most circumstances. But this was Reese, and the situation was extreme, and she couldn't risk an injury now merely for the sake of pride. She closed her fingers around Reese's hand and inched down the steep slope toward the scrub brush that dotted the dunes.

"What have you got?" Tory asked, her voice sounding very loud in the hushed night air.

"A girl—looks to be the same age as the boy we brought in. From the position of the body and the condition of the terrain, it looks like she was running from someone."

Tory's throat closed. "A homicide?"

Reese shone her Mag-Lite on a narrow sandy path that appeared through the darkness for an instant and then disappeared beyond the semicircle of illumination once again. "I'm not sure yet. She might have been running from the boy. Hell, they might just have been fooling around." She clamped her jaws tightly. "They certainly look the part to be playing silly kids' games. Barely more than children."

"Hide and seek? Win a kiss if you catch me?"

"Could be something as simple as that." Reese shrugged as much in comment as in an attempt to dispel the melancholy. *What a waste.*

They walked another twenty yards before Reese slowed. A

pair of sandaled feet appeared at the far edge of the spot of light that preceded them, then slim legs came into view, followed by narrow hips in white capri pants, a bare midriff with a glint of silver at the navel, and small, high breasts beneath a tight, light blue tube top. Tory's heart plummeted. The soft face beneath short blond hair was smooth and unmarred. An angel's face. *Oh God.*

"Have you moved her?" Tory stood at the juncture of light and shadow observing the body in the harsh artificial illumination.

"No. I just felt for a pulse. There wasn't one." Reese blew out a breath of frustration. "Allie Tremont found her. For a rookie, she did good. She kept her head and didn't contaminate the area, but she did check for a heartbeat. According to Allie, there wasn't one then either." Reese jammed her hands in her uniform pockets, her feet spread, her shoulders stiff as she stared down at the young girl's body. "I should've checked the area before I left with the boy. Maybe she was alive then. God *damn* it."

"If you had waited, *he* would've died." Tory didn't touch Reese because she knew that wasn't what her lover needed. "You made the right call, Sheriff. Now, is it safe for me to move around here?"

"Yes. We took photographs as best we could. We're not exactly equipped for a high-tech crime scene analysis here. We won't be able to really map the area and check for trace until daylight."

"Did you get 360-degree images of the body?" As she spoke, Tory opened the small satchel she kept in her Jeep for just such call-outs and cautiously knelt in the sand. The victim lay partially on her side, one leg drawn up and her body curled in on itself as if sleeping. Tory checked the muscle tone in the left arm, gently flexing and extending the elbow. It was stiff, but not in full rigor. "She's been dead for less than ten hours, but definitely for more than two." She looked up at her lover, silhouetted against the night sky. "You couldn't have helped her."

"Not in life, perhaps," Reese said quietly. She squatted down beside Tory, holding the light for her as she worked. "Do you see anything to suggest homicide?"

"Not yet," Tory replied, gently rolling the body flat onto its back. "But the best I'm going to be able to do here is recognize severe blunt or penetrating trauma. She'll need a full postmortem, and that's going to take someone more skilled than me to do it." She drew out a palm-sized Dictaphone and described the appearance of the body, indicating position, state of the clothing, presence and absence of identifying marks, evidence of trauma, and noted no apparent disruption in the surrounding area to suggest that a struggle had taken place. At least not there. When she'd finished the brief dictation, she removed a long, thin stylet that resembled a stainless steel knitting needle, pushed up the lower border of the clinging tube top, palpated the lower edge of the twelfth rib on the right side, and pushed the transcutaneous thermometer through the skin and into the right lobe of the liver. "The core temperature will give us a much better indication of time of death. The ambient temperature is fortunately still fairly close to body temperature, so we haven't lost much heat to the environment. Ask Jeff or Allie to get me a precise temperature reading now, please."

"Eighty-three degrees Fahrenheit."

Tory nodded, realizing that of course Reese would have already thought to do that. "Thank you."

"You're welcome."

"Have you identified her?"

"No," Reese said with a hint of irritation in her voice. "There's no wallet, no purse, and nothing in the car to indicate who she is. Hopefully, Robert Bridger will be able to tell us."

"She doesn't look like a street kid or a prostitute." Tory lifted one slim hand, staring at the slender fingers curled gently in her palm. "Her nails are clean and manicured. She's well nourished. Her clothes are expensive but tasteful. My guess is that Robert knows her and didn't pick her up on the side of the road somewhere."

"That's my thought too." Reese rolled her shoulders. "So far we haven't found anything useful in the vehicle. If this is an overdose, where are the pills?"

Without thinking, Tory reached out and braced her arm against Reese's thigh as she pushed herself upright, favoring her weakened leg. She didn't move away when Reese steadied her with an arm around her waist. Kneeling for extended periods still took a toll on her nerve-damaged calf. "Maybe they took them all?"

"And what, threw the bottles out the window?"

Tory shrugged as they made their way back to the road. "I

suppose that's possible. Perhaps they just grabbed enough for the night and got something stronger than they bargained for."

"Maybe. But if they didn't raid the drug cabinet at home, I want to know who supplied them with whatever almost killed them both."

"I'm sure you'll find out what happened." Tory's tone was far from placating. She spoke with quiet certainty. "Let me make some calls and find out who's available to do the post. Then we'll get an ambulance out here to transport her."

"Thanks. I'm sorry to have to bring you out here for this."

"Don't apologize." Tory lifted a hand and rested her fingers gently against Reese's cheek. "Try to get home sometime tonight, all right?"

"There's a fair amount of work to be done out here." Reese rubbed her face. "And I have to ID this girl. I may need to drive up to the hospital to interview the boy."

"Don't do that on no sleep, Reese," Tory said quietly. "Don't make me worry all night."

Reese sighed. "I won't. But if it gets really late, I might catch an hour or so at the station and then go."

"I understand. Come home when you can."

"Tory...I'm sorry about the way I left earlier..."

"It's all right, darling. You've got work to do." Tory allowed her fingers to trail over Reese's jaw before drawing away. "We'll talk soon. I promise. I love you."

"I love you, too." Reese opened the driver's door of Tory's Jeep so her lover could slide in. "Kiss the baby for me."

❖

"Is there anything I can do?" Bri stood by the side of Allie's desk, her hands in her pockets, her blue eyes dark with worry. Allie was pale and her hands shook as she filled out paperwork. It was three in the morning and they had both been off shift for over three hours, but Allie needed to document the details of finding the dead girl before leaving and Bri had stayed to finish her report on the boy. Now, she lingered out of concern and sympathy for her friend. She wondered how *she* would have reacted to coming upon a dead teenager in the brush in the middle of the night.

Allie looked up, dark eyes liquid with pain and fatigue. She forced a smile. "No, I'm okay. Almost done."

"Sure?"

"Yeah, thanks. You go ahead. It's late."

"How about I give you a ride home?"

"I've got my car," Allie said, but her expression belied her efforts to sound composed.

"This whole night has been a bummer," Bri noted truthfully. "I wouldn't mind company for a while."

A smile of thanks flickered on Allie's face. "Yeah?" At Bri's solemn nod, she said quickly, "Five minutes."

Even at the height of the season, the small town was deserted in the middle of the night. The bars closed at one and there was nothing much in the way of entertainment beyond that time. Bri, feeling as if they were the only two people in the world, powered the motorcycle through the twisting, narrow streets with Allie clinging to her back. Somewhere, though, she reminded herself, on the other side of the ocean that she could hear in the background even above the roar of her engine, Caroline was just waking. She missed her so much, especially now, when she hurt inside with feelings she couldn't put a name to. The warmth of Allie's body was comforting.

Gunning the engine, she took the bike in a low, sweeping dip around a turn onto the road to Pilgrim's Heights. Allie tightened her hold, and Bri felt a hand press low against the front of her uniform pants. Surprised, she covered Allie's fingers with her own before they could move anywhere else. She kept her hand there until she needed both to navigate the sharp turn into Allie's driveway. She cut the engine and put a leg down on either side of the big bike to steady it. "I'll swing by tomorrow and take you to the station to get your car."

"Can you come in for a while?" Allie asked, sliding off to stand by Bri's side. She rested one hand on Bri's thigh in a casual gesture, but her voice trembled. "I'm wide awake. I could fix us a drink or something to eat."

Bri heard the plea beneath the invitation and realized that Allie must be more upset than she wanted to let on. "Sure, for a bit. Thanks." She kicked down the stand and swung her leg over the wide tank, then followed Allie up the winding stone path to the small bungalow. Once inside, she waited while Allie turned on lights and rummaged in the kitchen.

"Here," Allie said, handing Bri a beer. She gestured to the sofa with her own bottle and the two young officers, both still in uniform, sat down side by side. They drank in silence for a few moments.

"You doing okay, for real?" Bri finally asked.

"I'm not so sure," Allie confessed in a small voice. She kept her eyes down, staring at the beer bottle that she turned around and around between her clasped hands. "It was weird. When I saw her, I thought she was sleeping. I thought, what a stupid place to sack out. Then it hit me. All at once. And I knew she was dead."

"That must've been hard." They had been in tough situations together, including a life-threatening fire. Bri had been in a takedown that had resulted in gunshots and death. But she'd never walked up on death alone. Secretly, she was glad.

"You know," Allie went on, "you always read about cops throwing up or something when they find a body, but I didn't feel that way. I felt...cold." She shivered, set her beer bottle down, and moved closer to Bri on the sofa. "I still do."

When Allie took her hand, Bri closed her fingers around Allie's in silent comfort.

"Reese and Jeff both said I did okay." Allie leaned her shoulder against Bri's and pulled Bri's hand into her lap, holding it between her own. In a low, tortured voice, she asked, "Don't you think I should feel something else? Like...maybe there's something wrong with me because I don't?"

"No," Bri said comfortingly. "No. I think you're tired and stressed and maybe...a little freaked out. I think that's pretty normal."

Allie laughed shakily. "Jeez, I don't feel normal."

"I think you did great too." Bri squeezed Allie's fingers. "I'm sorry you had to go through it, though."

"Part of the job, right?" Allie shrugged and tried to sound tough.

"Yeah. A really *rough* part."

"Thanks." Allie rested her cheek against Bri's shoulder. "For bringing me home."

"Maybe you should call Ashley," Bri suggested tentatively. "Tell her about it."

Allie shook her head. "No. We're sort of...cooling things off for a while."

"Why?"

"Oh, you know. Things run hot for a while and then..." She shrugged again.

"So you broke up?" Bri tried to remember the last time she had seen Allie with Ashley Walker, the private investigator with whom they had all worked a case earlier in the summer. She realized that it had been a few weeks at least. She'd *thought* that they were a couple, or at least headed in that direction.

"Ashley said...oh, fuck..." Allie moved one hand from Bri's, sat up, and grabbed for her beer bottle. She drained it in one long swallow. "Ashley's decided that she's too old for me. Do you believe that?"

"So she broke up with you?" Bri's voice held a note of incredulity. "For something like that? What is she, ten years older or something?"

"About that. So she's decided that I'm too young to make a commitment and that we should take things *slow*." She grunted derisively. "In my book, that means screw other people and forget about each other."

Bri frowned, recalling the attractive redhead who had not seemed like a woman who would be interested in casual encounters. "Did she *say* that?"

"She didn't have to. I got the message."

"Uh, maybe that's not what she meant. You know, sometimes, women are hard to figure out."

Allie regarded Bri with a slow smile. "Is that right? I never noticed that you had much trouble."

Bri blushed. "Half the time I'm not certain what Carre needs. I'm just happy to get it right whenever I do."

At the mention of Bri's girlfriend, Allie's smile wavered. "You're pretty crazy about her, huh?"

"Yeah. Totally."

With a seductive purr, Allie leaned close again, one arm sliding around Bri's waist and her lips close to Bri's ear. "But you're not married, right? I mean, she's going to be gone a long time."

When the warm breath tickled her ear and a very practiced hand smoothed over her abdomen and came to rest on her fly, Bri felt a familiar spark of arousal. This wasn't the first time Allie had touched her, and she remembered exactly how good that had felt. The last time they'd been naked in bed together, and she'd almost come while Allie touched her. Gently, Bri covered Allie's hand as she had done on the bike and moved it up a safe distance. "I'm not into fooling around. But if I was, I'd be begging at your door."

Allie grew very still, then after a minute, edged away until she could look into Bri's face. "That was a really nice thing to say. You're sweet, you know that?"

"Not really. It's the truth, what I said about you. You're hot. But I can't cheat on my girl."

Curiously, Allie asked, "Even if she never knew?"

"I'd know. I already don't deserve her." Bri shrugged and looked away, embarrassed. "But I'm trying."

"Will you stay here tonight?"

Bri's head snapped back. "Huh?"

"Not for sex. I just...I'd just like not to be alone."

"I can't sleep in bed with you." Bri wasn't crazy enough to think that she could sleep next to a gorgeous, hot woman who wanted her and not be tempted.

"You can take the bed, and I could sleep out here on the couch."

Bri laughed. "The couch will do me fine. But I'm only staying on one condition."

"What?" Allie asked playfully.

"You're making the breakfast."

"Oh, Officer Parker," Allie cooed, leaning close and kissing Bri's cheek. "You are *so* easy."

Chapter Five

Uh-oh," Nelson Parker muttered.

Reese followed her boss's gaze down the hospital hallway and saw a woman rise from a chair in the seating area outside the intensive care unit and start toward them. Swiftly, Reese took stock. Nearly her height, but not as muscular. Shoulder-length dark hair, looking as if it had been subtly cut to hold its casual style no matter the wind or weather. Light makeup, clear, pale complexion, hazel eyes gleaming even in the dim light. Piercing eyes—hard, unreadable eyes. A faint smile that might have been welcome or warning. At just after four in the morning, the woman, dressed casually in tan slacks and a cream-colored short-sleeved blouse, looked remarkably fresh and alert. She also looked, Reese thought, as if she were enjoying herself. *Uh-oh is right.*

"You must be here about Robert Bridger," the woman said in a rich, smooth alto, her eyes moving slowly from Nelson to Reese.

"I'm Chief Nelson Parker and this is Sheriff Reese Conlon," Nelson said. He held out his hand, which the woman took.

"How do you do? I'm Trey Pelosi, the Bridgers' attorney." She smiled again, and turned to Reese with an extended hand. "Sheriff."

"Counselor," Reese said quietly. "Vacationing in the area?"

"Why, yes," Trey answered, her eyes sharpening as she gave Reese an appraising glance. "I have a summer home in Truro."

"Yours must have been the taillights we saw ahead of us all the way up here."

Trey laughed. "Actually, I've been here a few hours."

His parents must have called you as soon as I finished talking to them, Reese surmised. *You probably got here before Robert arrived. Gives a new meaning to the term ambulance chaser.*

"We called the boy's doctors on our way up from Provincetown," Nelson stated. "They informed us that Robert was awake and could answer some questions. Are his parents here?"

"They are. Yes." She hadn't moved and her smile hadn't wavered. She stood comfortably, but quite obviously, in their path. "The doctors were partially correct. Robert is awake, but I'm afraid he won't be answering any questions."

"Is there some reason you don't want him to talk to us, Counselor?" Reese asked in a steady, even tone.

"Are you charging him with a crime, Sheriff?"

"At the moment, we're simply trying to find out what happened. He's the only one who can tell us."

"And at the *moment,* Robert isn't up to being questioned," Trey responded firmly without raising her voice.

"The doctors said—" Nelson began.

"I'm sorry that you both came all the way up here in the middle of the night," Trey interjected, her tone still reasonable. "However, I'm afraid that at the present time I can't allow Robert to answer any questions. Sometime tomorrow, I expect that his parents will retain permanent counsel. If you give me your contact information, I'll be certain that you're notified."

"You're not a criminal attorney, then?" Reese asked

Once again, a smile flickered at the corner of Trey's mouth and was quickly gone. "No. I'm a corporate attorney. Robert's mother is...an old friend. I was nearby, and they asked me to serve as temporary counsel."

"Ms. Pelosi," Reese said sharply, "I have a dead teenager whose name I don't know. Somewhere, that girl's parents are wondering where she is. I need to answer their question, and to do that, I need Robert to tell me who she is. That's all I want right now."

Nothing showed in Trey's eyes now as she met Reese's—not sympathy, not irritation, not anger. Her expression remained remote. "I appreciate your situation, Sheriff. I'm certain that Robert's attorney will do everything possible to assist you at the appropriate time. But for tonight, Robert is unavailable."

"Thanks," Nelson said quickly as he caught the rigid set of Reese's jaw out of the corner of his eye. She'd been up all night, and although she didn't look it, he knew she was wrapped pretty tight. He felt a little sick himself, and he hadn't been the one to find a dead girl in the dunes. When Reese had awoken him to advise him of the situation, the first thing he'd flashed on was the night they'd found Bri out there, beaten and nearly dead. The swift surge of nausea still hadn't left him, and he could only imagine what the frustration and distress was doing to Reese. Ordinarily, his second in command was the picture of equanimity in a stressful situation, but some things just got to you more than others. And being stonewalled at this point in the investigation was tough to swallow. "Here's my card. Please tell Robert's family that we'll be in touch tomorrow and will need to speak to him."

"Certainly," Trey said, taking the card and sliding it into her left breast pocket. She nodded before turning away. "Good night, Officers."

Reese watched her walk away with a combination of admiration and supreme irritation. It was difficult to be angry with someone who was simply doing her job very well, but at the moment, she was furious. Every minute that passed without her having a name for the girl lying under a white sheet in Tory's clinic awaiting transfer to the morgue in Barnstable for autopsy added to her sense of helplessness and rage. "Son of a bitch."

Nelson's eyebrows arched. Reese rarely cursed in his presence or, to his knowledge, much at all. It wasn't because she was too proper or too uptight; she was simply too controlled. "I'll bet she's hell in a courtroom."

"I suppose I should just be glad that I'll never find out," Reese muttered. Turning away, she rubbed a hand over her face wearily. "God damn it."

As they walked down the hall toward the elevators, Nelson clapped Reese briefly on the shoulder before putting his hands in his pockets. "Look, it makes sense for her to advise the family not to let him talk. Once we get a better handle on what happened out there—get some of the lab reports back, check the scene by daylight, get a little leverage on our side—we'll try again. We might have nothing to charge him with, and even if we do, in all likelihood the state boys will take it over anyhow."

Reese cut him a look of disgust. "I'm not thinking about the charges. I'm thinking about a dead girl with no name."

"I know."

His voice was edged with pain, and Reese sighed as they stepped out into the dawn. "Sorry, Chief."

"No need to apologize. It pisses me off, too." He slid into the cruiser and waited while Reese climbed into the passenger side. "I'll drop you off home." At her look of protest, he shook his head firmly. "Nothing is going to change in the next few hours, so you might as well get some sleep. If anything comes up, I'll call you."

"Yes, sir."

"Are the kids okay?"

She knew what he meant without asking. "Bri's fine. She handled herself perfectly during the vehicle surveillance and search. Allie, too. She was a little bit shaken up after finding the body, so we'll need to keep an eye on her for the next day or two. But she was solid in the field."

"Glad to hear it. Christ, how the hell did I end up with a force that's half women?" he muttered under his breath.

For the first time in hours, Reese grinned. "Just lucky, I guess, Chief."

❖

Forty-five minutes later, Reese let herself quietly into her house through the back door. She stopped in the kitchen and made a small pile of her equipment belt, keys, and hat on the breakfast counter. When she slipped as quietly as possible up the stairs, loosening her tie and unbuttoning her shirt as she went, she heard a tiny whimper from the nursery. Moving quickly, she entered the room and leaned over the crib. Reggie, waving one tiny fist in the air, regarded her with solemn eyes and the ghost of a smile.

"Hey, Tiger. You're awake already, huh?" Reese reached in and lifted her out. Cradling the baby on her left shoulder, she used her right hand to open a fresh diaper on top of the bassinet and arrange the other necessary supplies. Then she laid her daughter down to change her. "So, did you dream about something special last night? You have dreams, right? I bet you do. Exciting ones." With swift economy, she closed the sticky tabs to hold the diaper in place and maneuvered the baby into a clean onesie. "Hungry yet? Sure you are. You're always hungry."

Reggie made a gurgling sound of assent.

"Okay. Breakfast, then. What do you say we let Mommy sleep and get some of the stored stuff out of the refrigerator?"

"Mommy's awake," Tory said from the doorway where she'd been leaning watching her lover take care of their daughter. There were times that she looked at the two of them and feared her heart would burst.

Reese turned with the baby in her arms. "Hey."

Tory crossed the room and kissed Reese on the mouth. "Hi. Are you all right?"

"Yeah. Just a little tired."

"Why don't you get ready for bed, and I'll take care of her. I'll be there as soon as she's settled again."

"Feed her in bed. I like to watch."

Tory held out her arms for Reggie. "All right. Go get out of your uniform."

A few minutes later, Reese crawled under the covers and turned on her side next to Tory and the baby. She propped her head on one hand and rested the other hand on Tory's abdomen, her fingers just touching the baby's leg. "She looks so content."

"She is," Tory said with a small laugh. She ran the fingers of her free hand through the hair at the back of Reese's neck. "Want to tell me about last night?"

Reese shook her head. "Not until she's done. I don't want to think about anything except how beautiful both of you are."

Tory drew a sharp breath. "Honey, it's probably best that I not be aroused in the middle of this."

"You think she could tell?" Reese asked seriously.

"No," Tory laughed again, "but I can only handle so many conflicting stimuli at once."

"Oh." Reese was quiet for a few seconds. "That's a pretty sexy thought."

Tory tugged on Reese's hair. "I think your daughter isn't the only one who's hungry. Can you stay awake long enough?"

"I'm not the slightest bit tired."

"Give me ten minutes to get her fed and back to bed."

When Tory returned from the nursery, Reese lay on her back with both arms behind her head, watching Tory with an appreciative expression as she crossed the room. "That was eleven."

"Was it?" Tory asked as she drew the sheet aside and stretched out on top of Reese. She braced herself with her bent elbows on either side of Reese's head, once again threading her fingers into Reese's hair. With her mouth hovering above Reese's, she murmured, "Then I'll have to take a little longer doing what I plan on doing to you to make up for it."

Reese's moan was lost in the depths of Tory's mouth as their lips met and Tory settled her hips more closely between Reese's legs. Their joining was as seamless as two halves of a whole slotting together, their bodies and hearts blending effortlessly. Tory allowed the weight of her body to press into Reese's firm muscles and soft skin, loving the solid feel of Reese beneath her. Reese—so strong, so tender—everything she'd dreamed of, everything she counted on, everything she needed.

"Reese, I love you."

Almost dizzy with the heat of Tory's passion against her, inside her mouth, surrounding her, Reese opened her eyes and searched her lover's. "I need you so much."

Tory lifted her hips and slid her hand between their bodies, cupping Reese in her palm. Slowly, watching her lover's face, she slid into her, claiming her as she had been claimed. "I'm here, baby. Always." She settled her hips once again, her own wetness warming the top of her hand as Reese's flowed into her palm. When she began to thrust, Reese groaned and her eyelids flickered closed.

"Reese," Tory gasped, rocking harder, exciting herself as she entered Reese more deeply with each plunge, "watch my face. Watch my face and know how much I love you."

With supreme effort Reese opened her eyes. "I'll come just from looking at you."

"I want you to come watching me love you." Tory's voice was throaty and fierce as her hips bucked harder. Reese was everywhere—under her, around her, filling her heart to overflowing.

Reese caught Tory's breast in her hand, squeezing gently to the same rhythm that beat through her blood and her bones as Tory took her higher. Her skin burned, her belly was molten, and her mind filled with shimmering lights. She felt Tory's fingers inside her, filling her, holding her, owning her. "Slow down. Tor, slow down."

"No."

"Please. Come first," Reese implored. "Let me see you come."

Stilling her hand, Tory threw her head back and circled her hips faster between Reese's thighs, rubbing her clitoris harder over the back of her hand. "Oh God, soon." She caught her lower lip between her teeth and looked down into Reese's eyes as the first tendrils of orgasm floated free. The love and wonder she saw in their blue depths shot through her just as the orgasm exploded outward, and she crested on the twin peaks of unbearable pleasure. Crying out, she pushed her fingers hard into Reese, who immediately arched her back and came.

"Thank you," Reese groaned when she could finally talk. She held Tory tightly, cradling her lover's damp face against her shoulder. She kissed Tory's forehead and smoothed her hair away from her face. "You're so beautiful like that. Until Reggie I'd never seen anything that came close to being as beautiful."

Heart aching, Tory pressed her lips to Reese's neck. "I would never hurt you intentionally. You know that, don't you?"

"I know." Reese continued to stroke Tory's neck and shoulders as she reached with her free hand to pull the sheet over them. She closed her eyes for a second while she summoned her courage. "I'm afraid. I'm afraid that it will be too much, too soon. I still remember what it felt like riding in that goddamned ambulance the night Reggie was born and being afraid that I would lose you. Lose you both." Reese pressed her face to Tory's hair. "I couldn't stand it, Tor. I couldn't make it without you."

Tory gave a small cry and pushed herself up until she could see Reese's face. "Oh, baby. No. Nothing like that is going to happen. I promise."

"Sometimes I worry that I won't be able to take care of you. Christ..." Reese took a long, shaky breath. "The only things I'm good at—being a marine, being a cop—don't seem to be enough sometimes."

"I don't have any idea what you're talking about," Tory said gently. She kissed Reese's mouth softly. "You are strong and brave and gentle and kind and tender. You love me and you love Reggie and that's everything. *Everything.*"

"God, I hope so." Reese kissed Tory again, deeply, with near-desperate passion. When she drew away, she sighed with a conflicting combination of contentment and concern. "You have to get help at the clinic, Tor. It *will* be too much otherwise. It was already too much before Reggie was born, and now—"

"I will. I'll find someone. I promise."

Reese caught Tory's hand and brought it to her lips, then gently kissed each finger. "Promise that you'll take care of yourself. It won't help your patients if you get sick."

"I'll take care of myself for you and for Reggie." Tory slid to Reese's side and stroked her lover's neck and chest. "Go to sleep now, honey. Everything is going to work out."

Reese allowed Tory to gentle her into sleep, needing the strength of her lover's comfort to dispel the vision of a nameless blond girl who reached out to her through the dark.

Chapter Six

Bri squinted against the bright light dancing on the surface of her eyelids and tried to go back to sleep, but the combination of sun, the stealthy sounds emanating from the kitchen, and the sumptuous smell of coffee were too much to fight. She opened her eyes and rolled onto her side just in time to see Allie walk into the living room from the kitchen carrying two mugs of coffee. The next thing Bri noted was that Allie was wearing a T-shirt that came just to the top of her pale pink bikini panties. Bri rolled over in the other direction and pressed her face to the back of the couch.

"Hey," Allie said, her voice still thick with sleep. "It's almost ten. Want some coffee?"

"You can leave it on the table there." Bri felt the couch sway as Allie settled onto the far end. She heard Allie yawn just before she felt cool fingers drift over her bare calf. She'd taken off her shoes, socks, and uniform when she'd gone to sleep the night before. The only things she had on beside the thin comforter that Allie had provided were briefs and a T-shirt. Still, she was wearing more than Allie.

"As soon as I wake up a little bit," Allie mumbled, "I'll make us some breakfast." She rubbed the top of Bri's foot absently. "Did you sleep okay?"

"Uh-huh."

"Hungry?"

"Uh-huh."

Bri felt the couch dip again as Allie shifted. She felt bare skin against the bottom of her foot. Her toes tingled and her stomach did a whirly.

"Is there something wrong?" Allie asked drowsily.

"Uh-huh."

"Yeah? What?"

"You're practically naked."

Allie snorted. "Everything is covered."

"Everything should be covered with *more* than one layer. Go get dressed." Bri still lay on her side with her head practically in the crevice between the seat cushions and the back of the couch.

"You're serious, aren't you?"

With a sigh, Bri turned onto her back and opened her eyes again, squinting at the sudden brightness. "Allie. What part don't you get about me having a girlfriend and—"

"I *got* that, Bri," Allie said indignantly. "Jeez, you don't have to keep reminding me."

Bri's eyes widened. "You're serious, aren't you?"

"Huh?"

"Okay. Let me try to explain something." Bri pushed up on the couch and reached for her coffee, praying that the caffeine would clear her addled brain. She kept the comforter tightly secured around her middle and pulled her bare feet under the bottom edge as well. She could tell from the expression on Allie's face that Allie was truly confused. "We're not girlfriends, okay?"

Allie's eyes narrowed. "I know that, Bri. You and *Caroline* are girlfriends."

"No," Bri said, shaking her head. She took a long sip of coffee and although it burned the roof of her mouth, she was grateful for the pain. She was definitely awake. "Not that kind of girlfriends. *Girlfriend* girlfriends. You know, the kind of friends where you can walk around the house naked in front of one another."

"You don't want to be friends?" There was more than a little hurt in Allie's voice.

"I didn't *say* that." Bri blew out a breath. *Jesus.* "Let's pretend we're straight."

"*Please.*"

Bri laughed. "Just bear with me. Let's pretend we're straight and I'm a guy and you're a girl."

Allie tucked her feet up under her on the couch, her coffee mug cradled in her hands, and eyed Bri with interest. "I'm a straight girl."

"Right."

"Gotcha."

"So," Bri continued, "I'm a guy and I have a girlfriend. Not you. Some other girl."

"Yeah, yeah."

"But you and I work together. We like each other. We're friends."

"Yeah?"

"So would you walk around the house in your little teeny tiny practically see-through underwear in front of me?"

Allie grinned. "Only if I wanted to give you a great big hard-on and make you suffer for being so noble and refusing to fuck me."

Bri couldn't help but grin back. "Well, it's working."

"I didn't do it on purpose." Allie's expression for once was completely serious. "I'm sorry. I didn't think about it that way. I'm cool with us being friends. Well, not really cool. But I'd like to try."

"Me, too. But you have to keep all your clothes on."

"It's funny, you know," Allie mused as she sipped her coffee. "When you grow up having girlfriends who really *are* girlfriends, and then you find out you're a lesbian and that you like some of your girlfriends differently, it gets confusing."

"I never had girlfriend girlfriends."

"Really?" Allie gave that some thought. "How many girlfriends have you had in bed?"

"Just Carre," Bri said quietly.

"Holy shit. You're kidding."

Bri shook her head. "Nope."

"And you're willing to just…I don't know, settle for that? Like, you never plan on sleeping with another girl?"

"Well, you don't know Carre." Bri grinned. "She's, well, she's the best."

"Oh, puh-leeze." Allie groaned and dropped her head onto the back to the couch. "You are so whipped."

"Don't you believe in falling in love forever?"

Allie turned her head, her cheek still resting on the sofa, and regarded Bri solemnly. "I don't know. I don't think so, but I'm not sure. I don't know any couples like that. My mom and dad divorced when I was eight. My grandparents are still together, but I never got the sense they were really all that fond of one another."

"There's Reese and Tory," Bri said immediately.

"Yeah. They're cool." Allie purred and stretched. "And Reese is *so* hot."

"Jesus, Allie," Bri protested indignantly. "Don't say that about her."

"Why not? She's drop-dead gorgeous and built like—like Xena."

"Oh, *please.*" Bri made a choking sound. "Xena is such a girl. Reese would kick Xena's ass."

Allie threw a sofa pillow at her. "Would not."

"Would too." Bri threw it back. When they stopped laughing, Bri said solemnly, "Reese and Tory are special."

"I know." Allie leaned down and set her coffee cup on the table. She regarded Bri solemnly. "I bet you and Caroline will be like them someday. That's cool. I'm gonna go get dressed."

"How about I start breakfast?"

"Do you know how?" Allie asked suspiciously.

"Sure." Bri reached up and caught Allie's hand, squeezing it gently for a second. "And Allie? Thanks."

"Yeah, yeah. Don't burn anything in there, okay?"

"Don't worry. You can trust me."

"I know," Allie said softly as she disappeared into her bedroom and quietly closed the door.

❖

Reese surfaced to the sound of the phone ringing and Tory's muted voice in the background.

"Oh hi, Dan," Tory said in a whisper. "No, that's okay...I was planning on coming in this evening, why?...Really? Who?...*Now?* I don't know. Reese is still asleep and—"

"I'm awake, sweetheart," Reese said as she rolled over and wrapped her arm around Tory's waist. She opened her eyes and saw that Tory had been sitting up in bed reading with the baby asleep in her lap. She rubbed Reggie's back and kissed the side of

Tory's breast through the thin tee she wore. "What's going on?"

Tory covered the receiver with her hand. "Dan says the service left word about someone who wants to interview for the position at the clinic. For some reason he just got the message, and whoever it is wants to come in this morning while they're in town for another appointment. Can you take Reggie to Kate and Jean's so I can go over there?"

"Sure."

"Dan?" Tory said into the phone. "I can be there at noon. Do you have a number for me to contact this person?...A name?... Damn, the answering service gets worse and worse all the time. Never mind, I'll just come over as soon as I can. Thanks. Bye."

Tory hung up the phone and stared at Reese. "It looks like there's someone who's really hot for the job. I'm sorry I have to rush out."

"No problem. I should be getting up anyhow." Reese pushed upright and craned her neck to look at the clock. "Christ! It's almost eleven. I've got to get to work."

"Honey, you didn't get to bed until after six."

"Yeah, but what kept me *up* until six put me to sleep very nicely." She swung her legs over the side of the bed and stood, grinning down at her lover and their child. "I slept like a rock." Reese held out her arms. "Here, let me have sleeping beauty, and I'll get her and all the stuff ready to take to Grandmoms'. You wanna shower first, right?"

"Yes. Thanks, honey." Tory ran a hand distractedly through her hair as she gathered her clothes. "I wish I had some idea what I was walking into. It's very strange that someone just shows up for an interview without arranging things first. I hope they remembered to bring a CV."

"It's Provincetown. Everything is casual here." Reese leaned to kiss Tory's cheek on her way past to the nursery. "Maybe it's fate. It's certainly perfect timing."

"Fate. Yeah, right," Tory sighed.

❖

At eleven thirty, Tory walked through the front door into the waiting room at the East End Health Clinic, which was crowded as always. Randy sketched her a short wave as he talked on the phone and indicated with a roll of his eyes and a frantic motion of his head that her presence was needed in the back.

"What?" Tory asked sotto voce as she passed by the reception desk.

Annoyed, Randy pressed the mouthpiece of the phone to his shoulder. "In your *office.* Dr. Impatience has been waiting half an hour." Then he ignored Tory's question for details and went back to his call.

"Great," Tory muttered as she pushed through the dividing door into the clinical area beyond. Her office door was partly closed and as she pushed through, she put on her best professional smile. As her eyes took in the woman standing in profile studying the photographs on the wall, Tory stumbled to a halt and barely managed to suppress a gasp.

"KT? What are you doing here?" Tory was aware that her tone sounded accusatory, and not the slightest bit gracious, but her ex-lover was the last person she'd expected to find in her office. They'd barely seen each other in the nearly seven years since they'd separated, and almost all of those times had been during a medical crisis. Fortunately, the circumstances of those interactions had prevented them from having any true personal exchange, which was just as well. Tory had nothing to say to the woman with whom she had lived for twelve years, and whom she had loved with all her heart and youthful optimism, and who had betrayed their love and left her shattered.

Slowly, KT turned to face Tory fully. "Hi, Vic."

"Oh my God." Tory's stomach roiled as if she'd been punched, and for one terrifying second she was afraid she might be ill. She took one involuntary step forward, her hand raised as if for a caress, before she jerked to a stop. Her voice wavered as she asked, "What happened? God, KT."

"Bit of a dustup in the trauma unit about a month ago. I ran into a crackhead with a knife." KT shrugged and mustered up a smile. "Looks worse than it is."

It couldn't possibly look any worse than it does, Tory screamed inside. A fresh scar, red and faintly angry looking, crossed KT's right cheek, starting just below her eye and ending at her jaw. It wasn't the injury itself that Tory found so devastating, but imagining KT having been brutalized that way. But it was even more than the healing laceration that was so terribly upsetting. The physician part of her mind reminded Tory *that* would probably leave a scar that was only minimally deforming. It was the way KT looked. She was thinner than Tory had ever seen her, even when they had both been residents and KT was working like a madwoman 120 hours a week, barely sleeping and usually forgetting to eat. Tory remembered that young surgery resident, so charged with life, so aggressive and charismatic. The woman who faced her now, hollow-eyed and gaunt, wasn't even a ghost of that young warrior. Realizing she was staring, Tory forced her gaze away from KT's haunted eyes and looked down. Then she did cry out. "Oh God, *no.* Oh, what did he do to you?"

"It's okay, Vic," KT said gently. There was no place she could put her left arm to remove it from Tory's horrified stare. The hand surgeon had taken the cast off only days before, and she wore a molded plastic splint from fingertips to midforearm that kept her damaged fingers protected as well as immobilized with a complicated set of tiny pulleys and bands.

With concerted effort, Tory compelled her mind to rule her emotions. She'd seen every kind of human tragedy and senseless death and loss imaginable. She'd seen far worse than this. It was just the double shock of finding KT where she'd never expected her to be and seeing her so wounded that had penetrated her defenses before she'd a chance to throw up a shield. She took a breath and when she spoke again, her voice was controlled. "You'd better sit down."

The corner of KT's mouth quirked and she nodded wearily. "Yeah. I guess so."

Tory made her way around behind her desk. Just the act of sitting in the position where she always sat as she performed her professional obligations helped steady her further. "How bad is your hand?"

Tory had never seen KT look away from anything—not the horrors of a multicar accident or the guilt when Tory caught her in bed with one of the nurses in an on-call room. The fact that she averted her eyes now told Tory more than anything else possibly could. Once again, Tory's stomach threatened to rebel. She threaded her fingers together on top of the desk and leaned forward, her eyes never leaving her former lover's face. "KT?"

"He got the flexors to all four fingers and three of the digital nerves." KT lifted her left hand and let it fall back into her lap. "It's pretty useless."

"Oh, sweetheart," Tory murmured, uttering the old endearment before she realized what she was saying. "I'm so sorry."

"Well," KT said briskly. "My hand surgeon assures me that if I'm a good patient and work hard, I might get it all back." She grinned humorlessly. "Of course, that's what hand surgeons always say. That way, if you end up with a lousy outcome, they can always blame it on the fact that you didn't work hard enough in therapy."

"If working hard is what's required," Tory said quietly, "then you're going to be fine."

"Absolutely."

Once more, Tory reined in her distress and soul-deep sympathy for the woman whom she had loved so deeply for so long. "What are you doing here? Do you need something?"

"A job."

Tory gaped. "You can't mean *here.*"

"I can't operate, Vic. If I sit around doing nothing, I'm going to go crazy. I can still work, and I heard through the grapevine that you had a position open. Your name still carries weight in Boston, especially since you still work in the ER at Boston City part time."

"It's impossible," Tory said with finality.

"Why?" KT posed the question quietly. "Why, Vic?"

"Because..." *I'm still so angry with you that I can hardly bear to look at you. Because you hurt me so much, and I've wanted to hurt you back for so long. Because I can't stand to see you like this, and I can't believe that anything about you could still hurt me.* Tory merely shook her head resolutely.

For the second time that day, KT did something wholly unexpected. She leaned forward, her pain-filled eyes holding on to Tory's as if on to a beacon in a raging sea.

"Please, Victoria. I need this chance."

Why should I care what you need? I needed you. I needed us. *You threw it away for a woman you didn't even love. Do you even remember her name now? Damn you, KT.* Damn *you. Why did you come here? Why could you possibly think that I would care?*

Abruptly, Tory rose and walked to the windows at the opposite side of the room. There was nothing to see but sand and scrub. With her back to KT, she said, "I can't work with you. Besides, I don't think you can work with only one hand."

From behind her, Tory heard a small sound that might have been a gasp, or a groan. She turned, instantly regretful. "I'm sorry."

KT shook her head. "I know what you mean. I *can* work, though. I can see patients. I can write prescriptions. I can read x-rays. I can do almost anything that needs to be done." She shuddered as if with a sudden chill. "Except operate. I'd have to have help if someone needed suturing. But with a good medical assistant or a nurse, I could manage. I'd be pretty slow, probably, but—"

"Stop," Tory said softly. There was something that sounded terribly like begging in KT's voice, and for some reason, that nearly broke her heart.

"Sorry." KT stood and made a visible effort to straighten. "Well, thanks."

"What about your hand therapy? How can you work while you're in therapy?"

"I've made some inquiries. One of the nurses in the ER told me about a friend of hers who's an occupational therapist specializing in hand rehab. Apparently she got tired of living in the city and moved out here a year ago. She works primarily in the hospital in Hyannis, but I think I could set up something for private consults right here in town. Then I could fit my rehab into whatever schedule you needed me to work." KT gripped the back of the chair in which she had previously been sitting, the knuckles of her right hand white with strain. "You need someone, right? Do you have anyone else you're considering?"

"I have to think about it. I have to talk to Reese."

KT blinked. "How is she? And...Regina."

"They're fine." Tory's expression softened at the memory that it had been KT who had been there for her and Reese and the baby when everything had suddenly gone wrong. And that if it hadn't been for KT, Regina could very well have suffered. "The baby's beautiful, KT. Thank you."

"Yeah, well." KT smiled. "You're her mother. Of course she's beautiful."

Tory said nothing, torn between so many memories filled with so much happiness and so much pain. "Leave me your number. I'll call you."

"I'm ready to start today."

"I'll *call* you."

Nodding, KT extracted her wallet from the back pocket of her trousers and walked to Tory's desk. She placed the wallet down on the surface, fumbled it open one-handed, and finally managed to pull out a business card. "Got a pen?"

Silently, Tory handed her one, unable to look at the motionless fingers inside the splint on KT's left hand. KT turned the card over and scrawled a number on the back, then put down the pen and handed the card to Tory.

"My home number is on the front. I'm not there very often, and I usually can't remember how to check the answering machine remotely. I wrote my cell on the back. You can always get me on that."

Tory resolutely avoided thinking about where KT was probably spending her nights if she was rarely at home. "I'll let you know by tomorrow."

"Thanks. Goodbye, Vic."

"Goodbye, KT," Tory said softly as she watched the stranger whom she once had loved walk out the door.

Chapter Seven

KT walked out the front door of the clinic, stopped at the bottom of the stairs, and waited for the queasiness in her stomach to dissipate. She'd anticipated the difficulty in asking for a job. What she hadn't expected was how very hard it would be to see Tory again. This was the longest they had been alone together since that afternoon she'd returned home from her interrupted tryst in the on-call room to find Tory waiting in the living room, hollow-eyed and so terribly wounded. The apology she'd intended to make had died on her lips when she was faced with the enormity of Tory's pain. As had been the case just moments before, on that day she'd simply waited in silence for Tory's judgment. It had been swift and irrevocable.

"Get out, KT. Get out now and don't come back."

Get out, KT. Get out...Get out...

Involuntarily, KT fisted her hands. A river of pain surged in her damaged arm, nearly unbearable. Severed nerves screamed, and inflamed blood vessels pulsed and throbbed. Nausea rose in her already unsettled stomach, and she bit back a moan as she fought to stay upright. Unconsciously, she felt in her right-hand pants pocket for one of the small white tablets and dry swallowed it. Then she took a deep breath and forced herself to focus on her surroundings, relegating her regrets to the past and forcing the pain down to manageable levels.

The parking lot was crowded with patients' cars and enclosed by scrub pines, low bushes, and sand dunes. Overhead, the sky was clear blue with fluffy white clouds that were so postcard perfect they didn't seem real. As she watched, a seagull actually coasted by, wings spread, white body gliding on the air. The idyllic picture was a far cry from the bustling, exhaust-fume-sullied streets of

Boston and the pressure-cooker atmosphere of the trauma center. From the turmoil of her life. She'd been on a roller-coaster ride of highs and lows for fifteen years, from the day she'd started her residency in surgery. She'd battled for a place on the team with the big boys, and she'd bested most of them at the high-stakes game of life and death in the trauma ER. Along the way, she'd garnered a reputation for being decisive in a crisis, fast in the OR, and faster with the ladies. The pace and the challenge had suited her need for the adrenaline infusion that came with living on the edge. There was only one thing missing. One huge aching void. Tory.

As if to remind her that there was no going back, a police cruiser pulled into the gravel-and-sand parking lot and slowed to a halt twenty feet away, and Reese Conlon stepped out. The last time KT had seen the sheriff, they'd been standing side by side in the pediatric intensive care unit, gazing down in mutual awe at Tory's newborn daughter. *Reese* and Tory's baby daughter. KT braced herself as she held the gaze of the steely-eyed woman who approached.

"KT," Reese said evenly as she stopped two feet away. The brim of her hat was pulled low, obscuring her eyes. The rest of her face was unreadable.

"Reese."

Reese's gaze traveled from the laceration on KT's cheek down her body, lingering for a moment on her left arm, and then returning to her shadow-filled eyes. "You doing okay?"

"Managing." The corner of KT's mouth turned up in a rueful smile. "You?"

"Things are good. I won't bore you with the baby pictures."

KT's dark eyes flashed, even though Reese's voice held no hint of victory. "Tory says she's beautiful."

"Yes." Reese considered the earlier phone call and KT's presence at the clinic, and made the obvious connection. "Just finished your interview?"

"A few minutes ago." KT scrutinized Reese's face for some sign of anger or aggression. Nothing. Total control. *Impressive.* "Problem with that?"

"Not my call."

"If it was?"

Slowly, Reese shook her head. "It's not. I need to see Tory for a few minutes. Can I give you a lift somewhere after that?"

"No, thanks. I feel like a walk."

"Good enough. I'll see you around, then."

"Maybe." KT flashed a grin. "I guess that will be up to Tory."

Reese said nothing, merely nodding as she turned and walked toward the clinic. KT followed Reese's powerful form as she took the four stairs up to the front door two at a time, her movements graceful and quick. She was an imposingly attractive woman. Not the kind of woman KT was interested in bedding, but a worthy opponent, and therefore exciting nonetheless. She tried not to imagine Tory in Reese's arms as she made her way out to the street and headed toward the center of town.

Forty minutes later, KT realized that a two-mile walk in the middle of the day in early September wasn't the brightest idea. She was hot and thirsty and light-headed by the time she found the address she was looking for on the far west end of Commercial Street. A white half-Codder with baby blue shutters sat at the far end of a narrow driveway behind a much larger guesthouse that bore a historic sign indicating it was one of the original structures in the Provincetown settlement. At the end of the driveway fronting the street, a discreet, hand-painted wood sign hung from a curved wrought-iron post: Pia Torres, PT, OT, CMT.

KT was halfway to the small cottage before she noticed the woman kneeling by one corner of the small porch, tending a flower bed filled with day lilies and a profusion of brightly colored annuals. A wooden box holding garden tools rested by her side. At the sound of KT's footsteps, the woman looked up. KT's immediate impression was one of searching dark eyes, glossy midnight hair that glinted in the bright sunlight, and acres of smooth sienna skin. A sleeveless T-shirt and white boat shorts left her slender, well-toned arms and her shapely legs bare. KT stopped on the sidewalk and nodded in greeting. The answering smile was warm and open.

"Ms. Torres?"

Pia shielded her eyes from the blazing sun with her hand and stared up at the tall, dark stranger. It was hard to make out her features clearly with the sun casting her form in shadow, but the face beneath the thick, dark hair was pale, an unnatural paleness that made the pink scar on her right cheek stand out dramatically. It took only another second for Pia to register the Orthoplast splint with the metacarpal blocks and flexor tendon pulleys on the left hand. Pia stood. "Dr. O'Bannon?"

"Yes. We have an appointment."

"We do," Pia confirmed cheerfully as she checked her watch. "You're just a bit early. Why don't you come inside and have a drink while I get cleaned up. I'll be with you in a few minutes."

"Please don't hurry," KT said quietly. "I'll be happy to wait out here."

Pia wondered if the other woman even realized that she was swaying where she stood. Perhaps it was the undertone of weariness in her voice or her bold façade even in the face of obvious physical pain that put the gentleness in Pia's tone.

"It's ninety degrees out here and getting hotter every second. I can offer you a bit of shade and cool refreshment. It will make it easier for us to talk if you're not suffering from heatstroke."

KT hesitated, uncomfortable impinging on the woman's personal space, especially since she had pressured her for an urgent appointment and then arrived early for it. Still, she was feeling the effects of the heat and experienced a sudden urge to sit down. *It probably won't make a very good impression if I fall over in the woman's yard.* "Thank you. Something to drink would be very nice."

Pia favored her with another blazing smile and started toward the small porch and the front door. "Good. Just follow me."

❖

The door to Tory's office was partially open, and Reese stepped inside. Tory stood at the window on the far side of the room, looking out.

"Tor?" Reese said softly.

Startled, Tory jumped and turned quickly, her surprised expression instantly turning to one of pleasure. "Oh! Hello, darling. I didn't expect you."

Reese smiled and started toward her, noting the same dark

shadows swirling beneath the welcome in Tory's eyes that she had seen in KT's. "I decided to go in to work early, and I wanted to let you know. I just left Reggie at Kate and Jean's."

"Good. I need to stay here for a while and take care of some paperwork." As she spoke, Tory stepped up to Reese and wrapped her arms around Reese's waist, resting her head on her shoulder. "I'm so glad to see you."

"Mmm. Me too." Reese kissed the fine, soft hair at Tory's temple and rubbed her palm over her lover's back. Tory trembled and Reese pulled her closer. "I saw KT in the parking lot."

"Yes," Tory replied softly, not moving away from the solace of Reese's embrace. "She was the one inquiring about the position."

"I figured as much." Reese moved her hand to the back of Tory's neck and began to massage her gently. "She looked pretty beat up."

Tory flinched at the memory, and her voice was thick with emotion as she answered. "Someone...hurt her." She closed her eyes tightly and turned her face to Reese's neck. "God, Reese. An injury like that...for her? I can't imagine what she's going through."

But you can. And that's part of what's causing the pain in your eyes. Reese continued her gentle caresses. "She strikes me as being pretty tough. When she gets her fight back, she'll be okay."

"You saw quite a bit out there in the parking lot." Tory tilted her head back and studied Reese's face. Her blue eyes were calm and steady. Tory caressed her cheek tenderly. "You're very special, Sheriff."

"No." Reese cupped Tory's hand in hers and kissed her palm. "You and Regina are everything that matters to me, Tory. Everything."

"As simple as that?" Tory's voice held a note of wonder.

"Yes," Reese affirmed, kissing Tory lightly on the mouth. "Just exactly as simple as that."

"Oh, I'm so glad."

Reese looked down to Tory's eyes. The sight of the sadness there tore at her. "What did you tell KT about the job?"

"I didn't. I told her I'd get back to her about it." Tory stepped away and ran both hands through her hair, pushing the errant strands away from her face. "I wanted to talk to you."

"About what?"

Tory leaned her hips against the front edge of her desk and curled her fingers around the dark wood on either side of her body. She kept her eyes on Reese's face, watching her reactions. "I wanted to know if it would bother you if she were around."

"It depends," Reese said quietly.

"On what?" Tory steeled herself for the answer.

"On whether it's going to hurt you like this every time you see her."

Tory's lips parted in surprise and she breathed out slowly. "Me? I'm not hur—"

"Yes, you are." Reese stood without moving, holding Tory's gaze. "This time—just like all the other times."

"She stopped mattering to me the day I found her in bed with someone else." Fury rode just beneath the surface of Tory's insistent words.

Reese tucked her hands into her pockets, appreciating that anger was a much more acceptable emotion than disappointment and betrayal. "Can she do the job?"

Tory snorted. "She's one of the best doctors I've ever seen."

"If you weren't considering her, you would have told her no already," Reese pointed out reasonably.

"It's not like I have a lot of options. I have to come back to work. I *want* to come back to work. But I don't want to spend any more time away from you and the baby than I absolutely have to." Tory blew out an exasperated breath. "You're right. I *do* need the help. Dan is leaving tomorrow, and we're busier than we've ever been." She smiled, her eyes bright. "And in case you've forgotten, Sheriff, you and I are getting married in a few months."

Reese grinned. "Oh, I haven't forgotten."

"Jean and Kate have been wonderful about handling a lot of the arrangements, but there are still things I'm going to need to do myself. Plus, my parents will be coming in." Tory shook her head. "God, I can't think about all of that right now."

"You know I'll do whatever you need me to do."

"I know. But the fact remains, with me going back to work now, it's going to be a strain."

"And KT is available."

"Yes." Tory sighed. "She's ready to start tomorrow."

"If it doesn't work out, there's no reason you can't just tell her so."

"I know."

"But if she hurts you," Reese said quietly, "even just by *being* here, she goes."

"You're really all right about it?"

"I want you to have help. She's here and she's competent." Reese shrugged. "Seems like the thing to do." She didn't add that it might finally be the opportunity for Tory to truly put that part of her past behind her.

Tory moved away from the desk and back to Reese. She placed her palms flat against Reese's chest and leaned into her, her thighs pressed to Reese's as she kissed her. With her lips still close to Reese's mouth, she murmured, "And if anything about this hurts *you,* in *any* way, I'll send her away."

Reese slid her arms around Tory's waist and kissed her forehead, then her eyelids, and finally her lips. "While I have you, nothing can hurt me."

❖

Pia looked up from the copy of the operative report that KT had provided, her gaze unblinking. While she'd read, her face had revealed none of the compassion or sympathy she'd felt at witnessing the impersonal record of a woman's destruction. The harm was done; it was her job to undo it. "You haven't started any physical therapy yet?"

"No," KT replied. She was sitting at the kitchen table in front of the open back door, sipping iced tea and regarding the hand therapist intently. "I've only been out of the cast a few days."

"How much pain are you having?"

KT shrugged. "It's tolerable."

"It's important that I know," Pia continued reasonably. "Otherwise, it's difficult for me to fashion the appropriate treatment plan."

"Seven out of ten," KT grudgingly informed her.

Pia nodded, although she was willing to bet that the surgeon was underestimating her level of discomfort. She'd never met a surgeon without a healthy dose of machismo. Sometimes, in situations like this, that turned out to be *un*healthy. The worst thing that could happen in the aftermath of this type of injury would be to rupture one of the tendon repairs or avulse one of the reconnected nerves, and that could happen if the patient *or* the therapist pushed too hard or too fast. Such an event at this point would almost certainly guarantee a permanent loss of function, and for a surgeon, any loss of function was going to prevent her from resuming her career.

"I anticipate that you're looking at three to six months, possibly longer, of intensive therapy."

"Understood." KT planned to make her stay in therapy as short as possible. She'd work the program the therapist designed for her, and she'd work it hard. She didn't intend to be *disabled* for very long.

"We'll need to meet daily for the first six weeks," Pia added.

Again, KT nodded. "Whatever you say."

"I can see you here, but the schedule might be slightly erratic depending upon my responsibilities in Hyannis. I don't work a regular shift there, although I go in nearly every day."

"As long as I have a few days' notice, I'll fit myself into your schedule." KT hoped she wasn't being overly optimistic making these arrangements. After all, Tory hadn't *said* that she would hire her. Still, she'd seen the look in Tory's eyes. It wasn't the sympathy that she cared about or even the anger that she'd seen every other time she'd looked into her former lover's eyes. It had been that brief moment of tenderness, that precious instant when the past had faded and they had been nothing more than two women who cared about one another. The connection, no matter how fleeting, had felt so strong that it had obliterated the long years of loneliness and confusion. At least for her.

Pia tilted her head and smiled. "Are you always so accommodating, Dr. O'Bannon?"

KT smiled, but her eyes remained flat and without humor. "No."

"Can you start tomorrow?"

"What's wrong with today?"

Pia laughed. “Let’s say 9 a.m. Just leave me your number in case something comes up.”

KT provided her with her cell number and then rose. “Thank you.”

“Where are you staying?” Pia asked as she walked KT to the door.

“I’ve got a room at the Crown Point until I can find a condo to rent.”

Pia was about to offer a few suggestions about finding a place, and then thought better of it. It was usually best to keep things on a purely professional level, especially when a woman was as dangerously attractive as this one.

“Good luck. I’ll see you tomorrow, then, Dr. O’Bannon.”

“Please, call me KT.”

“And I’m Pia.”

“Thank you.” KT looked into the deep brown eyes and smiled. “Pia.”

Pia steadfastly ignored the slight flutter of her heart as she watched her newest client walk up the flagstone walkway and disappear down the street. She wasn’t particularly worried about her reaction. She had a heartbeat, and that’s all it would take to find KT O’Bannon attractive. But she’d had quite a few years of practice being attracted without becoming involved, and she had no intention of changing that now.

Chapter Eight

KT walked east on Commercial Street back toward the center of town. It was midafternoon on the Friday of Labor Day weekend, and she had nowhere to go and nothing to do. Despite her many years in Boston, she'd crossed Cape Cod Bay only rarely to visit the small village that had begun as a thriving Portuguese fishing community, evolved into a center for avant-garde artists in the early twentieth century, and finally emerged as a mecca for gays and lesbians. She hadn't visited at all since learning that Tory had settled there after their separation. She'd always expected that Tory would eventually return to Boston, believing that the quiet life of a small-town doctor could not possibly satisfy her for long. They had chosen different specialties, but they'd both been aggressive, determined physicians at the top of their respective fields when they'd shared a life.

Standing in front of Spiritus Pizza, surveying the narrow, crowded streets that teemed with tourists, gay and straight, she was struck by the energy humming in the air and wondered if she might have been wrong about what the tiny town had to offer. Wrong about that, as she had been about so many things. She shook off the questions that she had long since tired of asking, having no answers, and turned toward the sound of music on the opposite side of the street. The heavy beat of dance music emanated from the Pied, which she vaguely recalled had once been called the Pied Piper.

She smiled to herself, appreciating the irony, as she abruptly crossed to the wood deck pathway that led to the front door. When she saw the two young women in white T-shirts and jeans seated at a small table just inside, she grimaced and reached for her wallet. Another fumble-fest. Still, she managed to get the money out with reasonable aplomb and slid a twenty into her front pocket along with the change from her cover charge so that she wouldn't have to take her wallet out again. Her fingertips brushed the small pills, and she considered taking another one. The heat and the walk with her arm hanging down had caused her fingers to swell and throb viciously. There were only two tablets left out of the six she had counted out that morning. She made her way through the surprisingly large afternoon crowd to the bar and ordered a drink instead.

"Thanks," KT said with a nod to the stocky butch in the baseball cap behind the bar. She took a long pull on the draft beer, welcoming the slightly bitter aftertaste as the cold brew washed away some of the heat and dust of her morning. Perhaps after another, it would wash away some of the pain as well.

The large rear deck was visible through the oversized open window that connected the far end of the bar to the outside space, allowing those enjoying the sea and the sun to refill their drinks without coming back inside. Briefly, KT considered joining the women for a look at the sailboats on the harbor and the kayakers traversing the inlet in their red and yellow shells. Thinking about the water and the paddlers made her think of Tory and all the meets they'd been to. And then she saw again, as clearly as the day it happened, the final heat that Tory ever raced—saw the other scull blindsiding Tory's and the splintering shell, heard the screams, and relived those few agonizing seconds when she'd feared Tory would never surface. Her stomach clutched, her entire left side erupted into pain, and without even thinking, she reached for one of the two last pills. She washed it down with the beer and decided to stay inside in the cool darkness of the bar, away from the water.

"That looks nasty," a redhead about KT's age observed as she leaned against the bar and indicated KT's arm with a tilt of her chin. "Cut the tendons?"

Surprised, KT studied the newcomer, whose shapely figure was nicely accentuated by a turquoise, scoop-necked, sleeveless top and white hip-hugger capri slacks. "Yep. A couple of them. How did you know?"

"I'm a carpenter." The woman held up her left wrist to reveal the jagged scar that extended nearly halfway around. "Table saw—three tendons."

"Ouch."

The woman laughed. "Fucking ouch is right."

Now that KT looked more closely, she could see the muscles rippling beneath the smooth skin of her companion's arms. "It looks like you mended pretty well."

"Pretty much good as new. I've never quite gotten all the strength back, but I can handle my tools."

KT wondered fleetingly if she would ever again handle *her* tools, but she pushed the thought away and concentrated on the woman who was appraising her with obvious interest. She held out her hand. "I'm KT."

"Vicki."

KT blinked. Thankfully, the woman bore no resemblance to Tory, and she ruthlessly pushed the image of her former lover's face from her mind. "Can I buy you a drink?"

"Sure. Glenlivet on the rocks."

"Coming up." KT signaled the bartender over and ordered the drink along with another draft for herself. The room was filling up now that the afternoon tea dance was about to begin. Vicki moved closer as more people sidled up to the bar and as she did, turned her body so that her legs loosely straddled KT's thigh. KT could smell her perfume, the dark inviting aroma of rain on the wind. "Are you from around here?"

"No," Vicki replied, leaning into KT to be heard above the racket of drink orders being shouted from those nearby. Her breast brushed KT's arm. "Worcester. I'm just here for the weekend."

Inexplicably, KT felt a surge of relief. She wasn't certain exactly why, but she didn't want to spend the night with someone she was going to have to see on a regular basis in the small town where she might be living for an indefinite period of time. And if she was right about the signals she was reading in Vicki's eyes and the fact that Vicki's nipple had hardened the instant her breast had brushed KT's arm, then she didn't have to spend the night alone if she didn't want to. And considering the way she was feeling right now, a woman was probably the only thing that would drive away thoughts of past mistakes and future fears, at least for one night. The alcohol and painkillers didn't seem to be doing it. "Down here with friends?"

Vicki's smile widened and she placed her hand on KT's stomach, edging her hips a little tighter against KT's thigh. "All by myself."

And is there a woman at home? But that was not her concern, KT reminded herself. The fingers circling slowly over her abdomen felt good, as did the heat of Vicki's center pressed to her leg as the redhead undulated sensuously to the music in the background. As the arousal built in her depths, the pain in her arm, and in her heart, mercifully receded.

❖

Reese pulled into the parking lot in front of the sheriff's department just as Bri and Allie roared in behind her on Bri's big Harley. Reese climbed out of the cruiser and studied the two young women. Bri had on her uniform pants, which looked as if they'd been slept in, and the white T-shirt she usually wore under her uniform shirt. She'd filled out some since she'd been training heavily for her black belt test. The shirt stretched tightly over her small breasts, muscular chest, and ripped arms, accentuating her tapered torso and narrow hips. Allie, who straddled Bri's body with both arms around her waist and her cheek pressed to the back of Bri's neck, was in street clothes—impossibly tight, almost feloniously low-slung blue jeans and a minuscule, sheer white top that appeared to be suspended over her unrestrained breasts by a thread or two tied at the back of her neck. Considering their attire and the fact that Allie's car was parked exactly where it had been the day before, it didn't require much in the way of deductive reasoning to ascertain that Bri had spent the night at Allie's.

God damn it. Reese's jaw tightened as she leaned back against the patrol car, watching Allie climb off the bike and laughingly shove at Bri's shoulder. Bri merely grinned and shook her head no. Allie butted her hip against Bri's thigh and said something that made Bri toss her head back and laugh. They looked like a couple of healthy young animals in the midst of a mating ritual. *What the hell is wrong with her?*

Watching the pair continue to tease and banter, Reese chastised herself for approving Allie's transfer to the department.

She'd known that there had been some kind of attraction between the two earlier in the year, but she'd thought it was over. She'd trusted Bri to respect Caroline *and* her badge, and to keep things purely professional with Allie. *God damn it.* Out of nowhere, Reese looked at Bri and saw another darkly handsome, dangerous woman. One with the same seething, wild energy. KT. Fast on the heels of that inexplicable image, she remembered the shadows in Tory's eyes that morning and thought of how much greater her lover's pain had been when they'd met a few years before. Remembered, too, that Tory had withdrawn from everyone because of the hurt and disappointment KT's betrayal had caused. Reese pushed away from the cruiser and strode across the hard-packed sand lot to where the two young women now stood talking.

"You're both on duty in less than an hour."

Bri turned from telling Allie for the fourth time that she couldn't drive her bike, a smile on her face. "Hey, Reese."

"You're out of uniform, Parker. Where's your weapon and the rest of your gear?"

"In my bike bag, ma'am." Bri straightened, clearly confused by the tone of Reese's voice.

"Um—" Allie began, sensing that Bri was in trouble but not understanding why.

Reese silenced her with a quick look. "I want you to take personal time until further notice, Officer Tremont."

Allie straightened, her eyes flashing. "Why, ma'am?"

"Because I ordered—" Reese stopped in the middle of dressing down the startled young recruits. *They're not recruits. And Bri's not KT. Christ, what am I doing.* She took a breath, slow and controlled, her expression revealing none of her disquiet while she settled herself. She couldn't ever remember having behaved quite so irrationally. That it had to do with KT was clear, but why, she wasn't sure. She hadn't felt any particular animosity toward her when she'd seen her in the parking lot at the clinic, only a wariness that came from knowing that KT was a woman who had once hurt her lover. And knowing with absolute certainty that KT could *still* hurt Tory. *And you're probably not going to be able to stop it. And if you can't protect her...*

"Parker," Reese snapped.

"Yes, ma'am." Bri stood at rigid attention, her eyes unwavering, fixed on Reese's face.

"If you want to wear the uniform, treat it with respect."

"Yes, ma'am."

"Go home and change. Report back for your shift looking like you're ready to do the job."

"Yes, ma'am. I'm sorry, ma'am."

Reese shifted her gaze to Allie. "Come inside so we can talk."

"Respectfully, ma'am," Allie said, her voice steady. "I'd like to get ready for my shift as well. Could we speak later, ma'am?"

"We'll do it now. I'll make adjustments in your shift assignment if necessary."

"Yes, ma'am."

As Reese turned and headed toward the building with Allie beside her, she heard the roar of Bri's engine accelerate rapidly and then fade into the distance. She'd come down on Bri hard—for reasons that weren't altogether Bri's fault. She'd have to make that right.

❖

KT was dizzy, and she didn't think it was entirely due to the beer. Vicki's tongue was demanding, probing her mouth insistently, threatening to devour her. It felt unexpectedly good, being taken for a change. But before she completely lost control, she pulled away from Vicki's mouth and trapped the hand that was inching open her fly. "Hey, baby, slow down. I'm too old to do this standing up in a dark corner."

Vicki pressed hard with her whole body against KT's, rocking her hips between KT's spread thighs, her mouth on KT's neck, biting lightly. "Mmm, me too, but you've got me so hot. God, you're a great kisser. Tell me you're not going a little crazy, too."

"Oh, I wouldn't say that," KT said, breathing rapidly as Vicki continued to thrust her hips, working KT's blood up to a rolling boil. "Keep doing what you're doing, and I'm going to explode."

"Oh, yeah. I'd like that."

The bar was wall-to-wall people, and no one was paying them

any attention in the dark corner of the bar where they'd eventually migrated as their superficial conversation had given way to more in-depth physical explorations. Still, as aroused as she was, KT was long past fucking in public places. Vicki felt good in her arms, though, and with her body this turned on, she wasn't thinking about anything. That was the best part of all.

"Can we go to your room?" KT asked, circling her right hand over the base of Vicki's spine, matching the roll and thrust of Vicki's pelvis with her own. She felt teeth on her neck and carefully pulled away. "Easy."

"Mmm. God, I want to get naked with you." Vicki managed to get her hand between KT's thighs and squeezed. "And I want this."

"Then let's get out of here," KT urged, happy to surrender awareness to the pleasant euphoria of alcohol and the consuming burn of passion.

❖

Reese handed Allie a paper cup of coffee and leaned against the counter in the far corner of the squad room. The only other person present was Paul Smith, and he was busy with the phones. "How are you feeling about last night?"

Clearly surprised, Allie shrugged. "I'm okay."

"Is that the first time you found a victim like that?"

Allie hesitated, trying to decide the best answer. The sheriff never gave any indication of what she was thinking, but Allie knew that she always told the truth. It was something you could count on. Maybe the truth was the only answer. "No."

Reese sipped her coffee, wondering at the flicker of unease in Allie's eyes. "But it wasn't on the job, was it."

"No. It was my cousin. I was fourteen and he was seventeen." Allie swallowed around the sudden lump in her throat and put her coffee cup down before meeting Reese's unwavering gaze. "He OD'd on heroin. I found him in his room one afternoon after school. We lived next door to each other. We were pretty tight."

"I'm sorry." Reese tossed her empty cup into the wastepaper basket. "Last night couldn't have been easy."

"I'm not sure what it was," Allie said quietly. "I didn't feel a whole lot then and I don't feel very much now. I feel like I'm okay to work, though."

"Sometimes things like last night come back on us when we don't expect it."

Allie nodded. "I understand. I had nightmares for a while after Kevin."

"Provincetown is a small village, and we don't see a lot of action here. But that doesn't mean that we don't have to be alert."

"I know." Allie straightened. "I give you my word if I'm having problems, I'll tell you. I saw a shrink for a while when I was fifteen. It was okay—it helped. I'll do it again if I need to."

"Very well. Report for duty as scheduled, then."

"Thank you, ma'am." Allie made no move to leave. "Sheriff, about Bri—"

"I'll deal with Officer Parker, Officer Tremont."

Allie looked as if she wanted to say more, but wisely said nothing. "Yes, ma'am. Thank you, ma'am."

Reese watched Allie leave with new respect, impressed with her fortitude. She didn't want to lose her and hoped that she would be able to sort out the situation with Bri.

❖

"You'll have to make allowances for my performance," KT said, her breathing irregular and shallow as Vicki slid down the zipper of her fly. She was flat on her back in the middle of a double bed in a small motel room with a single window that faced Long Point, the final curve of sand before Cape Cod disappeared into the ocean. She couldn't get any further away from her demons if she tried. Vicki knelt naked above her, methodically undressing her. "I've only got one good arm here, and I don't quite know what to do with this contraption on my left."

"You don't have to do anything," Vicki assured her, her full breasts swaying as she worked to open buttons and buckles and zippers. "I'm going to take care of us both."

Not normally one to give up control under any circumstance, and particularly not in bed, KT felt an uncharacteristic surge of relief. She closed her eyes, distantly aware that her left arm throbbed and her head spun slowly. The breeze from the open window blew across her chest as her shirt was opened and the silk tee beneath was pushed up to expose her breasts. Her nipples hardened in anticipation.

"Lift your hips," Vicki urged as she pulled down KT's trousers and underwear. She stopped long enough to tease her fingers along the inside of KT's thighs until she was rewarded with a faint groan, then she leaned forward to slide an arm behind KT's shoulders. "Now sit up for just a minute."

KT pushed herself up with her right arm and helped free herself from the tangle of clothes, carefully drawing the garments down over her splinted left arm. She was no sooner completely bare than Vicki's hands were on her breasts, fingers closing hard over her nipples. KT groaned again and shivered. "Oh, yeah."

"Lie back, baby. I'm going to make you feel *so* good."

The light from the single table lamp that Vicki had turned on just inside the door flickered on the ceiling as KT stared upward through half-closed lids, surrendering to sensation. The mouth and hands that stroked and teased and fired the burn in her skin and stoked the hot need deep inside were talented and sure. Before long, the fingers of her right hand were tangled in Vicki's hair, and she was urging her down as her hips rose and fell with rhythmic urgency.

"Come on, baby," KT murmured. "I need your mouth."

As warm lips closed over her clitoris, KT sighed and closed her eyes completely. She moaned with relief as the orgasm slowly rose from her distant recesses to steal the last vestiges of thought. When her hips bucked with the first spasm, she whispered brokenly, "Oh, Vic. Baby. It's so good, so good."

Chapter Nine

When Bri arrived for her shift, Reese merely gestured to a nearby desk. "Settle in for a minute. I need to return a call."

In a freshly laundered and crisply pressed uniform, Bri sat quietly as directed while Reese spoke on the phone. Her leather equipment belt and silver badge gleamed. She didn't see Allie, so she figured that she was already out with Lyons on a tour through town. At least she hoped she was. She still didn't know what had gone down between Reese and Allie earlier that afternoon; in fact, she had no idea what had gone down between *herself* and Reese. Well. She had some idea. Reese was pissed that she'd been running around town with her uniform in a shambles. But there had been something else, and all through the ride to her apartment, and her shower, and the process of triple-checking her uniform to make sure that everything was in order, she still hadn't been able to figure out what that something else was.

She'd known Reese for a long time, and she couldn't remember her flying off the handle before, not ever. Her dad did that, and she was used to it. She knew he didn't mean anything most of the time when he lost his cool, and if she took the time to think about it, he usually only did it when he was worried about her. *But Reese—Reese is different. Reese always has it together. But she didn't this afternoon. She was pissed. At me.*

Bri had to force herself not to fidget. It made her uncomfortable knowing that she'd upset Reese somehow. In fact, it made her feel just a little bit sick.

Reese hung up the phone and reached for her hat. "Let's go, Parker."

Bri jumped to her feet. "Yes, ma'am."

As Bri settled into the passenger seat, Reese buckled up and started the engine. Bri stared straight ahead, her hands open, palms down on her thighs, unconsciously imitating her preparatory position to work out in the *dojo*. She was trying to settle her mind and banish the queasy feeling in her stomach.

"That was Robert Bridger's attorney," Reese said as she headed toward 6 East. "His *parents* want to talk to me."

"Huh," Bri said, forgetting her discomfort for a moment. "Why the turnaround, do you think?" She'd gotten the full story of the stonewalling attorney from her father and Reese late the previous evening when they'd returned empty-handed from Hyannis. She'd known then that Reese was really angry with the attorney and wondered if that had anything to do with Reese's behavior that afternoon. She fervently hoped so.

"Could be the attorney wants to find out what *we* know." Reese kept her eyes on the road, mulling over the possibilities. "Or she might be trying for some damage control by making a preemptive move."

"Controlling the information flow?"

Reese gave Bri a quick, appreciative grin. "Something like that. At the moment, I don't care, as long as *I* get some information. It's early still, but we haven't found anyone that matches the dead girl's description in the missing persons bulletins from any of the counties on the Cape. Leads from the mainland will be slower, because the larger departments don't disseminate missing persons information that quickly. Someone may already have put her data into the system, but we just haven't gotten it yet."

"Man, I hate to think of someone somewhere wondering where she is. Not knowing that she's..."

"Yeah. Same here."

They rode in silence another five minutes before Reese spoke again.

"You know, whether you're in uniform or out, you're still a peace officer."

Bri stiffened. "Yes, ma'am."

"When you walk down the street, when you ride through town, when you go to a party—you're still a peace officer." Reese spoke quietly, almost contemplatively. "Everyone who knows you, knows that."

"I know."

"And do you know what's the most important thing, the most powerful weapon, that you have as a law enforcement agent?"

Bri took a deep breath. "It's not my sidearm, I guess."

The corner of Reese's mouth flickered into a fleeting grin. "No. But I'm glad you know how to use it." She turned her head for a second and held Bri's eyes. "Respect, Bri. The respect of the community and the people you serve, and the respect of those you sometimes need to control."

"I understand," Bri said as she colored, embarrassed because Reese wasn't yelling at her. She wished she were.

"You're doing something to be proud of, and part of that pride is reflected in the uniform that you wear. I know that you'll respect it, because you're a good officer, Parker."

Bri blinked rapidly, horrified that her eyes had filled with tears. "I'm sorry."

Reese shook her head. "You don't need to be. The next time you...don't have a clean uniform to change into, go straight home."

"I know I should've done that, but Allie wanted to pick up her car—" Bri stifled the excuse. "Yes, ma'am."

"Now, about Officer Tremont." Reese's hands tightened on the wheel but her voice remained conversational. "There's a reason that we discourage interpersonal relationships among officers. In a crisis situation, you need to be thinking about two things: your own safety, and that of your partner. If everyone does that, everyone lives."

Bri frowned, shifting in her seat slightly so she could study Reese's face, intent on understanding the new direction of their conversation. "I know that. But Lyons is Allie's training officer."

"Correct. And it's his responsibility to ensure her safety. My point is that if you were worried about her, too, or vice versa, because you're..." Reese searched for a word that she could tolerate saying. "*...involved*, then—"

"Involved! You mean like *girlfriends*?"

"Well, yes."

"We're *not*. Jesus." At the sight of Reese's raised eyebrow, Bri hastened to add, "Sorry. I mean, we're friends. But we're not...why did you...?" She suddenly had a mental image of herself and Allie arriving at the station on her motorcycle that afternoon—her in the clothes she'd worn the day before, not counting her uniform shirt, which she'd balled up and stuffed into her motorcycle bag, and Allie wrapped around her wearing what she always wore. Skimpy little bits of nothing that Bri had yet to figure out how Allie kept on her body at all. It looked like they'd just crawled out of bed, which they had, except it looked like they'd crawled out of the *same* bed. *Oh fuck me.*

Bri had learned something from growing up on the brunt end of her father's tendency to jump in with both feet, or perhaps she'd merely absorbed it unconsciously. But somewhere, somehow, she'd learned to wait one extra second before saying what was on her mind. She had nowhere near the control that Reese had, but she was trying for it. She took a long, *long* breath, because after the first wave of acute embarrassment, she was righteously pissed. *How could Reese think that I would treat Carre that way? Doesn't she trust me at all?*

Before the bitter words could erupt, Reese spoke into the quiet, dense air of the suddenly crowded space. "I'm sorry. I should've known better."

"I...uh..." Apologies were foreign to Bri, at least in the heat of the moment, and she had no way to answer. "Okay."

"No, it isn't," Reese replied firmly. "If it had been someone else with Allie, other than you, then the conclusion I came to would've made sense." She looked to Bri again, her blue eyes dark with regret. "But it wasn't someone else. It was you. And I know how much you love Caroline. I'm sorry for forgetting that."

"Oh man," Bri muttered and turned her face to the side window, seeing nothing outside. The tears were back, and there were so many reasons for them she wasn't sure she could handle them all at once. She wanted to cry because she missed Caroline so much. Because Reese cared enough about her, about *them,* to get angry when she thought Bri was fucking up. Because someone believed in her feelings, believed in how much she loved Caroline. She bit her lip and waited for the tight fist that was squeezing the air from her lungs to relax enough for her to speak. "You know I almost did screw up, with Allie...last spring."

Reese waited, silent. She had a brief image of a much younger Tory and KT and chased it from her mind.

"I slept with her. Sorta. Seeing the way Carre hurt...the way *I* hurt her," Bri went on, the words sticking in her throat and finally coming out raspy and raw. She turned anguished eyes to Reese. "I could never do that to her again. Never."

"I believe you. And I know Caroline does too." Then, Reese did something she'd never done with a recruit in all her life. She reached across the space between them and rested her hand on Bri's thigh. She squeezed gently. "You're doing fine, Bri. I'm proud of you, on all counts."

Bri stared down at the hand on her leg, her own hands resting on the seat on either side of her body. She didn't move a muscle. Her voice was barely a whisper. "Thank you."

Reese put her hand back on the wheel. The tension that had been riding along her spine since she'd seen Allie and Bri together suddenly disappeared. "So, let me tell you about Counselor Trey Pelosi." She tossed a grin in Bri's direction. "And look sharp, because this one will kill the weak first."

❖

KT still lay on her back, still staring at the ceiling, but now Vicki was draped across her body, her head resting on KT's chest and one leg drawn up over her thighs. The redhead breathed softly, rhythmic excursions that sent soft puffs of warm air chasing across KT's left nipple. It felt oddly uncomfortable to hold her this way, perhaps because it was much more intimate than the hot-and-heavy sex they'd recently enjoyed. No sooner had KT's orgasm peaked than Vicki had climbed onto the bed and straddled her stomach, bracing herself with an arm on either side of KT's shoulders as she rubbed her wet, swollen clitoris over KT's skin until she'd come. Or perhaps what was the most unsettling was Vicki's vulnerability as she dozed in the aftermath of the orgasm that had had her crying out in an agonized scream of triumphant pleasure before collapsing on top of KT.

For the first time in longer than she could remember, KT

wondered what these last few hours had meant to the woman in her arms. She fervently hoped it had been only pleasure that Vicki had been seeking, because she knew that she had nothing more to give.

"Hey, baby," KT whispered, running her hand through the thick tresses that spread across her chest in a fiery blanket.

"Mmm?"

"I have to go."

Vicki burrowed her face into the hollow of KT's throat, kissing her neck as she snuggled closer. "Stay, can't you? I want you again."

KT laughed softly. "You might be able to get it up again, but I'm pretty sure I'm done for the night."

"Oh, I can get it up for both of us," Vicki murmured as she smoothed her hand down the center of KT's abdomen, between her legs, and into the waiting wetness. "And I know you'll like it."

Despite the fact that her legs tensed and her stomach clutched at the swift surge of pleasure, KT shook her head. "I'm beat. You wasted me." She kissed Vicki's forehead and shifted away from the teasing hand. "Plus, I've got an early-morning appointment."

Vicki raised her head and peered across the bed to the clock on the night table. "It's early. Sleep a little while, and I promise I'll wake you up nicely." As if to underscore her promise, she slid her fingers on either side of KT's clitoris and stroked languorously.

"Jesus," KT breathed in shocked surprise as she felt herself stiffen. "Keep it up, and I'll have a heart attack."

"Better yet, why don't you let *me* put you to sleep," Vicki crooned as she shifted and started to move down the bed. "I know just the thing to relax you."

KT caught Vicki's arm and held her back. Suddenly struck by an overwhelming need to leave, to be alone, she said as gently as she could, "I can't. I'm sorry."

"You're serious."

"Yeah," KT said softly as she stroked Vicki's cheek with her good hand. "You were great."

Vicki smiled, turned her head, and softly bit the base of KT's thumb. "Uh-huh. So were you." She sat up and pushed her hair back with both hands, regarding KT intently. "I'll be here for the rest of the weekend, but something tells me I won't be sleeping with you again."

KT held her gaze. "No."

"Wife back home?"

"No," KT said with a bitter laugh.

"But there is someone, isn't there." It wasn't a question.

"No," KT repeated with finality. "There isn't anyone at all."

❖

"Hi, Kate." Tory greeted her mother-in-law with a kiss on the cheek. "Sorry I'm late."

"No problem," Kate Mahoney replied as she ushered Tory into the small cottage situated behind her art gallery on Commercial Street. "Jean and I just finished dinner. It's Jean's Portuguese stew, and there are plenty of leftovers. Hungry?"

"Come to think of it," Tory said, "I'm starved."

Kate raised an eyebrow. "Forget lunch?" She knew that Tory often forgot to eat or simply didn't have time for a meal while she was working. She'd also known that Tory had been at the clinic, because Reese had told her so when she'd dropped the baby off earlier that day. They hadn't had much time to talk, but she'd sensed Reese's worry.

"Busted." Tory laughed. "How's the baby?"

"Gorgeous," Jean Purdy, Kate's lover, announced as she walked into the living room with Regina in her arms. "And perfect, of course."

"Is she ready for a feeding?"

"When isn't she? Ready for a nap again, too." Laughing, Jean handed the baby to Tory. "Here you go. I've got some work to finish in the studio. Don't forget to say goodbye before you leave."

"Thanks. I won't." Tory took her daughter into the adjacent bedroom to feed her. When Regina had finished, she put her into the baby seat to sleep and joined Kate in the kitchen.

Kate cradled a cup of tea between her large, paint-smeared hands and studied Tory while she ate. There were faint smudges beneath her eyes, and unlike most women who still carried some of their extra pregnancy weight at two months postpartum, Tory was thinner than she had been before she'd become pregnant. It occurred to Kate that her daughter had reason to be worried. "When's Dan's last day?"

"Today. In fact, he's already left for Boston and a late flight out to Pittsburgh tonight," Tory replied.

"So you're going back to work," Kate said carefully.

"Yes." Tory put down her soup spoon and regarded her mother-in-law. "Did Reese tell you?"

Kate shook her head. "No, but she told me you'd gone into the clinic today because Dan was leaving earlier than expected."

"I'm trying to find someone to take his place so I won't have to work full time."

"Any possibilities?" Kate knew that even part time for Tory would be very nearly a full workload by anyone else's standards.

Tory picked up the spoon and turned it between her fingers, thinking back to the morning. "KT O'Bannon came over from Boston this morning to interview for the position." She raised her eyes and met Kate's. "You remember her, of course, from when Regina was born."

"Yes. She seemed very capable." Kate regarded Tory steadily. "You have some history with her, don't you?"

Tory smiled briefly. "Along with her astonishing good looks, Reese seems to have inherited her ability for understatement from you."

Kate merely smiled and waited.

"KT and I were lovers when we were young." Tory gazed past Kate's shoulder out the window to the harbor. An artist's palette of purples and pinks and indigo was brushed across the sky by the setting sun. "We didn't part on good terms."

"She hurt you," Kate observed.

Tory brought her eyes back to Kate's, grateful that there was no sympathy in them, only kindness. "Yes."

"And how do you feel about her now?"

"I don't know." Tory frowned, surprised. "If you had asked me yesterday, I would've told you with certainty that I felt nothing whatsoever for her other than anger. Perhaps not even that. She was just someone from the past whom I had left there."

Kate tilted her head thoughtfully. "And what's changed?"

"I don't know that either," Tory said softly.

"Could you work with her, seeing her every day?"

"I've thought about that every minute since she left this morning." Tory leaned back in the chair, her dinner forgotten. "Actually, I think so. When I'm working, I'm so focused that nothing else really matters. And I've worked with her before. We were medical students and residents together. We know each other's...rhythm." She looked away, refusing to think about how well they had known one another and just how seamlessly they had fit together for so many years.

"I imagine there would be moments when it would be hard." Kate placed her hand on Tory's arm. "Only you can know if it would be *too* hard."

"Reese said that she would be okay with it."

"If she said it, then she means it."

Tory smiled. "Oh, I know. But still, I don't want to give her anything else to worry about."

"If you don't have help, she's going to worry a lot more," Kate said with certainty.

"What do you think?" Tory asked softly.

Kate took her time before answering. "I know you can trust Reese to support you in whatever you decide."

"She always does." Tory touched the scrolled gold band on her ring finger. "I love her so much."

"Yes, I know," Kate said with great tenderness. She covered Tory's hand with her own. "I also think that we never really leave the past behind, and the pain follows us until we find a way to forgive the people we used to be."

"I don't know if I can."

"None of us does until faced with it." Kate sighed. "But you said yourself that something's changed, and maybe that's all you need to know for now."

Tory squeezed Kate's hand in thanks, her mind on the silent plea in KT's eyes and the answering tug of her own heart. *Yes, something has definitely changed. For both of us.*

Chapter Ten

Trey Pelosi was waiting for Reese and Bri in a small alcove outside the ICU. She stood as they approached, a smile on her face and an appraising glance at Bri.

"Officers," Trey said.

"Ms. Pelosi." Reese indicated Bri. "Officer Parker."

"Ma'am," Bri said.

Trey nodded to Bri briefly before returning her gaze to Reese. "Thank you for coming. Mr. and Mrs. Bridger want to cooperate in any way they can with your investigation."

"Excellent," Reese said evenly. "When can I speak with their son?"

"Well," Trey said smoothly, "as you can see, he's still under observation and in no condition to be questioned. However, we might have some information that would assist you."

Reese raised an eyebrow but said nothing for a moment. She leaned one shoulder against the wall and studied Trey Pelosi. That evening, as on the previous one, she was impeccably dressed in tailored dark slacks, matching low heels, and a burgundy silk blouse with the cuffs rolled casually to midforearm. "Still on the case?"

Trey smiled again. "At this point, I'm here as a family friend and advisor. No charges have been brought, and I'm not anticipating that any will be since the boy hasn't committed any crime."

Bri shifted slightly, her equipment belt creaking as she moved. Reese shrugged off the first parry. "We're still gathering information."

"Yes," Trey agreed, indicating the tiny lounge behind her with a tip of her chin. "Why don't we sit down for a few minutes and perhaps I can provide you with some."

"At some point, Ms. Pelosi," Reese said without moving, "I'm going to need to speak to Robert Bridger."

"Since that won't be this evening, Sheriff, perhaps I'll do." Without waiting for an answer, Trey walked back into the lounge and took a seat in the otherwise unoccupied area.

"What do you think, Officer Parker?" Reese asked quietly.

"My guess is she won't let us talk to him until she's certain that charges won't be filed or, if they are, that she knows the specifics so she can protect him."

"Yes, I agree. I'd do the same thing."

Bri rarely thought about the fact that Reese was an attorney. It was weird thinking of Reese that way, because she was such a cop's cop. Everyone who knew her said the same thing. "So, if we can't talk to him anyhow, what's the downside of talking with *her*?"

"If we're not careful, she'll know everything we know, and we'll come away empty." Reese felt a little thrill of challenge and clapped Bri on the shoulder. "Come on, Officer. Let's go talk to Counselor Pelosi."

"There's a coffee machine down the hall," Trey said as she watched Reese and Bri approach.

"We're fine," Reese said, taking a seat on one side of Trey as Bri moved around to one opposite. "So what is it you'd like us to know?"

"Have you ID'd the young woman who was found near Robert's vehicle?"

"You mean the young woman who was with him?" Reese asked. Her thrust this time.

"I don't believe we've established that fact yet," Trey commented, sidestepping neatly.

Reese grinned, but a flicker of irritation hardened her gaze. "Counselor, we could fence all evening. I think it might even be enjoyable under some circumstances. But I've got a dead girl in a drawer in the morgue in the basement of this hospital. Right now, I'm assuming that she got into that vehicle voluntarily." Before Trey could speak, Reese held up her hand. "But if I don't start getting some answers, I'm going to start thinking maybe she *didn't*. Maybe your clients' son took advantage of a drug-impaired young woman, coerced her into the vehicle, drove her out into the dunes, and dragged her off where no one could see them for sex or something rougher. Maybe she resisted. Maybe he *thought* she would resist and he gave her more drugs to make her compliant. And now she's dead. And I *guarantee* we'll find evidence to support that she was in that vehicle with your clients' son."

"There are any number of explanations to account for her body being in the vicinity of the Bridger vehicle," Trey noted calmly. "It could even be a coincidence." *She* held up a hand as Reese started to speak. "Nevertheless, the Bridgers informed me that Rob had been spending this past week with family friends in Chelmsford. When I talked to them this morning, it sounded as if Rob heard about a party here on the Cape from the older brother of the boy he was visiting. We suspect he...borrowed...the family car so he and his buddy could go."

"They filed a stolen vehicle report," Bri pointed out.

"Yes, well, it seems that was premature." Trey smiled at Bri. "A simple miscommunication."

"Where was the party?" Reese asked.

"We don't know."

"What about the girl?" Reese asked sharply. "What do you *suspect* about her?"

Trey shook her head. "He doesn't have a steady girlfriend. The boys he was visiting don't know anything about her. But if you could get me a photo, I'll show it to his parents and the other family."

"Let me have the name of the family he was visiting." Reese took a small spiral notebook from her left breast pocket, along with a pen.

Trey looked apologetic. "Ah, they've retained my services, merely to facilitate matters at this point. For the moment, I'd like to keep their names out of this."

Facilitator, my ass. Covering their own asses. And their kid's. Reese's jaw tightened. "Look, Ms. Pelosi—"

"Sheriff," Trey said quietly, "I'm no happier about an unidentified dead girl than you are. For now, let me see what I can do. The Bridgers really do want to cooperate. *Both* families do."

Reese blew out her breath. She didn't like it, but until she had a clearer picture of what had happened, she couldn't blame the parents or their attorney for keeping the boy under wraps. "All right. For now."

Trey smiled, and it was a genuine smile of pleasure, not victory. "Good. When can you get me the picture?"

"It's a morgue shot," Reese said as she reached into her shirt pocket again and drew out a Polaroid. She passed it over to Trey and watched her face carefully as the woman looked down at the photo. The attorney's expression did not change. *She may be corporate now, but this isn't the first dead shot she's seen.*

"Thank you." Trey met Reese's eyes. "May I keep this?"

"Go ahead."

Bri leaned over and murmured to Reese, who nodded assent.

"Ms. Pelosi," Bri said. "When you talk to the boys about the party, ask if it was a candy-bowl party."

Trey looked at Reese, who shook her head. To Bri she said, "Translation?"

"It's a party where everybody brings whatever drugs they have, tosses them into a big bowl or just a pile, and everyone samples." She looked at Reese, whose expression was bland. "The parties move around. Usually in somebody's house, not a bar."

"Hard stuff?" Reese asked.

Bri shrugged. "Could be anything. Uppers, downers, crack, coke, sometimes even heroin."

"Christ." Reese rubbed her face in frustration. "Is it all...bring your own, or are their dealers there?"

"I don't know." For a second, Bri looked as if she might say more but did not.

"I'll see what I can find out," Trey said as she stood. She extended her hand to Reese and then to Bri. "Thank you for coming. I'll be in touch."

"Ms. Pelosi." Reese stood as well. "I'm not interested in hauling a boy into court on a DUI when he's already paying for his mistake. If that's all this turns out to be, we're not going to have a problem. But if it's anything more, the next time I come, I'm not standing outside in the hall."

"You two take care," Trey said calmly. "Good night, now."

"Good night, Counselor," Reese said.

"Jeez," Bri said so softly that only Reese could hear as she watched the attorney walk away. "I sorta liked her until I figured out she was kicking our asses."

Reese laughed. "She didn't kick them too bad. At least now we have a lead to work on." As they walked down the hall toward the exit, Reese glanced at Bri. "So when's the last time you were at one of these parties?"

Bri blushed and kept her face forward. "Last year. When I was still in school."

"Is there anything we need to talk about?"

"No, ma'am. I don't...partake." Bri got to the exit door first and held it open until Reese passed through. Walking briskly to catch up, she said, "Sometimes you don't know it's going to be that kind of party until you get there and it just sort of happens. Spontaneously. But other times, it's publicized in advance and an address circulates maybe a day or so ahead of time so you know where to go."

They settled back into the cruiser and Reese pulled out onto the highway. "And what about dealers?"

"I only went to two of them, and both were by mistake. At the second one, there were definitely guys selling hard street drugs."

"So," Reese mused. "We might be looking for a mobile drug party that's a front for dealers to move their stuff, probably to the kids of vacationing families who have plenty of money to spend. Jesus. Where do we start with that?"

"We have to talk to Robert Bridger or one of his friends to find out how they heard about it, how they got directions, and where it was."

"Yes," Reese agreed. "Unless Ms. Pelosi comes through for us."

"Think she will?"

"I don't know. She's too good to give her game away."

❖

"KT?"

"Yeah," KT mumbled, rolling over in bed without thinking. She caught her left hand in the covers and gasped sharply. "*God* damn it."

"KT? Are you okay?"

"Yeah, yeah." KT put her cell phone down, fumbled for the light switch in the unfamiliar room, and blinked into the sudden glare. Even through the haze of confusion, she recognized the voice. She found her phone again. "Vic?"

"I woke you. I'm sorry."

"It's okay." KT rubbed her face with the back of her arm and tried desperately to wake up. She'd taken two pain pills to get to sleep, and she was groggy. She glanced at the clock and saw that it was not quite 11 p.m. She'd only been asleep half an hour. "Sorry. Go ahead. What is it?"

"I...uh...wanted to tell you that you've got the job. Here at the clinic. If you still want it."

KT closed her eyes and let out a long sigh. "Great. Thank you."

"I know you probably need time to move your things and settle in, so I was thinking next week would be soo—"

"Tomorrow. I can start tomorrow." KT suddenly felt invigorated. She had work. She had some purpose. "I have a nine o'clock appointment with my therapist. I can start at eleven."

"I didn't ask you. Is it Pia Torres?"

"Yes," KT replied, surprised, although if she'd thought about it, she shouldn't have been. Provincetown—the entire Cape—was a small community, and it made sense that Tory would know about other medical professionals.

Tory was quiet for a second, then said, "Good. She's terrific. Does she know that you'll be working with me?"

"Not yet. I didn't know that I would be."

"No, of course you didn't."

Tory's laughter coming through the phone gave KT such a strong sense of déjà vu that she was nearly dizzy. How many nights had she lain awake in her on-call room down the hall from the trauma unit, talking to Tory on the phone? Hundreds? Thousands? Conversations about nothing. Something on the news. Some bill that needed paying. A movie they planned on seeing the following weekend. The aimless, easy conversations of people whose lives were one. *Jesus. How long has it been since anything has felt so right?*

"KT? Are you there?"

"Yeah," KT said quickly. "I told her I'd fit my schedule around hers. I'll try to get a better idea from her tomorrow about how that will shake out. You just tell me when you need me, and I'll work out the rest."

"Tomorrow at eleven will be fine for starters. We'll work out the rest of the details later." There were a few seconds of silence. "Good luck in therapy tomorrow. Don't push too hard, KT."

"Wouldn't think of it."

"Good night," Tory said softly.

"Good night, Vic," KT whispered. She didn't say what she'd always added at this point. *Sweet dreams, sweetheart.*

❖

"You're home right on time tonight," Tory said with pleasure, putting aside the newest Katherine Forrest mystery as Reese walked into the bedroom only a few minutes after midnight.

Reese leaned down and kissed her. "And you're up kind of late, aren't you?"

"I thought I should try keeping regular hours again since I'm going back to work. But I confess—Reggie and I took a little nap a bit earlier."

"Was she good with Kate and Jean?" Reese stripped off her uniform and laid it carefully across a nearby chair in case she needed to get dressed again before morning.

Tory smiled. "Her grandmothers told me that she was quite angelic."

"Of course she was. She looks like one asleep right now, too." Reese slid under the covers as Tory snapped off the light. She extended an arm for Tory to snuggle against her chest, threaded her fingers into Tory's hair, and kissed her forehead. "Hi."

"How was your night?" Tory tilted her chin up and kissed the corner of Reese's mouth. "God, you feel good."

"Mmm, you, too." Reese stretched and sighed. "Pretty routine. It seems like those kids were at some kind of drug party out here on the Cape somewhere. We're going to try to chase that down." She ran her hand down Tory's arm and back up again. "When will you have something from the pathologist in Hyannis?"

"The middle of the week, probably. I'll call him to check on Monday. Oh, that's a holiday. Tuesday, then."

"Thanks, baby."

"Reese," Tory said quietly as she stroked Reese's abdomen. "I called KT and offered her the job." She felt the barest flicker of muscles tightening beneath her fingers. "Okay?"

"It seems like a reasonable decision. What did she say?"

"She said yes. She's going to start tomorrow." The strange conversation with her former lover was still fresh in her mind. She'd never known KT not to awaken completely alert and totally functional. Of course, it had been a good many years since she'd had occasion to speak to KT in the middle of the night. Or at any other time, for that matter. Still, it had been disconcerting to talk with her at all. After so many years of relegating KT and everything about her to a past that she rarely allowed to taint her present, to talk to her twice in one day—and to talk to her at bedtime, the way they'd always done when they'd been together—it was so...Tory jerked, realizing that Reese had been talking and that she hadn't heard a word. "I'm sorry, honey. What did you say?"

"That I hope it works out."

"Yes," Tory said quietly. "So do I."

"But if it doesn't," Reese continued, her cheek resting against the top of Tory's head, "you'll let it go, won't you? Let her go?"

Tory tightened her hold on the most important person in her life. She pressed her face to Reese's neck, savoring her scent and her strength. "Of course. I promise."

"That's fine, then. Go to sleep, Tor. I love you."

"I love you too, sweetheart." Tory kissed her again and closed her eyes.

Reese held her in the darkness, listening to her soft, quiet breathing for a long time, thinking about the things she'd never imagined having and that now, she couldn't imagine living without.

Chapter Eleven

"Hey, did I wake you?" Bri murmured.

"Hi, baby!" Caroline sounded much more awake than Bri. "Did you just finish a shift?"

"Yeah. What are you doing?" Naked, Bri stretched out under the sheets and closed her eyes. She cradled the phone on the pillow next to her ear and idly drew her fingers up and down the center of her stomach.

"Just getting ready to go out for coffee and something to eat. Then I'm going to the studio later this morning to finish a painting I've been working on."

"Yeah? How's that going?" Bri tried to envision Caroline in the small studio apartment she'd seen in the pictures that Caroline had e-mailed her. She'd seen photos of the neighborhood too, but she had a hard time really getting a sense of what it was like there. It seemed pretty enough. Just—so far away.

"It's going good. Great, actually. They keep us really busy, and I'm glad." There were a few seconds of silence broken only by a very faint buzzing. "I miss you so much. When I'm painting, it's not so bad."

Bri's stomach tightened, and she fought a wave of sadness. "I know. I'd rather be at work than doing anything else. I love you."

"Oh, baby. I love you, too, so much." Caroline's smile came through in her words. "Are you in bed?"

"Uh-huh. You?"

"On the sofa—not dressed yet. I wish I was there with you. I miss sleeping with you." Her voice was silky soft as she added, "And other stuff."

"Jesus, Carre," Bri groaned as a wash of heat raced over her. "Don't make me think about that right now, okay? I have to get some sleep. There's a big weekend coming up, and I might be working a double shift for the next three days."

"Since when did a little sex ever stop you from sleeping?"

Bri brushed her fingers over the short, tight curls at the base of her belly. "It's not the same. Not even all that much fun."

Caroline laughed. "Yeah, I know."

"Do you...think about me? When you do?"

"Always." Caroline sighed. "You really okay?"

"No. I'll probably be begging you for phone sex in another week or so."

"Any time, baby. I don't want you to suffer."

"I'm already suffering." Bri stroked the inside of her thigh, but she wasn't really in the mood for anything more. When her body clamored for attention, she took care of it, but it didn't come anywhere close to making love with Caroline. Not just because Caroline was the hottest, most beautiful girl she'd ever known, but because when they were together that way, Bri felt better than she did at any other time. Even better than when she was working.

"I wasn't talking about just the physical stuff, you know." Caroline sighed. "I'm sorry it's hard for you."

"No," Bri said quickly. "It's okay. I mean, it's not *okay.* But I'm glad you got this chance. I think it's so cool."

"I don't think I could stand being here if I didn't have you," Caroline whispered. "I'm really lonely, but when I think about you, I feel better. It doesn't hurt so much to be so far away then."

"That's good, baby." Bri shifted aimlessly, tired, but not wanting to say good night. She hated the empty feeling right after she heard the click followed by nothing but empty air. "Reese has set up a date for my black belt test. In October, during Women's Week."

"Oh," Caroline gasped. "Oh, so soon."

"Yeah. I was surprised, too."

"And I'm going to miss it. Oh, I'm so sorry, baby."

"Yeah, well. It's just a test, you know."

"It's *not* just a test. It's a very big deal. You've been working so long, so *hard* for this." Caroline was silent for a moment. "Maybe I can get a supersaver flight or fly standby or something."

"No, I don't want you to do that," Bri protested, meaning it.

"Save your money to come home for the holidays. You have to come home then."

"Are you ready for your test?" Caroline asked, changing the subject.

"I don't know. I think so. If Reese thinks so, then I guess I am." Bri brushed a hand across her chest, toying unconsciously with a nipple. When it hardened beneath her fingers and her stomach clenched again, she moved her hand away. "I'll be ready by the time the test comes."

"You'll tell me when and everything, right?"

"Sure." Bri stifled a yawn. "I better go, baby. I just wanted to hear your voice."

"You be careful this weekend, you hear?"

"Don't worry, I'm always careful."

"Be extra careful. I love you."

Caroline made a small kissing sound and Bri smiled. "I love you bad, baby. Good night."

"Good night," Caroline said softly.

Bri waited for the final click, then set the phone down. She curled on her side, cupped one hand between her thighs, and closed her eyes, imagining Caroline's face and the sweet sound of her voice as sleep claimed her.

❖

KT stared at the ceiling. Her arm throbbed, her stomach rolled with the faint swell of nausea, and sweat streaked her face. The early September night was hot, and despite the air-conditioning, the room was stuffy. It felt as if a weight sat astride her chest, heavy and dark. It might have been loneliness, or sadness, or merely the fact that she'd awakened with the overwhelming urge for one of the small white pills. She turned her head and glanced at the red numerals on the cheap plastic clock radio by the bedside. 3:41 a.m. In less than six hours, she'd need to be at Pia Torres's for her first therapy session.

In less than six hours, the pain she was feeling now would double. Physical therapy was a difficult road, and she'd need her pain medication then. She had to wait.

Her mind raced. She tried not to think about the conversation with Tory. At least not beyond the fact that she would have a job. It wasn't the money she needed, but the sense of being valuable. Of doing something worthwhile. Her entire adult life, even *before* she could have truly been considered an adult, she had equated achievement with self-worth. The youngest child in a family of notables, she had set out to be the best at her chosen field because anything less would have made *her* less. In the eyes of her family, in her own eyes. She'd succeeded. In everything. In everything except in her relationship with Tory.

Tory. She'd gone for years barely thinking of her. She'd been so busy with work, and when she wasn't, she could easily fill the void that Tory had left behind in the arms of some other woman. There was always some other woman. Until she'd gotten to the point where the women became interchangeable and the temporary solace she found in their arms slipped away. Before the interlude with Vicki earlier that afternoon, it had been months since she'd been with anyone.

Tory. When she thought of her now, she remembered the bright-eyed, optimistic young woman she had been. The women they had *both* been. She thought of their lost dreams—Tory's of Olympic gold, hers of the pair of them taking the medical world by storm, co-chiefs of emergency medicine, battling death and winning. Always winning.

Well, I'm not winning now.

KT pushed herself up with her right arm and swung her legs over the side of the bed. In the tank top and briefs she'd been sleeping in, she crossed the room, opened the sliding glass door, and stepped out onto the deck. The moon was high, the sky clear, and in the distance through the trees she caught a glimmer of the harbor. The water was black, streaked with silver from the running lights of the boats moored on its glassy surface. The faint breeze dried the sweat on her face. She cradled her injured left hand against her chest and tightened the fingers of her right around the wooden railing that edged the deck. Moments of quiet were extraordinarily rare in her hectic life, and even now, surrounded by exquisite beauty, there was no peace.

She thought back to her interview that morning. Tory had

obviously been surprised to see her. The anger still simmered in her eyes, but she had managed it well. But it wasn't the anger or the distance that KT remembered most clearly. What she remembered was that when Tory had mentioned Reese and Regina, she had looked beautiful. Beautiful and happy. KT searched her heart and could not find it there to resent Tory the peace she had so clearly found.

Turning from the soul-wrenching view, KT walked into the bathroom and shook another pill from the small orange plastic container. Even more than she needed sleep, she needed respite from her thoughts.

❖

Pia Torres, dressed casually in a short-sleeved turquoise blouse, tan slacks, and sandals, opened the side door of her cottage at five minutes to nine on Saturday morning. She looked up at the slightly taller woman who leaned against the porch column in a shaft of morning sunlight. Dr. O'Bannon wore jeans and a white oxford shirt, the right cuff rolled to midforearm, the left unbuttoned and hanging loose over the molded splint. Pia couldn't help but register what a striking picture she made, but noted the shadows beneath her dark eyes and the faintly haunted expression on her face.

"Good morning," Pia said warmly. "Did you knock?"

KT pushed herself upright and shook her head. "No. Not yet."

"I don't stand on ceremony, Dr. O'Bannon. Please, just—"

"It's KT. Remember?"

Pia smiled. "Yes. And the next time, KT, just knock on the door, or better yet, stick your head in and holler." She pushed wide the screen door and gestured with her head toward the interior. "Please, come in. How are you feeling?"

KT stiffened, then forced herself to answer evenly. "Fine. I'm looking forward to getting started."

"Yes, I can imagine." Patients approached physical therapy with very different attitudes. Some resented it, feeling that they could do whatever needed to be done in terms of rehabilitation on their own. Some feared it, especially the possibility of pain. And others, and she suspected that Dr. O'Bannon would be one of those, approached therapy as a battle to be waged and a war to be won. Unfortunately, there was no standard time period for a particular campaign, as every individual needed to progress according to the particulars of their injury, their age, their pain tolerance, and their ultimate goal. A surgeon with a hand injury, like a musician, was one of the most difficult of all patients to treat. It wasn't just that incomplete recovery would make it difficult for Dr. O'Bannon to return to her profession—it would make it impossible. Most skilled laborers could still work with dysfunctional digits, but that was not going to be the case here.

"The treatment room is this way," Pia said as she led the way down the narrow hall to a large, sunny screened-in porch at the rear. Another garden, more luxurious than the small flower patch in front of the house, filled the entire yard behind the cottage. The flowers, a riotous panoply of color, danced in the breeze beneath the bright, clear sun.

KT didn't notice the beauty. All she saw were the strain gauges, the neurosensory filaments, and the goniometers arranged on a stand next to a picnic table with benches on either side that apparently was the treatment table.

"Should I take my splint off now?" KT asked as she sat on one side of the long, narrow table. A clear sheet of Plexiglas covered the top.

"In just a minute," Pia responded. "Let me review your medical history for a few minutes, and then we'll talk about where we're headed."

After KT confirmed Pia's understanding of her injuries, she listened politely as Pia laid out the treatment regimen, but she wasn't really absorbing the details of the plan. She'd slept fitfully the remainder of the previous night despite the sedating effects of the oral narcotic and had awakened inexplicably disturbed and agitated. Now, unexpectedly, Pia's voice, musical and rich, soothed her into a comfortable lassitude.

"Where are you from?" KT asked, struck by the barest hint of an accent underlying Pia's mellifluous voice.

Pia stopped abruptly in the midst of explaining the theory and practice of dynamic splinting. "Right here in Provincetown."

"Really?" KT barely noticed as Pia began to disengage the elastic bands attached to the ends of her fingers that protected them from unexpected motion.

"Mmm-hmm," Pia said as she worked carefully and efficiently to remove the Orthoplast splint. "My father was a fisherman, descended from some of the original Portuguese settlers. My brother still goes out on a fishing boat every day. My mother came here for the summer with her family thirty-five years ago, met my father at a party one night, and never left."

"I take it she was weal—ah, damn." KT flinched as a muscle in her forearm spasmed and an electric shock stabbed through her hand.

"What?" Pia asked quickly.

"Paresthesias," KT grunted, referring to the abnormal sensations commonly experienced after a nerve has been severed or badly injured. In the last few days, she had started to experience pins and needles, shooting pains, burning discomfort in her fingertips, and all other manner of abnormal nerve discharge as the damaged nerves in her hand attempted to heal. While in one respect it was encouraging, because it meant that the nerves in her fingers were starting to regenerate, the unexpected and often severe pain was wearing.

"It's about time for that." Pia cradled KT's hand in both of hers, examining the location of the incision, the texture of the skin, the condition of the muscles, and the adequacy of the blood supply to the injured fingers. She gently traced her fingertips over the healing laceration. "This looks good."

KT stared at the slightly raised, thick red ridge across her palm, remembering the instant when she'd held her hand out to ward off the blow and had felt the knife slice to the bone. She shivered and fought down a wave of nausea. "Yes. It's coming along."

"You understand that for the next few weeks we'll simply be concentrating on range of motion and scar desensitization. You can't flex your fingers actively or attempt any resistive exercises. The tendon repairs are still far too delicate to risk rupture."

"I understand."

"Good," Pia said with a smile. "I'm going to range each digit now. I'm sure the joints are stiff, so you can expect a little bit of discomfort." She cocked her head and studied KT's face. She was pale. "Have you eaten anything today?"

"I...uh..." Caught off guard, KT fumbled for an answer.

"These first few sessions are going to be difficult. It's been my experience that you will tolerate therapy much better if you're rested and not otherwise stressed. Breakfast..." She stopped when she saw KT smile. KT's lips were full and sensuous, and her smile might have been beautiful had it not been curved ever so subtly downward with bitterness. "What?"

"I was thinking about stress. I'm starting a temporary job at the East End Health Clinic today. It's not what I'm trained to do, but it's all that I *can* do. My hand is completely dysfunctional and might not improve significantly. I may never operate again. Somehow, I don't think a bagel is going to help."

"Yes," Pia said calmly. "I suppose you might be right." She held KT's eyes, her own gentle and without reproach. "But we won't know until we try, will we?"

We. It wasn't a concept that KT was used to contemplating. Even when she'd been in a long-term relationship, she'd always felt as if she were doing battle alone. Tory had supported her in her quest, but there had been only so much she could do to help. When it came down to succeeding or failing, the outcome had always rested squarely on KT's shoulders. KT stared at her hand still resting between Pia's long, deceptively delicate fingers. Her own hand, lifeless and pale, looked forlorn—nearly as forlorn as she felt. Nevertheless, Pia's darker, stronger fingers appeared capable. More than capable. Certain and sure. KT felt a flicker of hope and raised her eyes to Pia's. "I promise not to show up again on an empty stomach."

"Good." Pia resumed her gentle ministrations and, as she carefully massaged and manipulated the stiff joints in KT's fingers, continued the interrupted conversation. "My mother was a society debutante, I guess you could say. She'd just had her coming-out party the summer she arrived here." Pia laughed. "She always says she hated that party, but was glad she'd gone because it gave her a pretty good idea of the kind of man she *didn't* want to marry."

KT smiled. "I guess your father wasn't one of those guys."

"No," Pia agreed quietly. "He wasn't." She reached for the splint and set about reconnecting KT's fingers to the elastic bands and attaching the Velcro straps that held it around her wrist and palm. "You can take this off to shower. You probably already are. Be careful when the hand is unprotected."

"What kind of exercises can I do at home?"

Pia shook her head. "None for now." She caught the not-unexpected flicker of irritation cross KT's face, noting as she had the first time she'd seen her how extraordinarily good looking she was. Anger didn't diminish her appeal. It only made her look wilder, and a little dangerous. The fact that Pia found any of those things attractive surprised her, but she pushed the thought aside and said firmly, "It's too soon. You'll only delay the healing."

"All right. I get the message."

"If you cheat, I'll know."

KT felt the words like a blow and forced herself not to recoil. Then she admonished herself for the ridiculous reaction. Pia didn't know her. Didn't know a single thing about her. "I wouldn't think of it."

"I'll hold you to that, Dr. O'Bannon," Pia said mildly as she rose to show KT to the door. Out on the porch, she instructed KT to come again the following day at the same time.

As KT made her way slowly down the flagstone path toward Commercial Street, she felt Pia's gaze upon her back. Before she turned left to head into town, she glanced back toward the cottage. The tiny porch was empty. She felt a pang of loneliness, but this time there was a pleasant edge to it. It was the kind of missing that comes of having enjoyed someone's company and being disappointed to have that time come to an end.

For the first time in a long time, KT occupied herself with pleasant memories as she walked.

Chapter Twelve

Tory looked up in surprise as Reese walked in the back door shortly after 10 a.m.

"Hi, honey," Tory said. "Slow morning?" Reese had left for work over three hours before.

"Quiet enough." Reese quickly crossed the room and leaned to kiss Tory lightly on the mouth. Then she sidled around her, plucked Regina from her infant seat, swung her carefully into the air, and kissed her cheek. "Mmm, you smell good," she murmured before glancing back at Tory. "I thought I'd take this one over to the grandmoms."

"You didn't have to leave work to do that. I was going to drop her off on my way to the clinic." *On my way to see KT.* All through the morning's preparation, including feeding and bathing the baby, showering and dressing herself, and reviewing the preliminary work shift schedule she'd put together hastily the evening before, she'd thought about spending part of the day with KT. It was so unbelievable as to be impossible to absorb. More than six years had passed since they'd spent any personal time together, six years that reverberated still with all the things left unspoken between them.

"Nervous?" Reese asked gently.

Tory gave a small start, then shook her head with a wistful smile. "You are frighteningly perceptive, Sheriff."

Holding the baby against her shoulder with one hand, Reese efficiently gathered together bottles, diapers, a change of clothing, and the sundry other items required for the day's outing. She just as proficiently organized everything in a plastic carryall. "You didn't sleep very well last night. You tossed and turned a lot." She hefted the bag in her right hand and regarded Tory tenderly. "I figured you were worried."

"Oh, I'm sorry. I didn't mean to keep you awake. I—"

"Nothing to apologize for." Reese bounced Regina on her shoulder softly when the baby began to fret. "I think she's ready for a ride in the cruiser." She tilted her head and regarded the baby seriously. "What do you think, huh? Lights and sirens?"

Tory took the carryall from Reese and set it aside. Then she wrapped her arms around Reese's waist and rested her head on the opposite shoulder from their daughter. "I think she'd love it, but Nelson might object to you going Code 3 on the way through town to Grandmoms'."

"He'll never know."

"In Provincetown? Please." Tory kissed Reese's neck. "It wouldn't take five minutes."

Reese grinned. "Yeah, you're right. Besides, I should wait until she's a little bigger so she'll really enjoy it."

"So why did you *really* come home this morning?"

"You don't believe the part about me wanting to take the baby to my mother's?"

"Oh, I believe that." Tory snuggled closer. "It's exactly the sweet kind of thing that you would do. But it's Saturday morning on one of the busiest weekends of the year, and you're on duty. So what are you doing here, Sheriff?"

"I just thought you might be having a rough day," Reese said quietly.

"And you wanted to check?" Tory asked just as softly. She didn't need to hear the answer, she knew. She rubbed her cheek against the stiff fabric of Reese's uniform shirt, taking comfort from the simple strength of it, so like Reese. "Thank you. I'm fine."

Reese kissed Tory's forehead. "I knew you would be. I stopped by for me."

Tory lifted her head and regarded Reese somberly. "Are *you* all right?"

"Yeah, I'm fine." Reese smiled and snuggled the baby closer to her neck. "I better get going. I left Bri at the station chasing down missing-person leads." She picked up the bag with the baby's supplies. "Would you mind if I stopped by the clinic later?"

Tory's green eyes darkened. "You never asked before."

"I don't want you to think I'm being...overly protective."

"I like it when you worry." Tory tenderly stroked her fingers along the edge of Reese's jaw. "And you never need to ask if it's all right to come and see me. You might want to ask *Randy* if it's all right."

They both laughed.

"I already *know* what he'll say." Imitating his mildly exasperated tone, Reese said, "She's behind, and you've got thirty seconds."

"Well, I'm glad that you never listen to him." Still smiling, Tory linked her arm through Reese's and together they walked to the door. Her melancholy had disappeared, and when she thought ahead to her day, the prospect of seeing KT seemed far less daunting.

❖

Pia walked east along Commercial Street, enjoying the sunshine and the smell of the sea. She knew that within a few short weeks, summer would be gone and fall would be fast upon them. She didn't mind, because fall was her favorite season. The sun still held the power to warm her at midday, and the nights were cool enough for her favorite leather jacket—the one that had been her brother's when he'd been a teenager and that had been handed down to her when she was fourteen, despite her mother's protests. In addition to the weather, which pleased her, October brought Women's Week—seven days on either side of the Columbus Day holiday marked by a large influx of lesbians to town and a general atmosphere of celebration. Even though she'd grown up in Provincetown and had been exposed to the social and sexual diversity of the village since her earliest days, she still thrilled to the atmosphere of community when the town was filled with women in love. Or, sometimes, simply in lust.

As Pia climbed the wooden steps to Provincetown Realty, her mind suddenly skittered to KT O'Bannon. While she'd been working on the surgeon's hand, her attention had been completely focused on the wound and the challenges of rehabilitation. She hadn't allowed herself to think about the devastation, or the tremendous tragedy it would be if her treatment failed to overcome the damage. It hadn't been difficult to see what the injury had done to the surgeon. Beneath her undeniably self-possessed and forceful façade had run a river of pain.

Pia gave herself a mental shake as she pushed through into the large, single-room office. Her task was clear. She needed to bring to bear every ounce of skill and experience she had acquired over the last eight years in order to return KT O'Bannon to the life she had known before some maniac had taken it from her. If she could do that, she would be well satisfied.

"Pia!" the woman behind the desk exclaimed. Her blond hair was stylishly coiffed, her blue eyes were subtly highlighted with expertly applied makeup, and her tailored blouse and slacks accentuated a willowy figure. At forty-eight, she looked thirty-five. "What a nice surprise."

"Hi, Mom." Pia had her father's dark coloring and slender, wiry stature. Combined with her mother's elegant bone structure, they made her appear more exotically attractive than classically beautiful. "How's business?"

Her mother shrugged. "It's the end of the season. Rentals are down, but we're gearing up for the off-season maintenance projects." In addition to selling real estate in the increasingly competitive Provincetown market, her mother's business also managed several of the condominiums in the village. "You're in town early. Shopping?"

"No, I just dropped by to ask you a question about the third-floor unit. Is it still vacant?"

"Yes. Why?"

Suddenly, Pia was plagued with second thoughts. Just the day before she had decided it wasn't a good idea to get involved with KT O'Bannon in any way other than purely professionally. Now she was contemplating recommending to the surgeon that she rent a unit in her mother's guesthouse. The house that was twenty feet from her own front door.

"Do you have a possible tenant?" her mother asked curiously.

"Uh...I might." Pia rested her hip on the corner of one of the cluttered wooden desks opposite her mother's. The part-time agent who worked for her mother was not in, and they were alone in the warm, sunny room. "I have a new client, and I know that she's looking for a place to rent. It would be...convenient...I mean, she'd be close by and I know the unit is empty and she's going to be here at least for several months..." *And I don't know why, but I just wanted to help her out.*

"A client, you say?"

Pia nodded. "Yes. A surgeon from Boston Hospital. She has a hand injury."

Her mother grimaced. "Sounds serious."

"Very serious, I'm afraid."

"What is she doing while she's here?"

Elana Torres regarded her daughter intently, and Pia wondered what her mother might have seen in her face. Her mother was usually very good at reading her moods, often too good. As difficult as that sometimes was, Pia's inability to keep very much a secret from Elana had kept them connected even during the most chaotic periods of Pia's life. The first had been when Pia had realized she was a lesbian at the age of nineteen. She'd tried to hide it, only because her first crush on a fellow college student had been so intensely passionate that she hadn't wanted to share the feelings with anyone. She hadn't been ashamed, she'd been in awe.

But her mother had seen the truth the first time she'd seen the two of them together. After dinner the night that Pia had brought Rose home, her mother had taken her aside and asked pointedly about the nature of their relationship. Unwilling to lie, Pia had told her that they were in love.

"Are you sleeping together?"

"It's not about that, Mom."

Her mother hadn't been happy, and their relationship had been strained for several years. Gradually, however, their deep affection for one another had overcome the estrangement that had resulted from her mother's disappointment that Pia would not marry and produce grandchildren, at least not in the traditional fashion. In recent years, her mother's concern had shifted more to the fact that Pia wasn't married in any fashion whatsoever. It was one of the few topics they didn't discuss.

"Pia?"

"Hmm? Oh...what is she doing? I don't know. I've only met

with her twice."

"But you're finding her a place to live?"

"No," Pia said hastily. "I just thought of the unit, and it seemed like a reasonable solution."

"Here," her mother said, reaching into a drawer. She extended a set of keys. "The next time you see her, show her the unit. If she's interested, she can drop by and I'll go over the lease with her."

Pia backed up a step and unconsciously put her hands behind her back. "No. I'll just tell her to stop by—"

"Don't be silly. This will save a step." Elana tossed the keys to Pia, forcing her to catch them on the fly. "You must have a number for her. Just give her a call and ask her to drop by this evening and have a look."

"I, uh...all right," Pia acquiesced, feeling foolish. "I'll...I'll call her."

"Good." Elana narrowed her eyes. "Are you all right? You seem...distracted."

"No," Pia replied vehemently, ignoring the butterflies in her stomach at the thought of calling KT O'Bannon. "I'm just fine."

❖

When KT arrived at the East End Health Clinic at a few minutes before eleven a.m., there were already ten people in the waiting room. She nodded to Randy, who was seated behind the intake desk. His royal blue shirt matched his eyes, which were narrowed at her suspiciously.

"Is Dr. King in yet?" KT asked in what she hoped was a friendly tone.

"She's in her office."

KT extended her hand across the counter. "I'm KT O'Bannon. We met briefly yesterday. I'll be working here from now on."

"So I understand." Randy shook her hand, because it was required of him. "Today will be a good warm-up. We have fifty patients scheduled."

"Wonderful," KT muttered as she moved toward the doors leading to the rear. A minute later, she knocked on Tory's office door, waited for a response, and entered when Tory called out,

"Come in."

"Good morning," KT said.

"KT." Tory passed a single sheet of paper across the top of her desk in KT's direction. "This is the shift schedule for the next month. If you have a conflict because of your therapy or...anything, let me know as soon as possible so I can make adjustments."

Slightly surprised by Tory's formal and perfunctory manner, KT lifted the sheet of paper and studied it. "Looks fine to me."

"Good." Tory took a breath, surprised at the undercurrent of nerves. "The majority of the patients will have chronic, common medical problems such as hypertension or diabetes. If you have questions about the management, just check with me. I don't imagine it will take very long for you to catch on."

"All right."

"If there's anything you have a question about or are uncertain of—"

"Vic, I won't take any chances. I—"

"If you don't mind," Tory interrupted, "I'd prefer that you call me Tory."

KT blushed. She'd been the only one to ever call Tory *Vic*. It had begun in medical school when the computer had mistakenly listed her as Victor King on all of her class rosters. The teasing about Victor had led to KT calling her Vic, and it had just stuck. But the old endearment had no place in their present relationship.

"Of course," KT said stiffly.

"Well, I imagine we're already behind, and the day is young." Tory stood. "There's an empty office down the hall. You can use that. Feel free to ask Randy to get you anything you need in the way of supplies."

KT stood as well. "Sure. Thanks."

"Good luck, then," Tory said as she left the room without looking back.

Just as KT moved to follow, her cell phone rang. She checked the readout and was surprised to see that it was a local number. "Hello?"

"Dr. O'Bannon?"

"Yes. Can I help you?"

A soft chuckle came through the line. "It's Pia Torres. I

was wondering—well, there's an empty apartment—a condo, actually—in the main guesthouse adjacent to my cottage. I thought you might be interested—"

"I am. Definitely. Who should I call?"

"I have a key. I thought perhaps this evening—"

"Yes. That would be perfect." KT checked her watch. Seven hours and she would be off her first day of work as an internist. "How about we have dinner at seven and then go take a look at this place."

"Oh, I couldn't..."

"Sure you could. Just say yes."

There was silence on the line. KT found herself holding her breath as she waited for the woman's response, a wholly new and unusual experience.

"I'd like that," Pia said quietly. "Yes."

Smiling, KT breathed out slowly. "You pick the place."

"You might be sorry," Pia said teasingly.

"No," KT replied completely seriously, remembering the soothing tone of Pia's voice and the sensitive touch of her hand. "I don't think so."

Chapter Thirteen

Are you sure you can't stay for lunch?" Kate asked.

"Hmm?" Seated at the fifties-style Formica table in her mother's kitchen, Reese absently traced her index finger down the length of Reggie's arm, around the bend of her wrist, and over her tiny hand and even tinier fingers. She turned her own finger over and rested it in Reggie's palm, fascinated to see the little fist close around it.

Smiling, Kate placed both hands on Reese's shoulders and massaged the firm muscles, amazed still at the tall, strong woman her daughter had become. "Lunch?"

"Tory says she can't see things, but look at how bright her eyes are and the way she keeps looking all around. I'm pretty sure she knows what's going on."

"I imagine that Tory's right about her inability to focus just yet," Kate noted judiciously as she kissed the top of Reese's head. "But I'm also certain that she's taking in the whole constellation of sounds and sights and touches and smells in her little universe." She resisted the urge to kiss Reese's head one more time and merely squeezed her shoulders again. "And you and Tory are her whole world."

Reese glanced up from Reggie in her baby seat, grinning. "It's amazing."

"That it is." Kate moved across the small kitchen and leaned against the counter by the white enamel sink. "Tory's at work?"

"Yes. She's supposed to be working six hours today."

Kate said nothing.

"I suppose her first day back is going to be pretty hectic," Reese noted as she leaned over to kiss Reggie's forehead. "Did she tell you about hiring KT?"

"We talked about it last evening, but I didn't know that she had decided for certain." Kate took the coffeepot from the warmer and refilled her cup before gesturing to Reese, who shook her head. "I'm glad that she's going to have help."

"Me, too." Reese stood and walked to the window that looked out on a small wooden deck and a narrow strip of sandy beach leading down to Provincetown Harbor. A red kayak came slowly into view followed by a group of yellow ones—a class from the boat rental place in town—floundering along behind it like a disorganized line of baby ducks. She watched the leader, thinking how much she missed her morning drive to Herring Cove and the pleasant anticipation of waiting for Tory to appear on the horizon in her own red kayak. "It's funny how it turned out to be KT."

"Do you believe in coincidences?" Kate asked quietly.

Reese turned and met her mother's eyes. "I'm a cop. I learned a long time ago that there are no coincidences."

"Do you have a theory about what it means, then?" Kate studied her daughter's expressive eyes, thinking how like Reese's father's they were. Sharp and discerning and so, so intelligent. Reese saw everything with such clarity and didn't shrink from the sharp edges of truth. Kate imagined that had Reese been a combat soldier, she would have been a great leader, just like her father. But Reese was so very different from him in one critical way. One had only to see the way Reese looked at Tory or their baby to know that her heart was completely unguarded. As a woman, Kate appreciated that; as a mother, she worried.

"I don't think much about the metaphysical nature of things," Reese said with a wry smile, "but if I did, I'd say that when you're wounded, your instincts are to head for home."

Kate's eyes widened. "Does that bother you?"

Reese lifted her shoulder. "That KT came to Tory now?" Reese glanced at the baby, who in the midst of vigorously flailing her arms and legs was making small happy sounds. "I can't imagine not loving Tory, so I figure KT must still, too." She heard Kate's swift intake of breath. "Do you still love my father?"

"Oh, you have such a way of taking me off guard," Kate said with a shaky laugh. She glanced down at the wedding ring she wore, the one that Jean had put there only weeks after the two of them had fled from their lives, *for* their lives, leaving pieces of their hearts behind. She looked up at the largest part of her heart, realizing again the terrible sacrifice that had been forced upon her when her husband had made her choose between Jean and her child. "No, I don't love him. But I remember loving him. I was a different woman then, and he was a different man. I wouldn't go to him now under any circumstances, but I never loved him the way that KT and Tory must have loved each other."

"No, I guess not." Reese slid her hands into her pockets and rocked back and forth. "Tory loved her very much, and there are places in her that aren't...healed. She'll be better when she settles things between them...things they should've settled a long time ago but couldn't."

"How do you know about those things?" Kate asked curiously. "Did Tory tell you?"

"She didn't have to. When we first met, she didn't trust me, and she didn't trust love." Reese's jaw tightened, and her voice dropped a notch. "KT did that to her. There was a time I wanted to kick KT's ass because of that."

Kate laughed. "And now you don't?"

Reese laughed, too. "Not too much. Tory can take care of herself, and if she can't—if KT hurts her—I will personally put her on a plane back to Boston."

"You've turned out to be a remarkable woman, Reese," Kate said as she linked her arm through Reese's. "I'm so glad that you're my daughter, and that you and Tory are together."

"Thanks." Reese cleared her throat, which was suddenly tight. "It's...nice...to have you and Jean here for Reggie, for all of us. It's nice...being a family."

"Yes," Kate whispered, "it is."

❖

"And the next time you run out of medication," Tory said in a gently chiding tone as she opened the door of the treatment room, "call Randy and we'll phone in a refill. You need to take the blood pressure pills every day, or they're not going to work."

"All right, honey," the octogenarian called cheerfully. "I'll remember."

Smiling, Tory turned and nearly bumped into KT, who was leaning against the wall just outside the room. Her smile faltered as she pulled the door closed. "Yes?"

"It's a far cry from the ER on a Saturday night, isn't it?" KT observed.

"It's not without its occasional challenges," Tory remarked dryly, thinking of the variety of problems she saw. Patients of every description crowded her waiting room every day—young, old, male, female, representing varying ethnic and social backgrounds—and with all nature of problems, from the common cold to trauma and prenatal difficulties. "But I suppose it lacks the cachet you're used to."

"I wasn't putting it down," KT said quietly.

Tory took a deep breath. "No, you weren't. I'm sorry." She cradled the patient chart against her chest and pushed her hair away from her face with her other hand. "I'm a little thrown by this situation. I'm not used to working with anyone, and I barely had time to adjust to Dan. Now...you..."

"I guess I'll take a little more getting used to than he did."

"How's your hand?" Tory asked, noting that KT held the splinted appendage angled across her chest. From what she could see, KT's fingers were swollen.

"It's okay." Almost unconsciously, KT slid her right hand into the pocket of her navy linen trousers and counted the remaining pain pills. She'd need to wait another two hours at least. "But I have a three-year-old with a lip laceration, and I...can't handle it by myself."

"All right. I'll be right there. Just let me get the prescriptions for Mrs. Klein." Tory turned away, refusing to think about what that admission must've cost KT. "Just tell Sally to set up the suture tray."

"Already done."

Five minutes later, Tory joined KT and her clinic nurse, Sally, in the treatment room.

"Hi, Andy," Tory said to the small, young blond who cuddled a cherubic, tear-streaked towhead against her shoulder. "Patty been climbing trees again?"

"Swing set. She saw her brother do it yesterday and must have decided she could climb higher. I was hanging out the wash, and she was up the side like a monkey before I even noticed." There was a note of pride in the young mother's voice. "She only cried for a minute."

"Well then, we'll be sure not to give her any reason for more tears." Tory inclined her head until she was almost nose to nose with the child. "Hi, Patty. Are you going to let me fix your lip?"

Dark eyes observed her warily.

"I bet it was a very big swing set." Tory gestured to the treatment table. "Put her down over there, Andy."

Once the child was situated with her mother sitting on the far side of the treatment table away from the instruments, holding Patty's hand, Tory took her first careful look at the laceration. It was a little over a centimeter in length, vertically oriented, and extending through the vermillion border—the junction of the pink portion of the lip and the surrounding pale skin. That narrowed junction required precise approximation or else there would be a color mismatch at the edge of the lip, making the resulting scar very noticeable. Tory looked up at KT. "Pretty straightforward."

"Yes." *For anyone with two hands.*

"I'll take care of this if you wouldn't mind seeing the patient in four."

"Sure," KT said. She brushed her fingers over the small blond head. "See you later, kiddo."

When Tory finished fifteen minutes later, she walked down the hall and looked into the small office she had assigned KT earlier that day. KT sat at the desk, writing notes in a chart. "Got a minute?"

"Sure." KT pushed the chart aside and leaned back in the chair. "All done with the lip repair?"

"Yes. She was a trooper."

KT smiled. "Nice kid. Nice mother, too."

"Andrea's straight and happily married."

"Jesus, Vi—Tory!" KT tossed her pen down onto the desktop in frustration. "I wasn't going to ask her for a *date.*"

Tory bit back another careless response and sank into a metal folding chair opposite KT's desk. "Maybe your working here isn't such a good idea. I can't seem to be around you without being furious."

"You weren't furious in the hospital when Reese was hurt or when Reggie was born," KT snapped.

"I had other things on my mind—like the fact that my lover might be dying!" Tory looked away, the memories of Reese's accident still fresh, still painful, after half a year. "And I...appreciate all you did for us. Both times."

"Jesus." KT let out an exasperated breath. "I'm not asking for thanks. I *wanted* to help. It's what I do. And it was *you*, for Christ's sake. Don't you think I wanted to help you?"

"I don't know." Tory brought angry eyes back to KT's. "I really don't know anything about you."

"Yes, you do," KT said softly. "You know everything about me. Nothing's changed for me since the day you—since the day we separated."

"I'm sorry to hear that." There was no anger in Tory's voice now, only sadness. "Everything has changed for me." She closed her eyes, aware for the first time how tired she was. She'd only been working five hours, and she was exhausted. Her breasts were full and sore, and she realized that she needed to pump. With a sigh, she opened her eyes and smiled wanly. "We can't have this conversation here. There's work to be done, and neither of us is quite functioning at full power. Can we just agree not to discuss personal matters?"

"Sure." KT took in Tory's pale features and drawn expression. "Why don't you take off. I can handle the rest of the patients."

Tory laughed, genuinely amused. "You always did overestimate yourself, O'Bannon. You have no idea what you're in for here."

KT laughed with her. "I can be very resourceful when I need to be."

"Oh, I have no doubt." Tory stood. "I need to take a few minutes' break, but then I'll be good for another hour or so."

"Okay, but don't push. It's just your first day back."

Tory nodded. "Keep your hand elevated. Your fingers are swelling."

"Yes, Dr. King," KT replied lightly. She followed Tory into the hall and headed toward the reception area as Tory stepped into her office and closed the door. Randy looked up with his usual full-combat-mode expression as she approached, and KT held up her good hand to forestall any comments. Then she rested her elbow on the counter and leaned forward so that only he could hear. "Tory needs something to eat. Order something she likes and have it delivered, will you? Tell her you ordered it."

"Is she sick?" Randy's normally sultry voice hardened with concern.

KT shook her head. "No, just tired and too stubborn to admit it."

"Well, I'm glad to see that nothing's changed while she was away." Randy's elegant eyebrow arched as he regarded KT intently. "I'm really not prepared to like you."

"I got that impression. Is it something I said or do you just not like mainlanders?"

"It's because you must be an idiot to have let Tory go, and you hurt her besides."

"Guilty on both counts." KT's expression never changed, although her stomach abruptly tied itself into a knot. "Does everyone know?"

"No, only those people who love her."

"Will you please get her lunch?"

"Of course." Randy hesitated, then added, "What would you like? Sandwich or salad?"

"Roast beef, Russian dressing, black bread. Thanks."

"You're welcome." Randy picked up the phone to order and, as he did, said over his shoulder, "You should keep your arm elevated. Your fingers are swollen."

"Thanks," KT muttered as she headed back to work, wondering just what it was going to take to atone.

❖

"Do you really think Ms. Pelosi is going to let us talk to him this time?" Bri asked as Reese pulled into the emergency room parking lot at the rear of Hyannis Hospital for the third time in three days.

"She said he was ready to give us a statement."

"What do you think that means?"

Reese settled her cap over her brows as she climbed out of cruiser. Walking around to join Bri, she said, "I think it means she's pretty certain that Robert Bridger is innocent of any serious crime, and I think she probably wants to aid the investigation. She strikes me as a good attorney doing what good attorneys do, which is protect her client." She shouldered through the swinging door into the long, brightly lit corridor that ran from the emergency entrance toward the main hospital lobby. "It's just that good lawyers can sometimes be a pain in the behind for us."

"Were you a good attorney?"

Reese cast Bri a sidelong glance, then grinned. "I suppose I was. But the JAG Corps was too much talk and not enough action. Everyone was surprised when I switched to policing, but it suited me better. Still does."

Bri grinned, too. "Yeah. Nothing beats being out in the cruiser."

"Well," Reese said, "not *much* else does." She was about to add more when Trey Pelosi came around the corner, a cup of vending-room coffee in her right hand and a file folder in the other. Today, the attorney wore navy blue linen slacks, low-heeled, backless sandals, and a silk blouse with fine white and blue stripes.

"Hello," Trey said in greeting. "You made good time."

"Everyone is going in the opposite direction," Reese replied. "Thanks for calling us."

"I'm happy to. Robert is feeling much better and would like to speak with you."

"Really." Reese fell into step on one side of Trey while Bri walked on the other. "That's good news."

Trey effortlessly juggled the file folder and the coffee cup and extracted a single sheet of a computer printout. "You'll want to take a look at this."

Still walking, Reese quickly scanned what turned out to be the toxicology report, then wordlessly handed it to Bri. "Thank you."

"I just got it this morning." Trey slowed just before reaching the elevators. She glanced from Reese to Bri and back to Reese. "Robert is basically a very good kid. He's scared, and he's penitent, and he's willing to provide you with as much information as he can."

Reese appreciated that the attorney had lowered her sword for a moment of truth, and in appreciation of that fact, Reese lowered hers as well. "I'm not interested in going after him unless I don't have any other choice. I want the people behind this. I doubt that Robert and his companion are the first kids to run into trouble because of these parties, and I know they won't be the last. I want to shut them down."

"Then you and I are in complete agreement, Sheriff."

Reese smiled and Trey Pelosi's eyes warmed in response. "I'd rather you not advertise that, Counselor. It would be bad for my reputation."

"I imagine that your reputation would survive, Sheriff."

Reese pretended not to notice the brief brush of Trey Pelosi's fingers over the top of her hand as the three of them stepped into the elevator.

Chapter Fourteen

Tory ignored the sound of approaching footsteps until the familiar voice said, "Hey—okay to interrupt?" When she looked up from her paperwork, Reese stood framed in her office doorway. Surprised, she said, "Hello, darling. Of course. Come in."

"Busy?" Reese asked as she crossed the room and skirted around the side of Tory's desk.

"No."

Reese chuckled. "Liar. It's almost six and the waiting room is still crowded."

"News travels fast in our little world. I think half of them are here to check out the new doctor."

"I'll bet." Reese leaned down and kissed Tory softly on the lips. "How are you doing?"

"I'm fi..." Tory hesitated, because she knew that Reese would know. She always knew. "Actually, I'm tired." At her lover's immediate expression of concern, she added hastily, "But I'm all right. Really."

"Sure?" Reese ran her fingertip along the edge of Tory's jaw and kissed her again.

"Now," Tory sighed, leaned back, and closed her eyes, "I'm *definitely* fine."

Reese settled on the edge of Tory's desk. "Are you going to be able to leave soon?"

"Not too much longer," Tory replied as she slowly opened her eyes. "How about you? Are things hectic?"

"The village is jumping, like you'd expect." Reese shrugged. "And it's early yet. Bri and I just got back from Hyannis. We interviewed Robert Bridger finally."

Tory leaned forward, suddenly much more alert. "Really. What did he have to say?"

"He confirmed some of the things that we suspected. He *borrowed* his family's car to impress his friends and drove to a party in Wellfleet. He claims he had never seen the girl—she told him her name was Tina—before he met her there that night. No last name that he can remember."

"Do you believe him?"

"I do. Just gut instinct, but his story held up when I pressed for details. Usually if they're lying, they'll trip up over the small details right away. He didn't."

"How did he account for the drug overdose?"

Reese grimaced. "He swears that he only had one can of Budweiser. Somewhere in the course of the evening, his buddies disappeared. And someone slipped him a heavy dose of ecstasy. His tox screen confirms that he had a very small level of alcohol in his system and a great big dose of MDMA."

"So where does that leave you?"

"Well, we've got a first name for the victim, and we've got a general location for the party. Robert vaguely remembers hearing that the parties are a regular occurrence in the area, so we're going to do some discreet questioning in the bars and among some of our known area drug users. Chances are they'll at least have heard of these parties."

"You're going after the dealers, then?" Tory's voice was even, but her eyes were fathomless pools, swirling with dark undercurrents.

"No choice." Reese's tone was matter-of-fact, because the course of action was obvious. "They're responsible for that girl's death."

"You'll be careful, won't you?"

"I always am." Reese leaned forward and brushed her fingers through Tory's hair, letting her palm rest against the nape of her neck. "I've got two very good reasons to be *very* careful."

Tory leaned into the caress and wrapped her fingers around Reese's strong forearm. She turned her face, rubbed her lips over Reese's wrist, and murmured, "I love you so—"

"Hey, Tory, what's the deal with this new cholesterol—"

KT stumbled to a stop just inside the door. Her eyes moved from Tory—who leaned forward with half-closed lids and her parted lips against Reese's skin—to the woman who gazed down at her with undisguised adoration. The image was cuttingly beautiful, and KT felt a slash of pain as exquisitely sharp as the knife blade that had brought her there. "Oh. Sorry."

Slowly, Reese swiveled on the desk toward KT, giving Tory's hand a squeeze as she shifted away from her. "Hi."

"Hi."

"How's the first day going?"

"Actually," KT replied, smiling grimly, "I'm getting my ass kicked. Between the little old ladies who won't take their medication and the screaming kids who won't sit still long enough for me to listen to their hearts, I'm beat."

Reese laughed. "Tough crowd, huh?"

"Give me a multiple trauma any day." KT looked apologetically at Tory. "I just had a quick question about a patient's medication. I'm in exam room three when you get a chance."

"I'll be right there."

"Thanks." KT nodded to Reese. "Take it easy."

"You too."

When KT left, Reese stood and tucked her cap under her arm. "I should get back to work." She inclined her head toward the now-empty doorway. "Everything okay there?"

Tory stood and slipped an arm around Reese's waist, walking with her toward the hall. "A few minor bumps, but basically okay."

"Good." Reese kissed her one final time. "Don't stay too late, okay?"

"I won't. I promise." Tory stroked Reese's cheek. "Regina and I will see you at home, Sheriff. Be safe."

Tory rested a shoulder against the doorjamb and watched until Reese disappeared through the far door. When she finally turned away, she found KT contemplating her with an expression she had never seen on the surgeon's face before. It was a mixture of tenderness and sadness. Silently, she walked to join her. "Ready for that consult?"

❖

Pia paced, an extremely unusual activity for her. Ordinarily, she was calm, centered, and generally in control—not in a rigid, inflexible fashion, but merely in a studied, organized way. Her life was like her work—ordered and with a definite direction, but with no particular timetable attached. Consequently, she was able to adjust to small changes with alacrity. But now, she found herself unaccountably agitated. Actually, there was nothing *unaccountable* about her present mood. She knew exactly to what she should attribute the uneasiness and sense of foreboding. She had done something impetuous, something that probably skirted the edges of unprofessional at the very least. Although she wasn't a physician, she was a healthcare worker, and KT O'Bannon was her client. There wasn't the usual sort of power dynamic at work that made relationships between physicians or therapists and patients improper, but still, the surgeon had come to her in a professional capacity, and here she was—

What? What exactly am I doing?

Pia halted at her front door and looked out the window toward the street. At just before 7 p.m., there was still plenty of light, but the sun was low on the horizon, and the sky was tinged with the purples and pinks that preceded the midnight blues of impending darkness. Between the closely crowded houses on the opposite side of the street, she caught glimpses of the harbor and the white swatches of sails tilting in the wind.

She was about to go out to dinner with a woman—a client—she had just met and show her an apartment in the same complex where she lived. In the complex that her mother owned.

How many more ways can I impinge upon boundaries, I wonder?

As she contemplated informing KT that she would be happy to show her the apartment, but that she couldn't accompany her to dinner, the woman in question turned in the driveway and started down the flagstone path toward the house. Tonight, KT wore black jeans with a wide black belt, black boots, and a white shirt with the cuffs turned back twice. She looked like a knife blade turned edge on, glittering and sharp and enticingly dangerous. Unmindful of the danger, Pia opened the door.

❖

As KT walked the mile from her temporary quarters on Bradford to Pia's, she thought about her day, remembering the look on Tory's face as she'd kissed Reese. Try as she might, KT couldn't ever remember Tory looking at *her* in quite that way. They'd had passion and they'd shared dreams and they'd celebrated victories, but she didn't believe they'd ever had that depth of simple communion. So simple as to be profound. She wondered for the first time whose fault that had been. Hers, probably. She'd always had another goal to meet, another obstacle to overcome, another rung on the ladder to climb. There'd always been part of her that was somewhere else, so that she was never completely there with Tory. Never completely there *for* her.

Why didn't I ever know that?

The faint scrape of wood on wood brought KT out of her reverie. Pia stepped out onto the porch, and KT slowed to take her in. She wore a blue-and-white striped boatneck tee, white capri slacks, and sandals. Her bare arms and legs were a rich brown against the white, and her dark hair fell in loose velvet waves around her face. She was stunning in the earthy, sensual way of some women, and KT felt a welcome stirring of desire. Lust always chased the blues away.

"Hello," KT called as Pia came down the steps. "You look great."

"Thank you," Pia said easily, revealing none of her recent misgivings as she fell into step beside KT. "How was your day?"

KT laughed. "Humbling."

Pia smiled, liking the low, rich timbre of her voice. "Oh? How is that?"

"I discovered how much basic medicine I've forgotten in the last fourteen years. They say that you know as much medicine as you ever will on the day that you graduate from medical school, and that from that point on you know less and less. I never believed that until today."

"You're a surgeon. You're not supposed to know general medicine."

"Yes, well," KT said quietly, "for the time being, I'm a general practitioner. Maybe that's all I'll ever be again."

"Is that what you think?" Pia asked in surprise. "That we're not going to get your hand back?"

KT met Pia's eyes, finding the deep brown ones totally serious and startlingly intent. "Isn't that something I need to be prepared for?"

"Possibly. But certainly not now. We haven't even started." In a completely spontaneous gesture, Pia reached out and squeezed KT's right hand. "If there comes a time when I think we're not going to get you back into the OR, I'll tell you. Until then, I want you—*need* you—to believe that's *exactly* where you're going to be when we finish."

"You really believe that makes a difference? The mind-over-matter thing?" KT's voice was free of sarcasm. Pia's conviction was too genuine to castigate. And in addition to not wanting to criticize her beliefs, the warmth of Pia's fingers curled around KT's was too peaceful to risk losing.

"You must have seen it yourself," Pia replied quietly. "The ones who should have died but didn't because their will to survive was so strong, and the ones who gave up and slipped away even when there was no medical reason for it. What I know is that you and I have to share in the belief that we're going to bring you back. *All* the way back."

Bring me back. Back from where? To *where?* For the first time in her nearly forty years of living, KT didn't know where she was going, or more disconcertingly, where she wanted to go. She sighed. "I'm going to do something completely out of character."

Pia slowed and stepped away enough to turn and face KT on the sidewalk. Their hands were still joined. "What?"

KT smiled faintly and swung Pia's hand between them in a gentle arc as she allowed herself to relax in the warmth of Pia's dark eyes. "I'm going to let you be in charge."

Rather than laughing, Pia nodded solemnly, intuiting—without truly understanding why—that this was a momentous statement. "Thank you."

Suddenly self-conscious, yet another extraordinarily rare emotion, KT shrugged as if her heart had not just done a tiny cartwheel. "So. What about that dinner you promised?"

"Since I'm in charge," Pia answered as she gently withdrew her hand from KT's, "why don't you just follow me."

"All right." As she fell into step once more, KT found the feeling of *not* being in charge surprisingly pleasant.

❖

The restaurant turned out to be a tiny place tucked away in an unassuming building that was little more than a shack on the far end of MacMillan Wharf. There were eight tables, each of which had a stunning harbor view, and waitstaff who were friendly but unobtrusive. Pia was obviously a regular, and she and KT were immediately shown to a corner table that commanded the best vantage point from which to appreciate the spectacular sunset.

"I'll bet this place is a well-kept secret," KT commented as they were seated.

"It's one of those places the townspeople don't talk about. We don't want it to be taken over by the tourists." Pia smiled up at the small blond in black T-shirt and jeans who handed them menus. "Hi, Lor."

To KT's astonishment, the young woman leaned over and brushed a quick kiss over Pia's lips. "Hi, baby. We got the Dão Quinta Cabriz in today. Wanna try a bottle?"

"Red wine okay?" Pia asked of KT, who nodded in agreement. "Sure. That would be great."

"Girlfriend?" KT inquired as the cute waitress hurried off. She tried not to sound overly interested, but she'd found the casual kiss disconcerting.

"No," Pia answered evenly. "Cousin. This is my uncle's place."

"Ah. Convenient."

"Definitely." Pia leaned back in her chair. "This *is* Provincetown, but not everyone here is gay, you know."

"Including you?"

Pia smiled and shook her head. "No, not including me."

"Is there a girlfriend somewhere, then?"

"No."

"Hard to believe."

Lori returned at that moment with two glasses and an open bottle of red wine. Pia was grateful for the interruption, because she'd found the mild flirtation enjoyable and it hadn't been her intention to do that with KT O'Bannon. Her intention had been to keep everything between them on a friendly but professional level. For some reason, KT made her forget her best intentions with unnerving regularity. She fell silent as Lori poured a half inch of wine. She lifted the glass and breathed the bouquet before taking all of it into her mouth. Partially closing her eyes, she rolled the richly nuanced wine over her tongue, losing herself in the smooth taste and aromatic scent.

KT watched the wine tasting attentively. It was a ritual she had observed dozens of times, but watching Pia was an experience in itself. KT sensed her pleasure in the sensuality of the process—she could see it in the faint flush of Pia's skin, in the curve of her lips and the slightly unfocused look in her eyes. Watching her respond to the pleasures of the wine, KT couldn't help but imagine how Pia would respond to her touch. And she realized that she really didn't know, but that she wanted to—very much.

"That's perfect," Pia said to Lori, who nodded and moved away. As she set down her glass, Pia smiled across the table at KT. Her smile faltered when she saw the expression in KT's eyes. There was hunger there like none she had ever seen before. She wasn't a stranger to being desired, but the look in KT's eyes went far beyond desire. Her dark eyes were ravenous and so fiercely focused that Pia felt the heat on her skin. Softly, she murmured, "Stop."

"Stop what?" KT asked, her voice barely a whisper. The air between them danced with suggestion.

"You can't look at me like that in here. My uncle is likely to come out of the kitchen and thrash you."

The corner of KT's mouth lifted, and a second later, she laughed. "How big is he?"

"A lot bigger than you are."

"What about later? Can I look at you this way then?"

Forcing her gaze away from KT's painfully handsome face, Pia picked up the menu, which she knew by heart. "Everything on here's great, but I'd recommend one of the seafood-and-pasta dishes."

KT was unused to women putting her off. Moreover, she never gave in when there was someone she wanted, even if just for an evening. She did the playing, and she didn't like to be played. She knew—not cognizant of how but believing it completely—that Pia was not a woman who played or allowed herself to *be* played. Rather than being annoyed, KT was intrigued.

"You order for me." KT settled back in her chair, barely recognizing herself. "You're in charge, remember?"

Pia only smiled and gave their order.

They lingered over dinner, enjoying the exquisite food and the breathtaking sunset.

"It doesn't matter how many times I see it," Pia said, swirling port in a heavy glass as she watched night eclipse day over the water. "It's always so beautiful."

"Yes."

The contemplative tone in KT's voice drew Pia's gaze from the harbor back to the woman seated across from her. She had enjoyed talking with KT over the meal, finding her sharp, quick intellect challenging and her dry humor pleasant. And she couldn't deny that she'd enjoyed the undercurrent of sexual innuendo that charged their conversation. She wanted to tell herself it was harmless, and of course, it was, as long as she allowed it to go no further. But still, she couldn't remember the last time she had been so swayed by a woman's charms. The heat was back in KT's eyes, and Pia liked knowing she was the cause. "I like to walk through town after dinner. Would you mind?"

KT shook her head. "Not if it means spending more time with you."

"There's only one stipulation."

"What would that be?" KT asked as she slid her wallet from her back pocket. She managed to extract her credit card one-handed without undue difficultly. *Getting better at that.* Despite Pia's protests, she passed the card to Lori before Pia could grab the check.

"You don't have to do that," Pia said quietly.

"I know. But I want to, so please let me."

"Then I'll buy next time."

"Good enough." KT slid her right hand across the white cotton tablecloth and covered Pia's hand with hers. "What's the stipulation?"

Pia slowly slid her hand from beneath KT's and dropped it into her lap. "That you stop flirting with me."

KT's brows rose. "Why?"

"Because we have important work to do together, and I need to be able to concentrate on it. And so do you."

"We're not working now."

"No, but it's best that we keep things simple."

"Simple."

Pia nodded. "Yes."

KT grinned. "All right. I can do simple."

"Good," Pia replied as she stood, wondering why getting the response she wanted didn't feel very satisfying. Nevertheless, she said nothing more as she led the way from the restaurant and started toward the east end of the village with KT walking quietly by her side.

They spent two hours walking the length of Commercial Street, window shopping, people watching, and talking easily about the unique village's history and charms. It was nearly eleven when they turned into the path to Pia's cottage.

"The apartment is the top floor rear of the main house," Pia explained, pulling the keys from her pocket.

"Have you seen it?"

"Yes." Pia stopped just opposite the rear entrance to the house. "I'm very familiar with it. My mother owns the building."

They stood in a pool of moonlight that afforded them just enough illumination to see one another. KT laughed.

"Just how much of this town does your family own?"

Pia smiled. "On the Portuguese side of my family, quite a lot of it. Remember, we all stem from a few settlers, and most of us are related in some fashion."

"I'll take the place."

"Don't you want to see it?"

"Not at the moment," KT said quietly, stepping closer and slipping her arm around Pia's waist. She leaned forward, lowering her mouth toward Pia's.

Pia extended her arm, placing her palm flat against the center of KT's chest. "Stop." Her voice was tender and soft, as was her touch.

KT immediately grew still, relaxing her hold on Pia's waist but keeping her hand lightly on Pia's hip. "Earlier you told me not to look at you as if I wanted you. I tried very hard all evening, but it was a struggle. Now, no kisses either?"

"I'm sorry. It's just not a good idea."

"It's a *great* idea." KT stepped back a pace, no longer touching Pia. "If you tell me where to go, I'll sign the lease on Tuesday."

Pia gave her the address and held out the keys. "You can take these to check out the apartment at your leisure."

"You trust me with them?" KT took the keys and pocketed them.

"I trust you with anything, Dr. O'Bannon." Pia held out her hand. "Good night, and thank you for dinner."

KT took the offered hand and held it. Pia's skin was soft, her fingers as strong and gentle as KT remembered. She wanted to touch so much more of her and yet found this small connection supremely satisfying. Without thinking, she turned Pia's hand and lifted it to her mouth. She brushed her lips over Pia's knuckles. "I had a wonderful time. Good night, Ms. Torres."

Then, as Pia watched, KT turned and was instantly swallowed by the night.

Chapter Fifteen

Mid-September

Reese walked into the station house just in time to hear Nelson Parker say, "No way," in a tone that suggested no further discussion was welcome. She slowed just inside the door to reconnoiter. Bri and Allie, both in uniform, flanked Nelson at his desk. Both the look on Nelson's face and the fact that he was ripping the wrapper from a fresh roll of Tums indicated that whatever the two rookies had just said to him did not sit well.

"Afternoon." Reese edged through the dividing gate and crossed over to her desk across the narrow aisle from Nelson's. "Something up?"

Nelson grunted. Allie turned, her eyes glittering with barely contained enthusiasm, and said, "Bri and I had an idea about getting a handle on the dealers who are using the circuit parties to recruit new marks."

"No," Nelson growled again.

Reese's expression was noncommittal. "In two weeks, we haven't been able to get any kind of lead other than the fact that a few kids in town have heard rumors. The couple of local dealers we rousted either really didn't know anything about it or were getting paid off to keep silent."

"What *we* thought," Allie continued, apparently either oblivious or inured to her chief's obvious displeasure, "was that we could try picking up on these parties ourselves. Maybe by hanging out in some of the bars in Wellfleet or farther up the Cape, where no one knows us. You know, get invited."

"Undercover, you mean." Reese said the word evenly, as if it didn't represent one of the most dangerous assignments that a law enforcement officer could undertake. There was nothing harder than being on the front line with little backup in an unknown situation that could go from bad to worse in milliseconds. With inexperienced rookies like these two, it was a recipe for disaster.

Bri joined in. "We know that the people behind the parties have to have a way of getting the word out about where and when, or else no one would be able to find them. According to Robert Bridger's buddies, they heard about it in a bar. So," she went on, carefully not looking at her father, "Allie and I figured—"

"You figured *wrong.*" Nelson pushed back from his desk, stood, and paced the crowded space to the single window that looked out onto the blacktopped parking lot. It was late on Saturday afternoon, and Gladys had already left for the day. The four of them were alone in the station. "The case is going nowhere."

Unfortunately, that was the truth. Robert Bridger had been released from the hospital, and thus far, no charges had been brought against him. Tina, if that was even the dead girl's name, remained unidentified. It was not unusual for hundreds of young people from the United States and abroad to flock to Cape Cod in the summer to work and party. If she was in the country on a student visa or simply hadn't told anyone of her summer plans, she could remain unidentified for months, if not indefinitely. It rankled Reese to know that those responsible for a young girl's death and for turning on dozens of others to body- and soul-destroying drugs were operating unchecked within her province, but for the time being she was resolved to keeping an eye and ear out for potential leads while trying to be patient. She had briefly considered, and then discarded, the possibility of putting one or both of her young officers directly on the trail of the candy-bowl parties. She'd decided against it, even though the idea had distinct possibilities.

"There are plenty of people in the armed forces a lot younger than us who do things a lot more dangerous," Allie pointed out doggedly.

Nelson spun around, his eyes uncharacteristically hard. "You're not in the goddamn Army." He shot a look at Reese. "Or the Marines." Then he stomped out the front door.

"Oops," Allie said quietly.

"Your eagerness is commendable, Officer Tremont," Reese

said quietly. "However, arguing with one's commanding officer is generally not recommended."

"It's a good idea," Allie said stubbornly.

Reese nodded. "In some ways, yes. The problem is that it's very difficult to monitor you in a bar, and almost impossible at a party. We are not set up for that kind of surveillance here."

"But," Bri pointed out reasonably, "there isn't any real danger. It's a drug party. If we're careful about what we drink and make sure no one slips us anything, there's not really much chance that anything could happen."

Reese suppressed a smile. She was proud of both of them for their initiative and their drive, and it was never a good idea to discourage that kind of enthusiasm in a young officer. She thought of the many recruits she'd trained over the years and how she had had to think of them only as marines—not as eighteen- or nineteen- or twenty-year-old men and women who had barely begun their lives. They were marines. They would do what needed to be done, as would she. She wasn't entirely certain why she couldn't think of Bri and Allie in quite the same way. That, she realized, bore further consideration.

"Let me give it some thought. And the next time you two have a suggestion about an operation, follow the chain of command and come to me first."

Both Bri and Allie straightened perceptibly at the rebuke, although they couldn't hide their grins. "Yes, ma'am," they said in unison.

❖

"I was thinking I could go to the wristlet and get rid of this splint," KT said as she settled at the table in Pia's treatment room. She'd just gotten off shift at the clinic and it was nearly 7 p.m., almost exactly two weeks to the minute from the night they'd had dinner. In those two weeks, her life had settled into a routine that was surprisingly comfortable. She'd instructed her housekeeper in Boston to pack up a few essential clothes, books, and her stereo system and ship the entire lot by truck to Provincetown. Those personal articles were enough to make the small apartment she had rented from Pia's mother comfortable. She was working twelve-hour shifts at the East End Health Clinic, despite Tory telling her eight hours was adequate. She'd quickly realized that if *she* didn't work twelve hours, Tory would. And Tory obviously wasn't ready for it. She was too thin, too pale, and the circles under her eyes were getting deeper rather than fading.

"You're not ready to go to the light immobilizer yet," Pia said quietly, releasing the Velcro straps that held the Orthoplast splint in place. They'd met almost every day for the last thirteen days for an hour of treatment. KT had been prompt and eager. She'd also been perfectly decorous in her comportment, with no repeat of the attempt at a kiss. Pia was relieved about that—at least, that's what she told herself. She turned KT's hand palm up and began to massage the scar with both thumbs. She stopped when she saw KT wince. "What?"

KT unclenched her jaw. "Paresthesias. Ring finger. Man, it burns like fire."

"Here?" Pia tapped very lightly on the scar.

"No. A little more distal, toward the metacarpal-phalangeal joint."

Pia tapped slightly closer to the base of KT's finger, watching KT's face carefully.

KT jumped slightly and nodded. "Yep. That's the spot. Damn." She wanted to take another pain pill, but she'd taken one just prior to the session. Unfortunately, the pain was almost constant in her fingers, and the pills didn't seem to be doing as much good any longer. Even if she doubled up on them, it only dulled the shooting pains, pins and needles, and intermittent burning sensation that accompanied the nerve regeneration in her injured digits. At least she was able to work if she medicated herself enough to ignore most of the discomfort.

"From the location of the trigger points," Pia noted, "it looks like the nerve repair is on schedule. Anticipating a millimeter of regrowth a day, that's about where the healing nerves should be at this point."

"How much longer can I expect the pain?"

Pia saw the faint mist of perspiration on KT's forehead, and her stomach tightened in sympathy. She was accustomed to her work sometimes causing her clients discomfort, because effective physical rehabilitation was often impossible to achieve without forcing stiff joints to move and tight tendons to stretch. The sight of KT's obvious pain affected her more than she was used to. She caught herself just as she was about to reach out and stroke KT's cheek. *What am I doing?*

"It varies," Pia said softly. "If it doesn't let up soon, you might want to ask your hand surgeon about prescribing Tegretol. It sometimes quiets the nerve irritability enough for it to be tolerable."

"Thanks. I will." KT watched as Pia gently manipulated her finger and wrist joints through a complete range of motion. She looked forward to the hour that she spent with Pia almost every day. Not just because their time together was essential for her recovery, but because as Pia worked on her hand, they chatted about current events or local gossip or sometimes unusual cases they had seen and treated. KT brought Pia up to date on the changes at Boston Hospital in personnel and protocol. When she'd asked Pia why she had left the busy big-city hospital for the quiet life of her hometown, Pia had merely smiled and said that the pace suited her better and she liked the independence of her private practice. KT thought there was something more that Pia wasn't saying, but she hadn't pushed. And although it went contrary to her nature, she found that being with Pia was teaching her to tolerate, if not almost enjoy, waiting. At the moment, however, the throbbing pain that hadn't diminished was making patience difficult.

"I think if I don't have to wear the heavier splint," KT insisted, "it will take some of the stress off my hand."

Pia shook her head, but before she could speak, KT went on.

"Look, I know you're being conservative, but—"

"It's not about being conservative," Pia said quietly, raising her head and meeting KT's eyes. "It's about making sure that you don't inadvertently stress the tendons and rupture them. Six to eight weeks after the repair is the critical period for delayed rupture, and you're right in the middle of that time. You're seeing patients every day, and if one of them slips and you reach out to catch them and rupture those tendon repairs, we could be right back to square one."

"I'll be careful."

"I know that you'll *try* to be, but—"

"How about this," KT interrupted. "I'll wear the Orthoplast splint at work and the wristlet the rest of the time."

"This isn't *Let's Make a Deal.*" As they talked, Pia continued to hold KT's hand, unconsciously rubbing her thumb up and down the inside of KT's forearm, caressing her softly even as she argued. When KT rested her right hand on Pia's, Pia reflexively intertwined her fingers with KT's.

"I'll be good," KT whispered.

Pia looked down at their joined hands, aware that her heart was thudding painfully in her chest. KT's fingers were supple and strong. And warm. Very warm as she slowly slid her fingers in and out between Pia's. "You have beautiful hands."

"Have dinner with me tonight."

"We have a half hour left of the session."

KT lifted their joined hands and rubbed the back of Pia's against her cheek. "After that."

"I'd need to shower and change." Pia was helpless to stop the words as she felt herself surrendering to the intensity in KT's dark eyes. She sensed the danger but had no desire to flee.

"So do I."

"I want to do some ultrasound on the scar."

KT nodded, resisting the urge, but just barely, to brush her lips over Pia's knuckles as she had that night two weeks before. She could smell the citrus scent on Pia's skin, and she hungered for the taste of her. "All right."

"You have to let go of my hand."

"No."

Pia laughed shakily, and a second later, so did KT. Finally, Pia was able to break the spell of KT's mesmerizing gaze and leaned back, gently withdrawing her fingers from KT's grasp. "Doctors make the most difficult patients."

"Oh?" KT's brows rose. "Have you had many doctors ask you out for dinner?"

Pia blushed. "I wasn't talking about that." She reached over for the small ultrasound probe, dabbed a bit of the gel on KT's palm, and began to work the oscillating probe back and forth over the scar to aid in softening the healing ridge of tissue. She kept her head down as she worked and could not see KT's appraising glance.

"I bet you had a lot of offers, though," KT said playfully.

"Not the kind I wanted," Pia replied before she could censor her comment.

KT heard the undercurrent of what sounded like sadness in her voice. "Is that why you're here? To leave the memory of someone behind?"

"Not everyone comes home to escape something painful," Pia answered quietly.

"What about you?" KT persisted.

Pia sighed and set the probe down. "No. No one hurt me. I'm not running from a disastrous love affair. This is where I'm happiest. Simple story."

KT studied her seriously. "Why hasn't anyone claimed your heart?"

"Because no one has ever asked for it."

"How can that be?" KT was genuinely confused. "You're beautiful, you're sexy, you're smart."

Pia laughed. "It's not about those things."

"Then what?"

Pia reached for the splint and gently placed KT's hand into the curved plastic mold. She reattached the elastics to the small hooks glued to each of KT's fingernails, drawing the fingers down into a protected position. Then she carefully closed the Velcro straps. When she was done, she met KT's eyes. "It's about forever."

"Forever." KT turned the word over in her mind, wondering where along the way she had stopped believing in it. It might have been when she'd lost Tory, but when she recalled her life in the years just before that final irreparable event, she realized that she had lost sight of what she had with Tory in the shadow of her unrelenting drive, her overpowering need, to excel. Almost before she knew it, it was all gone. "Is that what you're holding out for? Forever?"

Pia nodded. She'd seen the shadow pass over KT's face and wondered what painful memory the word had evoked. "Still interested in dinner?"

"Absolutely." Even as she said it, KT wondered if she had anything more than a casual evening to offer, knowing with certainty that that would never be enough for this woman. Still, even knowing that Pia wanted something she'd once had, then squandered, and finally forgotten, KT couldn't bring herself to walk away.

❖

Reese pushed through the back door with two bags of Chinese takeout in her arms. Tory looked over from the sofa where she'd been half asleep watching the evening news.

"Tell me that I smell dinner," Tory said with a note of reverence in her voice.

"Kung Pao chicken, Moo Shu shrimp, and wonton soup, at your service, madame." Reese set the bags down on the breakfast counter. "And enough for leftovers, including breakfast, if you should so desire."

Tory grasped Reese around the waist and turned her so her back was to the breakfast counter before pressing full-length against her. As she wrapped both arms around Reese's neck, she murmured, "I adore you."

Reese had no chance to reply before Tory's mouth covered hers. Surprised, she closed her eyes and enjoyed the welcome heat of Tory in her arms. After twenty seconds, she forgot that she was hungry. After thirty, she forgot that she had to be back on patrol in half an hour. She slid her hand beneath the loose T-shirt that Tory wore and caressed her palm up the center of Tory's back until her fingers rested against the nape of Tory's neck. With the other hand, she cupped Tory's rear, pulled her closer, and rocked her hips into her lover. "Mmm. You feel so good."

"Reese," Tory murmured, moving her mouth away an inch. "You don't really want to do that."

"Yes, I do," Reese answered, her voice thick and deep.

"Well...I can always eat later," Tory whispered, pulling Reese's shirt from her trousers.

"Baby asleep?" Reese asked breathlessly as she hurriedly unbuttoned her pants and jerked down the fly.

"Uh-huh." Tory stripped off her T-shirt and dropped it on the floor. She wore nothing beneath.

As Reese reached for Tory's breasts and Tory slid a hand down the front of Reese's abdomen and under the waistband of her briefs, the phone rang. They froze, listening to the mechanical voice announce the caller ID. It was a Boston prefix.

"Who?" Reese gasped.

"Don't know," Tory replied desperately. "Hospital, maybe."

"Better answer."

"Yes." Tory snatched up the phone in frustration and snapped, "Dr. King."

She stiffened and, after a second, held out the phone to Reese. "Your father."

Reese encircled Tory's waist with one arm as she reached for the receiver with the other. Holding Tory near, she said crisply, "Hello, sir."

Chapter Sixteen

"Tory?" KT narrowed her eyes and studied Tory contemplatively. "Is something wrong?"

"No," Tory said quickly, running her hand through her hair distractedly. She glanced at the clock opposite her desk and then back to KT. Seven p.m. "I'm sorry. You were saying that Mr. Abbot is complaining of increasing intermittent claudication?"

"Yes. According to him, there's been a big change in the last six months." KT glanced down at the chart in her hand. "By history, he used to be able to walk..." She couldn't suppress a grin as she read from her notes. "From the Lobster Pot to the Coast Guard station at a pretty steady clip, but now he has to stop in front of the town hall and 'rest a spell' because his right leg cramps so bad." She looked up from the file in time to see Tory glance at the clock again. KT closed the folder, tucked it under her arm, and settled her hip on the edge of Tory's desk. "What's going on?"

"Sorry," Tory muttered. She leaned back in her chair and sighed. "It's nothing. It's silly. It's just that...it's nothing." She was getting used to seeing KT every day, at least to the extent that her heart didn't give a painful lurch whenever she looked up and saw her former lover's face. After the first few days, she'd come to realize that her reaction wasn't one of anger or even pain, but of pure and simple *surprise*. She had effectively, or nearly effectively, erased KT from her consciousness. Suddenly seeing KT daily, having her so much a part of her life again so abruptly, reminded her forcefully of all the things she had once liked about her. Despite her growing comfort with KT's presence, however, she hadn't quite gotten to the point where she was able to confide in her. Their conversations had been strictly limited to patient care.

"Come on, Vic," KT prodded with a grin. "Oops. Sorry. *Tory.*"

Tory waved a hand at the offered apology. "Reese went to Boston today to meet her father. That's all. I just thought she might be home by now."

KT recognized the undercurrent of worry in Tory's voice. Despite their years of separation, she hadn't forgotten how to read Tory's moods. "Some kind of problem there?"

"You could say that," Tory said with a grim chuckle. Forgetting that she hadn't intended to talk to KT about anything personal, she went on, "Reese's father is a Marine Corps general. Very by the book. He raised *her* to be a Marine Corps officer as well. Until four years ago, she was everything he ever expected her to be. Then she left active duty, came here, and came out."

"I guess *Daddy* isn't entirely pleased."

"That would be an understatement." Tory rose and walked around to the front of the desk until she stood by KT's side. She rested her hips against the front edge of the desk and folded her arms beneath her breasts in an unconsciously self-protective posture. "He actually threatened to have her court-martialed at one point if she didn't stop seeing me."

"Jesus. Her own father?"

Tory nodded. "I have a feeling he expected that threatening her career would bring her into line." She smiled. "He doesn't really know her very well."

"She wouldn't choose her career over you, I take it." KT spoke softly, watching Tory carefully.

"No, never. There's nothing more important to Reese than Regina and me."

The absolute certainty with which Tory spoke astonished KT. Astonished and humbled her. She knew with the sudden clarity that accompanies an epiphany that she had never been able to give Tory that unshakable security. Even had she not destroyed Tory's trust, eventually she would've been faced with the choice of sacrificing her career for her relationship. She doubted that she would've been able to change her course then, even had she wanted to. She believed in her heart that she would've *wanted* to keep Tory, but she also knew she would not have been able to forgo her goals in order to do it. She understood now, too, what lay beneath the look that had passed between Tory and Reese the day she'd seen them embracing in the office. Their devotion was mutual, their commitment unshakable. Observed from a distance, beyond the reach of her own personal pain, it was a wonder to behold. She cleared her throat and reached down deep beyond her own sense of loss for the love she had always had for Tory and always would. "I'm glad for you, Tory—for what you have with Reese. You deserve that kind of love."

Surprised at the quiet sincerity in KT's voice, Tory turned until they faced one another, only inches apart. Closer in many ways than they had been in years. "Thank you."

"So what do you think he wants?"

Tory shook her head. "I don't know. He called last night, said that he was in town for thirty-six hours, and ordered her to present herself for a meeting."

"She doesn't strike me as the type who can be ordered around very easily."

"Well, he's her father, he's a general, and she's a marine through and through." Tory blew out a breath. "And in all fairness, she loves him. Despite his blindness about her being gay, according to her, he did a good job of raising her. And I have to believe her about that, because she's—well, she's wonderful."

KT grinned. "Jesus. You're really pretty hopeless about her, aren't you?"

Surprising herself, Tory laughed. "Apparently so." She reached for the file that KT still held. "Mr. Abbot? From what you say," she remarked as she leafed through the lab reports, "it sounds as if his peripheral vascular disease is escalating. I've tried to get him to stop smoking that pipe, but he just 'there theres' me, pats my head, and ignores my advice."

"Well, I guess since he's ninety-two, he figures the smoking isn't going to hurt him too much."

"He's probably got a point, but it certainly isn't helping his circulation either."

"He needs to have an arteriogram and either an angioplasty or bypass." KT indicated the notes that she'd made in the chart that day. "I'm not getting any pulses below his popliteals, and if that artery occludes acutely, he's going to lose his foot."

"I agree," Tory said. "I'll call him tonight and talk to him about going to Hyannis to see a vascular surgeon."

"I can do it if you want." KT checked her watch. "We were supposed to be out of here two hours ago."

"I know, but I should probably do it. He *might* listen to me."

"You need to start letting me do more of that kind of follow-up, Tory. Otherwise, there's just too much work for you to handle," KT suggested gently, setting the file down on the corner of the desk.

"You're only here for the short term, KT," Tory pointed out reasonably. "The patients are just more used to me."

"According to Pia," KT said, the muscles in her jaw tightening perceptibly, "I'm not going anywhere any time soon."

"Is there a problem with your hand?" Tory still found it difficult to look at the splint and the tendon outriggers on KT's arm. In the years they'd been together, she'd seen KT operate dozens of times. Her hands had been so facile, so sure, so beautiful to watch. It hurt her physically to imagine what KT was going through now.

"Nothing too bad. A lot of paresthesias." KT shrugged. "But Pia seems to think it's going to slow my recovery down because she doesn't want to irritate the nerve endings and risk the chance of neuromas forming." She couldn't hide her frustration. "So she's sitting on me to go slowly."

"Pia's very good. She's taken care of a number of my patients." Tory placed her hand on KT's shoulder, squeezing gently to reassure her. "You can trust her judgment. She's the best."

KT thought about sitting across the table from Pia the night before at dinner—of how much she'd enjoyed herself and how very much she had not wanted to say good night at the end of the evening. This time, Pia hadn't even given her the opportunity to try for a good-night kiss, surprising her by leaning forward and brushing her lips softly over KT's cheek as she whispered good night. It was still hard for KT to believe that she'd stood rooted to the spot, unmoving, and watched Pia walk away without a word. Every smooth line and practiced gesture she'd acquired unconsciously over the years had fled with the first sweet touch of Pia's lips to her skin. She could still feel the memory of that brief, warm caress.

Tory watched the emotion play across KT's face with a sudden sense of foreboding. She knew the look in KT's eyes. She'd seen it often enough, and it would take more than a few years for her to forget what that smoldering heat meant. The words were out of her mouth before she even had time to consider them. "You can't possibly be thinking about making a play for Pia."

"What?" KT jerked as if Tory had struck her. Her surprise was followed swiftly by anger. "*Make a play* for her? You mean as in seducing her into bed for a quickie? I suppose you think that's the only thing I'm interested in where women are concerned."

"Isn't it?"

KT reached for the file she'd dropped on the desk. Through clenched teeth she snapped, "I'll call Mr. Abbot."

Tory reached out swiftly and stopped KT with a hand on her arm. "I'm sorry. That was completely uncalled for." When KT turned to face her, Tory smiled wanly. "You didn't deserve that."

"I don't know. Maybe I did deserve it." KT held Tory's gaze unwaveringly. "Maybe I *did*, once, Tory. But it's not like that with Pia."

"There *is* something going on, then." Tory shook her head. "KT, Pia...God. Pia is just...so...*not* the woman for you."

"What's that supposed to mean?" KT asked, half astonished and half angry. "We have a lot in common. We get along really well. What's so wrong about that?"

"Oh, come on. Pia is a sweet woman, but hardly your type."

"My type." KT's voice was flat, her eyes expressionless. "And what would that be, exactly? As I recall, *you* were my type once."

"Yes, and look how well that turned out."

"Jesus. Are you ever going to forgive me?"

The anger mixed with hurt in KT's voice brought Tory up short. *Forgive her. Is that what this is really about?* "I don't know." She reached out and touched her fingers gently to KT's cheek. It was the first time she had touched her in almost seven years. "I think eventually I'm going to need to."

The touch of Tory's hand was so unexpected and so welcome that KT closed her eyes and leaned into the caress, resting her uninjured hand against Tory's hip. She hadn't realized how much she longed for simple tenderness and comfort. "God, I'm sorry, Tory."

"Oh, KT," Tory sighed. "I wish—" She stopped at the sound of footsteps and turned to see Reese framed in her office doorway, watching them. She dropped her hand and stepped away from KT as she smiled at Reese. "Darling, you're back."

KT jerked slightly, as if awakening from a dream. She looked from Reese to Tory and then rapidly retrieved the file from the desktop. "I'll take care of this right away."

As she passed Reese in the doorway, she nodded and said hello.

"Hello, KT." Reese's voice was quiet and steady, her eyes on Tory. To her lover she said, "Do you have time for a break?"

Quickly, Tory crossed the room and kissed Reese on the mouth. "I'm pretty much finished. We only opened for a few hours this afternoon because tomorrow's schedule looked so full that I had Randy bring some of the patients in today for routine exams. I can leave the rest of it to KT." She threaded her arm around Reese's waist. "Let's go."

On their way out of the building, Tory instructed Randy to have KT see the last few patients in the waiting room. It was already close to eight on Sunday evening, and for once, there were no emergencies. Outside in the parking lot, Tory climbed behind the wheel of the Jeep while Reese slid into the passenger seat. Neither spoke until Tory reached Route 6 and headed toward Herring Cove. Then Tory reached across the space between them and rested her hand on Reese's left thigh. "How are you?"

Reese covered Tory's hand with hers, cradling Tory's fingers in her palm. "I'm okay. How's KT?"

Tory glanced over briefly before looking back at the road. "Why?"

"She looked upset back there in the office. So did you. Is everything okay?"

Tory turned right along the coast road and then made a quick left turn into the long, narrow parking lot that overlooked the beach at Herring Cove. She pulled to a stop at the far end and turned off the engine. They were alone.

She turned in the seat and regarded Reese with a gentle smile.

"Most women would want to know what the hell I was doing with my hand on my ex-lover and hers on me."

A small crease formed between Reese's brows as she gave the notion some thought. "Are you upset that I'm not jealous?"

"No. Just...curious." Tory brushed her fingers through Reese's hair. "By the way, you have nothing to be jealous about."

"It's not that I don't think you're the most beautiful woman in the universe—or the sexiest," Reese noted seriously. "I still have no idea how KT ever let you go. I don't imagine there's one woman in Provincetown, married or not, who doesn't have a crush on you."

Tory laughed self-consciously. "Stop it. You're embarrassing me."

Once more, Reese regarded her lover intently. "It's true. Every word."

"*Stop,*" Tory whispered, her fingers trailing down Reese's neck and over her chest. "Because God help me, I'm not going to be able to keep my hands off you if you don't."

Reese shifted in her seat, caught Tory's hand, and drew it to her lips. She kissed Tory's palm and then cradled her hand between her own. "I love you. You make me feel like the luckiest woman in the world. I know that whatever was going on back there was about one of you, or both of you, hurting." She lifted Tory's hand again and brushed it against her cheek. "If it's you, I want to help."

"I'm all right," Tory murmured, struggling with unanticipated tears. "Let's go sit on the beach. If we stay in here, I'm going to forget myself."

Reese grinned. "Yeah?"

Tory leaned over and kissed her—a slow, deep kiss. "*Yeah.* Grab the blanket out of the back, will you?"

"Uh-huh," Reese muttered, her stomach tight and the conversation with her father forgotten. Almost.

Chapter Seventeen

Reese spread out the blanket in one of the many bowls of sand carved into the dunes by the wind and the rain. Once they were inside the natural shelter—ten feet across and just as deep—they were invisible to anyone passing by on the beach below, even had the night not been fast closing around them. The sky was so clear, the stars overhead so bright, that it seemed she could reach up and touch one. Fifty yards away, the ocean lay before them, its black surface broken by the crests of waves that sparkled like diamonds in the moonlight.

Carefully, Tory lowered herself to the blanket and stretched out on her side facing Reese. The crash of the surf and the swirling wind forced them to lean close together to be heard. Tory wrapped an arm around Reese's waist and snuggled against her. She knew Reese's body so well that she recognized the knots in her back as an unmistakable sign of tension.

"Tell me what happened with your father, sweetheart," Tory said, starting to knead the tight muscles.

Reese shifted and settled Tory's head against her shoulder. She sifted strands of Tory's hair through her fingers as she spoke. "He came to talk to me about the wedding."

"Ah, I guess he got your letter, then," Tory remarked, recalling the note Reese had sent to her father telling him of Regina's birth and their plans to be married. She'd enclosed a picture of the baby and had invited him to come to the ceremony. That had been almost a month ago, and they'd received no reply. "I can't believe he came in person to discuss it."

"He said he was on the east coast for an appropriations meeting."

"Uh-huh." Tory rubbed her hand up and down Reese's back.

"So what did he say about it?"

Reese sighed. "What you might expect. He repeated the military's stance on homosexuality, warned me that I was putting my commission at risk, and argued that there was no point in doing that since our marriage had no legal standing anyhow." She pressed her lips to Tory's forehead briefly. "He was very reasonable and rational."

"He didn't threaten you with any kind of official action again, did he?" Tory was struggling to remain calm despite her fury that her lover should have to face this kind of irrational discrimination from her own father.

"No." Unconsciously, Reese tightened her hold on Tory.

"I take it he isn't coming?"

Reese laughed humorlessly. "Ah, no. 'Fraid not."

"I'm sorry, sweetheart." Tory felt impotent, unable to offer her lover the one thing that Reese provided *her* so effortlessly. Comfort.

"It's okay," Reese murmured, closing her eyes and savoring the aroma of the sea and the delicate sun-kissed meadow scent that was uniquely Tory. "It's not important whether he comes or not. What's important to me is you and Regina."

Tory heard the undercurrent of concern in Reese's voice and had the sudden sickening sense that there was something even more serious at stake than Reese's military position. "He came for some other reason too, though, didn't he?"

Reese hesitated. "Nothing definite."

Tory shook her head. "Don't do that with me. Don't try to protect me. I love you for it, but it's not what I need."

"I know." Reese nestled her cheek to Tory's. "He was circumspect because he had to be, but his message was clear. What we've been hearing about the unrest in the Middle East is only the tip of the iceberg. The situation is much worse than we think. That rumbling in the distance is war coming."

"War." Tory turned the word around in her mind. She didn't remember much about the Vietnam War. Desert Storm had been over so quickly and, due to the strange immediacy of being able to watch it unfold nightly on CNN, had seemed almost unreal. "What does that mean?"

"I got the impression from the general, although he wouldn't say anything specific, that a significant mobilization and deployment is likely within the next year." Reese took a long breath. "If that happens, my reserve unit will be one of the first called. No matter what the situation, the Marines, especially the military police, always go in first."

Tory shivered. They were sheltered in their little hideaway, and the air was still warm, but she couldn't remember ever having felt as cold inside. "Do you really think this is going to happen?"

"I don't know." Reese heard the unsteadiness in Tory's voice, and her heart ached. Tenderly, she stroked Tory's shoulders and arms, cradling her lover against her chest. "But I think so. High-ranking military personnel like my father often know about these things well before anything is made public." She felt Tory tremble. "Still, anything could happen."

"Would you go?"

"Tory, I'd have to go."

"Would you *want* to go?"

Reese thought about the question, the same question that had been in her mind since her father had warned her that her military career might be derailed by this wedding just as the opportunity for significant advancement was around the corner. "All my life, Tor, I've trained to serve my country. When the call comes, it's not something a marine thinks about. It's just something that we do."

"I think I understand," Tory said quietly, "but you're going to have to give me a while to absorb all of this. I never expected to be married to a marine."

"I know. And I never expected to have a wife and a baby, either." Reese worked the tail of Tory's blouse from her slacks and slid her hand over the warm flesh of her back. She murmured softly as Tory, mirroring her actions, loosed her shirt from her trousers and pressed her palm to Reese's abdomen.

"Would it have made a difference?" Tory asked softly "If you'd always had us—or even had us ten years ago?"

"I don't know. Nothing could have diverted me from my course when I was eighteen or twenty-five. Now, the one thing I'm certain of is that I don't want to be separated from you."

Tory found the entire conversation surreal. She had anticipated many things for their future, but never that Reese would not be by her side. At least not for decades. As a physician, she understood in her rational mind that life was fickle and that anything could happen, but it was human nature to believe that those things would not happen to you or the ones you loved. And she was human, just like everyone else. She had visions of sharing the milestones of Regina's life with Reese and growing old with her. Even the inherent dangers of Reese's job as a law enforcement officer didn't seem as ominous or frightening as the possibility of her going off to some foreign land to engage an enemy whom Tory could not even bring into focus in her mind. It just didn't seem possible.

"I don't want you to go anywhere." The words were out before Tory could censor them. Before she could even imagine their impact on her lover. All she knew was that she would do anything within her power to keep her family intact, and that Reese was the very heart of her life.

"We don't know that's going to happen," Reese whispered. She'd told Tory about her father's predictions because she couldn't keep something of that magnitude from her lover. But she understood the vagaries of politics and power as well and appreciated that in six months, the world picture could be very different. "We don't have to worry about it now."

Tory inched closer until she was stretched out on top of Reese, braced on her elbows with one thigh between Reese's. She could see Reese clearly in the moonlight and thought she had never looked more beautiful. "Is there any possibility that you could get out of going? If you decided that?"

"Not unless I resigned. And I'd need to do it soon. Once something happens and we're officially at war, that won't be possible."

"Would you do that for me?"

Reese threaded the fingers of her left hand through Tory's hair and pressed her right to the small hollow at the base of Tory's spine. She could feel Tory's body all along her own—not just against her, but inside of her. This woman was her life; she was the reason Reese lived and breathed, hoped and dreamed. There had never been a need in her life as powerful as the one she had for Tory. She would give anything to her, do anything for her.

"Yes."

"I cannot imagine a day without you," Tory murmured, leaning down and brushing her lips over Reese's. "I need you. Regina needs you. You're everything for both of us." She slipped her hand beneath Reese's shirt again and smoothed her hand over the hard planes of her abdomen and the gentle curve of her ribs until she found the softness of her breast. There, she stilled her hand and simply held her.

"Tory—"

"I love you so much." Tory claimed Reese's mouth, exploring gently at first with the tip of her tongue over the silken surface of Reese's lips before dipping into the sweet heat beyond. She pressed her hips down when she felt Reese rise beneath her, gently rocking into her. The wind was all around them, and in the distant silence, the threat of thunder hovered.

When Reese lifted her arms to clasp Tory to her, Tory caught her wrists and pressed Reese's arms back down, holding her forearms close to her shoulders. She moved her mouth from Reese's lips to her jaw, then along her neck, and finally to the soft hollow between her collarbones where her heart beat so close to the surface. Closing her eyes, Tory felt the precious life pulse through the vulnerable vessels just beneath the skin. The power and the wonder that was Reese filled her, and that flood of love rushed through her, heating her blood and stirring her desire.

"If what we talked about ever happens," Tory murmured against Reese's throat, "I'm likely to say almost anything to keep you with me. But I want you to remember what I'm going to tell you now."

She let go of one of Reese's hands and unbuttoned Reese's shirt, then pushed up the light silk tee beneath it to expose Reese's breasts. Pressing her face to the inner curve of one small, firm breast, she heard Reese gasp as her lips found a tight nipple. She kissed the erect nub gently. "I'm not going to ask you not to go. I'm not going to ask you to resign. I know who you are, Reese. I love you for every single thing about you—your bravery, your valor, your dedication. I want you to do what you need to do, whatever that is."

"Tory—" Reese's voice was husky and low, her body quivering

beneath Tory's. "Whatever you want—"

"No. Just remember what I'm saying now, because if there ever comes a time when you need to go, I don't think I'll be strong enough to say it then."

As she spoke, Tory loosed the buckle at Reese's waist and opened her trousers. She pushed herself down between Reese's legs until her face was against the taut abdomen. Then she splayed her fingers along the arch of Reese's rib cage, her thumbs meeting in the center as she massaged the trembling muscles. Reese shifted restlessly beneath her, her hips lifting rhythmically against the weight of Tory's body.

"Lie still, darling," Tory whispered as she kissed the soft hollow where Reese's abdomen joined her thigh. She caressed and tormented the delicate skin at the base of Reese's belly until Reese was moaning continuously, and then she grasped Reese's trousers and tugged them down far enough to press Reese's legs open. Continuing her kisses along the inside of Reese's thigh, she tasted Reese's desire. When she closed her lips gently around the prominence of Reese's clitoris, Tory moaned with wonder and helpless longing. She'd made love to Reese hundreds of times, but every time she was struck anew by the overwhelming splendor of their passion. Beneath the star-filled night sky, surrounded by the wonder of the land and sea that nurtured her, Tory paid homage to the love that had resurrected her life and defined her destiny. As Reese's cries drifted to her on the wind, the sound as primitive and wild and achingly beautiful as the roar of the sea beyond, Tory closed her eyes against her tears.

Soaring, Reese threaded trembling fingers through Tory's hair and through glazed eyes watched the stars dance overhead. As Tory brought her steadily and exquisitely to orgasm, she melted beneath Tory's lips and surrendered to the demands of Tory's mouth, knowing that she had never been so perfectly loved. For those moments out of time, all that she was belonged to Tory.

❖

"You need a ride somewhere?" Randy asked KT.

KT hesitated, then nodded. "I wouldn't mind a ride into the

center of town. I can get a cab, though, if you're not going that way."

"Nothing in this town is out of the way," Randy noted as he locked the front door and indicated a black Mazda Miata parked in the far corner of the gravel lot. "It's no problem."

It took less than five minutes to reach the center of town, where KT climbed out, thanked Randy for the ride, and headed toward her temporary home. Along the way, she replayed her conversation with Tory, recalling Tory's assessment that Pia was not *her type*. She couldn't help but wonder if Tory really believed that she could only be interested in a shallow sexual relationship with a woman.

When KT considered what her life had been like the last five years or so, she supposed that conclusion might seem valid. She'd had no long-term relationships since Tory, and even her affairs had been relatively brief. But as attractive as she found Pia, the thought of a night or two in bed with her left her feeling unsatisfied. That in and of itself was a departure for her. Casual liaisons had been her staple, providing both a release from stress and a diversion from introspection. For whatever reason, that wasn't what she was looking for with Pia. They'd *already* shared more than she'd shared with most of the women with whom she'd slept in recent years.

The entire train of thought left her uneasy, because she wasn't certain why she felt differently about Pia or if it was even wise to try to find out. She'd had a difficult conversation with Tory, her arm ached, and she'd forgotten both lunch and dinner. She felt around in her pants pocket for the last pain pill she'd counted out that morning—the one she should have saved until midnight—and swallowed it dry. Then she detoured down the sidewalk to the Pied for something to wash it down with and for a little company to help turn her thoughts from her past mistakes and future uncertainties.

Two hours later, she'd had two drinks and had turned down one very promising offer to spend the evening with an extraordinarily attractive, but very young, art student from Brown who was spending the fall semester painting on the Cape. As lovely and eager as the young woman had been, KT was simply not interested. She left a ten-dollar tip on the bar and decided it was time to go home. When she eased down from the bar stool, she was nearly overcome by a sudden wave of dizziness. She staggered back a step and clutched the curved edge of the bar with her right hand to steady herself.

Two drinks. I only had two drinks. I can't be this drunk on just two drinks. Must be because I didn't have dinner.

She blinked and tried to focus on the faces across the room. Unfortunately, the room and everyone in it were spinning.

"Looks like you could use a little air," a smooth voice murmured in her ear as a firm arm came around her waist.

"Dizzy," KT muttered. "Just a little dizzy."

"I can see that, darlin'. Now come on outside with me."

Too disoriented to argue, KT allowed herself to be led through the bar and onto Commercial Street by the willowy brunette who guided her. She shook her head and tried to focus on the woman's face, but found it impossible. She could tell, though, that she was beautiful. As beautiful as her mellow voice with its soft Southern accent.

"I'm okay," KT stated emphatically, trying to walk a straight line and failing. "I just live up the street a few blocks."

"Well, it's a nice night for a walk, so why don't we head that way. What's your address?"

KT had to think for a minute, but she was finally able to recall the numbers on the front of the guest house. She shook her head, but it didn't clear the cobwebs from her brain. *Must be tired. Too much stress.*

"What's your name?" the brunette asked.

"KT. You?"

"Allie. You must be new in town, KT, because I don't know you, and I can't imagine that I would have missed you. I don't usually miss good-looking women like you."

KT would've laughed at the pick-up line that should have been hers, but she suddenly felt as if she might vomit. She concentrated on controlling her heaving stomach and remained silent. Ten minutes later they turned down the driveway toward the rear entrance to KT's building. KT had draped her arm around Allie's shoulders for support, and the smaller woman still guided KT with an arm around her waist.

"That's it," KT muttered, indicating the rear stairs. "Up there."

"Well, I brought you this far. I'm going to make sure you get inside." Carefully, Allie guided KT to the stairs. "Besides, I'm getting kind of fond of you."

❖

From the shadows of the porch across the way, Pia watched the two figures come arm in arm down the path and climb the stairs to KT's apartment. As soon as they disappeared inside, she got up, entered her own small, tidy home, and closed the door gently behind her.

Chapter Eighteen

"Keep going," Pia said to the teenager who sat on the weight bench doing straight leg lifts with a three-pound weight strapped to his ankle. "Four more reps and then stop and we'll ice it."

"We've got a big game coming up next week," the handsome boy said. "Am I going to be able to play?"

"I think so, but the final word will be up to your surgeon. You're seeing him on Wednesday afternoon, right?"

"Yeah. But *he* won't let me do anything unless *you* say it's okay."

"Well, I'll give you a written report to take with you to the office visit, just like always. I think if you agree to stretch out before the game..." She saw the fleeting look of disdain cross his face before he quickly squashed it. "I know, I know. It's not considered cool to stretch, but if you don't, you're going to be right back here again with another ligament tear and that will be the end of your football career."

"I hear you." He sighed, then met her gaze fully. "I promise."

"And ice it as soon as the game is over."

"Yeah, yeah."

She smiled and wrapped an ice pack on the knee in question. "Let me see you Wednesday morning for a half-hour session." She checked the appointment book that she kept on the small desk under the windows overlooking the garden. "Eight thirty."

At his nod of assent, she began to pencil his name into the book when the phone rang. Distractedly, she reached for it. "Pia Torres."

"Pia? Tory King."

"Tory? What's up?"

"I have a strange request."

"Go ahead. What do you need?" Pia held up a hand signaling five minutes to the boy, who nodded and leaned back as if he were about to take a nap.

"KT O'Bannon is renting a place from your mother, right?"

At the mention of KT's name, Pia stiffened. She'd gone to bed the night before and awakened that morning with a lingering image of KT and the strange woman arm in arm. There was no earthly reason why the sight of KT with *any* woman should have bothered her, because—well, because there was nothing between the surgeon and herself to have warranted her being upset. And KT with a woman shouldn't have been a surprise. Pia had heard the same rumors that most of the town had heard—namely, that KT was a high-profile Boston surgeon known to be friendly with the ladies, with the emphasis on *ladies*—plural. She also happened to know, though it *wasn't* common knowledge, that KT had once been Tory's lover.

"Pia?"

When she realized that Tory was still waiting for an answer, Pia quickly said, "Yes. The condo unit in the rear."

"Would you mind very much checking to see if she's there?" Tory gave a self-conscious-sounding laugh. "I'm probably overreacting, but she was due at the clinic an hour ago, and she hasn't shown up or called. She doesn't answer her cell phone, and I don't know of any other way to reach her. I suppose she might have left a message with our answering service that I never received, because messages *have* been known to slip through the cracks, but I just want to make sure there's not a problem. If there's one thing I know about KT, it's that she's never late."

"I don't mind checking, but she probably just overslept." *And considering the way she arrived home, completely wrapped around that woman, there's probably a good reason for it.*

"That's great. Thanks. I'm sorry to bother you with this."

"It's no bother. It's right next door, and I was just ending a session. Really, it's no trouble."

"If she's there, have her call me. Thanks again."

"Will do. Bye, Tory." Pia replaced the receiver and crossed the room to the town's star quarterback. She removed the ice, gently ranged his knee, and mentally approved of the absence of swelling or tenderness. "You're finished for the day, Rocko. Do we have a deal about you taking care of your knee before and after the game?"

Wordlessly, he nodded.

"All right, then. Come on, I'll walk you out."

After bidding the boy goodbye, Pia climbed the stairs to the rear deck of the main building and knocked on the screen door to KT's condo. When she got no answer, she opened the screen and knocked harder on the inside door. She was about to turn away when Tory's remark about KT never being late for anything repeated itself in her mind. Feeling foolish, and slightly intrusive, she cupped her hands around her face and pressed against the glass window. There was a light on in the kitchen, a set of keys on the breakfast bar that she recognized as the ones she had given KT for the condo, and a single shoe lying on the tile floor, abandoned. The rest of the kitchen appeared neat and tidy, as if nothing had been cooked or eaten in it since KT moved in. Typical bachelor flat.

"If her keys are inside, then she must be, too," Pia muttered, wondering what to do next. From everything she'd gleaned of KT as a surgeon, it seemed completely out of character for KT not to have gone to work for any reason—even a particularly hot liaison with a woman. And certainly not without having called the clinic to let someone know. Still, she hesitated, loath to walk in on KT in the midst of a tryst. *You don't really* know *that she'd call in. She could be too* involved. *She could be in there right now romping with some woman and just not answering the phone.*

Still, Tory King was not a woman to jump to conclusions or to be overly dramatic. Tory had asked her to check on KT, and that was reason enough to be concerned. Pia twisted the doorknob. It turned easily and the door opened. She took one step inside and called, "KT? It's Pia. Sorry to bother you."

Her voice echoed oddly in the apartment; were it not for the keys on the counter, she would have thought the condo empty. Her sense of disquiet increased, and she moved further into the kitchen, listening carefully for any voices or sound of movement. "KT?"

She was familiar with the layout of the apartment and started down the hall toward the master bedroom at the far end. It was then that she heard a soft moan. *Oh God, she really is with someone. How humiliating.*

About to beat a hasty retreat, she heard the unmistakable sound of retching and then a groan. In less than a minute she passed through the empty bedroom to the bathroom. KT, shoeless and in a rumpled, half-opened shirt and wrinkled trousers, was on her knees, arms braced on the toilet, gasping for breath.

"Oh my God," Pia murmured, bending down to brush the sweat-drenched hair from KT's face. "What's wrong?"

KT turned her head, her eyes glazed. "Pia? Hell. What are you doing here?"

"Tory called." Pia stood and ran cold water on a washcloth, then wiped KT's face with it. "You're supposed to be at work."

"Fuck," KT whispered weakly. "What time is it?"

"It doesn't matter," Pia said, taking in KT's ashen pallor, the sunken appearance of her eyes, and her trembling hands. "You're not going anywhere."

"Need to." KT attempted to push herself upright and failed, sinking down again with her back against the commode. She leaned her head back and closed her eyes, both hands lying limply in her lap.

Pia noted absently that KT had kept her splint on. As she turned back to the sink to rinse out the washcloth, she saw for the first time the open container of prescription medication sitting on the counter. The *empty* container. Her heart sank and her stomach seized. She picked it up and read the label. Oxycontin. *Oh God.*

"How many?" Pia was astounded at how calm her voice sounded when inside, she was screaming. "How many did you take?"

"What?" KT opened her eyes and struggled to make sense of the question. When she saw the pill bottle that Pia held in her hand, she wanted to laugh, but she was too close to vomiting again. "None of them."

"The bottle's empty, honey," Pia said gently, squatting down beside KT. She picked up KT's right wrist and felt for a pulse. It was rapid but strong. KT's skin, however, was clammy and damp.

"Maybe you don't remember taking them. Try to think. We have to know how many you took."

KT shook her head, which immediately caused her to retch again. She turned her head and vomited what little remained in her stomach. When she caught her breath, she said hoarsely, "Threw them out. Down the toilet."

It took a moment for Pia to compute the significance of that statement, but then suddenly the scene in the bathroom made horrifying sense. What she had at first taken to be the aftereffects of too much alcohol mixed with pills wasn't the case at all. KT was demonstrating all the signs of narcotic withdrawal—dilated pupils, increased respiratory rate, vomiting, sweating. "How are the muscle cramps?"

"Tolerable," KT mumbled.

"We should get you to the hospital."

KT's head snapped up, and her eyes suddenly focused. Her voice was surprisingly strong. "*No.* I'll be all right in a few hours."

"You won't be all right by then, and you know it." Despite her words, Pia's tone was tender. She used the washcloth again to wipe KT's face and neck. "Let me get you into the shower and then to bed. We'll talk after that."

"Go away. I don't want you here."

"I know." Pia eased her arm around KT's shoulders and gently guided her to her feet, switching her grip to encircle KT's waist once she was standing. "But you can't do this by yourself."

"There's nothing to do. It's not that bad." Despite her best efforts, KT shivered violently, and her teeth chattered. "I'll just sleep it off."

"Shower first. Let's warm you up."

KT leaned her back against the wall and held her good arm out straight, keeping Pia at a distance. "I don't want you to take care of me. I want you to go." She took a breath, her eyes pleading. "Pia, please."

"All right," Pia said quietly. "I'll call Tory."

"Oh, Jesus," KT moaned. "That's all I need." She struggled not to shake, but a surge of nausea and dizziness swept over her. She figured she had about thirty seconds before she fainted.

Surrendering, she turned her hand palm up. "Help me get to the bed."

❖

"I'm so cold."

"Here, honey," a soft voice said. "Let me hold you."

KT turned her face to the comforting warmth of the woman beside her and wrapped her arm around Pia's solid strength as if she were a life preserver in the raging sea. Still shivering, her stomach rolling, KT moaned quietly. A hand brushed over her hair and massaged the muscles in the back of her neck.

"It's okay. It's going to be okay," Pia murmured.

Fully dressed, Pia sat half upright with her back braced against the headboard and KT against her side. She drew the other woman closer, encircling her shoulder with one arm as she pulled the blanket higher over them with her other hand. KT's cheek rested against her shoulder. After she'd gotten KT to bed, she'd called the clinic with the excuse that KT had a stomach bug and wouldn't be in for at least a day. She hadn't intended to do any more than stay until KT was settled, but after an hour of seeing the semiconscious woman toss and turn and shiver and shake, she couldn't stand it anymore. She'd climbed onto the bed to hold the struggling woman, and the instant she had, KT had quieted. Fortunately, she had no other appointments herself until the next afternoon.

"I'm sorry," KT mumbled, dizzy and disoriented. "I'm so sorry for everything."

"You're doing fine," Pia whispered, resting her chin against the top of KT's head and rubbing her back soothingly. "You're going to be all right."

In a moment of clarity, KT lifted her head, finally able to focus on the woman who comforted her. "You should go."

Pia merely shook her head and smiled gently. "You should close your eyes and get some sleep."

"I'm glad you're here," KT confessed as she dropped her head once more to Pia's breast and closed her eyes.

❖

When next KT awoke, the room was completely dark except for a small lamp burning on the dresser. Pia stood in the doorway, a tray in her hands. KT blinked at the light.

"What time is it?" KT croaked, her throat unbelievably raw and sore.

"Nine o'clock."

"When?"

Pia set the tray with a bowl of soup and a glass of room-temperature water on the bedside table and eased her hip onto the mattress next to KT. "Same day. You've been sleeping on and off for about eight hours." *If you could call it sleeping. Mostly you've been thrashing and moaning.*

"You've been here the whole time?"

Pia nodded.

"Why?"

Pia regarded KT curiously. "Because I wanted to be."

"I don't understand."

"Don't you?" Pia slowly reached out and brushed the back of her fingers over KT's cheek. "You need to eat a little bit, and then we should get you into the shower."

KT grimaced. "You're right about that. I'm disgusting."

"How do you feel?"

"Pretty ragged." KT tried to take the bowl of soup that Pia extended to her but was unable to manage it. Her left hand was useless and her right hand shook so badly she couldn't even hold the spoon. With a sigh, she dropped her head back against the pillows. "I'm not really hungry."

"Yes, you are. Besides, you need to get something into your system after everything you've tossed out in the last eighteen hours." Pia spooned up a small amount of soup and brought it to KT's lips. "Come on."

Obediently, KT sipped. After a few minutes, she lay back, exhausted. "Thank you."

"You're welcome." Pia set the bowl aside. "Think you can make it to the shower?"

"Probably. Yeah." KT rested her fingers on Pia's knee. "I don't want you to stay any longer. I appreciate everything you've done. Another twenty-four hours and the worst will be over."

"It's going to be a difficult twenty-four hours." Pia saw no reason to pretend other than the truth. KT knew what was coming, and she knew that Pia knew. Addiction to pain medication was not that uncommon, especially in patients whose physical injuries required prolonged physical therapy and whose pain level was high for extended periods of time. Fortunately, the withdrawal from such drugs was intense, but short-lived. Thirty-six to forty-eight hours was usually the extent of the severe symptoms, and KT was almost halfway through.

KT was about to say she would be okay when her stomach gave a warning rumble.

"Oh, fuck," KT muttered as she pushed off the bed, swayed unsteadily for a few seconds, and then lurched into the bathroom to lose the small meal she'd just eaten. She held one hand behind her back to ward off Pia's assistance. "Stay out there. I don't want you to see this."

"KT," Pia protested gently from the bathroom doorway.

"Just give me a few minutes. I'll be out as soon as I get cleaned up."

When Pia finally relented and closed the bathroom door, KT pulled off her clothes and dropped them on the floor. She turned on the shower, staggered into the stall, and leaned against the wall, shivering beneath the hot spray. When she'd managed to wash her hair and soap away twenty-four hours of sickness, she stepped out and brushed her teeth. Finally feeling clean, she reached for the robe that usually hung behind the bathroom door and realized that it was somewhere in the bedroom. It was almost impossible to wrap a towel around her body one-handed, but she finally managed to cover the essentials. When she reentered the bedroom, she saw that Pia had changed the sheets on her bed.

"Thanks," KT said, heading toward the bed. The slight effort of getting cleaned up had exhausted her.

"Here," Pia said, lifting up the top sheet so that KT could slip inside. She held out her hand. "Let me have that towel. It's wet and you can't get into bed with it."

KT hesitated, and then realized that there was no point in being modest. Pia had already seen her humiliated and pathetic. Naked was the least of her concerns. She pulled the towel off and held it out to Pia

Carefully, Pia kept her eyes on KT's face as she took the towel. Nevertheless, she couldn't help but look down as KT settled onto the bed and tried to get her injured arm into a comfortable position. The quick glimpse of the nude form confirmed what Pia had felt as she'd held KT in her arms. KT was muscular and firm, with subtle curves at her breasts and hips. Her body was every bit as beautiful as her striking face, and Pia knew that the image would stay with her always.

"Try to get some sleep," Pia said as she placed a pillow beneath KT's splinted left arm. "This hand has been dependent too much of the time for the last day. Your fingers are swollen. How do they feel?"

"Without the benefit of the Oxycontin, they hurt like hell," KT confessed. She was too damn tired and too damn sick to pretend she didn't hurt. "Once my stomach settles down, I can try taking some nonsteroidals."

"That should help some." Pia stood and stretched the sore muscles in her back. "I've got some ibuprofen at the house. I'll bring it over for you."

"Go home now, Pia. I'm going to be all right."

"I just want to stay until you fall asleep." *You're going to have a difficult night, and I'm not going to be able to sleep worrying about you.*

"It's not—"

Both women jumped at the distant sound of a knock on the door.

"I'll go see who that is," Pia said.

A minute later, she pulled open the door and came face to face with a very surprised Tory King.

Chapter Nineteen

Tory!"

"Pia?"

"Uh, hi." Pia stood in the doorway, uncertain of what to do next. She saw the questioning look in Tory's eyes, saw her gaze travel from the damp towel that Pia still held in her right hand to the rumpled appearance of her clothing, and saw an uncomfortable expression cross Tory's face. Although KT hadn't said so explicitly, Pia had gotten the definite impression that KT did not want anyone at the clinic to know what was wrong. Awkwardly, she asked, "What's up?"

"I stopped by to see how she's doing." Tory knew from personal experience that subterfuge was not something that Pia was very good at, and Pia's discomfort was apparent. From the look of things, it seemed that she'd just interrupted an intimate moment, and although she didn't doubt KT's powers of seduction, she couldn't quite believe that KT had managed to get Pia into bed. Still, something was obviously going on. Feeling that she needed to explain her presence, although not entirely clear why, she said, "She didn't look sick yesterday, so I was concerned."

Pia considered her options, which were few. She could lie and say that KT was asleep and doing fine, or she could let Tory evaluate the situation for herself. Her better judgment suggested the truth, because she feared that KT would need more than a comforting hand before this ordeal was over, and Tory was a physician as well as a friend. She pulled the door wide. "Come on in. She's in the bedroom."

"Thanks."

Pia led Tory to the bedroom. "KT? Tory's here."

KT made an effort to sit up, and failing that, tried for a smile.

"Hey. Making house calls now?"

Tory hid her shock as she approached the bed, her clinical eye swiftly taking in KT's obvious weakness and debilitated state. Considering her fragile physical condition and the fact that Pia had obviously been there all day, it didn't require much deductive reasoning to conclude that there was more than a stomach virus at work here. She looked from KT to Pia. "What's going on?"

Pia backed toward the bedroom door. "I'll leave you two alone."

"KT?" Tory repeated again as she reached down and rested her hand against KT's forehead. "You look like hell."

"Thanks, Vic."

"Don't try to put me off," Tory said sharply. "You're sick as a dog, and I want to know what's going on."

"Would you believe—" KT was suddenly taken with another round of severe cramps and began to shiver, barely able to finish her sentence. "A really...bad...hangover?"

"No."

Shaking violently, KT gasped, "Too much Oxycontin. Time to quit."

"Like this? Are you *crazy?*" Tory looked closely at KT's eyes and then pressed two fingers lightly to her carotid artery. "Your heart rate is at least 120. Are you having any chest pain?"

"No," KT said with a groan. "Just muscle cramps."

"When did you last take any kind of medication?"

"I don't know. About twenty-four hours ago." Moaning, KT curled on her side. "I think I'm going to vomit again."

Hurriedly, Tory looked around the room and grabbed the wastepaper basket just in time. Supporting KT's head while she vomited, she called over her shoulder, "Pia!"

Pia appeared almost instantly. "Oh, no. Again?"

"How long as this been going on?" Tory asked abruptly.

"Since last night."

"Why didn't you call me?" Tory eased KT back against the pillows, watching her rapid breathing with a frown. "She doesn't have to suffer like this."

"She didn't want me to call."

Tory whipped her head around, her eyes flashing. "Do you

really think she's capable of making that decision?"

Before Pia could answer, KT grasped Tory's hand with unexpected strength. Although her voice was weak, her tone was forceful. "Tory, let it go. It's not Pia's fault."

"God damn it, KT." Tory covered KT's fingers with her own, rubbing the back of KT's hand with surprising gentleness. "You are so *frigging* hardheaded."

A faint smile curled KT's lips as she took a shuddering breath. "Yeah. You just noticed?"

"I'm going to go back to the clinic for some Catapres and a couple of bags of saline," she said, turning to Pia. "Can you stay with her until I get back?"

"I wasn't planning on leaving," Pia replied evenly.

"I'm sorry for jumping on you." Tory met Pia's eyes. "I don't know how it's possible, but for a few seconds there, I forgot just how stubborn she is."

"That's putting it mildly." Pia glanced at KT tenderly, unaware of just how revealing her expression was, before giving Tory a smile. "It's okay. I'm glad you're here. Maybe between the two of us we can handle her."

"Maybe. Just." As Tory passed Pia, she grasped her hand and squeezed lightly. "I'm honestly sorry."

Pia shook her head, her voice low as she walked out into the hall with Tory. "It's really all right. It's hard, seeing her like this."

"Are you okay?" Tory asked gently. For the first time, she noticed the circles under Pia's eyes.

"Yeah." She pushed a hand through her hair and shook some of the tension out of her shoulders before leaning back against the wall. "I've been watching her carefully. I would have called you if things had gotten worse. She's just...so proud, you know?"

The corner of Tory's mouth lifted into a weary smile. Another barrier that she had tightly constructed around her heart to bury the memory of what she had once felt for KT fell away. Surprisingly, the only thing she now felt was gratefulness that Pia had seen past KT's façade. "Yes, I know."

"This is all so terrible for her—the damage to her hand, the constant pain, and now this." Pia's eyes drifted back to the bedroom. "I just didn't want to make it any worse."

Tory realized with a sinking feeling that she had seen KT every day for weeks and hadn't noticed what she had been going through. Hadn't really allowed herself to see KT's struggles or her pain. *My God, I missed a drug addiction in my own colleague. A woman I once knew as well as I knew myself. Is that what my anger has done to me?*

"You haven't made anything worse. On the contrary." Tory slid her arm around Pia's shoulders and gave her a hug. "I think you being here is just what she needs."

Pia blushed, suddenly aware that they were discussing Tory's ex-lover. "I'll wait until you get back. Then if you want to stay with her..."

"Actually, Reese is picking Regina up from Kate's, so I've got a little time. I'll get the things from the clinic, and then we can decide." She tilted her head and regarded Pia seriously. "Do you need a break?"

"No. I just want to stay with her." As it was, even being out of the room was making Pia uneasy. What she really wanted to do was climb back onto the bed and hold KT. She didn't bother to analyze her feelings. She was too raw emotionally to even try. All she knew was what she felt, and what made her feel right was having KT in her arms.

"Then you should stay. You can always call me if there seems to be a problem. Once she's hydrated and we counteract some of the adrenergic symptoms with the Catapres, she'll be more comfortable."

"I hope so. I can't stand seeing her like this."

Tory gave Pia's hand another squeeze. "Go on back to her. I'll run over to the clinic and get what we need to make her comfortable."

❖

"Thanks," KT said quietly as Tory finished taping the intravenous line to her right arm. She looked down and lifted both hands an inch off the bed before letting them fall back. "Well, now I'm well and truly fucked."

"As soon as a second bag goes in, Pia can put a cap on this IV line, and you'll be able to use your arm a little bit more freely." Tory began removing the detritus left on the bed from the containers that had housed the IV tubing, intravenous catheters, and the bag of normal saline. She stopped moving when KT caught her wrist.

"I guess you're pretty angry, huh?" KT asked.

Tory finally looked up into KT's anguished eyes. "Why in God's name didn't you come to me? Do you have any idea how bad this could've gotten, especially if Pia hadn't come by today? What were you thinking?"

KT winced under the verbal onslaught. Despite the intravenous hydration and the sedative that Tory had given her, she hurt all over, her stomach threatened to revolt at any second, and her head reeled with dizziness. On top of that—worse than that, really—was the knowledge that both Tory and Pia had seen her so helpless and pathetic. She didn't think things could get much worse. "I didn't know. I should have, but I didn't. I just...since the accident...I just wasn't thinking."

Carefully, Tory sat on the bed, her hip against KT's. "*I* should've noticed."

"It's not like I've been walking around stoned, Tory," KT pointed out wearily. "But the damn drug sneaks up on you. I definitely had a physical addiction, and I'm sure the psychological dependency wasn't far off." She leaned her head back against the pillows and sighed. "If I hadn't almost OD'd after two drinks last night, I probably wouldn't have figured it out until it was too late."

"God," Tory murmured, reaching out to stroke KT's cheek. She stopped herself with a jolt just before her fingers made contact and quickly drew back. "I'm sorry. If I had been paying more attention, this wouldn't have happened."

"Bullshit," KT said with as much conviction as she could manage.

Tory smiled wanly. "I'll stop by in the morning to see how you're doing."

"Make Pia go home."

"When pigs fly." Tory laughed. "I could barely get her to go home for something to eat and a shower. I don't think she trusts me to look after you."

KT smiled softly. "She was great today."

"I'm glad she was here," Tory said, surprised at just how much she meant that. It had shaken her badly to see KT so debilitated and frightened her even more than she wanted to admit to realize that KT might have succumbed to an overdose. She stood up and gathered her gear. "Pia should be back any minute. I'm going to head home."

"You won't tell anyone about this, will you, Tory?"

"God, of course not." Tory looked shocked. "This isn't your fault. And I know you well enough to know this isn't going to be a long-term problem."

"I should have seen it coming. And...it didn't help to add alcohol on top of the meds."

"No, it didn't," Tory agreed. She brushed her fingers over KT's arm. "But you recognize that now, and you're more than paying for that mistake. I trust you not to repeat it."

"Thanks." With a sigh, KT closed her eyes.

Tory made her way quietly through the house. When she stepped out on to the back deck, Pia was just climbing the stairs. "I think she just fell asleep."

Pia leaned against the railing, a book under one arm. "Good. What should I do tonight?"

"If she wakes up before morning in pain or agitated, you can give her another dose of Catapres. Keep the IVs running at the present rate until the second bag is in. Hopefully in another eight hours she'll be able to keep something down. If not, we'll give her a third liter of saline. Can you handle that?"

"Yes. When I used to work at Boston Hospital, most of my patients were in the ICU or step-down units. Changing IV bags was something I did routinely in the physical therapy department."

"Good. And don't let her tell you that she doesn't need the medication. She's going to be very uncomfortable as it is. Without it, it'll be hell."

Pia's hands tightened on the book she held. She hated the thought of KT suffering. "Don't worry. I won't let her pull that macho stuff."

Tory laughed. "How is it that you've got her figured out so quickly?"

"I don't know that I do, but it's not very hard to tell how much she's been hurting." Pia looked at Tory kindly. "Inside and out."

"What happened between KT and me is ancient history. I told you that when we first met."

"Yes, I remember." Pia smiled. "In fact, you told me that the first night we had dinner together. I didn't believe you then." She squeezed Tory's arm affectionately. "I *do* believe you now."

"It's easier to give up the anger now. When I think of Reese, I can't imagine being without her. Looking back, I'm beginning to think it might not have been all KT's fault that we didn't work out."

"Does it matter who was at fault?" Pia asked gently.

"I don't know." Tory leaned her back against the building opposite Pia and shook her head. "I'm beginning to think it doesn't. I look at her now and my memories seem to be from a different lifetime."

"Maybe that just means that the past is finally becoming the past for you."

"And what about you?"

"Me?"

"And KT?"

"Ah," Pia said softly. "I...like her."

"Mmm-hmm."

"What can I say that you don't already know? She's smart and funny and gorgeous. And so sexy it's criminal." Pia laughed. "What's not to like?"

"Uh-oh. Sounds like more than *like* to me," Tory teased gently, realizing that it didn't bother her to think that Pia, whom she'd always had a fondness for, was interested in KT. And seeing the way KT had looked at Pia that evening had made her forget why she'd been opposed to the idea when KT had first mentioned Pia's name the day before.

"Well, until KT is back on her feet and we finish our therapy together, *like* is all it's going to be."

"Uh-huh." Tory saw no point in reminding Pia that KT O'Bannon was not the kind of woman who sat back and waited for much of anything, especially a woman in whom she had an interest. And if the looks that had passed between Pia and KT throughout the evening were *not* an indication of strong mutual attraction, Tory couldn't imagine what was. The two of them were deep in denial, but she didn't think that would last much longer. "I'm going to go home to my own gorgeous, sexy woman. Call me if there's any problem at all. Any time."

"Thanks, Tory. I will." Pia waved good night and let herself into the condo. It was after 11 p.m., but she wasn't tired. The anxiety and worry of the long day had hyped her up to the point where she wasn't sure she would be able to sleep at all. When she reached the bedroom, she stepped quietly to the chair that she'd drawn up to the bedside earlier.

"Tory leave?" KT asked drowsily.

"Yes. How are you doing?"

"Better. You?"

"Fine." Pia lifted the book. "If you don't mind the light, I thought I'd just sit here and read for a while."

"You don't need to stay. Go home and get some sleep."

"We've had this conversation before."

KT sighed. "And Tory called *me* frigging stubborn."

Pia laughed quietly. "Comparatively speaking, I think I just qualify as plain stubborn."

"You and Tory are pretty good friends, huh?"

"Yes, we are." Pia settled into the chair and inched it forward until she could see KT's face as they talked. Unconsciously, she reached out and stroked KT's hair. "You really should sleep."

"Did the two of you used to...date?"

"Very briefly, a long time ago." Pia rested her hand on KT's shoulder, rubbing her fingers lightly over KT's skin. "How did you know that?"

"Something about the way Tory yelled at you. There was a certain degree of familiarity to it."

Pia laughed. "Very observant."

"So what happened?"

"Tory was still in love with someone else." She spoke gently, her fingers drifting to KT's jaw.

"Did she break your heart?"

"No," Pia said with conviction. "No one broke my heart."

"So why—"

"You're supposed to be sleeping."

"Just tell me what you're waiting for."

Pia sighed, and had she not been so exhausted from the day, she might not have answered. But KT's skin was so soft beneath her fingers and her face so unguarded that Pia forgot her usual caution. "I want the woman I'll spend the rest of my life with to be the only one."

"Forever," KT said drowsily.

"Yes."

"I screwed up pretty badly back then," KT murmured.

"That's between you and Tory."

KT turned her face until her cheek rested against Pia's palm. The cool strength of Pia's fingers gave her comfort. "Do you think I'm a lost cause?"

"No," Pia whispered. *I think you're beautiful, in every way.* "Go to sleep now, honey."

Nearly asleep, KT asked what she never would have let herself ask had she been fully in control. "Would you hold me again like you did this afternoon?"

Pia didn't stop to think what it might mean—that KT asked, or that she couldn't for one second imagine saying no. She set her book aside and eased onto the bed. In a motion that felt as natural to her as breathing, she settled KT's head against her breast.

Chapter Twenty

"Why don't you go check on her?" Reese said quietly as she drew the soft strands of Tory's hair through her fingers. It was just after 5 a.m., and the room had begun to lighten as the sun rose over the harbor. She knew Tory was awake, even though she hadn't moved her head from Reese's shoulder where she'd fallen asleep the night before. There was a stillness in her body that wasn't there when she slept and a tightness in her muscles that belied her restful pose.

"Have you always been able to read my mind?" Tory touched a kiss to Reese's shoulder while tightening her hold around Reese's waist.

"Not at the very beginning." Reese moved her hand from Tory's hair to the center of her back and massaged her gently, the movement pressing Tory's bare breasts to Reese's chest. "I didn't realize for the longest time that you lusted after me."

Tory laughed. "I should think it would have been obvious to you when I couldn't keep my hands off you, even when you'd been shot." Recalling that night, and her terror, she tensed.

"Freak accident," Reese murmured, turning until Tory lay beneath her. She braced herself on her elbows and framed Tory's face in her hands. Then she kissed her forehead. "If you're worried about KT, you should go see her."

"Pia is with her. She would have called me if there was a problem."

Reese nodded. "I know. But you're still worrying."

Tory smiled softly and opened her legs so that Reese could settle more comfortably between them. She loved being able to hold her while they talked, about anything, it seemed. Reese made it possible to discuss the really hard things because she never allowed distance to come between them, no matter what had transpired. Tory counted on that, in the moments when she was most uncertain. She caught the thick hair at the base of Reese's neck and tugged Reese's head down until their mouths met. She took her time with the kiss, because it was the first of the day and it might be hours before they could share a moment as private and wholly theirs as this one. The baby would awaken soon, needing to be fed and readied for her day at Kate and Jean's, Reese would leave for the early-morning class at the *dojo*, and she would head for the clinic after dropping Regina off. None of those thoughts was foremost in her mind, only the distant sense of urgency to connect, to renew herself through the love that sustained her. She didn't notice when her grip on Reese tightened, or when she hooked her heels over Reese's tight thighs and arched her pelvis into her lover. She wasn't aware of her heart beating wildly or the soft undulations of her hips or the sudden tension in Reese's body. As she stroked her tongue over Reese's, she savored the warmth that began in her heart and settled deep in the core of her, transforming with each second from the quiet comfort of belonging to the sharp edge of pleasure. When she felt the first hint of the pressure coalescing between her thighs, she drew her head away with a gasp. "Oh my."

Breathing fast, her eyes the navy blue of the sunset over the dunes, Reese grinned. "Yeah. Oh my."

"Do we have time?"

Reese shifted enough to allow a hand between their bodies and smoothed her fingers between Tory's legs, coating her fingers with the evidence of Tory's desire. When Tory arched her back with another sharp gasp, Reese groaned quietly. "Plenty of time."

"And it's *about* time." Tory moaned as she caught Reese's hand and pressed Reese's fingers inside.

"Tor?" Reese said anxiously.

Already contracting around Reese's fingers, eyes nearly closed, Tory shook her head restlessly. "Eight weeks, sweetheart. Eight weeks and I've missed you so much."

Reese could feel Tory's orgasm gathering and couldn't have abandoned her then for any reason. She rested her forehead against Tory's shoulder and carefully moved within her, following the demanding thrust of her lover's hips with gentle replies of her own.

"I love you."

"So good," Tory whispered, digging her fingers into Reese's strong back. "So good, so good."

Reese closed her legs tightly around Tory's as she stroked Tory to climax, feeling her own release build swiftly through her trembling limbs. When Tory threw her head back and convulsed around Reese's fingers, Reese exploded. She cried out once before burying her face in Tory's neck, coming hard and deep.

"Oh my," Tory sighed after a moment.

"Uh-huh."

"I think that was a record."

Reese laughed, then shifted some of her weight off her lover and rolled onto her side. Gently, she eased her fingers out but kept her hand cupped lightly between Tory's thighs. "You're wonderful."

Tory leaned her forehead against Reese's, tracing her fingers along Reese's jaw. "I realized something last night. Something that should have occurred to me a long time ago."

"What?"

"That you're the person that I belong with. Just you. Always you—yesterday, today, and tomorrow."

"Tory," Reese murmured reverently. She drew Tory close, fitting their bodies together until nothing separated them. "I'll do everything I can to always be here for you."

"I know."

"About what my father said the other day—"

"No." Tory put her fingers gently to Reese's mouth. "I don't want to talk about that right now."

"All right." Reese kissed Tory's fingers. "What about KT? Is *she* going to be all right?"

"It depends on what you mean." Tory sighed. "I don't think she's going to have a long-term problem with substance abuse, but she's so..." She struggled to express what she hadn't wanted to admit but what had been so clear to her the night before. "God, she is so *lonely.*"

"I was lonely too, before I met you." Reese rocked Tory unconsciously. "It took meeting you for me to know that. Maybe it works that way for some people."

"Oh, baby," Tory said gently. "Sometimes, you break my heart."

Reese frowned. "Why?"

"Because I worry that I won't be able to love you well enough."

"Oh yeah," Reese responded with a laugh. "That was pretty obvious a few minutes ago."

Tory slapped her lightly on the shoulder. "I wasn't talking about that."

"The only reason it happens the way it does—the reason that I can't hold back when we make love, is because you love me just the way I need to be loved." She kissed Tory softly. "Don't ever doubt it."

The faint sound of fretful, waking noises came to them through the baby monitor next to the bed. Both turned instinctively toward the sound.

"Guess the *other* reason I'm so happy just woke up." Reese kissed the tip of Tory's nose and drew away. "I'll get her and bring her in here for breakfast."

Tory caught Reese's hand before she could get out of bed. "Thanks for being so good about KT. A lot of women wouldn't understand."

"If I thought she could or *would* hurt you, I'd feel differently."

There was an unwavering edge in Reese's voice that made Tory realize that for all of Reese's gentleness, she would fight for anything that threatened what was hers—Tory, Regina, and, Tory knew in her heart, her country.

"Go get the baby, sweetheart," Tory whispered, refusing to think about what that might mean for their future.

❖

KT opened her eyes to the absence of pain for the first time in over thirty-six hours. She lay still, aware of Pia's arms around her and Pia's shoulder cushioning her head. She hadn't awakened with a woman in months, and none in her memory other than Tory whom she'd wanted to remain next to after their few hours of mutual release. Pia's chest rose and fell with comforting regularity beneath her cheek, and the curve of Pia's breast pillowed her face. She never wanted to move.

"Pia," KT finally whispered.

"Mmm?" Pia stretched and sighed. As she came more fully awake, all of the events of the long night came back to her. The middle-of-the-night shower after KT shivered and sweated and soaked the bed linens as well as the two of them. The retching that finally ended in dry heaves. The apologies that KT had managed to make despite being barely able to stand. Reflexively, Pia tightened her hold and drew KT closer in an unconscious attempt to protect her. "How are you feeling?"

"Okay. You?"

"Stiff," Pia admitted, moving carefully, not wanting to disturb the woman in her arms. *In my arms. God, how did this happen? Twenty-four hours ago I woke angry with her for sleeping with another woman.* She was suddenly flooded with an even more irrational surge of anger. "How could she have left you in that condition?"

"Who?" KT rested her palm on Pia's abdomen, over the thin white tank top Pia wore. She noticed that Pia's legs were bare beyond her pale blue bikinis and that she herself wore nothing at all. *Holy Christ, we're practically naked in bed together.* Despite her abysmal discomfort, she felt a twinge of desire.

"The woman you were with the other night. How could she have just left when you were so sick?"

KT struggled to follow the question. "Woman? What woman?"

"The woman you brought home—the night before last," Pia said quietly. "I saw you with her."

"Oh, man. I remember. She walked me home and came up here, and—"

"I don't want to hear the details."

Frowning at the clipped tone of Pia's voice, KT tried to raise her head to see Pia's face, but the sudden movement made her stomach lurch dangerously. She rested her cheek against Pia's breast again. "I sent her away."

"What?"

"I said thanks and sent her on her way. I didn't sleep with her."

"You don't have to expla—"

"Pia," KT said gently, "I didn't want to sleep with her. Even if I'd been *able* to, I wouldn't have wanted to. I've been trying to tell you it's you I wa—"

"Hush," Pia said, stroking KT's cheek. "Not now."

"God, you have wonderful hands," KT sighed. "Why not talk about it now? You said there isn't anyone else, and you know there's something between us. I just have to look at you and I get—"

"KT," Pia interrupted, "I'm not going to sleep with you."

"Not talking about sex." KT's head throbbed just enough to make her brain a little slow. "Well, not *just* sex. I want to go out with you—date, you know." She frowned, snippets of the previous evening's conversation coming back to her. *I want the woman I'll spend my life with to be the only one. The only one. Forever.* "Holy Christ." KT finally managed to sit up enough to look into Pia's face. "You were telling me you aren't sleeping with *anyone* until what—you get married?"

Pia held KT's gaze. "Yes."

"And you've never—?"

"Don't sound so surprised."

"Does Tory know?"

"Why?" Pia asked, confused.

"Because she was so sure you weren't my type."

Pia flushed. "Oh really?"

"It wasn't a comment about you," KT said gently. "It was a criticism of me. I'm not—worthy, in her eyes. Not of that kind of trust."

"She didn't tell you—"

"Hell, no. Tory is the soul of discretion." KT laughed, and even though her throat was so parched she could barely swallow, it felt good. Good to feel something besides pain. "She just intimated that you were too good for me."

Pia smiled and threaded her fingers into KT's hair before gently pulling KT's head back down to her chest. "Being a virgin doesn't make me a saint."

"It makes you some kind of miracle." KT sighed. Rather than

being challenged by the prospect of a new conquest, she felt oddly intimidated. "You weren't kidding about forever, were you?"

"I don't kid about the things that matter to me," Pia murmured, her voice low and husky. As they'd talked, she'd slowly become aware of KT's bare leg against hers, of the heat of her body, of the press of KT's hand to her abdomen. Her stomach tightened beneath KT's fingers, which lightly stroked up and down and around her navel. Everything about lying next to KT felt good, and talking about sex made her acutely conscious of the fact that she was practically naked with a gorgeous woman who *was* naked and who, sick or not, made her heart race. She flashed on the memory of KT standing nude beneath the shower spray in the middle of the night, water sluicing over her breasts and belly, the dark triangle between her thighs standing out in stark contrast to her smooth, pale skin. She'd been too worried about KT's health then to do more than register in an abstract way how beautiful she was. Now, with that soft skin against hers and a firm breast molded to her side, she couldn't think of anything else. Except the tingling in the pit of her stomach and the unmistakable pressure between her thighs. When KT's fingers drifted to the bottom of her tank top and onto her bare abdomen, Pia's legs trembled and wetness slicked her center. She tried to dampen her desire, reminding herself that KT was ill, that they hardly knew one another, and that KT was a woman who was easy about sex. All you had to do was look at her to know that sex was as natural to her as breathing.

And Pia wasn't. Breathing. Her heart threatened to pound out of her chest.

Looking down, she watched KT's fingers stroke the strip of skin just above her bikinis. She should have left her jeans on, but they were soaked from helping KT get in and out of the shower, and who would have thought...KT traced a fingertip beneath the waistband of Pia's panties and her hips lifted involuntarily. Pia's fingers tightened in KT's hair.

Oh my God. If she touches me, I'll die. If she doesn't—

"Pia," KT said softly.

"Mmm?"

"Can you tell how much I want to make love to you?"

"KT," Pia whispered, her voice tinged with regret and

longing.

"I've wanted to since that first night we had dinner. Every day, seeing you, feeling your hands—so gentle, so sure—"

"Oh," Pia caught her bottom lip in her teeth, holding back a moan. Her nipples hardened painfully, and all she could think was that she wanted KT's mouth on them. When KT shifted and pressed her pelvis against Pia's hip, Pia thought she might whimper with the need that rode roughly over her defenses. KT's body was hot; hers was nearly in flames. She couldn't think now why it mattered to wait for anything, not when just being next to KT made her melt. "KT...oh, I—"

KT rubbed her cheek over the prominence of Pia's nipple, loving the soft moan Pia made in response. "I want to feel you move under me. I want to brush my lips over your breasts and lick my way down your belly and taste you. Jesus, I want my mouth on you."

Pia's fingers fisted convulsively in KT's hair; her breath tore from her chest; her clitoris pulsed with each beat of her heart, aching and so, so ready. She turned, wanting KT's body against hers everywhere, shivering when she felt KT's skin meet hers along her legs and abdomen.

"How can I be so aroused when you haven't touched me?" she whispered.

"Because," KT drew her fingertip over Pia's lips, swollen with desire even in the absence of kisses, "I'm about to explode from wanting you, and it's catching." She touched her lips gently to Pia's mouth, closing her eyes at the incredible softness. She trembled and drew away. "Get up, Pia."

Pia's eyes were dazed, her mind clouded with pleasure. "What?"

"Get out of bed, baby," KT murmured against Pia's throat. "I can't move very well right now, but I can touch you, and I will in just another second—so you have to get up."

"I want...oh, I want you to touch me. Put your fingers on me." Pia's voice was a plea.

"No." KT couldn't help herself. She closed her lips over the taut nipple tenting the thin cotton. She groaned, desperate to slide her fingers beneath the silk and into Pia's heat. When she heard

Pia's cry of pleasure, she pushed herself onto her back, panting. "No, you don't. Pia, this isn't the time."

"Are you crazy?" Pia gasped in disbelief.

"*Yes.*" KT gritted her teeth and ignored the painful pressure in her depths. "Fuck."

Pia fell onto her back and stared at the ceiling, every breath an effort. "No, *you're* not crazy. *I* am. You can't even stand up, and I'm trying to have sex with you."

KT laughed shakily. "I can do it pretty well lying down, too."

Pia turned her head, her face flushed. "I'm sorry."

"Oh, man. So am I." KT met Pia's eyes. "Don't be sorry for wanting me to touch you, okay? Please?"

Pia cupped her fingers under KT's jaw and ran her thumb over KT's chin. "Let's neither of us apologize, okay? It's been a crazy few days."

"Okay," KT replied, aching in every cell to caress her again. "I'm going to want another chance, though."

With a shake of her head, Pia rolled away and feigned a control she didn't feel. "Let's get you back on your feet first."

"I'm gonna need one more day for that," KT said wearily.

"I know." Pia stood, aware of the lingering stir of arousal, and averted her eyes from the line of KT's hips and thighs beneath the sheets. With effort, she banished the image of KT on top of her, between her legs, so gentle and fierce. "I...I'm going to rearrange my patient schedule today so I can stay."

"Pia—" KT protested.

"No," Pia said definitively. "I'm not leaving you."

KT watched her cross the room and disappear down the hall, replaying those words and wondering why they both terrified and thrilled her.

Chapter Twenty-One

"You could've taken a few more days off," Tory said quietly when she came upon KT leaning back in her office chair, eyes nearly closed.

"Nah." KT smiled wanly as she straightened up. "I can feel crappy at work as well as I can sitting in my condo. My brain is working all right. It's just going to take another week or so for my body to catch up."

"You could have done half-shifts."

"I'm okay." KT held up her left arm. The awkward, heavy splint was gone, and in its place was an elastic wrist wrap with thin, flexible bands attached to each injured finger, holding them in a safe, flexed position. "Look—Pia finally let me go to a wristlet. I've been to therapy every day except for those few days I was... indisposed last week."

In truth, KT had insisted on returning to therapy even when Pia had wanted her to wait a few more days. Despite some muscle cramping and a persistent headache, she needed the return to routine. She needed to feel in control again, and most importantly, she needed to get her relationship with Pia back onto familiar ground. Even though Pia had stayed with her most of the day after they had awakened in one another's arms, she had been distant and cautious, and KT had found the distance maddening. They'd gone from a degree of intimacy, both physical and emotional, that KT hadn't experienced in years to careful formality in a matter of minutes, and she was left with an empty feeling that it seemed only Pia could fill. At least during therapy, Pia was relaxed and easy with her. They'd resumed their casual conversations as well as their frequent debates about the speed and direction of KT's therapy, verbally sparring over how much KT could do and how quickly. KT found that she enjoyed the power that Pia wielded with surprising gentleness. In fact, there was nothing about Pia that she didn't enjoy.

"Indisposed," Tory said dryly. She noted that KT's eyes were clear despite the fact that she looked exhausted still. "How are you handling the pain?"

KT blinked, and a muscle jumped on the edge of her jaw. "Not with narcotics, if that's what you're asking."

Tory kept her voice even. "What I'm asking is if you're doing all right without them."

"Sorry," KT said quietly. "It was rough for the first week or so. Besides feeling like I was going to puke any second, my hand felt like it was going to fall off. I've started to take Tegretol and that, along with the Naprosyn, is keeping things to a tolerable level."

"Good. Are you staying well hydrated, because you look a little shaky. That's easy to fix, you know."

"Don't even *think* about coming near me with an intravenous needle. That lasted about seven hours the last time, and when I managed to dislodge it in the shower *by accident*, I thought Pia was going to kill me."

"Really?" Tory raised an inquisitive eyebrow and was astounded to see KT blush. "Well, well."

"It's not like that, Tory." KT sounded defensive even to herself and laughed softly. "I can't believe I'm explaining that I'm *not* sleeping with someone."

Tory checked her watch, saw that she had at least five minutes before the next patient, and settled into the chair across from KT. "It sounds to me as if you're defending her honor."

"Pia's honor doesn't need defending."

"You sound like that matters to you," Tory remarked neutrally. It was an odd experience discussing an intimate relationship with a woman with whom she had once been intimate herself. To her amazement, she felt no animosity, jealousy, or even criticism, probably because she had never heard KT sound the way she did now—at once protective and perplexed. "She really has you confused, doesn't she?"

"She's got me pretty much in a tailspin, yeah," KT admitted ruefully. She regarded Tory cautiously. "You're not mad?"

"About what?"

"About me being...interested...in Pia."

Tory sighed. "Pia is an adult. So are you."

"That's not what I asked you."

"God, you are relentless."

"You've forgotten?"

Tory laughed quietly. "There were a lot of things about you I had forgotten. A lot of things that I liked." She regarded KT steadily. "A number of things that I loved."

Caught off guard, KT jerked. "Christ, Tory, I made a mess of things back then. I'm sorry."

"So am I. And it wasn't all your fault." Tory smiled, feeling a hard, cold place inside of her break apart and drift away. "And you know what? I'm tired of talking about it. It was a long time ago, and we're both different people now."

KT sat forward, resting her good arm on the desktop. "You mean that?"

"I do."

"Thank you."

Tory nodded, wondering if it wouldn't be possible for them to someday be friends. She wasn't ready to declare that immediately, but as each day passed, she grew more comfortable with the woman KT had become in the years during their separation. "So, about Pia."

"I don't want to talk about Pia," KT replied evenly. "She wouldn't like it."

"Well. That says a lot all by itself."

KT looked confused. "It does?"

"Even when she's not around, you're thinking about what's important to her."

"Oh," KT moaned quietly. "That sounds bad. Very bad."

Amused, Tory said nothing. She had very rarely seen KT O'Bannon when she wasn't completely on top of her game, *any* game. *Oh, this is going to be fun to watch.*

"Why are you smiling?" KT asked suspiciously.

"No reason," Tory said lightly as she stood. "No reason at all."

"A little advice wouldn't hurt," KT called after her.

"'Fraid not," Tory called back. "Where's the pleasure if you don't suffer first?"

KT tilted back in her chair again and closed her eyes, thinking of Pia's skin beneath her fingers and Pia's sounds of pleasure when she'd touched her. She had no doubt of the exquisite pleasure making love with Pia would bring, nor did the throbbing in the pit of her stomach leave any doubt as to how much she was suffering right that minute. What she wasn't certain about was whether she dared, or even had the right, to seduce Pia away from her dream of forever. Because forever was something that KT no longer believed in.

❖

"And then I thought I'd sell the business, move to Trinidad, and find a tireless young lover."

"That's nice," Pia said absently.

"Of course," Pia's mother mused as she nibbled on a corner of a sandwich, "I haven't talked to your father about the idea yet."

"Talk to Daddy about what?"

"About where you've been for the last ten minutes," Elana noted conversationally.

Pia blushed. "I'm sorry, Mom."

"Is everything all right?"

"Yes. Of course."

Elana sipped her tea and regarded Pia thoughtfully. "Are you seeing someone?"

"No!" Pia sighed. "Sort of. Not exactly. I'm not sure."

"Well, I can see why you're preoccupied, then. Is it Dr. O'Bannon?"

Pia stiffened. "Why do you ask? Are people talking?"

"No, but there aren't that many new faces in this town, other than tourists, and forgive me for saying so, but I've never known you to have a...fling."

"That's what it would probably be with KT. A fling."

"Why do you say that?" Elana asked with interest.

"I don't think she's the type to settle down." Pia tried to keep her tone light, but her eyes were sad.

"People change, Pia. Or maybe they just reach a point in

their lives when they want something different." Elana stood and began to clear the dishes from the table. When Pia rose to help, she waved her down. "Don't worry so much about who she was, and concentrate on who she is with you. That's all that matters."

"Can I ask you something personal?"

Elana laughed. "We haven't been talking about personal things?"

"This is about you and Daddy."

"All right." Elana set the dishes in the sink and leaned against the counter, her large dark eyes compassionate and curious. "Go ahead."

"Did you ever regret not having other lovers?"

"I won't ask why you think I haven't had others," Elana said with a small smile. "I was eighteen when I met him and totally in love from the first moment. There's never been anything that I could have wanted in that regard that I haven't had with him."

"I always sort of got that feeling." Pia rose and walked to the door that led out to the deck. Her parents' home stood on one of the highest points of Pilgrim's Heights, and from there she could see the wetlands, the dunes beyond, and just a sliver of the bay. It was a beautiful view and one of which she never tired. "I never consciously decided to wait—not at first. It just seemed right."

"And now you've changed your mind?" Elana joined Pia in the doorway and slid her arm around her daughter's waist.

"I'm not sure."

"But the very attractive Dr. O'Bannon has you reconsidering."

Pia rested her head against her mother's shoulder. "She makes it hard for me to think at all."

"Ah, well." Elana rubbed Pia's back much the way she had when Pia was small, in comfort and companionship. "What's she like? Other than sexy, that is."

Pia laughed. "Very intense. Aggressive. Focused. And..." She took a long shaky breath. "And she hurts inside, and I want to make that go away."

"How does she make *you* feel?"

"Beautiful. Competent. Interesting. Sexy. Aggravated and annoyed." Pia smiled self-consciously. "Wonderful."

"You haven't brought anyone home for a long time," Elana remarked. "And I can't remember the last time you sounded this excited about anyone. Bring her to dinner tomorrow night so I can get a look at her."

"Mom."

"Don't worry, I'll be subtle."

"All right. I'll ask her."

"There's nothing wrong with changing your mind about the things you want in life." Elana gave Pia a firm hug. "I just want you to be happy with whatever choice you make."

"I know." Pia kissed her mother's cheek. "I'm just not sure if what makes me happy now is going to make me happy down the road."

"That's something we sometimes need to take on faith."

Faith, Pia thought. *Trust and faith.* She remembered the way she had felt with KT in her arms and with KT's hands on her body. More than she'd ever wanted anything, she wanted to believe that those things were possible with the only woman who had ever touched her so deeply, or stirred her so completely.

❖

"Come on, you should dance with me," Allie said.

"Again? We just danced," Bri complained. It wasn't that she minded dancing. She loved dancing with Carre. Except then, it was more about feeling Carre in her arms—the way Carre's body fit just right into the angle of her belly and thighs, the way Carre's breasts molded to hers, and the way Carre's leg fit so naturally between her own. She always got hot when they danced, and more than once, she'd sweet-talked Carre into discreetly easing her discomfort in a dark corner of the bar or the backseat of the car because she couldn't wait until they got home. Carre always seemed to know when she really needed her, and she never said no. *Jeez, I miss her so much.*

"We can't look like we're just sitting here spying on people," Allie pointed out reasonably while settling her hand on the inside of Bri's thigh a few inches above her knee. She caressed the firm muscles beneath the soft leather, stopping a few decorous inches below Bri's crotch. Leaning close, she whispered in Bri's ear, "And we're supposed to look like we're, you know, a couple. So it's good if we dance, since you don't want to make out."

Allie laughed when Bri gave her a cutting look. "Come on. I've been good. This is our third time out together, and I haven't put the moves on you once."

"Maybe this isn't such a good idea," Bri mumbled. Neither her father nor Reese had explicitly said that she and Allie couldn't check out the area bars for signs of drug dealing or some word about the candy-bowl parties, but she had a pretty good idea that her father would be pissed. She thought maybe Reese would be proud of their initiative, and that helped ease her guilt a little bit. What wasn't helping her guilt was the fact that dancing with Allie tended to make her horny. She consoled herself with the thought that that was natural, but it still made her feel a little unfaithful. It also made her a *lot* uncomfortable, and taking care of things herself was getting old pretty fast. "Maybe we should try another place."

"This place is perfect. It's a nice mix of gays and hets with plenty of money. You know these guys are looking for easy marks who are going to drop a bundle without thinking twice about it." She took Bri's hand and tugged her up from the bar stool. "Come on. I like this song."

It was one of those songs that you could dance to either fast or slow, and when they made it to the edge of the crowded dance floor, Allie wrapped her arms around Bri's neck and snuggled into her.

"Mmm, you really are a good dancer," Allie purred.

"Cut it out," Bri hissed.

"What?"

"You know what. The thing you're doing with your hips in my crotch."

Allie laughed. "Jesus. Carre better come home soon, or you're going to burst into flames. I'm just *dancing*."

"That's not dancing, that's practically fucking."

"You wish." Allie laughed again but eased away until there were a few inches between them. "I must be crazy to cut you a break when you're in such a weakened condition."

Bri grinned. "Yeah, yeah."

Allie was about to make another smart remark when someone pressed close to them in the crowd.

"Hey, you girls looking for a little something to spice up the ride?"

Instinctively, Bri stiffened, but Allie just turned slightly in her arms and regarded the preppy-looking guy with studied disinterest. He was dancing with a woman whose face she couldn't see. With casual coolness, she replied, "If you're volunteering, we're *so* not interested."

He laughed, his gaze traveling to Bri's face and darting quickly away. "Do I look crazy? I can see you two don't need any help in that department." He leaned over, his voice low. "I was thinking more along the lines of chemical enhancements."

"We're not in the market," Bri said sharply, moving them away from the interloper. To Allie she said, loud enough for him to hear, "Come on, baby—he could be a narc."

"Hey! No, no!" He followed them persistently. "I'm not trying to *sell* you anything. I just thought you might like some party favors. You know, an exchange of gifts, so to speak."

"Sorry," Allie said regretfully. "We didn't come prepared." She hooked her fingers over Bri's belt and smiled at her seductively, then licked her neck. "But we like to play, don't we, baby."

Bri slid an arm around Allie's shoulders protectively and narrowed her eyes at the man who watched them. "We don't share some things, got it?"

"I'm telling you, that's not what this is about." He slid a business card from his pocket and tucked it into the back pocket of Allie's tight jeans. He very carefully kept his fingers from touching her body. "There's a phone number on there. Call it Wednesday night at nine o'clock and ask for Jimmy."

"And then what?" Allie asked, bumping her hip rhythmically between Bri's legs in a distinctly proprietary move. She directed her question at the stranger but kept her mouth on Bri's throat. She looked as if she was about to swallow her whole.

"Then we'll party."

Chapter Twenty-Two

Pia leaned over and curled her fingers around KT's forearm. "Doing okay?"

KT looked over her shoulder toward the kitchen to be sure that they wouldn't be overheard. "I don't know. Am I?"

Laughing, Pia nodded. "Beautifully."

"Your father hasn't said more than two words to me all night," KT said in a low, anxious voice. She couldn't remember the last time she'd felt so compelled to make a good impression. Maybe when she'd been interviewing for medical school. Actually, thinking back, that hadn't been half bad. This was much worse.

"That's one more word than he usually says before he's finished dinner and read the newspaper." Amused by KT's obvious dismay, Pia shifted closer still and kissed KT lightly just below her ear. "Relax."

"Oh, *that's* really going to help," KT muttered as she turned her head and sought Pia's mouth for another quick kiss. She nearly jumped out of her chair when Pia's mother spoke from behind them.

"I can save this dessert until later, if you'd like," Elana said.

Slowly, holding KT's gaze, Pia drew away. She wondered if her own eyes were as heavy and hot as KT's appeared right then. She certainly felt that way inside, as an indolent, simmering heat stole through her limbs and coiled in her core. "No. We should have it now. I'll take some in to Daddy."

KT wanted to protest about being abandoned but couldn't find an acceptable way to do it. A second later, she found herself alone in the dining room with Elana Torres. "Dinner was wonderful. Thank you very much for inviting me."

"I'm very glad you could come." Elana poured coffee and

inquired with a raised brow if KT would like some. At KT's nod, she filled another cup. "Do you mind me asking what happened to your hand?"

"Pia didn't tell you?"

Elana shook her head. "No, only that she was working with you in therapy."

"Yes. She's the only thing that's keeping me going, I think." KT blinked, stunned at her own admission. "I mean..." She was very aware of Elana watching her carefully with a kind, gentle expression, and it was the complete lack of judgment in her face that allowed KT to voice the thought she hadn't yet fully admitted to herself. "She has a way of making me believe that I can make it back to the way I was before."

"I would wager that she makes you work pretty hard for that, too."

KT laughed. "Oh yeah. She can be pretty tough."

"Where is it that you want to get back to?"

"My life," KT said automatically. Then, with a frown, she amended, "I'd like to be able to operate again."

"I can only imagine how difficult it must be for you not to be able to."

"It is, but I'm so busy at the clinic that most of the time I don't think about it." KT was surprised yet again. Her days were so full that she rarely had time to miss the adrenaline-charged, high-pressure world of the trauma unit. "I can't believe I just said that, but it's really true."

Elana cut a wedge of the deep-dish apple pie she'd made earlier, set it on a plate, and slid it across to KT. "So you'll go back to Boston when your hand is healed?"

"Yes," KT said absently, her mind still turning over the fact that she didn't miss her life in Boston nearly as much now as she had a month ago when she'd arrived. Although her nights were too long and her bed far too lonely, she'd settled into a routine that actually suited her, and she was frighteningly content. She enjoyed her work at the clinic; seeing Tory every day had restored a huge part of her past that she had been forced to deny because it had hurt too much to acknowledge; and, as each day passed, she was more and more drawn to Pia. She counted on seeing her each morning for their therapy session and considered it a victory when Pia agreed to have lunch or dinner with her. She hadn't touched her again since that morning in the bedroom, and that was something she couldn't entirely explain. Because she *wanted* her—in the natural, instinctive way she'd always been drawn to beautiful, passionate women. She loved the way the light shimmered over her ebony hair in the sunlight, and the full, throaty sound of her laughter, and the tender, knowing touch of her hands. Desiring her because of those things made sense to KT, and perhaps if that had been the entire basis for her attraction, she would have pursued Pia with her usual vigor. But it was Pia's unwavering belief in *her,* and what they could accomplish together, that held her captive most of all. Without intending it, she had come to count on that strength and, without realizing it, had allowed Pia's faith to become hers. It was precisely *because* Pia meant so much to her that she hadn't tried again to seduce her.

KT emerged from her musings to find Elana still studying her quietly. "Pia is something of a miracle worker."

"What a nice thing to say." Elana smiled. "I can certainly see why she finds you so charming."

To her utter consternation, KT blushed. Even worse, she was suddenly tongue-tied, aware that she was speaking to the mother of a woman for whom her intentions might be considered less than honorable. "Uh..."

Laughing, Elana rose and squeezed KT gently on the shoulder. "I'm sorry. I promised Pia that I wouldn't put you on the spot, and I'm afraid that I have."

"No, you haven't." KT grinned. "I'm just out of practice. It's been an awfully long time since I've been taken home to meet the family."

"Really? How long?"

"About twenty years." KT stared at Elana, stunned at her reflexive admission. Twenty years ago she'd been practically an innocent. A lifetime had passed since she and another young college student had discovered the wonders of passion in a dorm room late one Saturday night. *Tory. So long ago. So young—both of us.*

"Well, if that's the case, then Pia must be special." Elana spoke softly, with calm conviction.

"She is."

"Good."

"Mrs. Torres—" KT began, suddenly needing to tell her that Pia was more than special and that she would do everything she could to be worthy of Pia's affections.

"Mom," Pia said from the doorway. "You're not interrogating her, are you?"

"Absolutely not." Elana patted Pia's cheek affectionately as she passed on her way into the living room to join her husband. "We were just chatting."

Pia looked after her mother with fond exasperation and then turned back to KT. "I'm sorry. I got caught up talking to my father about some business things."

"No need to apologize. Your mother is terrific."

"I was going to get myself some coffee," Pia said. "How about I refill yours, and we can have it out on the deck?"

"Sounds great."

A minute later they stood leaning side by side against the railing. It was a typical early-fall evening—the air just crisp enough to be invigorating and the ink-black sky overhead littered with thousands of stars. KT was acutely aware of Pia's bare arm lightly touching hers.

"Cold?" KT inquired quietly.

"A little, but I don't mind. It's so beautiful."

"It is." KT put her coffee cup on the railing and slid her arm around Pia's waist. "So are you."

Pia rested her cheek against KT's shoulder. "Thank you for coming tonight."

"I like your parents. I'm sorry I didn't get to meet your brother."

Pia laughed softly. "Believe me, if he'd been here with his brood, it would've been chaos. My mother and her questions were probably enough to subject you to for the first visit."

"She was fine. I think she just wanted to make sure I was worthy of your affections," she said lightly.

"I already told her that you were."

After shifting until Pia was in front of her, KT threaded both arms around her waist and held her loosely against the front of her body. With her cheek caressing the side of Pia's face, she murmured, "I'm really not." She kissed the angle of Pia's jaw. "But I'm hoping you won't notice."

Carefully, Pia cradled KT's left hand in her own, supporting it against her body. "Be careful with this."

The tenderness of the gesture made KT want to weep. Brushing her lips over Pia's ear, she tightened her embrace. "It's okay. I have it on very good authority that it's nearly healed."

Laughing, Pia turned her head and nuzzled KT's neck. "That's *not* what I said. What I said was that you are beyond the danger of delayed rupture and that you could start resistive exercises on Monday. That does not equal 'nearly healed.'"

Suddenly, KT's head was filled with the sight and sound and scent of Pia. Her next conscious thought, striking KT as swiftly and undeniably as anything in her life ever had, made her want to flee. *I'm falling in love with you.* Then she was no longer thinking at all. Her breasts and belly ached where they pressed against Pia's body, longing for more contact, desperately seeking a deeper connection. Her thighs trembled, and she struggled not to push her pelvis into Pia's firm backside. Her stomach was in knots and her heart was a mass of confusion and joy. Wordlessly, helplessly, she buried her face in the curve of Pia's neck.

"What?" Pia asked gently, rubbing her hands up and down KT's forearms as they crossed her midsection. "What is it? KT? You're shaking."

"I love the way you feel."

There was something in the quiet urgency of KT's voice that struck at Pia's heart. Turning carefully within the circle of KT's arms, she wrapped her own arms around KT's neck. "Mmm, I like the way you feel, too."

Then, leaning back against the deck railing, Pia drew KT to her until their bodies joined. With one hand behind KT's neck, Pia guided KT's head down until their lips met, and then she treated herself to a slow, luxurious exploration of KT's warm, clever mouth.

It was the first time they had kissed, *really* kissed, and KT lost track of time. She lost all awareness of the brisk sea air and the distant roar of the surf and the brilliant glitter of the stars overhead. Everything was heat and thunder and a raging peace that stole through her like the breathless calm just before the heavens opened. It was wondrous and wild and far, far too long since she had been touched so deeply. Groaning, she edged her hips between Pia's thighs and pressed hard into her, her good hand smoothing up Pia's side to the undersurface of her breast. When Pia quivered and moaned tremulously, KT froze. It wasn't just that they were standing on Pia's parents' deck, ten feet from the brightly lit kitchen, that brought her up short, but more the fact that she was about to cross a line from which she would never be able to turn back. Until now, the promise of Pia's body had been only a dream. Once she had felt her, flesh on flesh, she would never be able to banish the wanting.

Shuddering, KT pushed away. "Dangerous territory."

"Touching me?" Pia asked, her breath short and ragged, "Or touching me out here?"

KT grinned weakly. "Both."

Pia stroked KT's face, her fingers shaking. "Why did you really stop?"

"I seem to have an embarrassing lack of self-control where you're concerned," KT murmured, taking Pia's hand in hers. "Translated, that means I can't seem to keep my hands off you." She grimaced and lifted her left hand. "Well, one hand anyway."

"Is there some reason that you think you should?" Still leaning back against the railing, Pia swung their joined hands in an easy arc between them.

"You don't understand." In the moonlight, KT's face was a study in sharp planes and angles. Her voice held an edge as well. "I *don't* want to stop, and every time I touch you, it gets harder. One of these times, I'm not going to be able to stop."

"And one of these times, I won't want you to."

"That's not what you said you wanted, Pia." KT closed the distance between them and cupped Pia's chin in her hand, tilting her face up until their mouths nearly touched. "*Forever,* you said."

Pia's vision blurred as she tried to hold KT's fierce gaze. The energy pouring off KT's body slammed into hers and lightning streaked through her depths. "I still want that. I always thought I would have forever with someone I wanted as much as I want you.

Maybe I won't. Right now I don't care."

"*I* care. Damn it," KT muttered as she took Pia's mouth again. *I care.*

The force of KT's kiss stunned Pia almost as much as her subsequent turning and walking away shocked her. "Where are you going?"

"To thank your mother and father," KT said without turning around. "Then I'm going for a walk."

"KT," Pia called after her, but she had already stepped through the doorway into the kitchen and did not turn back.

❖

A few minutes later, Elana found Pia on the deck. She joined her at the rail and together they watched the night.

"Well, your description was certainly accurate," Elana said after a few minutes.

"How so?" Pia asked dully. Once her body had quieted, which had taken far longer than she ever could have imagined, she tried to make sense of KT's departure. She supposed it could simply be for the obvious reasons. KT wouldn't be the first woman who had become angry at or frustrated by Pia's desire to go slowly with the physical aspects of a relationship. *Except I've been doing anything but going slow. She only has to touch me and I'm ready to explode. She has to know that.* Shaking her head in frustration, Pia suddenly remembered her mother's presence. "I'm sorry. What were you saying?"

"I was saying that she's very attractive, and very intense, and somewhere, very wounded."

Pia caught her breath. "She's been hurt."

"Yes, I'd say so."

Suddenly energized, Pia turned to look at her mother. "Do you think that's the reason she's afraid to make love to me?"

Startled, Elana's lips parted but she made no sound. With a small jerk, she cleared her throat and replied, "I'm afraid I don't have an opinion on that. Perhaps she's just being—chivalrous?"

"Yes," Pia said smiling. "That would suit her, wouldn't it?"

"You do realize that any kind of relationship with her would be challenging."

Pia laughed out loud. "Oh, what an understatement." She leaned forward and kissed her mother's cheek. "I had a great time, but I've got to run."

"You'll be careful, won't you?"

"I don't know," Pia called back over her shoulder as she hurried into the house. "But I'll be okay."

❖

"What are you drinking?" Pia asked as she slid onto the bar stool beside KT.

"Ginger ale."

Waving to the bartender, Pia called, "I'll have what she's having." Then she edged closer on her stool until her thigh rested along the length of KT's. "I like that you want to, but I don't need you to protect me."

"Protect you?" KT turned, her expression wary. "From what?"

Pia rested her hand on KT's leg just above her knee. "From you."

"How do you know I'm not trying to protect myself from you?"

"Are you afraid of me?"

Solemnly, KT nodded. "Oh yeah."

"I thought you might be," Pia said contemplatively. "I haven't figured out why yet. Until I do, I can't know if you have any reason to be." She leaned forward and gently kissed KT's mouth. "But I don't think you do."

"It's complicated," KT murmured.

"I know. For me too."

"Are you afraid of *me?*" KT asked softly.

"No," Pia answered immediately.

"Why not?" The question was asked with genuine seriousness.

"Because you've never given me any reason to be."

KT found Pia's hand and threaded her fingers through Pia's. "You tie me up in knots."

Pia smiled. "Good. Want to walk me home?"

"Yeah. I do."

Fifteen minutes later, KT stopped on the sidewalk in front of Pia's porch and kissed her softly. "Good night, Pia. Thank you for tonight."

Gently, Pia brushed her palm over KT's chest before turning to ascend the stairs. "Good night. I'll see you at 9 a.m. for your session."

KT laughed softly and watched until Pia disappeared into the cottage, aware of something she hadn't felt in so long that she almost didn't recognize it. Happiness.

Chapter Twenty-Three

"If there was any place lower than traffic I could bust you down to, I'd do it," Nelson Parker growled as he stood, legs spread and hands fisted on his hips, glaring at his two youngest officers.

Wisely, neither Bri nor Allie commented, but both remained at rigid attention, staring straight ahead. Reese stood behind them and slightly to one side, her hands lightly clasped behind her back.

"The answer is *no*. I've a good mind to put you both on probation for that little stunt you pulled." Nelson glanced at Reese. "Did you know anything about this before this morning?"

"No, sir."

Nelson stared at his daughter. "What the *hell's* gotten into you?"

Bri's posture grew even stiffer, and she answered in a clipped, formal tone of voice. "In my opinion, it was a reasonable investigative—"

"Oh, horseshit. Just what do you know about investigations? And your *sidekick* here," he snapped, giving Allie a blistering glare, "knows even less."

"Actually, sir," Allie replied with a hint of indignation, "it was my idea, not Bri's. And it worked."

"That remains to be seen," Nelson shot back. "And *neither* one of you is going to see anything but the intersection at Commercial and Standish for the next six months." He turned his back and stalked across the room to the window.

Reese turned to the pale young officers. "You two step outside."

"Yes, ma'am," came their very subdued replies.

After waiting until they were alone in the room, Reese said

quietly, "You have to give them credit for devising and executing an excellent plan."

Nelson didn't turn around. "I don't have to give them credit for anything. It was a damn fool idea, and we're just lucky the two of them didn't end up out there in the dunes somewhere like that girl." His shoulders shuddered as he took a breath, apparently searching for control. "Just because these are white-collar criminals with lots of money doesn't mean they aren't dangerous. When you're moving 10 or 20K worth of drugs in an evening, you don't take kindly to having your operation interrupted."

"I agree." Reese crossed the room to join him and looked out the same window at the unremarkable view of the rear corner of the parking lot and a huge sand dune. "We're going to have more dead bodies if we don't shut down this operation. If not here in Provincetown, then in Truro or Wellfleet or Eastham or Chatham. It's only going to get worse."

"Are you saying you support their crazy plan?" Nelson eyed her angrily. "They're goddamned *rookies*." His expression grew even more fierce. "They're kids."

"No sir," Reese said quietly. "They're officers of the law, and they've been well trained, and they're eager to do their jobs. I'm proud of them."

Nelson said nothing, his eyes focused on something far beyond the mundane panorama. Reese wondered if he was remembering the night they had found Bri in the dunes, and she was grateful once again that she had not called him until they had transported his daughter to the clinic. He wouldn't have to live with the memory of finding her battered and bruised and half naked as Reese had.

"Of course," Reese mused, "I don't intend to tell *them* that. I intend to kick their metaphorical asses. Sir."

Despite himself, Nelson laughed. "Good. Coming from you, it will probably mean something."

"So does your opinion, Chief. It means a lot to them." Reese considered her next words carefully. "Especially Bri. What you think of her as her commanding officer's one thing. What you think of her as her father is something far more critical."

"Your father's a general or something, right?"

"Yes sir. He is."

Nelson turned and leaned his shoulder against the window frame, contemplating his second in command. He'd worked with her for years and still felt that he barely knew her. She was calm, controlled, steady under any circumstances. He'd never seen her rattled, not unless it had something to do with Tory. When Tory's pregnancy had gotten difficult, he'd thought that Reese might just crack. But she'd held steady—steadier than he would have. "Can you separate the commander from the father?"

Reese blinked. "No, sir. There's never been any difference for me. But that's not true for Bri."

"Damn." He ran his hand through his thick hair, tugging at it as if the pain would clear his mind. "I don't think about something happening to any of my people when I send them out on the street. I can't think about that and command."

"I understand, Chief."

"I know you do," Nelson agreed readily. He met Reese's eyes, and his were troubled. "But I can't do it with Bri. I can't send her out there knowing the risks."

"That's why you have me," Reese said quietly. "I'll give the order, and I'll see that they're *both* all right."

Silence descended as they held one another's gaze. Finally, Nelson spoke.

"Do it."

❖

"How much danger are they likely to be in?" Tory asked. Reese had come home later than usual from work and had been unusually quiet during dinner. When she'd said that she had to go back to the station house at 8:30 p.m., Tory had asked why. And now she knew. Allie was to call the number on the card at 9 p.m. to receive information about the drug party.

"Danger tonight? Probably none." Reese scrubbed her hands over her face and rolled her shoulders to ease some of her tension. "I expect they'll just be given an address or maybe even another phone number to call closer to the weekend to get the final location of the party. It's the middle of the week, and I doubt there's going to be a big party anywhere tonight."

"And what about when they're at the party?"

"They're both going to be wired. We'll be able to hear everything." Reese shifted on the couch and curved her arm around Tory's shoulders. "These parties aren't known for violence, and all Bri and Allie are going to do is verify that there are drugs in quantity on the premises, make a buy, and give us a reason to go through the door."

"What if someone suspects who they really are?"

Reese shrugged. "There's no reason to think that they do or will. Why would they invite Bri and Allie to the party thinking that they were law enforcement officers? They just look like a couple of kids with too much money in their pockets, which is what got them the invitation in the first place."

"Do you trust them to do this?"

"Yes. They're both bright and resourceful. And when the time comes, they'll follow orders."

Tory looked slightly doubtful. "Are you sure? Sounds like they haven't followed orders very well so far."

"No, they didn't," Reese agreed. "But we've discussed that, and I expect they'll exercise better judgment in the future."

"Ah," Tory said with a ghost of a smile. "Was your 'discussion' followed by them cleaning large areas with toothbrushes?"

Reese looked affronted. "You've been watching too many movies." Then she grinned. "But every cruiser in the department has been washed and hand waxed, right down to the gleaming wheel wells."

"It's not as if I don't know that any of the *ordinary* calls that you take during the day might be dangerous. Most of the time, I try not to think about it." Tory picked up Reese's hand and cradled it in her palm, running her thumb over the long, strong fingers. "But *knowing* that you're going to be involved in something that's potentially dangerous makes it impossible not to worry and imagine the worst."

"Tor," Reese said gently, moving closer on the sofa. "We'll be well prepared. This is likely to be nothing more than a few hours of surveillance, a quick roundup of a few midlevel dealers, and a long night of paperwork."

"I don't imagine that Nelson's very happy about Bri and

Allie's part in it."

"No, but he's behind the operation."

Tory sighed. "I'm sorry. You shouldn't have to defend your professional decisions to me."

"Hey," Reese protested, "you have every right to ask about my work, and if it makes you feel better for me to explain, then I will." She kissed Tory's temple and then her mouth. "I love you."

"I love you, too, Sheriff," Tory murmured, turning to tuck her head beneath Reese's chin and holding her close with an arm wrapped around her waist. "Promise you'll wear your vest."

"I will." Reese kissed Tory's hair and smoothed a hand up and down her back comfortingly. She'd wear the Kevlar, but she wouldn't be the one who'd really need it. And Bri and Allie, who *might*, wouldn't be able to. They'd be lucky to get inside wired up without blowing their cover.

❖

"You nervous?" Allie asked as she sat in the windowless interrogation room in the rear of the sheriff's department.

"No. You?" Bri paced back and forth in front of the chipped and scarred table that was flanked on either side by matching pairs of equally decrepit slat-backed wooden chairs.

"No. Uh-uh."

Bri stopped walking and stared at Allie, who stared back. Silence stretched between them for thirty seconds before Allie giggled.

"OK. Maybe a little," Allie admitted.

A smile twitched at the corner of Bri's mouth and then she laughed quickly. "Me too."

"But I'm psyched, too," Allie added quickly.

"Yeah. I know. It's weird, huh?"

"I never expected to be doing this." Allie drummed her nails on the top of the table, her only outward sign of nervousness. "I figured, you know, we'd be doing mostly community service and keeping the peace. But not—really catching criminals."

"I don't know," Bri mused. "My dad has arrested a few people who were really...bad. Someone held up the Cumberland Farms market when I was about ten. And then there was the guy burning down buildings for insurance. And there's always, you know, the domestic stuff. That can get pretty crazy when you have to get in the middle."

Allie nodded solemnly. "I know, and I'm not putting down our job. I love doing what we do. But..." Her eyes sparkled. "This is undercover. This is the real deal. Man."

Before Bri could reply, the door opened and Reese walked in with a small cardboard box, which she put in the middle of the table. She looked from Allie to Bri. "Who's first?"

When Allie quickly stood up, Reese motioned for her to come around the table. Then she reached into the box and extracted a wire so thin it was nearly invisible from several feet away. At the end was a round disk slightly smaller than a watch battery. She held it up. "This is the microphone. I want you both to see how and where it's attached in case there's a technical problem and one of you has to switch mics or try to fix this one." Glancing at Allie, she said, "It'll be easier if you take off your top."

Without a second's hesitation, Allie reached for the hem of the sleeveless, low-cut silk tee and pulled it off over her head. She wore nothing beneath it. Bri, who had come to stand beside Reese, turned bright red. Reese's expression never changed.

"I can't wear a bra with one of these," Allie explained nonchalantly. "The straps just ruin the look."

Reese dabbed a tiny amount of skin adhesive just below Allie's right breast and slightly off center toward the midline. After waiting twenty seconds, she carefully pressed the tiny microphone to the spot. Her movements were precise and certain, and she managed the maneuver without touching Allie's body anywhere. When she gave the thin wire a brief tug, the microphone remained securely in place.

"Good." Then Reese applied the adhesive in two or three more spots leading down Allie's abdomen and around her flank to the middle of her back, fixing the wire in place. The transmitter was a box about the size of a deck of playing cards.

"I can't wear that back there," Allie said matter-of-factly. "My jeans are cut low and if my blouse rides up, that's going to show."

"It's the most secure spot."

Bri shook her head. “That might work on a guy, but not a girl. Not at a party. Someone’s going to put their hand there. It’s just natural.”

Reese frowned and surveyed Allie’s outfit. Her jeans were skintight, and if they were any lower, they would be illegal. “You’re going to have to change into something a lot looser.”

“I can’t. It’s not my style, and if whoever was watching us in the bar is there, they’re going to know something’s up if I walk in wearing a baggy T-shirt and cargo pants.” Allie looked from Reese to Bri. “Just wire Bri. We’ll be together, so I won’t need one.”

“Not possible,” Reese said shortly. “If you get separated, I won’t be able to monitor you.”

“I’m not letting her out of my sight,” Bri said immediately.

“You don’t know what’s going to happen once you get inside,” Reese insisted. “You both go wired or you don’t go at all.”

Allie shrugged. “OK. Put it on my back, but higher up. Not where you’d put your hand if we were dancing. That’s—”

“I think I can figure that out,” Reese said dryly.

Bri glared at Allie, who smiled sweetly back.

❖

At shortly before 10 p.m. on Saturday night, Reese followed Bri’s motorcycle along Route 6 East into Wellfleet. Nelson sat silently beside her in the Blazer, his hands pressed flat to his thighs, his eyes riveted to the two figures on the bike as they were intermittently illuminated by the headlights of the SUV.

“You sure we’ll be able to hear them the whole time?”

Reese answered his question exactly the same way she had the previous four times he’d asked. “Yes. These are powerful transmitters, and we should be able to get very close. I imagine there are going to be plenty of cars around, and one more won’t matter.”

“If the locale they gave Allie over the phone is legit, we’re going to be in a sparsely populated area very near the ocean side of the Cape. There might not be much in the way of cover. It could be one of those big solitary beach houses, which makes sense, if there’s a lot of money involved.”

"We'll be able to hear them," Reese repeated with certainty. Allie had been given directions but no specific location. *Just follow the crowd, honey,* the anonymous male had said. So Nelson and Reese hadn't been able to do any advance planning beyond placing cruisers in the general area to move in once the target was identified.

"I don't know why I ever thought I could stand having her on the job," Nelson mumbled as he chewed a Tums.

"How about because she's a natural at it, and you're proud of her."

"Hmmph."

"Here we go," Reese said quietly as the big Harley in front of them turned off 6 behind several other vehicles onto a much smaller road like so many that wound through the dunes along the coastline. Nelson turned on the receiver and adjusted the volume. All they could hear was the roar of the engine. Ten minutes later, Bri banked into a driveway that presumably led to a house that was hidden from view by a thick stand of trees.

"Damn it. We're not going to be able to follow them up there," Nelson said in frustration.

Reese drove another fifty yards until she could pull off the road and nosed the SUV into the trees so that it was less visible to casual inspection. "Looks like we're going for a walk."

Chapter Twenty-Four

"I could do this a lot better if I took the wrist immobilizer off," KT grumbled.

Pia tightened her arms around KT's neck and settled more closely into the curves of her body. "You're doing just fine."

KT nestled her face into the lush thickness of Pia's hair and closed her eyes, reveling in the sensation of Pia pressing everywhere against her—Pia's soft, warm skin brushing over the curve of her neck, Pia's breasts caressing teasingly against her achingly sensitive nipples, Pia's abdomen and thighs cleaved to hers. Everywhere so good, everywhere so breathlessly exciting. She rubbed the fingertips of her right hand in the hollow at the base of Pia's spine, gently echoing the circular motion with her hips. When Pia sighed into her neck, a soft low moan of pleasure, KT's heart lurched and her blood raced toward the boiling point.

"God," Pia murmured, "you're good at this."

"You should see what I can do with two hands."

Pia leaned back in the circle of KT's arms and gave her a heavy-lidded, hazy-eyed look, her full lips parted into a lazy smile. "Considering that we're in a room with a hundred other people, it's probably better that you only have the use of one."

KT was dimly aware of the other dancers and of the low, heavy beat of music keeping time with the pulse of blood deep in her belly, but her senses registered only the heat of Pia's body and the fine mist of excitement on her skin and the hunger in her eyes. "You're all I can see, all I can feel." She brushed her lips over Pia's forehead, then her lips. "You're all I think about."

"I like that," Pia whispered. She combed her fingers through KT's hair and caressed the back of her neck with one hand while bringing the other to rest between them in the center of KT's chest.

As they swayed to the music, she danced her fingers over the inner curves of KT's breasts. "I like that a lot."

"You're driving me out of my mind, Pia." KT's voice was a desperate groan. Her thighs trembled with the effort it took not to pump her hips in response to the insistent pulsations between her legs.

Marveling at the hard point of KT's nipple against her palm, Pia skimmed her lips along the curve of KT's ear. "I like *that* a lot, too." It was true. So true. Never before had she taken such delight in another woman's desire for her. Never before had she felt the exquisite pleasure of being wanted with a force that equaled her own. She'd had relationships with women she'd cared for, women whom she'd admired and respected and liked, women who had excited her with their kisses and their caresses, but never—*never*—a woman who made her yearn so desperately to give of herself and to take from *her* until she was empty and completely filled.

"Baby, stop," KT implored when Pia's fingers closed around her nipple and gently squeezed. She couldn't breathe. She could barely see. "I can't take it."

Pia wanted more, not less. She wanted to feel KT quiver again the way she just had. She wanted to hear that swift intake of breath and the barely stifled moan. She wanted KT to touch her and quench the fires that threatened to consume her. She wanted. Oh, how she *wanted.* "We can either go outside on the deck and cool off, or we can go back to my house and do what we both want."

Summoning every ounce of resolve left to her, KT found Pia's hand, turned, and led her through the crowd toward the rear of the dance floor and the deck beyond.

❖

"You ready to party, babe?" Bri inquired as she and Allie walked hand in hand up the sidewalk to the front door of a multistory, rambling wood-framed home that stood on a tree-studded knoll above the beach and the Atlantic Ocean beyond. She wondered briefly as she spoke the prearranged words to signal that they were about to enter the house if Reese or her father could actually hear her. Then she put the question from her mind. They were out there. They said they would be.

"Can't wait for the fun to begin," Allie replied, squeezing Bri's fingers as much for her own reassurance as Bri's.

At Bri's knock, a sandy-haired man in his thirties opened the door and greeted them with a wide smile. He stood with his body blocking the entrance, one arm extended along the door, sweeping his gaze over them with practiced calculation.

"Hey, girls! Glad you could make it. Tom tell you about our little gathering?"

Allie wrapped her arm around Bri's waist and gave him a disdainful look. "Nuh-uh. Jimmy. And *he* said that Karl would take care of us."

"You got that right, honey," their host responded, apparently satisfied with the information since he pushed the door all the way open. "I'm Karl. Come on in."

❖

Tory leaned back into the corner of the couch in Jean and Kate's living room, glancing at the baby monitor by her elbow as she stretched her legs out to the hassock at her feet. She fidgeted, unable to get comfortable and irritated by a nagging headache that just wouldn't go away. When she heard Jean's voice coming through the monitor, singing softly to Regina in the other room, her throat suddenly felt tight. She glanced at Kate, who was smiling tenderly. "I don't know how I'd manage without the two of you looking after Regina. I can't imagine how women without family to help out survive."

"Believe me," Kate said, "we couldn't be happier doing it." A hint of sadness tinged her eyes. "Jean and I would've loved to have had children together, but it just wasn't to be."

"Well, I'm eternally grateful. Dinner tonight was great, too."

Kate propped her feet on a matching footstool and studied Tory intently. "Reese is out on some kind of operation, isn't she?"

Tory nodded. "Yes. How did you know?"

"Because you were very quiet during dinner, and Reese left immediately after, and you haven't been able to settle since then even though you're clearly exhausted."

"I can't rest when she's out doing something like this."

"The baby is asleep and is likely to be for a good part of the night. Why don't you at least close your eyes and rest."

"I'm not sure if it's having Regina and all the responsibility that goes along with that or if it's just that the longer we're together, the more I realize how much I need Reese, but it seems to be getting harder for me to tolerate her job." Tory grimaced. "Reese would hate that if she knew it."

"You know she's very, very good and very, very careful. She wouldn't do anything that would hurt you or Regina."

Not if she could help it. The words hung in the air as Tory nodded, suddenly very tired. "Do you know that her father met her in Boston a few weeks ago?"

Kate gave a startled gasp. "No. She didn't tell me. Is everything all right?"

"For the time being, I think so." Tory hesitated, but she'd been keeping the secret too long, and she couldn't bear to continue to carry it alone. "He hinted that a major military action was coming and that Reese might be activated."

"Every time I hear about the escalation of violence somewhere in the world, I think about Reese going," Kate confided. "But then, I was married to a marine and was always prepared for him to be gone. Before Reese was born, he did two tours in Vietnam."

"Was that hard?" Tory asked quietly.

"Yes," Kate answered truthfully, holding Tory's gaze. "It was very hard. But as much as I wanted him to come home, I was proud, too. It was a very tumultuous period in my life."

"I can't get used to the idea," Tory admitted. "I'm used to her going away for her reserve weekends and the two weeks during the summer, but I never really thought about her serving in a war zone. God, I just can't imagine it."

"There's no reason you should be able to," Kate said kindly.

"I don't want her to go." Tory said evenly as she met Kate's eyes without flinching. "I want her here with me and Regina. Where she belongs."

"Did you tell her that?" Kate asked calmly.

"Yes." Tory drew a long breath. "Then I told her that if the time ever comes, I want her to do what she feels she needs to do."

"That was a gift. She would have needed to hear that from you."

Tory laughed without humor. "I wish I'd screamed and hollered and told her absolutely no way was she going. That she was to march right down to the Marine Reserve office and resign immediately."

"Why didn't you?"

"Because of who she is. Because I love her so much." Tory's voice broke, and she looked away. When she looked back at Kate, her eyes glistened with tears. "If it happens, do you think she'll go?"

Kate's expression softened. "Yes."

"So do I," Tory whispered.

❖

"How's the reception?" Nelson whispered, puffing only slightly from their rapid traverse over the hilly ground to a point where they could see the front door.

"Should be excellent." Reese surveyed their surroundings. "Depending on the terrain, we're good for up to two thousand feet with the SR-697."

The SR-697 was a portable, multichannel audio body-wire receiver designed for the field. With it, Reese could monitor several audio bands and listen to both Bri's and Allie's conversations. Depending on ambient noise levels in the house, she could also pick up a fair amount of background chatter as well. The device had recording capabilities, and the tape was time and date stamped. Nelson had gotten a special warrant allowing them to employ wireless surveillance, so anything recorded would be admissible in court. "This location looks good. We have a sightline to the door and no major obstacle interference." She toggled the frequency indicator, an expression of intense concentration on her face. "Got them both."

"I'll radio Wellfleet and key them to our location." Nelson had organized the joint operation with the Wellfleet sheriff's department, insisting that he and Reese take the lead and Wellfleet back up with cruisers around the perimeter, waiting to move in if a bust went down. Because it was Nelson's people undercover, Wellfleet had readily agreed.

"They're not going to be able to set up on this road," Reese observed, listening to Bri and Allie introduce themselves to what sounded like a group of college students who had come over to the Cape from Boston for the weekend. "Maybe a parallel road where they can access the rear of the house to cover that exit. Failing that, at the junction with the main road. The last thing we want is for someone on the way to the party to see them."

Nelson merely grunted. They both knew that the more people involved in an undercover surveillance operation, the more likely the chance of exposure. Although they regarded the risk of violence to be relatively low, that was far from certain. And Allie and Bri were unarmed.

"How long do you figure to get to them from here?"

"Thirty seconds."

He clenched his jaw and said nothing. Thirty seconds was a lifetime.

❖

Pia leaned back against KT and lifted her face into the breeze. The rear deck of the Pied stood directly on the beach overlooking Provincetown Harbor. At high tide, the water rose under the deck. The tide was out now, and reflections from the running lights of the many sailboats moored in the shelter of the breakwater shimmered and danced off the dark surface of the water, blending with the paler glow of the moonlight bathing the sea. Thousands of times she'd witnessed the eerie beauty of the ocean as it slumbered beneath the stars, but she had never tired of it. Tonight, with the warmth of KT's body surrounding her, she felt the rhythm of the tide flowing in her blood and the steady cadence of the waves pulsing in her depths. That wonder was echoed by the sweet harmony of passion and peace that settled in the very heart of her.

"I've fallen in love with you," Pia said simply.

"Pia," KT moaned, her mouth against Pia's temple.

Pia intertwined her fingers with KT's and guided KT's palm to the undersurface of her own breast, where she pressed it gently over her rapidly beating heart. "You are not required to answer. I just wanted to...say it."

"You know I'm a decade older than you are?" KT murmured.

"Is there some significance to that?" Pia asked quietly, folding her arms over KT's, holding KT even as KT held her.

"I've made a lot of mistakes in the last ten—no—make it twenty years."

"I don't want to minimize your past," Pia replied, leaning her head back against KT's shoulder, "but your past is not about me. This moment, last weekend with my parents, tomorrow—those are about me. About us."

"I'm trying to tell you that I'm a lousy risk, Pia. And you're—God, you're—"

"What?" Pia turned around and put both hands on KT's shoulders, looking intently into her eyes. "I'm *what,* KT? Incapable of making a mistake? Incapable of being selfish or stubborn or foolish? Do you think because no one ever made me want to give everything, to *feel* everything..." She pressed close to KT, her lips skimming KT's mouth, and when she spoke again her voice was low, husky with desire. "Just because no one has ever made me want their hands all over me the way I want yours, that I'm special?"

"I can't think when you're this close," KT groaned. "When you say these things, all I want is to be inside you. Pia, God, I want you so much."

"Feel me," Pia whispered, her arms tightening around KT's neck again, her lips hungry on KT's mouth.

KT was lost. She had no defense against Pia's words repeating in her mind. *I've fallen in love with you.* Pia's voice. Her own heart, echoing. With supreme effort, she broke the kiss. "Let's go."

"Yes. Yes."

❖

"Your girlfriend's really hot," a small, tight-bodied Asian woman in skintight black Lycra slacks and a spandex top nicely displaying her small, high breasts commented to Allie. Bri had just left to investigate the house under the guise of searching for fresh beers.

"Yeah." Allie sipped her beer and regarded the woman nonchalantly. "This is a kinda weird deal, you know? The secret code phone calls and stuff." She laughed and sipped her beer again. "After all, it's just a party."

"Well, you know, there's a lot of stuff hanging around and you don't want just *anybody* crashing." The tone of the woman's voice indicated that she considered the party to be an elite gathering.

Allie shrugged. "I suppose—although I haven't seen anything too special in the way of *party favors* yet."

"Is this your first time?"

"Hardly," Allie snorted. Then she gave the other woman a knowing smile. "But I haven't been around *this* circuit before. Just down by Providence. Do they have quality stuff?"

To Allie's surprise, the smaller woman edged closer and snaked her arm around Allie's waist before rubbing her cheek against Allie's arm, almost like a cat twining itself around its human. "Mmm, usually." She nuzzled her face against the curve of Allie's breast. "I know who to ask. We can party, the three of us."

"I want to know what I'm getting," Allie said softly, stroking her fingers up and down the woman's bare arm and shifting so that the woman's hand settled on her butt. She didn't want her to feel the transmitter. "I don't want to get numbed out, you know? Especially if we're going to play."

"Play at what?" Bri asked as she edged up to them in the crowd. She caught the quick flicker of caution in Allie's eyes and leaned in to kiss Allie on the mouth. Then she put her arm around Allie's waist between the strange woman's hand and the transmitter. "Who's your friend, babe?"

"Hey, baby," Allie purred to Bri, still caressing the other woman. "This is..." She turned her head and brushed her lips over the Asian woman's ear. "What's your name, beautiful?"

"Tamara." Tamara extended an arm and trailed her fingers down the center of Bri's chest and abdomen until she reached Bri's belt. Then she curled her fingers inside. "Hi."

Bri nodded warily. "We don't usually do threesomes."

"I can just watch," Tamara replied, rocking her pelvis against Allie's thigh. "Or I can help you do her—or you can both do me.

Whatever works."

"Tamara says she can get us what we came for, baby," Allie said soothingly. She kissed Bri's neck, then along her jaw. When she saw Tamara's hand drift lower down Bri's fly, she caught Tamara's wrist. "Ask permission first, honey. That's private property."

"Sorry," Tamara whispered, looking anything but. "You want me to score us something? I can get us E or coke—just about anything you want."

Allie looked at Bri. "Come on, baby. Let's play."

Bri hesitated, then finally nodded. "Let's all go get it together. If this is gonna be a night to remember, I wanna be sure I do."

❖

"What?" Nelson whispered urgently when he saw Reese stiffen and frown.

"They're about to score the drugs," Reese muttered. She was a little uneasy about the third party being involved. Allie and Bri had been particularly careful in not suggesting anything that could be considered entrapment, more careful than she would have expected them to be in light of their inexperience. Nevertheless, the sexual propositions might come back to haunt them if they weren't careful. "They've hooked up with another woman who's going to make the connection for them. I don't think she's a dealer. She's just interested in...them."

"Them?" Nelson asked, confused. When Reese said nothing, he bunched his shoulders and muttered, "Jesus Christ."

"We're going to have to be very careful with a civilian in the middle of this if we make the arrests inside."

"What about—"

Reese held up a hand, interrupting him, the fingers of her left hand pressing the earpiece as if to make the transmission clearer. "Call Wellfleet. It's going down any minute."

Chapter Twenty-Five

KT pulled Pia down beside her on the wooden love seat that swung gently on Pia's front porch, suspended from ceiling hooks by thick braided ropes. "Let's talk for a second."

"We've been talking every day, sometimes *several* times a day," Pia said, her voice silky and low as she pulled her legs up onto the cushions and curled against KT's side, "for almost a month." She wrapped an arm around KT's waist and nestled her head against KT's shoulder. "And as much as I enjoy your mind, I'm more interested in your body right now."

Despite her persistent unease, KT laughed, rubbing her cheek against Pia's hair. "How is it that two weeks ago you told me quite emphatically that you weren't going to sleep with me?"

"Two weeks ago you needed every ounce of your strength to get the drugs out of your system and your feet back under you," Pia said softly. "You needed me to be your friend then, and I...I wasn't ready to want you this much."

"And what about now?"

"We're still friends, aren't we?"

"Yes," KT murmured, realizing it was true and knowing that the last time she'd felt that way with a lover, it had been Tory. Thinking of Tory reminded her forcefully of just how bad she was at relationships. Still, Pia's nearness invoked a familiar stirring in her body—the growing knot of tension deep down inside her that always came when she held a woman, smelled a woman, imagined the glide of smooth skin under her fingertips. It was a hunger, a longing so profound—to immerse herself in the mystery and wonder of all that was female—that she'd often followed her desire without thinking. Now, when a beautiful woman—a woman she wanted as fiercely as any she'd ever known—told her not once, but repeatedly, that she wanted her, she did nothing. She held herself back while her body screamed for release, aching and close to breaking. And still, she waited. "Yes, we're friends. That's why I haven't touched you, when I want to so much."

Pia shifted until she could look up into KT's face, shadowed in the moonlight. "Let me get this straight. You *don't* want to go to bed with me because you *like* me."

No, because I love you. KT caressed Pia's side, sliding her palm up and down the curve of her flank and over her hip. "You've waited all this time, Pia. Waited for something...*someone*...special." She drew a deep breath. "I'm not special."

"Tell me why you think you aren't." Pia rested her hand in the center of KT's chest and slowly circled her fingertips, loving the subtle tensing of KT's body when she touched her. She'd been aware of other women's excitement before, of their need, but she'd never thrilled to the knowledge that she had created it. Not like she did with this woman. KT's desire made her feel powerful in a way she had never experienced, powerful and humbled at the same time. It was all she could do to refrain from sliding her leg over KT's, from cupping KT's small, firm breast, merely millimeters away from her burning palm. "Tell me what I'm missing, because I think you're very special."

"I've spent most of my life meeting someone else's expectations and never even questioning if those goals were my own. In the process, I was so focused on satisfying my own needs that I destroyed the most important thing in my life." KT leaned her head against the wooden seat back and stared at the darkness overhead. "I didn't even know it at the time, that's how out of touch I was with everything that should've mattered."

Pia didn't answer; she merely held KT tightly.

"Since then—well, let's say I've been selfish when it comes to relationships."

"Did you make promises you didn't keep?"

KT shook her head.

"Did you lie about your feelings?"

"No," KT rasped.

"Were you only concerned with your own pleasure?"

KT laughed wryly. "I don't know. I don't think so."

Pia kissed KT softly, then drew back until she could look into her eyes. "Then I don't think you've been selfish. And I'm not asking for promises."

KT brushed her fingers through Pia's hair and closed her fist gently around the heavy richness of it. "You deserve promises."

"Would you be so worried if I hadn't told you that I've never slept with anyone before?"

"I don't know," KT answered truthfully. "But you did tell me. And one thing I know for sure. I never want you to regret anything that happens between us."

"You have to trust me when I say that I won't." Pia shifted until she straddled KT's thighs, her knees on the cushions on either side. She framed KT's face in her hands and lowered her head until their mouths met. When KT's hand came to her waist, then under her blouse to tremble against her flesh, Pia murmured, "Please."

❖

"Well, you three look like you're ready for some real partying," Karl said with forced friendliness as he surveyed Allie, Bri, and Tamara.

"We were ready when we walked in the door," Allie replied in a tone halfway between sarcastic and seductive. Tamara's hand was still firmly attached to her hip, and she was afraid that any second the other woman was going to take a bite out of something vital. "And so far, all we've seen is beer. Pissy beer, actually."

"Looks like you've scored a little more than that," Karl smirked, his eyes on Tamara.

"*That* isn't what we came for," Bri growled, releasing her grip on Allie's hand in case she suddenly needed both of hers.

"Come on, Karl," Tamara crooned. "Why are you being such a prick?" She insinuated her other arm around Allie's waist and ran her tongue over the point of Allie's nipple, leaving a small wet spot on the material before smiling up at the big man. "Be nice to my friends."

Karl's eyes narrowed for a fraction of a second, and then he smiled again. "Well, we like to welcome newcomers." His eyes flickered from Bri to Allie and then back to Bri. "Tonight everything is on sale."

"So show me the merchandise," Bri said steadily, her eyes on his.

❖

"That's it," Reese said abruptly, removing her earpiece. "Put Wellfleet on the rear door now and another team behind us. You and I will go first through the front as planned."

As she spoke, Nelson translated the orders into his radio, and then they were both moving through the low brush and taller scrub pines, ducking as much to avoid the swinging branches as to keep from being seen from the house.

"Maybe we should've brought more people," Nelson panted, slightly winded.

"We've got the perimeter shut down," Reese reminded him. "No one is going anywhere and we've got six going in. Two inside. We're covered."

Yeah. And the two inside are unarmed rookies. Nelson saved his breath and tried to ignore the sick knot of tension that had centered in his chest.

❖

Inside the house, Bri closed her hand around the six tabs of ecstasy and extended the wad of folded bills she'd pulled from her jeans. "Next time we're going to want more."

"Any time. Just call." Karl grinned. "You're on my VIP list now."

"Come on, stud," Tamara urged, tugging on Bri's belt. "We've got everything we need. Let's go find someplace to do it."

Bri and Allie followed Tamara down the hall. With an arm still cinched possessively around Allie's waist, Tamara peered into several rooms until she found an empty one. She stepped across the threshold of the darkened space and looked around. "Mmm, nice big bed." She tugged on Allie's hand. "Tell your girlfriend to pass out the goodies. I'm so, so ready."

Bri said loud enough for Tamara to hear, "I'm going downstairs for a beer, babe. Why don't you two get ready for me."

"Uh-uh, lover," Allie said, dropping Tamara's hand and grabbing Bri's. "I'm not letting you go off by yourself. Not now." She smiled and bumped her hip against Tamara's thigh. "This one's already got me awfully hot, and I don't want you getting distracted when you should be taking care of me."

Bri looked put out. "Then come with me if you want to. But let's go."

Allie kissed Tamara's cheek and stroked her as she might a favored pet. "We'll be right back, beautiful. You can even start without us, but don't you dare come."

"Hurry," Tamara demanded, one hand absently toying with her nipple.

"Oh, we will," Allie replied as she turned away with Bri. In a voice too low to be overheard, she said, "You take the back, I'll get the front?"

"Yeah. Be careful."

Allie grinned. "See you in a few minutes."

❖

"Pia," KT gasped, "we're going to break this swing." Somehow, they'd managed to end up lying down on the narrow porch swing with KT beneath Pia, one leg still on the floor and Pia between her spread thighs. Pia's hand had edged down beneath the waistband of her trousers, and, minutes before, her own hand had found Pia's breast. "If one of us doesn't break something first."

Pia threw her head back and braced herself on the swing with a hand on either side of KT's shoulders. She thrust her pelvis gently between KT's legs, reveling in the pressure building in her stomach and the harsh, ragged sound of KT's breathing. "Are you ready to stop resisting me now?"

"Baby," KT groaned, "if I don't get my mouth on you soon, I'm going to die."

It was Pia's turn to gasp as KT's words—*the image*—struck like lightning searing through her nerve endings. She moaned as her clitoris quivered in anticipation. "Oh God." She pushed away to stand on unsteady legs and held out her hand. "Please come upstairs."

Wordlessly KT followed, knowing only that she couldn't go a moment longer without being as close to Pia as she could possibly get.

❖

There were a few partyers in the kitchen when Bri arrived. She walked straight to the back door that led out to a fenced patio-pool area and unlocked it. She stiffened infinitesimally when a hand closed on her shoulder.

"Going for a swim?" Karl asked congenially.

"Thought I'd check it out in case the girls need to cool off later," Bri replied, turning to him with a grin. "I expect they're going to get awfully hot."

He snorted. "Too bad I'm working. I could help you out with them."

"I don't need any help." As she spoke, Bri moved back into the kitchen, hoping to draw his attention away from the rear of the property. She expected to see officers approaching any second since she knew that Reese was only waiting for money to exchange hands to make the bust solid. She also knew that Reese wanted her and Allie to stay clear of the arrests if possible, rather than identifying themselves as police officers. Their only function at this point was to facilitate entry and help calm the partygoers if needed.

"Sometimes," Karl said in a flat, hard tone as he moved closer to Bri, "you don't know what you need until you've had a taste."

Bri stood her ground, even though Karl's crotch brushed hers. "Karl, don't be an asshole."

"Bet you thought I'd go for the *girls*," he said softly, placing his index fingertip gently between the subtle swell of Bri's breasts and pressing her T-shirt against her breastbone in tiny circles. "But I don't. You know what I like, *stud?*"

Out of the corner of her eye, Bri caught a flicker of movement as the shadows in the yard coalesced into human form. At the same time, she heard surprised shouts from the front of the house.

Karl jerked, swiveling his head around. "What the hell?"

Before he could move, the back door burst open and two

officers came through, shouting, "Sheriff's Department. Everybody down. Everybody down."

"Fuck this." Karl never hesitated as he reached past Bri and lifted a carving knife from the counter. At the same time, he threw an arm across Bri's chest and dragged her back against him, his elbow crooked beneath her chin, the blade swiftly at her throat. "I'm going out the back door, and she's coming."

There were several indelible rules that Bri had learned in the academy. Never give up your weapon. Never become a hostage. Had she never learned those rules, her reaction would have been the same. She had been taken by force once, and it would never happen again. No one was ever taking her against her will again, no matter the price.

Even as she clamped her fingers around his knife hand, she felt the first bite of the steel.

❖

KT stood in the soft glow of the bedside lamp and lifted her left hand. "I want to take this off tonight, when we're together." Anticipating Pia's protest, she hurriedly added, "I'll be careful. I promise." She held Pia's eyes. "I want to come to you whole. I *need* to."

"Oh," Pia whispered, resting her fingertips against KT's cheek where the barest hint of a scar remained. "You *are.*" Closing the fingers of her free hand around KT's wrist, she lifted the damaged hand and kissed a spot that she knew KT could feel. "This doesn't make you less. This makes you hurt." She stroked KT's face. "Hurts can be healed."

"You're healing me," KT whispered.

"No." Pia moved closer until their bodies touched. "You're doing that all by yourself." She kissed KT, a gentle kiss of soft lips caressing soft lips. "And that's one of the reasons I fell in love with you. That stubborn persistence of yours."

Feeling anything but strong, KT wrapped her arms around Pia and returned the kiss. She covered Pia's mouth harder than she had intended, entered deeper than she had meant, but she had waited so long to be touched inside, waited without even knowing she was waiting. Now she felt open and exposed, and only Pia's tender strength could soothe the raw edges of her soul. Pia's arms were around her neck again, and they were both moaning.

Pia got a hand between them and pushed KT away a fraction. "The bed. I have to lie down with nothing between us and feel your skin on mine, everywhere. I've thought about it, I've dreamed about it." She took a step back and tugged on the tail of KT's shirt, urging her to follow. "I've done other things, imagining your hands."

"Oh, Christ," KT groaned, fumbling with the buckle on her belt. Her head was reeling, her heart nearly bursting. She'd just managed to work the button free on her fly when another sensation penetrated her consciousness. A faint throbbing at her hip. For a moment she didn't recognize it, although until a couple of months ago it had been an everyday occurrence. She looked down in disbelief. "Oh, no."

Pia followed her gaze and then laughed shakily. "Please tell me this is not happening."

"It is," KT said grimly as she pulled the beeper from her belt and blinked, trying to clear her vision to read the numbers. "It's the service, and they never call unless it's an emergency." Desolate, she looked at Pia. "I have to answer."

Pia sank down to the side of the bed, gripping the mattress on either side of her body to steady herself. She was shaking all over. "Of course you do."

❖

"Tory," Jean said softly. "Tory, honey."

"Hmm?" Tory murmured, rolling over onto her side. She opened her eyes, disoriented, and struggled to focus on Jean's face. "I fell asleep, didn't I." She sat up and ran a hand through her hair. Still fuzzy, she looked around the dimly lit room. "What time is it?"

"About two," Jean said apologetically. "Kate and Regina are both asleep, and I wouldn't have bothered you, except..." She held up a small rectangular object. "This was on the kitchen table with your keys, and it was going off."

Instantly awake, Tory stared at her beeper, a cold hand closing around her heart. It could only mean one thing. With a steady hand, she reached for it. "Thank you."

She read the number as she walked through the house to get her cell phone. It wasn't the service, and she felt a faint stirring of hope. *Just a wrong number.* Then she realized where she'd seen the number before. KT's cell phone.

Sick dread flooded her senses as she calmly punched in the numbers. On the second ring, Tory heard the clipped response that took her back fifteen years.

"O'Bannon."

"KT, it's Tory."

"The service called," KT said immediately. "Wellfleet paramedics are bringing someone to the clinic because we're closer than the hospital. Knife wound."

"Someone?" Tory repeated. Her heart trembled when she sensed hesitation from a woman who never hesitated over anything.

"KT?"

"It's a police officer, that's all I know."

"I'll be right there." Matter-of-fact, controlled, professional. Inside, Tory had already begun to bleed.

"I'll meet you there."

Grateful for the absence of meaningless platitudes, Tory nodded, then realized that KT couldn't see her. "Yes. Good. Thanks."

As she grabbed her keys and rushed for the door, she realized just how glad she was that KT would be there. If it was Reese they were bringing in, she wouldn't be able to handle it. Not again. If it was any of the others, she just *might* be able to manage. But every time, it took more from her, and she wondered just how much was left.

Chapter Twenty-Six

Tory drove with her eyes fixed on the dark road ahead, her hands clenched on the wheel, her gaze narrowed to the flickering columns of light cast into the shadows by her headlights. Her mind was blank. She forced it to remain empty, not to contemplate what she would do, how she would hold the terror at bay, if it were Reese.

"Set up the IVs, prepare the instrument tray, draw up the Valium, morphine, and lidocaine..." She spoke aloud to dispel the thundering quiet, and in the process made the ingrained transition to professional mode. By the time she pulled into the parking lot and saw a single car parked close to the front stairs, she had obtained the practiced calm required of her to deal with an emergency.

The door to the clinic opened as Tory stepped from her vehicle and Pia looked out.

"Hi," Pia said quietly. "KT's in the back. She thought I might be able to help. Is that okay with you?"

Tory didn't hesitate. "Sure. You can stand in for Sally."

As she followed Pia down the hall, Tory gave only a moment's thought to why KT and Pia had arrived together in the middle of the night. She wasn't entirely certain how much KT would be able to do one-handed in the midst of a true emergency, and having another medical person available made sense. The paramedics would be able to help as well, but they would be busy monitoring vital signs, managing the airway and fluid resuscitation, and administering meds.

KT turned at the sound of Tory and Pia's arrival in the treatment room. "Hi, Vic."

"Where are we?" Tory asked.

"Pia's setting up the IVs, and I just pulled a major suture

tray." She indicated a large sealed tray that bore the small sticker indicating that it had been autoclaved and the contents were sterile. She placed it on a tall Mayo stand, which resembled a stainless steel TV tray. On wheels, it could be pushed up to or even over the treatment table so that the surgeon could easily reach the instruments.

Tory nodded absently. "Did you draw up the drugs?"

A brief flicker of discomfort crossed KT's face as she lifted her left hand. "No, I couldn't."

"I'll get them ready, then," Tory said, brushing her hand lightly across KT's shoulder as she passed.

"Thanks." KT glanced across the room at Pia, who met her eyes and smiled gently. She had no time to think about how that smile settled in her chest and seemed to leave no room for pain or uncertainty, because suddenly the building was filled with the noise of clattering wheels and a cacophony of voices talking over one another. The treatment room was the only brightly lit room in the rear of the building, and it wasn't hard for the emergency team to find them.

All three women turned to the door, braced for the imminent blur of activity and the adrenaline-charged moments that could spell the difference between life and death.

❖

The first thing Tory saw was the irregular swatch of maroon in the center of Reese's chest. She had tried to prepare for that, but the shock ran through her, leaving numbness in its wake. For one pain-filled second, her mind closed down, refusing to acknowledge what her eyes had registered. Then, with the next breath, her vision cleared. There was blood soaking Reese's shirt, but Reese was walking, running, really, with her hand on the end of the stretcher being pushed by the paramedic.

It's not Reese. It's not Reese. She focused on the lean body recognizable even beneath the mountain of resuscitation equipment. *Oh no. Not again. Bri!*

"What do we have?" KT asked the paramedics, reaching out with her right hand to guide the stretcher alongside the treatment table as Tory placed a stethoscope on Bri's chest.

"Lungs are clear," Tory said.

"Knife wound to the neck," the paramedic said, holding the oxygen mask against Bri's face with one hand and a pressure dressing to the left side of her neck with his other. The gauze beneath his gloved fingers was soaked with blood, and a steady trickle ran down onto the stretcher.

"Airway?" KT knew that any knife wound to the neck could injure the trachea, causing blood to seep into the windpipe, fill the lungs, and prevent oxygen exchange. Many victims of penetrating trauma to the neck died from asphyxiation, not blood loss.

"Oxygen saturation is excellent, 99% on four liters," a second paramedic noted, balancing the multiple monitoring devices on the far end of the stretcher with both hands as they moved. "No blood in the posterior pharynx either."

"Good," KT observed. The other structure at risk—in addition to the many huge blood vessels in the neck—was the esophagus, and if it were perforated, blood would back up into the mouth and eventually compromise the airway as well.

"Bri?" Tory said quietly, moving the oxygen mask aside enough to look at Bri's face. Bri's eyes flickered open, dazed but aware. "Hey, sweetie. Can you hear me?"

"Yes," Bri whispered hoarsely.

"Are you hurt anywhere else? Your chest, back, belly?"

"No." Bri's eyelids flickered closed, and then she opened them again with effort. "Neck hurts."

"I know. We'll take care of that." Tory reached across the treatment table for the sheet beneath Bri. "Let's get her over here."

Many hands grabbed the sheet from both sides of the stretcher while one of the paramedics stabilized Bri's neck.

"One, two, three," Tory counted and everyone lifted, swinging Bri in the makeshift sling onto the treatment table. Then Tory took her first look around the room and saw an ashen Nelson and shell-shocked Allie standing inside the door. She looked up at Reese. "Take them out of here."

Reese looked hesitantly from Bri to Tory, as if she might protest, but nodded grimly. "Okay." She put her hand on Bri's thigh and squeezed. With the barest hint of tremor in her voice, she repeated, "Okay. See you in a minute, Bri."

As Reese turned and shepherded Nelson and Allie out into the hall, Tory moved to the head of the table next to KT. She met KT's eyes and saw in them the steady focus and intensity she'd always found so comforting in the midst of a trauma. "Ready to take a look?"

"Let's get the suction hooked up first and load the sutures. You're going to have to be ready to clamp and tie."

Tory shook her head. "There's nothing wrong with your dominant hand." Her gaze never moving from KT's, Tory said over her shoulder to Pia. "Can you glove KT's right hand, please."

"Of course," Pia replied. She looked at KT. "Size?"

"Seven and a half." KT stepped over next to Pia, removing the immobilizer on her left hand as Pia, wearing sterile gloves herself, opened a second pack of gloves. "Glove them both."

Without a word, Pia held up the left glove, stretching open the cuff so that KT could slide her hand inside. "Careful not to extend your fingers when you push in here."

"I've got it," KT said as she eased her damaged fingers into the tight latex. "At least I won't contaminate the field with it now."

"You'll be fine."

"Thanks," KT replied sincerely. Then she turned back to the table and said briskly, "Let's get this bleeding stopped."

"Give her four milligrams of IV morphine," Tory said to the paramedic before reaching down, suction cannula in hand, and removing the pressure bandage from Bri's neck. Immediately, a heavy stream of dark blood poured out of a five-inch laceration that extended along the side of her neck, parallel to her jaw, two inches below her ear. Precisely along the line where a knife being held by someone from behind would have rested.

Immediately, KT pressed the fingers of her right hand over the wound, squeezing it closed with her fingers. "From the location, it's probably the external jugular."

"Flow is pretty brisk," Tory murmured. The external jugular vein was a relatively low-pressure vein almost 5mm wide, a quarter the size of its deeper partner, the internal jugular vein. She didn't say what they both knew—that the external jugular vein alone wouldn't produce this much bleeding.

"Might be a partial transection preventing it from constricting and closing off," KT observed. "Get the 3-0 ties ready, Vic, then take over the compression on the wound." She motioned to the second paramedic. "You're going to need to suction for us."

"Sure," he said as he moved closer to the field and took the suction from Tory.

KT picked up a hemostat in her right hand and glanced from Tory to the paramedic. "All set?" At their nods, she said, "Put the retractors in and let me have a look."

For the next two minutes the room was entirely silent except for the gurgle of the suction machine pulling a steady stream of blood from Bri's neck through the plastic tubing and into the container. Once, KT said steadily, "Suck right there. Over just a little bit. Good."

While Tory and the paramedic stared into the depths of the laceration, struggling to clear the blood and hold back the subcutaneous tissue and divided muscle edges, KT used the hemostat to dissect out the external jugular vein from the surrounding tissue, identifying the segment that had been partially divided and that gaped open, accounting for the rapid hemorrhage.

"Got it," KT muttered, clamping the proximal portion leading from the head toward the chest. Without taking her eyes from the other end of the vein that she needed to control, she held out her right hand. "Hemostat."

Pia placed the instrument into KT's hand, and KT clamped it around the distal end of the vein. The bleeding from the wound stopped.

"Scissors," KT requested, again extending her open hand, palm up. The scissors settled smartly against her palm, and she closed her fingers automatically on the instrument. She finished dividing the vein so that the two ends were now free and could be ligated. After setting the scissors aside, she held up the first hemostat. She couldn't tie with only one hand. "You'll have to tie these off, Vic."

"Vicryl okay?" Tory asked, reaching for the suture.

"Should be."

Tory looped the suture around the end of the hemostat and,

using both hands, tied off the vessel. She repeated the procedure as KT lifted the second hemostat. When she was done, the wound was nearly dry. Looking into KT's dark eyes, Tory said quietly, "Beautiful."

"Thanks. Let's look around to make sure there isn't anything deeper."

With the paramedic retracting and Tory gently suctioning, KT delicately explored the wound, lifting tissue layers with her forceps until she had identified the carotid sheath—undamaged—and the nearby internal jugular vein, also inviolate. "Fortunately it doesn't extend to the midline, so the trachea and esophagus should be fine. Looks like it nicked the submandibular gland. I should close the capsule just to prevent delayed bleeding." She straightened and turned to Pia. "Can you load up that 3-0 Vicryl on the short needle holder for me."

"Got it." Pia opened the sterile suture package and clamped the jaws of the needle holder onto the semicircular needle. She passed it handle first into KT's right hand.

"You're pretty good at that," KT murmured.

Pia smiled and nodded toward the wound. "You too."

Twenty minutes later, Tory and KT had finished closing the laceration. Bri, only semiconscious due to a combination of shock and sedation, remained unaware of the procedure.

"We should ship her to Hyannis for observation, I guess," Tory said reluctantly. "I know she's going to hate that."

"She's stable. We can watch her here until morning," KT suggested. "She's already had antibiotics, the wound is closed, and if you're worried about blood loss, we can do a fingerstick hemoglobin. But I doubt she's going to need transfusion."

Tory hesitated.

"Why don't I talk to her father?" Pia suggested. "Then one of you can fill him in on the medical details, and you can make a decision about the next step."

"Now there's an idea," Tory said with a shaky laugh. "Thanks. Let me just check her blood count, and I'll be out."

When Pia stepped out into the hallway, Nelson, Reese, and Allie rushed forward.

"She's doing fine," Pia said immediately, aware that that was all they really needed to hear and that they probably wouldn't remember anything else from the initial explanation.

"The bleeding?" Nelson croaked. Christ, there had been so much of it. When he'd followed Reese into the kitchen and seen Bri on her knees, blood pouring from her neck, he thought he'd pass out. While he'd stood rooted to the spot in helpless fear, Reese had jumped forward and clamped her hand over the wound in his daughter's throat. "Jesus Christ."

"It's stopped. KT and Tory found the bleeder and controlled it." Pia surveyed the small group. Nelson was obviously a wreck; Allie was deathly pale, her eyes dark pools of anguish; and Reese—Reese vibrated with tension so palpable Pia felt it even though their bodies did not touch. "Are any of you hurt?"

"No," Reese replied abruptly. She glanced toward the treatment room. "We were just a little too far away."

"It was my fault," Allie said. "I was behind Bri on the stairs, and I didn't see him follow us. I let that fucker get to her." Her voice was hollow with self-recrimination and pain.

"We'll talk about that when we debrief," Reese said quietly. She looked at Pia. "What's the plan?"

Tory appeared in the hallway, announcing as she approached, "She's stable. Her hemoglobin is just a bit above eleven. I'll check again in a few hours, but she's not going to need a transfusion." She walked directly to Nelson and put both hands on his shoulders, forcing him to look only at her. "She's awake. She's all right. She's going to be fine. She wants to see you."

Tears finally streaked his cheeks. "You're sure—about her being okay?"

"Yes. We need to keep an eye on her, make sure she doesn't develop an infection, but the knife didn't strike anything vital. She's going to be completely fine."

Nelson gave a shaky laugh. "Then she might be the only one of us." He rubbed his face. "Jesus. That kid..." He trailed off as his throat closed around another unanticipated swell of tears. When he finally managed to find his voice, he said, "Well. Let me go see her."

"Go ahead, but expect her to be drowsy." Tory looked from Allie to Reese. "You can both see her, as well. But just for a few minutes. I'm going to keep her here until morning. I'll check her hemoglobin again then, and if she's stable and everything else looks good, I'm going to take her home with us, Reese. There's nothing they would do in the hospital but keep an eye on her. And I can do that."

"Good," Reese said gruffly. "I'd rather have her here."

For the first time, Tory touched her lover. She took Reese's hand and squeezed. "So would I. Sweetheart, change your shirt before you go see her."

Reese glanced down and winced. "Yeah. I've got clothes in the Blazer. I'll do that now."

Tory watched Reese walk away, the relief so acute now that the crisis had passed and she knew that her lover was safe for another day that her legs felt weak. She leaned one shoulder against the wall and took a long breath.

"She's really going to be okay?" Allie asked in a small voice.

"Yes." After a second, Tory turned and put her arm around Allie's shoulders, giving her a hug. "She really is." To Tory's utter surprise, Allie pressed her face to Tory's shoulder and wept. Soothingly, Tory rocked her. "It's okay, honey. It's okay."

"That fucker," Allie sobbed into Tory's shirt. "That fucking bastard. I'm so glad she broke his goddamned arm."

"Did she?"

Allie nodded, breath hitching as she struggled to contain her tears. "Dislocated his shoulder too."

"Good," Tory said vehemently.

"Yeah," Allie said with a sigh, stepping away and brushing the tears from her cheeks with both hands. "The guys said she never even hesitated. Took him down with a shoulder throw even though he'd..." Her voice broke. "...cut her."

Tory stroked Allie's cheek. "She won't remember very much about it. She'll remember, but thankfully, the mind has a way of dealing with horrible things like that. She'll need to talk about it—you all will—but you're *all* going to be okay." She lifted Allie's chin and smoothed away the last of her tears. "All right?"

Allie nodded, then turned at the sound of Nelson's voice.

"She wants to see you, Allie," Nelson said, his color considerably better, the torment gone from his eyes. He smiled crookedly. "She sounds like a bullfrog, but she doesn't look too bad." He glanced at Tory. "The other doc says there won't be too much of a scar."

"She should know," Tory replied with certainty. "She's the surgeon."

Chapter Twenty-Seven

Tory slumped, eyes closed, in the leather chair behind her desk. At the touch of a soft kiss on her forehead, she opened her eyes. Reese bent over her, her arms braced on either side of Tory's body. Murmuring a soft hello, Tory reached up and wrapped her arms around Reese's neck, burying her face against Reese's shoulder. "Are you sure you're all right?"

"Yes." Reese knelt, sliding her arms around Tory's waist and cradling her against her chest.

"When I got the call, driving here—" Tory halted, collecting herself. "All I could think was that you'd been hurt again. I can't stand it when you're hurt."

"I know you must have thought it was me. I'm so sorry, Tor."

"Oh God," Tory whispered, her voice trembling. "It's not your fault."

"I scared you. I don't ever want that. And Bri...I put her in there. I thought I could cover her fast enough." Reese shuddered. "I promised Nelson I'd take care of her, and I almost let her get killed."

Tory leaned back, her arms still around Reese's shoulders, and fixed her with an intent stare. "That is *not* your fault. If Bri hadn't been as well trained as she is, who knows what could've happened. And *you* trained her."

"The command part of my brain knows that—I'd make the same decision again about the execution of the operation." Reese rested her forehead against Tory's wearily. "But I don't mind telling you, I was scared there for a minute."

"Me too. But she's going to be okay." Tory lifted an arm to check her watch. "I should go relieve KT. In another couple of hours, if Bri is still stable, we can take her home."

Reese kissed Tory, gently but firmly, running her hands up and down Tory's back possessively. "I love you. Thank you for taking care of Bri. Thank you...for Reggie and..." Her voice failing, Reese turned her face to Tory's neck to hide the tears that blindsided her.

Shocked, Tory stroked the back of Reese's neck, her lips pressed to Reese's temple. "Darling, what is it?"

"When I saw her down...the blood everywhere, I thought we were going to lose her. I couldn't let her die—I couldn't even fathom it." She lifted her head, her blue eyes black with stunned awareness. "Because I don't know what I would've done. All my training, all my *life,* I've been prepared to lose people. But you and Regina...and Bri...I couldn't handle it." Embarrassed as well as tired and stressed, Reese put her head down on Tory's shoulder again.

"It's all right, darling." Tory held her tightly. "It's all right."

Finally, Reese straightened, smiling faintly. "Why don't *you* get some rest? I can watch Bri as long as you tell me what to look for. Then KT and Pia can go home too."

"I'm fine for a few more hours. I got a *little* sleep last night." Tory stood, bringing Reese up with her. She kissed her lover and stroked her cheek. "But you can sit with us if you don't think you can sleep."

Reese took her hand. "I don't want to be away from you right now."

Tory linked her fingers with Reese's. "Good. Then let's go take care of Bri."

❖

It was very nearly dawn as KT and Pia walked down the path to Pia's cottage. When they reached the porch, KT stopped and took Pia's hand.

"I don't quite know how to tell you what it meant to me that you were there tonight." Struggling to put words to emotions so foreign to her, KT kissed Pia gently. "I felt you—your faith in me and your certainty—inside. I...needed that."

"I'm glad I was there, too," Pia replied, moving closer and

wrapping her arms around KT's waist. She settled her head on KT's shoulder. "You would've been fine no matter what, but if I helped, I'm glad. You were wonderful."

KT laughed and kissed the top of Pia's head. "For a one-handed surgeon, I guess I did okay."

Pia lifted her head and tapped KT's chin with a finger for emphasis. "You won't be one-handed forever."

"Somehow, I think we've had this conversation before." KT kissed Pia again, a longer, more probing kiss, before she drew away. "I know you're probably tired, but I don't want to say goodbye right now."

"No," Pia said softly, "neither do I."

Holding one another securely, they made their way inside.

❖

"Nelson," Tory murmured, shaking the sheriff gently.

"Huh?" Nelson's eyes opened, and he shot upright, instantly looking toward his daughter, who slept a few feet away. "What?"

"She's fine. You need to go home and get some sleep." Tory tilted her chin toward the other officer curled up on a portable stretcher nearby. "And Allie needs the day off, at least. I'll take her home with me. She's only going to be hanging around the house asking after Bri anyhow."

"Yeah," Nelson said, his voice rough with sleep and worry. "The two of them are going to wear me out."

Tory laughed quietly. "I won't disagree with you."

As they talked, Reese leaned over the patient and whispered, "Hey, Bri."

After a moment, Bri opened her eyes and frowned, struggling to focus on Reese's face. "Hi." Her voice was weak, but her eyes were clear. "He didn't...get away...did he?"

"Not a chance." Reese squeezed Bri's shoulder. "He never moved after you put him down. They've got him up at Wellfleet while we sort out all the details. How are you feeling?"

Bri appeared to give that serious thought. The sheet covering her twitched as she moved her arms and legs. "I'm okay, I think. What happened?"

"You got dinged up, but Tory and KT took care of things. It's not bad."

"I feel...sort of weak." To demonstrate, she tried to sit up and failed.

"Hey," Reese cautioned. "You're not ready to move around yet. We're going to take you to our place so you can recuperate for a while."

"Nobody told Carre about this, did they?" Bri said anxiously. "I don't want her to be scared."

"It's okay. There's nothing to worry about." Reese bent down close to Bri's ear, one hand smoothing back her damp hair. "I'll take care of talking to Caroline. I'll make sure she's okay."

"Thanks. Okay...thanks." Bri closed her eyes and, a moment later, drifted off.

❖

Pia and KT faced one another across the bed, the room aglow in the dawn light, the air alive with the fresh scent of the sea. The town still slept.

"You must be exhausted," Pia said quietly as she unbuttoned her blouse, her eyes on KT's face.

"You too." KT unbuckled her belt, then opened her pants. She hesitated before removing them. "Everything?"

"Yes," Pia replied with a soft smile.

KT pushed down her trousers and underwear, then stepped free of the crumpled clothes along with her shoes and socks. Deftly, she unbuttoned her shirt but left it hanging open as she watched Pia's blouse drift down her arms and fall away behind her.

With a hand behind her back, Pia loosed the clasp on her bra and drew it from her breasts. She watched KT's face, saw her eyes flicker down. When KT's lips parted with a quiet sigh, a flush of heat kindled in Pia's belly. Slowly, she lowered her jeans and underwear over her hips. The corner of her mouth lifted in a smile as KT stood frozen in place, her expression one of stunned pleasure. "Your shirt."

"What?" KT asked, her tone befuddled. Pia was beautiful, just as she knew she would be. But it wasn't the loveliness of her body or the wondrous smoothness of her skin that made her head spin, but her own amazement that she should be so lucky. So lucky that Pia should allow *her,* with all her failings and failures, to be the one to touch her first. She sought Pia's eyes. "Thank you."

It was Pia's turn to grow still, her heart hammering wildly as the flutter of pleasure in her depths soared into a thousand wings beating through her blood. "If I feel this way from just your eyes on me, I won't survive your hands."

"Before I touch you," KT whispered, shrugging her shirt from her shoulders to stand exposed, "I need to tell you something."

"You don't," Pia whispered gently. She extended her hand across the bed.

KT took a step closer, her fingertips a breath away from Pia's. "Pia."

"Just come to me."

KT took Pia's hand, her eyes holding Pia's, and said, "I love you."

❖

Naked, Tory slipped into bed with a long sigh. She slid across the cool crisp sheets toward Reese and fit herself to the curve of her lover's body. She kissed Reese's shoulder, then settled her cheek against Reese's chest.

"Are they both asleep?" Reese asked quietly, curling her arm around Tory's back and resting her hand just beneath Tory's left breast.

"Yes. Allie's sacked out on the couch and Bri seems to be resting pretty comfortably. How was Regina?"

Reese smiled. "Hungry. Once she ate, she went right back to sleep. I'm surprised, since Jean said she slept all night."

"I think she senses that we're all going to be sleeping late today."

"Do you think she really can tell if there's something going on?"

"Babies are intuitive. The house is quiet, our routine is different. She'll sense that."

"That's amazing." Reese nuzzled her face in Tory's hair,

breathing the fresh scent of her shampoo. "You were great last night with Bri. With everyone."

"*Everyone* was great. KT did an incredible job with Bri's injury, even with only one hand."

"Do think she's going to be able to operate again?"

"I think if Pia has anything to do with it, she will." Now that she had a moment to reflect on the tumultuous evening, Tory realized there had been an unspoken communication between Pia and KT that was obviously strong and unexpectedly tender. "Ah."

"What?" Reese asked drowsily, smoothing her palm over the arch of Tory's breast.

"KT and Pia."

"KT and Pia what?" Reese shifted, sliding one leg between Tory's and brushing her lips over Tory's. She was about to deepen the kiss when she made the connection. She pulled back and studied Tory's face. "You mean KT and Pia as in...together?"

"I think so. KT mentioned something about being interested in Pia, but I didn't think it would go anywhere."

"Why not?"

Tory was silent, absently drawing strands of Reese's hair through her fingers. She thought about the woman she had known so many years ago, before the relentless pace of KT's singular drive to succeed had come between them. She remembered tenderness and laughter and the warm sense of belonging. KT had had all of those qualities and even moments of uncertainty when she had turned to Tory for encouragement and support. Tory had seen glimpses of that woman tonight. "I was wrong, thinking that KT and Pia wouldn't be good together."

Reese settled onto her back and pulled Tory into her arms, cradling her close. "People change."

"You won't, will you?" Tory murmured, circling her palm over Reese's chest.

"My life already changed forever when I met you. And nothing will ever change the way I feel about you."

"I love you so much." Tory kissed Reese's neck and closed her eyes, certain, secure, and forever safe in their love.

❖

Still holding hands, KT and Pia slid beneath the sheets and turned to face one another. KT leaned forward and softly kissed Pia. The only points of contact between them were their lips and their fingertips. Despite the minimal physical connection, KT felt her body roar to life. She pulled back, her breath nearly deserting her.

"I should say something like, 'I know you're tired, and we can just hold one another and go to sleep,'" KT murmured, her voice thick and low. She shivered and grinned weakly. "But I can't. I just can't hold back anymore." She let go of Pia's hand and placed her arm around Pia's waist, slowly drawing her forward in the same motion until their bodies touched. Groaning, KT brushed her mouth over Pia's. "I'm dying for you."

"Oh, I don't want to wait anymore. I want *you.*" With a nearly inaudible whimper, Pia clutched KT's shoulders, slipped her tongue into KT's mouth, and pressed as close as she could.

At the touch of Pia's skin to hers, KT's mind filled with searing white light and every barrier—physical and emotional—disintegrated. She slid her hand down Pia's back to her hips and turned Pia beneath her, moving over her to settle upon her. As she kissed her, probing kisses that teased and claimed, her fingers drove into the rich fall of her hair, twining in the soft, thick waves. Pia was everywhere, filling her senses, drowning her in a flood of desire. When Pia's hand found its way between them and cupped her breast, lightning struck between KT's thighs. She jerked her head away. "Christ. God, you feel so damn good."

"Tell me what you like," Pia gasped, closing her fingers on the erect nipple beneath her palm. Her heart skipped when KT groaned. "I want to touch you everywhere. I love to make you want me."

KT laughed, shivering beneath the onslaught of sensation. "*Want* you?" She dipped her head and nipped at the skin just above Pia's collarbone. While Pia tormented her breast with tiny tugs and pinches, making her pulse stutter and soar, she eased her thigh between Pia's. Pia was wet, hot against her skin. The unbridled evidence of Pia's desire made KT desperate to be inside her. "Pia. God, Pia."

Pia sensed the storm brewing in KT's taut body as the nipple hardened beneath her fingers. She loved the way KT's breath caught and fled as she worked her teeth over KT's breast. More. She wanted more. She wanted KT to feel the ache she had inside for her. She wanted to infuse KT's body with the terrible, wonderful pressure she felt building inside her own. She wanted things she couldn't describe and barely knew how to contain. She dug her fingers into KT's back and pressed her face hard to KT's breast. "Help me. Help me make love to you."

Nearly out of her mind from the pleasure flowing from her breast through her belly and pooling between her thighs, hungry for the taste and feel of Pia's body, KT was beyond thought. "You are. Baby, you are. Can't you feel what you're doing to me?"

"I want..." Pia dragged her hands over KT's shoulders, fisted in her hair, pulled KT's head back until she could stare through glazed eyes into her face. "I want to make you come. Tell me how."

"I think..." KT pulled in great gasps of breath, trying to form sentences. Pia's desire cut through her, a sweet piercing pain that made her bleed from the beauty of it. "I think I'm supposed to... please *you*...the first time around."

Pia laughed, a wild, urgent laugh. "Says who?" She placed her palms against KT's chest and pushed gently. "Lie down. I want to touch you."

KT had waited so long—so long to hear those words and all that lingered in their depths. Even more than her body craved the blessed relief of Pia's hands, her heart longed for Pia's tender solace. She didn't struggle, couldn't resist, wanted to shed the past—all of it: all the long, empty nights; all the frantic, desperate days; every regret and sorrow and shame. She wanted another chance. As she turned onto her back, she cupped Pia's cheek, brushing her thumb across Pia's mouth. "There are things I want to say. I can't—I don't know how."

"You will," Pia whispered, her mouth moving along the column of KT's throat. "We both will. Not now."

KT eased her fingers into Pia's hair, gently now, unhurried, almost peaceful despite the frantic beating of her heart in her chest, in her belly, in her loins. She guided Pia down, back arching, muscles tightening, as Pia's lips and mouth explored her breasts and her abdomen and finally the tender hollow at the juncture of her thighs. In the last thinking part of her brain, KT worried that it was too fast or too soon, but the low hum of pleasure that reverberated through Pia's chest and throat and into KT's flesh drove all thoughts of caution from her mind. She nearly screamed when Pia gently parted her thighs and kissed the very heart of her need.

"You're so beautiful," Pia murmured, tracing her thumb between the flushed and swollen folds. She hesitated for an instant before pressing the base of KT's clitoris and moaned softly at the sudden jerk of KT's hips. "I want to taste you."

"Please." KT's hand trembled against Pia's face as she raised her head, urgently seeking Pia's eyes. "I need you so much."

Pia clasped KT's hand with hers, intertwining their fingers as she lowered her head and drew KT inside her mouth. KT's hand tightened around Pia's as she surrendered to the spell of passion and sweet, tender promises.

"Take me," KT whispered. "Oh, Pia, please...just take me."

❖

Pia wasn't certain when she started breathing again. It seemed like forever that all she knew, all she heard, all that filled her senses was KT. The wonder of KT exploding beneath her hands, between her lips, inside her heart. She wanted more. She wanted it never to end. She might not have stopped exploring, taking, driving KT higher and higher, beyond reason, if KT had not finally twisted away with a hoarse plea.

"Baby...stop, before I have a heart attack."

Shakily, Pia laughed and rested her cheek against the inside of KT's thigh. She couldn't bear not to be touching her, though, and ran her fingers lightly over KT's clitoris. KT twitched and groaned. "You feel amazing."

"I don't think I've ever felt so good," KT muttered, weakly stroking Pia's hair.

Pia raised her head and peered at KT. "Yeah?"

"Oh yeah." With effort, KT turned on her side and curled around Pia's body, gently urging Pia up until they lay side by side. She traced Pia's lips with her fingers. "I'm going to get addicted to your mouth."

"I hope so," Pia said fervently, kissing KT lightly. "Because

I'm already addicted to you."

"How do you feel?" KT asked gently, smoothing her hand over Pia's breast and down her belly. She felt the muscles in Pia's abdomen quiver beneath her fingers. She knew what Pia had not yet sensed. She was ready. And KT wanted her, wanted her enough to go slowly.

"Fabulous." Pia's voice held a note of wonder. She was reliving the sounds of KT's pleasure, the taste of her, the incredible sense of awe she'd experienced as KT climaxed again and again beneath her demanding mouth. As she felt it all, *heard* it all again, she didn't realize that her hips had begun to thrust against the palm that KT had laid between her thighs. As her clitoris swelled with remembered pleasure and the soft steady brush of KT's fingers, Pia's belly tightened and her nipples grew taut. When KT lowered her mouth and caught one between her teeth, Pia cried out. "Oh. I—oh, I want to come!"

"I know," KT soothed. She gentled her fingertips just on the verge of entering and let Pia push against her, drawing her in, setting the pace. She wanted more, she wanted fast, she wanted deep...and she waited. "Take me inside, Pia. Let me please you."

Pia braced both hands on KT's shoulders and rested her forehead against KT's. With her eyes holding KT's and her breath shuddering, she pushed down slowly, another small cry of wonder escaping as KT filled her. She wanted to let go, she wanted to scream and thrust until the pressure between her thighs exploded, but even more she wanted to fix in her memory that first miraculous instant when they were completely joined. She tried to hold back, but the orgasm caught her by surprise and wiped her consciousness clean in a single wild rush of heat.

Chapter Twenty-Eight

Allie woke to the sound of insistent tapping somewhere nearby. It took her a moment to place her surroundings. *Couch? Sunlight...ugh. Bri!*

She sat up in a flash, the memories flooding back. The party, the raid, Bri and all that blood. Her stomach lurched, and she pushed the faint nausea away. Bri was okay. Would *be* okay. She looked around the room, her fears abating. *Tory and Reese's. Everything is okay.*

She'd fallen asleep almost immediately, despite her protests that she wouldn't be able to relax until she was certain that Bri was all right. Tory had simply handed her a T-shirt, said, "Stretch out on the couch and close your eyes," and the next thing she knew, the sun was streaming in the double glass doors that led to the deck and someone was outside, wanting very badly to get in. Still a little groggy from the combination of stress and fatigue, Allie rose and stumbled to the door, scrubbing a hand over her face to wake herself up. She slid open the door and stared at a very frantic blond.

"Oh!" Allie said. "How—?"

"Is she here? Reese said she would be here." Caroline Clark peered past Allie anxiously. "Is she all right?"

Allie stepped aside, automatically reaching for the overnight bag Caroline carried. "She's asleep in the guest room. How did you—?"

"Reese got me the tickets." Caroline took a step inside, her eyes tracking across the room to the hall that led to the bedroom as if she would able to see Bri through the walls. Then she turned her attention to Allie, her expression narrowing briefly as she took in the oversized T-shirt and the apparent absence of any other clothing. Evenly she asked, "Did you stay with her?"

"Couch," Allie muttered, tilting her head toward the sofa. "I just wanted to be sure she was okay."

Caroline studied her, saw the shadows beneath her eyes. "Thanks. It's good to know she has a friend."

Allie grinned briefly. "She does." She met Caroline's appraising glance. "There was a time—well, you probably know."

"Yeah."

"That was before we started working together and got tight." Allie shrugged. "She's only ever gonna be yours."

Caroline's eyes flooded with tears, but her smile was brilliant. After a few seconds, she blinked away the moisture and took a deep breath. "Tell me what happened."

"Uh..."

"Reese didn't give me the details—only that Bri had been hurt and that Reese thought I should come home. But she said Bri was all right." Caroline's voice trembled. "Is that the truth?"

"She's okay," Allie said immediately. "She got...injured... during a drug bust last night. But Tory and another doctor took care of it. They said she's going to be fine."

Caroline's face was white. "Injured. What do you mean, *injured*?"

Allie stalled. "You should probably talk to Tory."

"No. I want to see Bri right away," Caroline insisted, "and I need to know what happened before I do. I need to know what she needs."

"You're here," Allie said softly. "I think that's just about everything she needs."

"Thanks. It...it goes both ways."

"Then you're both lucky," Allie said, no trace of envy in her voice.

"Yeah. I know." Caroline touched Allie's arm. "So, tell me what kind of trouble my girl got into this time."

❖

Without opening her eyes, Pia stretched, gave a contented sigh, and murmured, "That's an amazingly nice way to wake up."

"Mmm," KT agreed, continuing to run her tongue over Pia's nipple while softly stroking Pia's other breast. She'd awakened feeling better than she had in years. Fresh, energized, and with the warmth of Pia's body against hers, instantly aroused. The October air from the open window was brisk, invigorating, and as she'd drawn a deep breath, a wave of desire that felt very much like life returning to the long-dark recesses of her being coursed through her. Pia. Pia had brought light back into her life, dispelling the shadows and the loneliness. As she'd marveled at that unexpected gift, she'd smoothed her fingers over Pia's body, meaning only to satisfy her need to be near her. But when Pia's nipple rose beneath her fingertips and Pia murmured softly in her sleep, KT needed more. Needed her inside. And she'd put her lips to Pia's breast.

"Astonishing." Pia rested her hand lightly on the back of KT's head, caressing her neck and shoulders languidly. The tantalizing attention to her breast had ignited the first tendrils of heat deep down inside, but she was enjoying the slow rise of pleasure too much to want to hurry. "It's even better than I imagined."

KT laughed softly and raised her head. "Sex?"

"No," Pia remarked lazily, opening her eyes and fixing them on KT. "Making love with you. I knew it would be wonderful, I just didn't realize how very much."

"Pia," KT whispered. "Pia. I can't seem to think of anything but you. You do the most amazing things to me." As she spoke, she leaned on her left elbow, her injured hand still protected with the wristlet, and smoothed her other hand over the soft hollow of Pia's abdomen—up and down, up and down—until finally her fingers rested between Pia's thighs. When Pia caught her breath and lifted her hips, KT slowed her explorations.

"Don't stop," Pia said thickly. "Feels so good."

"To me, too. And you aren't the only one who's been imagining this." KT lowered her head and nipped at Pia's breast, laughing again when Pia gave a cry of pleased surprise. "So I don't want to rush."

"What if I want you to?" Pia rocked her hips insistently beneath KT's hand. "I like the way you made me feel last night."

KT feathered her fingers over the tender folds between Pia's legs, watching Pia's expression intently. "I want to learn everything about you. What makes you happy..." She traced a finger up and down the warm, moist valley—just a little bit harder, just a little bit deeper—smiling when Pia caught her bottom lip between her teeth. "What makes you excited..." She caught Pia's clitoris between her fingertips and squeezed ever so lightly.

Pia trembled and closed her fingers hard around KT's wrist. "There. Oh, like that."

"Yes." KT's voice was heavy with desire as she moved away, away from the spot that she knew would take Pia too high too fast. When Pia moaned in protest, KT lowered her head and kissed her, swallowing her moans and soothing her need with gentle strokes of her tongue. When she drew away, Pia's breathing had deepened and her eyes had grown liquid with the desire spreading within like a flame banked beneath a layer of coals. "I want to know you," KT whispered. "Inside." She pressed a fingertip, then two, just inside, waiting for Pia to relax enough for her to move deeper. "Inside the way you've touched me. Not just in my body..." Deeper now, nearly filling her. "But all the way to my heart."

"I love to feel you like this," Pia murmured, both hands twisted in the sheets, back arched to take KT deeper. "Everywhere inside me."

As KT slowly eased almost all the way out and then back in, she inched down on the bed until she could put her mouth over Pia's clitoris. She swept her tongue in long, smooth strokes that matched the rhythm of her fingers sliding in and out, ignoring Pia's increasingly frantic pleas to go faster, harder, deeper. Her need for Pia to climax was an ache in the pit of her stomach, her hunger for the sound of Pia's pleasure ringing out in a breathless cry all but consuming her, but she held back. She was desperate to feel each pulse of Pia's excitement building beneath her lips and to thrill to the clench of Pia's passion around her fingers. Then, when they were both poised to explode, *then* she would take her.

Her heart thudded wildly in her chest; her stomach quivered with the need to come. If she caught Pia's leg between her own and pressed her clitoris to Pia's warm, smooth skin, she knew she would. But despite the piercing urgency for release, she didn't want anything to cloud her awareness of Pia, not even her own pleasure. Pia was everything. Everywhere. All she wanted.

"I'm almost there," Pia moaned, her head rocking with each labored breath. "You're making me come...oh, yes. Oh yes. Oh. Now."

At the first quiver of Pia's orgasm, KT thrust harder. Eyes fixed on Pia's face, she was beyond stopping now. Pia's pleasure was her own, and with each sharp cry, she drew closer to her own release. She knelt astride Pia's thigh, hips pistoning along taut muscles as each thrust of her arm lifted Pia's body from the bed. "Come, baby. Come."

When Pia reared up on the bed in the throes of her orgasm, clutching wildly at KT, KT buried her face against Pia's breasts and soared over the edge.

❖

Bri was having the nicest dream. Carre was whispering in her ear, telling her how much she loved her and how she couldn't wait to be with her all the time. Carre's voice always gave her a rush. But it was even nicer when Carre not only talked to her but touched her. And Carre was touching her now. Stroking her face and her hair and her arm. It was all so real, she could even smell the scent of fresh air and bright sunlight that she always associated with Carre.

"Yeah," Bri muttered. "You feel so good, babe."

"Don't wake up, baby. You just sleep, and I'll be right here."

Smiling, Bri rolled to her side, wanting to feel Caroline against her body, even if it was just a dream. The movement triggered a stabbing pain in her neck that shot deep into her chest, and with a cry, she jerked awake.

"It's okay," Caroline said quickly, placing the hand that wasn't stroking Bri's face on her shoulder to hold her still. "Bri, baby. It's okay. Just lie still."

Despite the pain, Bri could only think of one thing. Caroline was leaning over her, inches away, and she seemed...real. "Carre?"

"Yes, baby. It's me."

"Carre?" Bri blinked, and then she remembered the night before. She remembered feeling pretty righteous about the way she and Allie had orchestrated the bust, and then she saw Karl's face again as he snarled in the direction of the officers coming through the door and then lunged for the knife. In the next instant, she felt the bite of steel slice through her skin, sharp and hot. "Oh, Jesus, Carre. He cut me."

Caroline's face lost all color, but her voice remained even and soothing. "Tory took care of you. Reese told me you'll be fine."

Bri stared, unseeing, still caught in those few terrifying seconds before she had done what she had practiced hundreds of times. Before she'd pulled her chin down hard to her chest to protect her windpipe and the big vessels in her neck. Before she'd wrapped both hands around his knife arm and held it back with all her strength, despite the agony in her neck. Before she'd dropped her center of gravity below his and then pushed up with her legs, the strongest part of her body, to flip him over her shoulder and onto the floor. The maneuver replayed in her mind like a video, stark and clear, but the cold lump of terror in her stomach was all she could feel.

As the panic flashed across Bri's face, something Caroline had never witnessed before, her heart nearly broke. She leaned down and kissed Bri gently, then murmured against her mouth, "I love you. You're all right. I promise."

"Don't leave me," Bri whispered, tears streaking her cheeks.

"Oh, baby. Never." Carefully, Caroline settled onto the bed next to Bri and curled one arm around her waist. Gently drawing Bri closer, Caroline stroked and kissed and petted her until Bri fell asleep. Then she merely held her, determined never to let her go.

❖

"We have to get up," KT said quietly. "I need to go check on Bri."

"Mmm. Okay." Pia lay with her cheek on KT's chest, tracing a fingertip in a small circle around KT's navel. It was two in the afternoon and they had spent the day in bed, waking only long enough to make love and then drifting off again. "Tory would have called, though."

"Uh-huh." KT brushed her fingers down Pia's neck. "I'm not

sure how it's possible, but you're turning me on again."

Pia chuckled contentedly and sketched a line down the center of KT's abdomen with a fingernail. "From this?"

"From everything. Anything." KT's legs twitched. "Jesus. Yes. Stop that."

"I think that's a mixed message."

"Tell me something," KT gasped, grabbing for Pia's wrist just before Pia's fingers closed around her clitoris. "How is it possible that you're so good at this, and seem to like it so much, and you've never done it before?"

"That's *two* questions." Pia cupped her hand between KT's thighs but just rested there without teasing her. "It's not as if I've been living in a nunnery, you know."

KT laughed.

"And there has been more than one woman who's made me pretty hot, so I know what I like."

"I don't want to hear about them," KT growled.

"My point is," Pia said with exaggerated patience, "that it wasn't from lack of interest or some archaic innocence that I didn't sleep with someone before now." She raised up on an elbow and kissed KT. "I just couldn't see myself with anyone for longer than a few weeks, and it didn't seem worth it. Too many complications."

KT grew very still, and Pia felt it.

"KT, you don't owe me anything."

"What the hell does that mean?"

"It means that we slept together and it was great and—"

"Bullshit."

Pia blinked. "Excuse me?"

"I said," KT replied in clipped tones, "bullshit." She placed her hand over the one between her thighs when she felt Pia start to withdraw, and her expression softened. "Don't talk to me as if last night didn't matter. It meant everything to me."

"Oh." Pia's lips parted and her eyes grew large. "I...you..." She shrugged helplessly, her throat too tight for words.

"I told you last night that I love you. I mean it. I'm crazy about you. Totally, certifiably nuts."

Pia smiled shakily. "Is that good?"

"It's good for me," KT replied seriously. "You'll have to be the one to decide if it's good for you."

"I already know it's good for me."

"Well, we know *one* part of you it's good for." KT's tone was light but her eyes were serious.

"If you so much as *hint* that you think I'm in it only for the sex," Pia said threateningly, "I will be not only furious but insulted. And you, even *you*, couldn't possibly be that arrogant."

KT lifted an eyebrow.

Despite herself, Pia laughed. "All right, *Doctor* O'Bannon, perhaps you could. And I admit there was a time when I was so attracted to you that I *did* intend to sleep with you just for the sex." She leaned down and slowly bit KT's lower lip, tugging at it gently until KT groaned. "But between the time I realized I couldn't look at you without getting hot and last night, I fell in love with you."

"I like to hear you say that," KT murmured as she pressed down on Pia's hand, guiding Pia's fingers through the wetness that had gathered again while they were talking and inside. She sighed. "Say it again."

Pia stroked her tongue over KT's lips as she buried herself inside her. She waited until she knew that KT felt her everywhere—body and soul—before she spoke.

"I love you."

Chapter Twenty-Nine

Looks like they're having a party," KT remarked as Pia pulled in behind a line of cars double-parked in Tory and Reese's driveway.

"I'd say we arrived just in time for visiting hours." Pia turned off the ignition and leaned across the seat to kiss KT briefly. "That's to hold me until I get you alone again."

KT edged closer and ran her right hand up and down Pia's thigh. "When we're done here, maybe we can have dinner out someplace and then go back to bed."

"Maybe we can skip dinner."

Laughing, KT opened the car door and stepped out. She looked across the top of the car at Pia, glad for the distance between them. It seemed that when they were anywhere within touching distance, she felt compelled to put her hand on her. It was a disconcerting and wholly enjoyable sensation. "There's always takeout."

"Now *there's* an idea. Let's go see Bri." Pia walked around the side of the car and joined KT, taking her hand as they walked up the stone path to the rear deck. "I know this sounds silly, but I'll miss you."

"No," KT said quietly, closing her fingers tightly around Pia's. "It doesn't sound silly at all. It sounds wonderful."

Tory answered the knock, her expression registering no surprise at finding KT and Pia waiting on the deck together. So together they appeared not to notice that they were holding hands. *KT holding hands?* She tried not to stare. "Hi."

"How is she?" KT asked.

"She's doing great. Temp is normal. She's tired, probably more from stress than blood loss." Tory stepped aside so the two could enter. Across the living room in the kitchen alcove, Reese and Allie were cooking. Nelson sat at the breakfast bar, a cup of coffee cradled in his hands. Kate and Jean relaxed on the sofa with Reggie between them on a blanket.

"Full house," KT remarked as she glanced around.

"Bri is everyone's sweetheart."

"Did you check the wound yet?" KT realized that she and Pia were still holding hands and, after giving Pia's fingers one more squeeze, let go.

"No. I thought I'd wait for you to change the dressing the first time. I knew you'd be by eventually."

Tory caught Pia's grin out of the corner of her eye and smiled. "Come on, let's go see the patient."

"I'll wait out here," Pia said. "I'm sure Bri has seen enough people for one day."

"I'll be back in a few minutes," KT said as she and Tory turned away.

"Tell her I said hi," Pia called after them, while nodding hello to Kate and Jean on her way to the kitchen. She took a seat next to Nelson and rested her hand on his arm. "How are you doing?"

"Not bad," he said, his voice gravelly from lack of sleep but his expression relaxed. "She looks good. A little beat up, but good."

"That's terrific."

"Want a cup of coffee?" Allie asked Pia as she refilled Nelson's.

"That would be great. Thanks." Pia waved at Reese, who nodded back as she dropped a pound of pasta into a huge pot of boiling water.

"Tory said that O'Bannon is some kind of hotshot surgeon over from Boston," Allie commented as she passed a mug to Pia.

"I suppose you could say that," Pia replied carefully.

Allie waited to speak again as Nelson took his coffee and left to join Kate and Jean in the living room. Then she leaned across the breakfast bar, her voice pitched low. "I heard about her hand. Is that going to ruin her career?"

"Hopefully not." Pia regarded Allie thoughtfully, trying to figure out what about the young officer was ringing bells in her subconscious. She supposed the questions could just be idle curiosity, but there was a note of concern in Allie's voice that belied simple inquisitiveness. As if her concern for KT was more personal.

Allie glanced down the hall toward Bri's room. "Tory said it was really good that she was here last night. I'm glad she's going to be okay, because an injury like that—it can really mess you up. That would be a shame. She's...cool."

There it is again—that undercurrent of concern and sympathy. And then Pia finally made the connection, remembering the woman she'd only seen shadowed in moonlight, but who, in retrospect, had looked very much like Allie. "Did you by any chance walk her home a few weeks ago? When she was a bit...under the weather?"

"As in...sick?" Uncertain, Allie hesitated.

"You probably thought she'd had a few too many, but she was actually ill, not drunk." Pia's voice held an edge. She knew that Allie hadn't intentionally abandoned KT in such a dangerous condition, but she would never forget KT's suffering.

"I didn't know that," Allie said in surprise. "Jeez. I never would have left her alone if I'd realized."

"Well," Pia relented, her tone softening, "she's fine now. And you may have saved her life by helping her get home. So... thanks."

Now Allie regarded Pia intently. "Ah."

Pia laughed. *"Ah?"*

"You and the surgeon. Cool."

"Me and the surgeon," Pia repeated contemplatively. "Yes. Very cool."

❖

"Hi," Bri said uncertainly as she watched KT approach with Tory just behind her.

"You won't remember me," KT said easily. "I'm the surgeon who helped Tory take care of your neck last night." She held out her hand. "KT O'Bannon. Good to see you awake, Officer Parker."

"Bri." Bri's eyes flicked to KT's injured left hand as she took her right in a firm handshake. "Thanks a lot."

KT followed her gaze. "Wrong end of a knife."

Bri swallowed and met her eyes. "Tough one."

"Yeah. But it's mending. These things do."

"Yeah." Bri smiled weakly. "Look, thanks for not making me go to the hospital."

KT smiled. "You can thank Tory for all of that. Like I said, I was just helping out." She gestured to the square of white gauze taped over the laceration in Bri's neck. "I'd like to check your incision."

"Okay." Bri glanced at Caroline, who still sat beside her on the bed. "You don't have to stay for this, babe."

Caroline carefully climbed off the bed and stood where she would have an unimpeded view of Bri's neck while KT worked. She put her hand on Bri's hair and stroked softly. "I'm staying."

"This shouldn't hurt much," KT remarked as she carefully detached the tape. "Looks excellent."

"Good," Bri sighed. "So now what?"

"Usually at this point, we leave the incision uncovered. The bandage really isn't doing any good and can sometimes be irritating. It's up to you."

Bri inched around until she could locate Caroline. "Carre?"

"It's okay," Caroline said in a thin but steady voice as she studied the incision. "Just a red line with…" She leaned down, her eyes narrowing. "*Blue* stitches?"

KT laughed. "Prolene. They only come in blue."

"Cool," Caroline and Bri said simultaneously.

Still laughing, KT gently palpated Bri's neck, checked the carotid pulse and the function of the facial nerve branches running through the area, and declared Bri "doing fine."

"So," Bri said again. "Can I go back to work before the stitches come out?"

"Ah, no." KT glanced at Tory, who was shaking her head and muttering something about having heard *this* story before. "You're looking at about ten days before you're ready for work."

"Ten days!" Bri croaked. "But I—"

"If she says ten days," Reese interrupted from the doorway, "it's ten days." She entered carrying a tray with a plate of pasta and a glass of iced tea and set it down on the bedside table. Then she asked, looking at Tory, "What about desk duty? If she doesn't drive or leave the building?"

"KT?" Tory punted, having no desire to negotiate with both her lover and her stubborn young protégé.

"One week. Nothing before then." KT's tone indicated it was not an issue open to discussion.

"Good enough," Reese pronounced. She turned her attention to Bri. "Try to eat something and make sure you at least drink. And take advantage of the fact that Caroline is here for a few days. Work will keep."

Bri reached for Caroline's hand and nodded as much as she was able. "Yes, ma'am. I got it."

"Very good." Reese smiled at Caroline. "Tory and I want both of you to stay here while Bri's recuperating."

"Thanks," Caroline said softly as she reached for the plate and silverware. "For everything."

"What about my black belt test?" Bri asked suddenly, ignoring the food that Caroline offered. "It's next week. I need to train."

"We'll talk about that later," Reese replied.

"But—"

"Honey," Caroline chided gently. "You have to get well first."

Bri looked as if she were about to protest, but as she focused on the faces of those around her, she seemed to accept that she was outnumbered. Grouchily, she muttered, "Okay. Right. Fine."

Caroline prevented her from saying anything else by sliding a forkful of pasta into her mouth.

❖

KT and Tory walked out onto the deck where they could discuss Bri's case in private.

"What do you think?" Tory asked. "The incision seems fine, don't you agree?"

"I do." KT leaned her elbows on the railing and studied the harbor beyond the low dunes that separated the house from the beach. "The only real danger at this point is delayed bleeding. As long as she's relatively quiet for another day or two, that shouldn't be a problem. I said a week because it's been my experience that the young, aggressive types like her are hard to hold down."

Tory laughed. "That's an understatement. But let me tell you, it has nothing to do with age. Reese is the same way whenever she's injured."

KT glanced at Tory. "You sound as if that's a common occurrence."

"Unfortunately," Tory said with a wince, "it is."

"That's hard."

"Very."

"And I guess there's nothing you could say to make her give it up."

Tory shrugged. "She would, if I asked her to. But I can't. It would take too much from her."

"You're happy with her, aren't you?"

"More than I can say."

"Yeah. That's what I thought."

"And how are things going for you?" Tory inquired gently.

"At the rate I'm going," KT said quietly, "I'll know in another month or two if I'm going to be able to operate again."

"And then?"

KT blew out a breath. "I guess it depends on what the answer is. If I can operate—then I'll go back to work."

"In Boston." Tory said it as if it were a given, not a question.

"Well, yes." KT sounded far less certain. She kept her eyes on the water. "But there's Pia."

"Yes. I noticed."

"I know what you think about me and her, but—"

"I was wrong." Tory lightly grasped KT's forearm. "I was wrong to make judgments concerning something I knew nothing about. About *people* I don't know as well as I thought I did."

KT turned, her eyes searching Tory's again. "You know me. The good and the bad."

"Yes, I do." Tory smiled faintly. "But not as well as I once did. And for a while, I couldn't see the good. Or maybe—maybe it's that falling in love with Pia has brought all those good things out."

"How did—?"

"I know?" Tory laughed. "It's pretty obvious to anyone who's looking. Pia is a wonderful woman. She'll be good for you."

"She already is."

Startled by KT's humble tone, Tory spoke without thinking. "Then why are you thinking about going back to Boston?"

"I—what would I do here?" KT asked in frustration. "You have to admit, I'm only a passable family doctor."

Tory laughed. "The patients love you."

"Well, it takes more than personality to do your job, and I don't want them to find out the hard way."

"KT," Tory said gently. "Don't lose her because of a job."

"Like I did you?"

Tory shook her head. "Maybe—I don't know, and even if I did, it doesn't matter anymore. What matters is *now*. I don't know what you want in your life. I don't know what Pia wants. But you need to find out before it's gone."

KT closed her eyes for a second, then slowly nodded. "Thanks. I'll try."

"I've never known you to fail at anything you've tried." Tory leaned close and kissed KT's cheek. "My money's on you."

An hour later, Pia backed out of Tory's driveway and headed west on 6A toward town. She reached across the space between them and stroked KT's thigh. "You've been awfully quiet. Something happen with Tory?"

KT turned on the seat, covering Pia's hand with her own and holding it against her leg. "What do you mean?"

"The two of you looked like you were having a very serious conversation out on the deck. Since then, you've been somewhere else."

"Sorry."

Pia glanced at her quickly and then back to the road, shaking her head. "You don't need to apologize. *Is* there something wrong?"

"No," KT said solemnly. "Everything is...great."

Pia laughed quietly. "You don't sound like it." She rubbed her hand in a gentle circle on KT's thigh. "Is it Tory?"

"Tory?" KT's voice held a hint of confusion and surprise. "Why?"

Still staring straight ahead, Pia asked, "Are you still in love with her?"

"I'm in love with *you,*" KT said immediately. "Only you. And that's the problem."

Pia frowned and looked at her quickly. "Why?"

"Because it isn't simple. Because for the first time in my life, when I try to see my future, I don't see anything."

"Do you see us?"

"I *want* to."

"Then that's enough," Pia said gently.

"How can that be?" KT's frustration made her voice harsh. "I've always known where I was going, what I needed to do to get there. Now I...I'm not even sure where I'm going to be in two months. *Who* I'll be."

While they'd talked, Pia had driven through town. She pulled into the parking lot at Herring Cove and stopped on the long stretch of blacktop that fronted the beach. It was sundown, the air had grown cold as it did near the water at night, and only a lone walker far up the beach shared the solitude. Pia turned on the seat, wrapped her arms around her raised knee, and regarded KT seriously. "Who are you, KT?"

KT ran a hand through her hair distractedly. "I used to be a surgeon."

"And if you can't be?"

"I don't know." KT shrugged her shoulders. "That sounds pathetic, doesn't it?"

"No. It just sounds like you haven't been paying attention to much of anything else for a while."

KT laughed shortly. "For a while? Try fifteen years."

"Maybe." Pia regarded KT evenly. "You're also bright and determined and focused. You could do almost anything you wanted to do." At KT's expression of dismissal, Pia laughed. "I know. Medicine is what you do. Would you consider working with Tory at the clinic?"

"Oh man, I don't know. It takes a certain kind of person to be good at that. Not just the medicine part, but the people part. That's never been my strong suit."

"Everyone has their own style. Some of us like the strong, self-assured type."

The corner of KT's mouth twitched. "I thought we were talking about doctoring."

"I am—among other things." Pia stretched out her arm and ran a finger along the edge of KT's jaw. "You could work in the ER in Hyannis."

"I've thought of it. I could probably work in the ER in Boston, too."

"But," Pia reminded her, "you and I still have a long way to go on that hand, and I think you'll be operating again before the beginning of the year."

"If that happens, I think I want to go back to the trauma unit." KT said it quickly, as if to get the words out before she changed her mind.

Pia was silent for a few moments, and when she spoke again, her voice was carefully neutral. "That makes sense. You've been there a long time, and that's what makes you happy."

KT's head snapped around. "*You* make me happy. Being a trauma surgeon satisfies a need in me—to do what I'm good at, to make a difference with my own hands. But you...*you* make me happy."

Pia smiled. "I'm glad. You make me happy too."

"Well hell, then. What are we going to do? You live here."

"Are we talking about that future that you can't see clearly now?"

KT laughed. "Yes, God damn it. I'm not comfortable unless I know where I'm going."

"I want you in my future. I want to be in yours."

"I want that too." KT's gaze was fierce. "I want you, more than anything."

"Well, then, you'll commute. It's only twenty-five minutes by plane. Plenty of people do it." Pia edged closer, sliding her arm beneath KT's and cupping her palm on the inside of KT's thigh. She rested her cheek against KT's shoulder. "You come home when you can, and I'll be here."

"I already hate the thought of being away from you," KT confessed.

"Good. Then you'll be sure to come home often."

KT kissed Pia slowly, enjoying the soft liquid heat of her

mouth. "I love you."

Pia snuggled closer. "I love you too. *That's* the picture I see when I look ahead."

"Yes," KT murmured. "So do I."

Chapter Thirty

Reese halted in the parking lot of the Wellfleet Sheriff's Department and waited while the driver of the Jaguar XKR parked, got out, and walked over to her. "Hello, Counselor."

"Hello, Sheriff," Trey Pelosi replied. "Congratulations. I hear you got your man."

"Thanks, but we only got a little piece of the great big pie. There's a lot more where Karl Smith came from, I'm afraid."

"There always are." Trey shifted her briefcase and tilted her head toward the building. "I understand you also got a name for the girl in the dunes."

"Is this an official inquiry?"

Trey smiled. "Just a favor for the family. They don't want their son to live under a cloud for the rest of his life, and the less mystery surrounding the case, the better. I told them I'd find out what I could."

"In the last three days we've interviewed three dozen of the kids we rounded up at the party Saturday night. Two of them recognized both the dead girl and your client. We made a positive ID this morning from information they provided us—Angela Fisher." Reese grimaced and shook her head. "I notified the family as soon as I got a name. They thought she was living with a cousin in Boston and going to school at night. Maybe she was. The family didn't know she was missing, and the cousin assumed she'd just taken off with some 'dude' she'd run into somewhere."

"So there's no evidence to suggest that their meeting was anything but coincidental."

"Your boy's story holds up. In fact, no one remembers him doing anything heavier than drinking a beer. Nobody's going to be charging him in Angela's death."

"Thanks for the information. I'll just put in an official appearance inside." Trey regarded Reese speculatively. "Why do I think you're overqualified for your job and probably wasted out here in the middle of nowhere?"

"I can't imagine." Reese laughed. "Believe me, Counselor, I am precisely where I want to be."

Trey's eyes dropped to Reese's left hand and the gold band she wore there. "I see that." She extended her hand to Reese, who took it. "I've enjoyed working with you, Sheriff. I hope we meet again someday."

"Same here," Reese replied, watching while the attorney walked away. As Trey disappeared inside the low building, Reese had a feeling their paths would cross again.

❖

"I don't need a babysitter," Bri grumped.

"You sure don't. You need to get your ass out of this house." Allie sauntered into the kitchen and rummaged in the refrigerator. Looking over her shoulder, she called, "Coke?"

"Yeah. Sure." Bri flung herself, albeit gently, onto the sofa and kicked her feet up onto the coffee table. "Besides, Caroline has to go back to Paris in two days, and I don't see why she has to go out shopping now."

"Ooh," Allie crooned, settling a hip on the arm of the couch and handing Bri the can of soda. "Someone's *very* cranky. Is someone getting bored? Is someone maybe not getting enou—"

"Cut it out," Bri snapped, but she was grinning. "*You* try sitting around here all day long with nothing to do except read."

"Uh, well gee, hot stuff, I bet *I* could think of something else to pass the time."

"Ha ha. I'm not supposed to..." Bri blushed, which made Allie laugh again. "*...exert* myself, okay?"

"I'm sorry," Allie said, still laughing. "It's just that you're so cute when you're all out of sorts like this."

"Fuck." Bri dropped her head onto the back of the couch and stared at the ceiling. "I can't believe I let that bastard get hold of me."

Allie's laughter instantly disappeared and her face grew serious. "I missed it totally. I never got violent vibes from him. Who knew he was going to freak out?"

"I should've been ready for it. Reese hasn't said anything, but she must think that I screwed up."

"No!" Allie leaned forward and rested her hand on Bri's shoulder. "If it was anyone's fault, it was mine. I saw him come down the stairs behind you and head toward the kitchen. I just didn't think he was going to be that kind of problem. But *I* was your backup. *I* screwed up. Not you." Her eyes glistened but she kept the brimming tears at bay. "I'm so sorry."

Bri's brows furrowed as she regarded Allie in confusion. "You were handling the front, just like we'd been briefed. You weren't supposed to be in the kitchen backing me up."

Allie shook her head, refusing to listen. "I saw him follow you, but I was so focused on meeting the team in the front that it just didn't register. At least, not as something I should worry about. God, Bri, I let him get to you."

"That's crap. We both had jobs to do, and we were doing them. There are some things you can't plan on, and he was one of them. He freaked out; I handled it. It's done."

"I was scared, Bri," Allie whispered. "I was so scared when you got hurt."

Bri reached up and took Allie's hand, squeezing it gently. "I'm sorry. It's tough, working with people you care about so much, especially when they might get hurt."

Allie nodded wordlessly.

"I think if it was you or Reese or my dad, I'd be really really scared, too. You're all special to me."

"Caroline's got you pretty well trained." Allie smiled weakly. "You know just the kind of thing a girl likes to hear."

"Well, yeah." Bri grinned. "But it's *true.* And I like us being partnered, so just forget about apologizing. It's part of the job, right?"

"Yeah. It is." Her eyes clearing, Allie looked across the room at the clock. "You know, sitting around here is starting to make me kind of nuts. Let's go for a drive."

"A drive?"

"Uh-huh." Allie stood and extended her hand. "Come on. It won't *exert* you too much to sit in the car, will it?"

"Ha ha," Bri muttered, but she followed willingly. Anything for a change of scenery. On the way to the door, she abruptly stopped. "Wait. I need to leave a note for Carre."

Allie groaned, but grinned good-naturedly while muttering something about being whipped.

"Yeah, yeah. Don't you wish," Bri grumbled back.

Surprisingly serious, Allie answered, "Yeah. Sometimes."

Ten minutes later, Allie pulled into the parking lot shared by the New Provincetown Playhouse and the Provincetown Martial Arts Center.

"What's going on?" Bri asked, frowning.

"I forgot some of my gear here earlier today. Come on in while I get it."

"Who knows when I'll be able to train again," Bri groused as she followed Allie inside. Despite the fact that it was almost 9 p.m. and no classes were scheduled, a light burned in the practice room. Bri narrowed her eyes and looked around. Something felt off. "Allie, what—?" She halted abruptly as Tory, in her *gi*, stepped from the shadows near the door.

"You need to get changed, Bri," Tory said quietly, extending a pristine tournament-weight *gi* top in Bri's direction.

"Whose is this?" Bri whispered, not even knowing why she kept her voice down. She *did* know that a *gi* jacket like this cost a quarter of her weekly take-home pay.

"Yours," Tory replied.

Bri looked in confusion to Allie, who was quickly changing into her own uniform. Then, not knowing what else to do, she stepped out of her jeans and took the new white pants that Tory offered her. Once fully dressed, she followed Tory and Allie into the practice room. Her entire class knelt in a single line along the edge of the practice mat. What shocked her into a stumbling standstill, however, was the fact that her father and Caroline sat on a bench on the far side of the room. She could feel Caroline's smile all the way to her heart. Her stomach suddenly fluttering, she followed Tory to the mat, bowed, and knelt wordlessly by Tory's side. Then, as she always did when she prepared herself for this place, for these moments when thought was abandoned and harmony flowed between mind and body, she placed her hands palm down on her thighs and closed her eyes. In some distant part of her consciousness, she registered the faint rustle of fabric and a whisper of air brushing past her face. Then, as if summoned in the silence, she opened her eyes.

Reese, dressed in a similar snowy white jacket and black billowing *hakama*, knelt facing Bri and the rest of the students. Folded in front of her on the mat lay a black belt bearing the symbol of the *dojo* embroidered in gold on one end. She looked directly at Bri.

With her eyes fixed on Reese, Bri placed both hands forward on the mat, fingertips touching, thumbs spread, and knelt slowly until her forehead touched the mat in the triangle formed by her hands. In response, Reese placed first her left and then her right hand in precisely the same position and returned the bow. Then she straightened, rested her hands on her thighs, and spoke while continuing to look into Bri's eyes.

"We train for many reasons. For peace of mind, for health of body, for harmony of spirit. But always, we train for the moment when we will be challenged."

Bri's heart pounded, and she was afraid that everyone in the room would see her tremble. But she kept her eyes on Reese's, one of the safest places she had ever known.

"Sun Tsu said, 'If you know yourself but not the enemy, for every victory gained, you will also suffer a defeat. If you know neither the enemy nor yourself, you will succumb in *every* battle. But if you know the enemy *and* know yourself, you need not fear the result of a hundred battles.'" Reese lifted the black belt and balanced it between her outstretched palms. "You have trained hard. You have been tested in battle."

Reese's voice, strong and deep, resonated in Bri's body and settled in her chest, at once soothing and yet so powerful she could barely breathe.

"You have earned this. You have made us all proud."

Breaking with custom, which dictated that Bri should come to her, Reese glided across the tatami to Bri's side in a fluid movement designed hundreds of years before when the samurai fought by necessity from a kneeling position in the courts of their masters. She passed the black belt to Tory, who held it in the same position as Reese had, across her outstretched hands, while Reese reached down, untied Bri's white *obi*, and removed it. Then Reese took the black belt, wrapped it around Bri's waist, and knotted it in place herself.

"Well done, Parker *sensei*."

"Thank you, *sensei*," Bri managed, although her voice was barely audible, it was so thick with tears.

Never taking her eyes from Bri's face, Reese moved back to her original position, bowed, then left the totally silent room.

The minute Reese was gone, pandemonium erupted. Students swarmed Bri, and if it hadn't been for her recent injury, she would have been inundated with back slaps and hugs.

"Way to go, Bri," Allie said exuberantly. "Man, that was awesome."

"Yeah." Bri was still too stunned to take it all in. "Yeah. Wow."

While her classmates continued to celebrate, Tory was the first to kiss Bri's cheek.

"Congratulations, sweetheart."

Bri grabbed Tory's hand and held it almost desperately. "Thank you. *Thank you.* Do you think it's okay? This way? That I didn't test?"

"If Conlon *sensei* promoted you, you can be absolutely certain you deserve it."

"Did you know?" Bri asked.

Tory shook her head. "No. She doesn't discuss those decisions with me. In this room, we are all students." Then she held out a folded black *hakama*. "From me. Ready to put it on?"

"Will you...show me?"

"Of course." Tory helped Bri step into the flowing ceremonial pants that covered the white *gi* pants and demonstrated the proper cross-over pattern to tie the four strands of the waistband. Then she stepped back and surveyed the *dojo*'s newest *shodan*. "Very handsome."

"I'll say," Caroline pronounced, wrapping her arms around Bri's waist in a fierce hug.

"Hey, babe," Bri said, turning to see her father's eyes shining with pride and her girlfriend's wet with tears. That was enough to bring on her own. Embarrassed for anyone else to see, she pressed her face to Caroline's neck. "I'm so glad you were here. It wouldn't have been the same without you."

Caroline held her tightly, stroking her cheek and back. "I would have come no matter what. I'm so proud of you. I love you so much."

"I'm so lucky." Bri raised her head when she felt her father's hand on her shoulder. She grinned at him. "What do you think, Dad?"

"I think your fellow officers are going to be damned jealous. I wouldn't be surprised if the *dojo* gets a few new students." He touched her face, his eyes on the healing wound in her neck. "I think you're a helluva police officer and the best kid a man could have."

"Oh man," Bri whispered as she felt tears starting again. "I gotta cut this out."

Caroline brushed her fingers beneath Bri's eyes. "It's been a tough few days, baby. It's okay."

At that moment, the room went silent as Reese entered, still in her *gi* but without her *hakama* now. Then, seconds later, conversation began again. Reese crossed the room directly to Bri and extended her hand. As they shook, she asked, "Are you ready for the job of assistant instructor?"

"Yes, ma'am," Bri said instantly. "I should be able to start this weekend."

Reese laughed. "I believe your doctors said two weeks for that."

Bri looked as if she were about to protest, but after one glance at Tory, Reese, her father, and Caroline, she surrendered. "Okay."

"Good," Reese responded. "Remember, responsibility—to those you love, to those who love you, to yourself, to your community, to your country—that is one of the most important things you must teach." She cast her eyes around the room at her students and her friends. "And here, we live what we teach."

Quietly, Bri whispered, "Yes, *sensei*."

❖

"That was beautiful," Tory said as she and Reese headed for home. "I thought Nelson was going to burst with pride."

"I didn't tell him until today because I was pretty sure he'd give it away. And I wanted it to be special for her." Reese smiled. "I remember when she first came to me and declared that she wanted to train. She reminded me so much of myself at that age."

Tory shifted in the seat and put her back to the door so she could watch her lover as she drove. "I've always thought of her as a younger version of you."

"No," Reese said with a shake of her head. "She's much braver than I ever was." She glanced quickly at Tory and then back to the road. "She'll take Nelson's place in the department some day. She has the heart of a warrior, and others will follow her gladly."

"You underestimate yourself, Sheriff," Tory said softly. "Bri is an amazing young woman. Brave and strong and valiant, true. But she looks to you to stay the course. Not that Nelson doesn't love her, or Bri him, but it's your hand that has guided her into adulthood, and it will be your example that shapes her life. She loves you."

Reese's voice was husky as she said, "I love her."

"I know, and I think it's wonderful." Tory smiled, watching the moonlight play on her lover's handsome face. It was one of those moments when she couldn't think of a single thing about her life that she would change. "Regina is very lucky to have you for a parent."

"Thank you. That means...everything to me."

"Mmm. You mean everything to us." Tory sighed. "It seems like forever since we've had a chance to talk alone."

"Is something wrong?" Reese asked in concern.

"No. Everything is right."

Reese stretched out her hand between them and Tory took it. When their fingers intertwined, Reese asked, "What did you want to talk to me about?"

"The wedding."

Epilogue

Thanksgiving Weekend

Bri emerged from her dreams to the sensation of warm lips against the back of her neck. She lay on her stomach with her arms curled around her pillow and Caroline's mouth against her skin. When she shifted to turn over, a firm hand held her down.

"Don't move, baby," Caroline whispered, smoothing her palm down the center of Bri's spine as she nuzzled her face in the curve of Bri's neck. She traced her lips over the faint red ridge of scar tissue, the persistent reminder of all she had nearly lost. "I don't get to wake up with you very often, and I want to remember everything about the way you feel right now."

"I feel good," Bri muttered. "I'd feel a whole lot better if I could turn over and get my hands on you."

Caroline laughed. "I know. Which is why you're not going to." She nudged her leg between Bri's, settling her pelvis on Bri's hip. "I got here first."

Bri made a sound between a growl and a groan. "Come on, baby. Don't torture me."

"Sorry, too late." Caroline leaned down and set her teeth into the fleshy triangle between Bri's neck and shoulder. She nuzzled her breasts against Bri's back, moving slowly from side to side as her nipples hardened, drawing the sensitive tips across the firm planes of her lover's body. "Oh, I love the way that feels. My nipples are connected directly to my—"

"Let me suck them." Bri's hands were fisted in the pillow, her voice urgent, but she did not try to turn although she easily could have. "I can make you come that way."

"I know," Caroline whispered, sliding her hand between

their bodies and into the cleft between Bri's thighs. "But you have somewhere important to be this morning, remember?" She pressed gently with her thumb as she fanned her fingers over the tender folds.

"Not for hours." Bri moaned softly and lifted her hips, urging Caroline deeper.

Caroline curled around her lover, resting her cheek in the hollow above Bri's hips as she slowly entered her, taking what was hers with gentle reverence. "I love you."

Bri closed her eyes as Caroline claimed her, allowing the certainty of those words to ease her fears and fill her heart. This was the woman who loved her. This was her safe harbor.

❖

Above the steady drum of the water against the shower walls, Pia heard her name. Smiling, she slid the glass door open and peered through the steam into the bathroom. KT stood on one leg, kicking off her trousers. She was already shirtless, and the sight of her bare breasts and stomach made Pia's thighs tighten with instant arousal. "You made it."

"Said I would," KT replied, grinning. "Want some company?"

"If it's yours."

"Better be." KT stepped into the shower and wrapped her arms around Pia's waist, drew her close, and kissed her for a long moment as water cascaded over their heads and shoulders. When she finally relinquished Pia's mouth, she tilted her forehead to Pia's and kissed the tip of her nose. "Miss me?"

"Nope. How was the drive?"

KT laughed. "Fine."

"Long night?" Pia reached around KT for the shampoo and squeezed a ribbon onto the top of KT's head. As she worked her fingers through the short, thick hair, she leaned her thighs and pelvis against KT's.

"I got some sleep."

"How's your hand?"

"A little better than useless, but still not worth much."

"It will come. You're not overusing it, are you?"

Eyes closed, KT leaned into Pia's hands, which had moved to her back and were slowly massaging her tight muscles. "Don't see how I can. I can hold a few instruments for a minute or two, but I can't really operate with it. Still, I can triage and handle most emergencies."

"Good. Rinse." Pia waited until KT was suds free, then leaned back against the shower wall and pulled KT with her, dropping her hands to KT's hips and guiding KT's thigh between her legs. "Because if you're going to spend four nights a week in Boston, I don't want you to be wasting your time."

KT braced her elbows against the wall on either side of Pia's shoulders and rhythmically thrust her leg between Pia's. Pia moaned and KT smiled. "You did too miss me."

"Maybe." Pia tilted her head back, her eyes hazy and her smile soft. "You?"

"Every minute," KT growled as she lowered her mouth to Pia's. She kissed her hard this time, her tongue insistent as she drew her thigh in and out between Pia's. She found Pia's breast, closing her fingers around it as she thumbed the nipple. She felt Pia's fingers dig into her buttocks, urging her to pump harder, and she knew that Pia was ready. When she moved her left hand down, eager to satisfy her, Pia caught her wrist.

"No," Pia gasped. "You can't."

"*Damn* it," KT muttered, angling her body to fit her right hand between Pia's legs. "I need both hands to touch you. I need *all* of you."

On a laugh that was nearly a sob, Pia guided KT inside her. "Touching me or not, you have all of me."

"I love you," KT whispered, reveling in the heat of Pia's body. She thrust more gently than she had intended, her hunger sharp but her pleasure tempered by awe. She was where she wanted to be, needed to be, and she was desperate for this moment never to end. "Tell me. God, Pia, tell me."

Pia drew one leg up, circling KT's hips, taking her even deeper inside. She knew what her lover asked, and she never tired of answering. It was no hardship to bestow what she wanted so very much to give. She would come for her in a minute, holding nothing back. But before that, she would give her what they both needed. "I love you. Always."

❖

"It's quiet here without her, isn't it," Reese said, softly running her hand up and down Tory's arm.

"Almost too quiet."

"Yeah."

"I wonder how long it will be before she can stay overnight with her grandmothers and we won't miss her." Tory drew one leg over Reese's and curled into the side of her body, murmuring contentedly as she nuzzled Reese's neck. The windows were open, and the breeze carried winter on its wings.

"Not ever, I don't think." Reese kissed Tory's forehead, her fingers drifting lazily along the curve of her lover's breast. "But it is nice that it's just the two of us now and then."

"Especially today." Tory raised up on an elbow, kissed the tip of Reese's chin, and smiled. "Nervous?"

Reese laughed and pulled Tory on top of her. She bent one leg at the knee so that Tory could settle between her thighs. "No. Excited. You?"

"Mmm. Excited and happy." Tory smoothed her cheek over Reese's breast, absently brushing the nipple with her lips. "It's funny," she mused, unmindful of the quickening of Reese's breath. "We've been together for years now and have a child, but I still feel like a bride."

"It's special, standing up in front of our friends and family to pledge our love."

"Are you okay that KT will be coming with Pia?"

"Of course. I like her."

"Funny, me too." Tory made absent circles on Reese's stomach with her fingertips, aware now of the tension humming in Reese's body. "And I love that Bri is going to stand up with you. The two of you will look so handsome."

Laughing, Reese threaded her fingers into Tory's hair, unconsciously guiding Tory's mouth back to her nipple. "Everyone knows how much I love you, but I want to say it out loud for all the world to hear." Her voice was husky, deep with emotion and desire. "I want everyone to know that I belong to you."

"And I to you," Tory murmured even as her focus shifted from the upcoming ceremony to the woman in her arms. Always, always there was Reese, and only Reese. Reese kept nothing from her, not her tenderness or her fears or her devotion.

No matter where they were, no matter what convention said of them or what circumstance befell them, the only thing that truly mattered was what bound them, heart and soul—the love they had forged. Reese was her answer and her hope, her home and her destiny, her partner and her passion. Reese was her heart, as she knew she was Reese's. She would say that aloud to all who would listen—today, tomorrow, and every day to come. They would live with their love as their shield and their banner, for all the days of their lives. This was their truth.

The End

About the Author

Radclyffe is a member of the Golden Crown Literary Society, Pink Ink, the Romance Writers of America, and a two-time recipient of the Alice B. award for lesbian fiction. She has written numerous best-selling lesbian romances (*Safe Harbor* and its sequel *Beyond the Breakwater, Innocent Hearts, Love's Melody Lost, Love's Tender Warriors, Tomorrow's Promise, Passion's Bright Fury, Love's Masquerade*, *shadowland,* and *Fated Love*), two romance/intrigue series: the Honor series *(Above All, Honor, Honor Bound, Love & Honor,* and *Honor Guards*) and the Justice series (*Shield of Justice,* the prequel *A Matter of Trust, In Pursuit of Justice,* and *Justice in the Shadows)*, as well as an erotica collection: *Change of Pace – Erotic Interludes*.

She lives with her partner, Lee, in Philadelphia, PA where she both writes and practices surgery full-time. She is also the president of Bold Strokes Books, a lesbian publishing company.

Her upcoming works include: *Justice Served* (June 2005); *Stolen Moments: Erotic Interludes 2*, ed. with Stacia Seaman (September 2005), and *Honor Reclaimed* (December 2005)

Look for information about these works at www.radfic.com and www.boldstrokesbooks.com.

Other Books Available From Bold Strokes Books

Distant Shores, Silent Thunder by Radclyffe. Ex-lovers, would-be lovers, and old rivals find their paths unwillingly entwined when Doctors KT O'Bannon and Tory King—and the women who love them—are forced to examine the boundaries of love, friendship, and the ties that transcend time. (1-933110-08-2)

Hunter's Pursuit by Kim Baldwin. A raging blizzard, a remote mountain hideaway, and more than one killer-for-hire set a scene for disaster—or desire—when reluctant assassin Katarzyna Demetrious rescues a stranger and unwittingly exposes her heart. (1-933110-09-0)

The Walls of Westernfort by Jane Fletcher. All Temple Guard Natasha Ionadis wants is to serve the Goddess, and she volunteers eagerly for a dangerous mission to infiltrate a band of rebels. But once away from the temple, the issues are no longer so simple, especially in light of her attraction to one of the rebels. Is it too late to work out what she really wants from life? (1-933110-24-4)

Change Of Pace: *Erotic Interludes* by Radclyffe. Twenty-five hot-wired encounters guaranteed to spark more than just your imagination. Erotica as you've always dreamed of it. (1-933110-07-4)

Fated Love by Radclyffe. Amidst the chaos and drama of a busy emergency room, two women must contend not only with the fragile nature of life, but also with the mysteries of the heart and the irresistible forces of fate. (1-933110-05-8)

Justice in the Shadows by Radclyffe. In a shadow world of secrets, lies, and hidden agendas, Detective Sergeant Rebecca Frye and her lover, Dr. Catherine Rawlings, join forces once again in the elusive search for justice. (1-933110-03-1)

shadowland by Radclyffe. In a world on the far edge of desire, two women are drawn together by power, passion, and dark pleasures. An erotic romance. (1-933110-11-2)

Love's Masquerade by Radclyffe. Plunged into the often indistinguishable realms of fiction, fantasy, and hidden desires, Auden Frost discovers a shifting landscape that will force her to question everything she has believed to be true about herself and the nature of love. (1-933110-14-7)

Beyond the Breakwater by Radclyffe. One Provincetown summer three women learn the true meaning of love, friendship, and family. Second in the Provincetown Tales. (1-933110-06-6)

Tomorrow's Promise by Radclyffe. One timeless summer, two very different women discover the power of passion to heal and the promise of hope that only love can bestow. (1-933110-12-0)

Love's Tender Warriors by Radclyffe. Two women who have accepted loneliness as a way of life learn that love is worth fighting for and a battle they cannot afford to lose. (1-933110-02-3)

Love's Melody Lost by Radclyffe. A secretive artist with a haunted past and a young woman escaping a life that proved to be a lie find their destinies entwined. (1-933110-00-7)

Safe Harbor by Radclyffe. A mysterious newcomer, a reclusive doctor, and a troubled gay teenager learn about love, friendship, and trust during one tumultuous summer in Provincetown. First in the Provincetown Tales. (1-933110-13-9)

Above All, Honor by Radclyffe. The first in the Honor series introduces single-minded Secret Service Agent Cameron Roberts and the woman she is sworn to protect—Blair Powell, the daughter of the president of the United States. First in the Honor series. (1-933110-04-X)

Love & Honor by Radclyffe. The president's daughter and her security chief are faced with difficult choices as they battle a tangled web of Washington intrigue for...love and honor. Third in the Honor series. (1-933110-10-4)

Honor Guards by Radclyffe. In a journey that begins on the streets of Paris's Left Bank and culminates in a wild flight for their lives, the president's daughter and those who are sworn to protect her wage a desperate struggle for survival. Fourth in the Honor series. (1-933110-01-5)